Praise for Karen Kay's *Brave Wolf and theLady*

"This is an incredibly awesome book!...I was so extremely touched by this story…there are parts of this story that…(will make) you cry so much your heart will hurt, and other parts that will fill you with joy.

(Karen Kay)…is an amazing story writer and if you haven't read her stories yet, please do yourself a favor and start.

I very highly recommend this book to you and I know that you will enjoy it as much as I have."

Review by Starr Miller

Look for these titles by Karen Kay

Now Available:

Lakota Series
Lakota Surrender
Lakota Princess
Proud Wolf's Woman

Blackfoot Warriors
Gray Hawk's Lady
White Eagle's Touch
Night Thunder's Bride

Legendary Warriors
War Cloud's Passion
Lone Arrow's Pride
Soaring Eagle's Embrace
Wolf Shadow's Promise

The Warriors of the Iroquois
Black Eagle
Seneca Surrender

The Lost Clan
The Angel and the Warrior
The Spirit of the Wolf
Red Hawk's Woman
The Last Warrior

The Clan of the Wolf
The Princess and the Wolf
Brave Wolf and the Lady

Brave Wolf and the Lady

The Clan of the Wolf, Book 2

Karen Kay

PK&J Publishing
1Lakeview Trail
Danbury, CT 06811

Brave Wolf and the Lady

Print ISBN: 978-1-98335-0-320

Cover by Angela Waters

Acknowledgements

Because one does not write a book without great inspiration, I would like to acknowledge the following people:

Musically, I would like to thank Keith Whitley for his musical genius and inspiration, as well as James Paul McCartney. I do believe that the song, "Love in the Open Air" might very well be the most beautiful song of the last century.

To Tom Brown, Jr. and his book,
The Way of the Scout.

To Myra Elliott, always a kind word.

To Jeanne Miller, always an inspiration and friend.

To my husband, Paul, my love, my inspiration for this story.

And to the following Warriorettes, who have helped:

Starr Miller, a special mention for she has helped very much

Yvette Poulin
Carolyn Benton
Christine Martin
Pam Hamblin

BRAVE WOLF AND THE LADY
1871
Washington D.C.

PROLOGUE

The man with clipped, soot-colored hair and shadowy, drab-tinted eyes scowled as he swirled the red liquid around the crystal-clear wine glass. His thoughts were sour, his mood dangerous.

How dare they do this to him. How dare that little flirt and her casanova insult him in this manner.

Hadn't Sheehan told her? Hadn't the senator drilled into her the fact that her family would be ruined if she didn't act in a style befitting her station? After all, he held enough ammunition on the senator to cost him his position.

But it appeared that Sheehan was immune to blackmail when the matter concerned his daughter. Blackmail. Such an ugly word. It was business. Business with the promise of harm.

The man took a sip of the blood-red wine, then smiled. However, the gesture was hardly a cheerful affair. Indeed, for a moment, a light of insanity shown broadly in his blackened gaze.

Well now, they believed they had escaped him. They actually had the gall to consider that they could start their lives elsewhere, with nary a thought for him, his family or his reputation.

But they had both reckoned without consideration of his great—and moneyed—influence. Certainly, they would learn of their mistake—to their detriment.

His grin broadened. He only wished he could be there to watch the woman's abuse, in particular, at the hands of his henchmen. With that thought, an exquisite sort of pleasure stirred within him. Setting the crystal glass down onto a side table, he entertained the vile idea, since the notion of inflicting pain upon some helpless creature stirred his passion.

Ah, yes. They would learn...and none too soon...

CHAPTER ONE

Smoky Hill River Area, Border of Colorado and Kansas

Summer, 1871

Boom! Crack! Bang! Rat-a-tat! Blast!

Guns!

As Brave Wolf looked up from his inspection of the earth and the tracks left over it, he sensed that this hunting party of four would have no choice but to investigate the trouble. Turning his attention back to the earth, he studied the clues left upon its face, tracing the indentations of the trail with his hand.

"What do you see there, my son?" asked White Buffalo silently, squatting beside his son and speaking to him with a series of graceful hand motions.

Brave Wolf answered his father in the same manner, saying, "Two large groups of white men made these prints, and they are fresh—this morning. One is a band of the 'sea of white' people...pioneers. The other is a war party."

White Buffalo, whose name in his own language was Tahiska, nodded.

"The war party means the 'sea of white' people harm," continued Brave Wolf. "It is all here: the pausing of their mounts, the short distance between each track, which shows a cautiousness and stealth." Brave Wolf looked off in the direction where the tracks led. "The guns we hear will be from these people."

Brave Wolf rose up to his full height—which was almost a head taller than those of his two uncles, who surrounded him. He paused, watching his father closely as White Buffalo also gained his feet. White Buffalo, however, didn't return his son's look. Instead, the Lakota chief directed his attention toward his brother, Strikes Hard.

Still utilizing the language of sign, he said, "We must investigate. We will cache our kill here, so that we may return later to bring it home."

Strikes Hard frowned. "It is not our concern what these white people do. Let them kill one another if they must. It might save our own young men, since we are often at war with the white man."

White Buffalo nodded solemnly. "You speak wisely and you speak well, my brother. But it is curious that two parties of whites are in conflict."

"Perhaps," replied Strikes Hard. "But recall that we have often puzzled over the stupidity of these white men, for they are known by us to act in ways that are loco."

White Buffalo nodded briefly, yet he drew his brows together, the only indication that his thoughts might be weighty. He spoke silently, utilizing only the Plains language of sign, "Careful, brother. Do not forget that she who holds my heart is from that same race."

Strikes Hard had the decency to look abashed. Immediately, he responded with gestures alone, "I meant no offense, my brother. Your wife has been with us so long that I forget that her face is that of a white woman."

"As do I," signed White Buffalo. "Yet, the light color of my son's eyes remind me of his pale-faced heritage." White Buffalo stepped forward and gestured to Brave Wolf to squat down beside him. Gingerly, White Buffalo ran his hands over the numerous prints. But what his thoughts were as he knelt there remained a mystery to Brave Wolf, for his father was a master at hiding his musings.

At last, White Buffalo came up to his full height which rivaled that of his son's. With quiet dignity, he signed, "I agree that these tracks show treachery. I fear we must discover if these persons mean danger to our people, since the white soldiers wage war in a way that we Indians do not understand. If you, my brothers, do not wish to be part of our investigation, take the meat that we have hunted, and return home. There is no dishonor in doing this."

Boom! Crash! Boom! Crack!

But this time, the noise didn't stop.

Bang! Bang! Rat-a-tat-tat.

"I agree with White Buffalo." It was Watapah "speaking," also in the language of gesture. "We must protect our people. We must see for ourselves what danger, if any, these white people might bring to us."

Strikes Hard scowled, but he made no further protest.

So it was that in this manner it was decided. Quickly, each man cached the meat from their hunt, then each mounted his own pony, and all three of the hunters were away, sprinting over the prairie in the direction toward the trouble.

Brave Wolf, however, followed the others at a slower pace, since he was this party's *toŋwéya*, a scout; thus, it was his duty to continue his study of the earth, if only to ascertain any other clues here upon the ground. That his relatives had so recently spoken about his white heritage bothered him not even a little, although it might have given cause for a lesser man to pause and pursue his thoughts on the matter.

But to Brave Wolf's way of thinking, the mix of his blood proved nothing. He had always been, and would always be Indian -- and a *toŋwéya*, a scout. It was as a scout that he knew he had no place in his mind for wayward notions. There was only the here and now, and the future, of course. That the immediate future might hold trouble only served to show that he must concentrate. After all, it was his duty to ensure that he and his relatives returned home safely. In this, he would not fail....

***

Eighteen-year-old Mia Sheehan-Carlson smiled at her husband,

Jeffery Carlson, as he handed her the whip he used to guide their two oxen. She watched as Jeffrey jumped from the seat of their prairie schooner onto the grassy knoll of the plains, and when he spun back toward her, she basked under the heat of his gaze. He grinned up at her, and Mia was reminded of the fervor of their passion from the previous evening. Remnants of that devotion were still alive upon his countenance, for that fervor echoed lavishly in Jeffrey's gaze at her.

Warmth and the sense of belonging to this man stole over her, bringing her pleasure. She sighed as she smiled back at him. She and Jeffrey were newlyweds, of course, having tied the knot only a few short months earlier, four to be exact.

"You watch the rig for me, darlin'," Jeffrey said as he plopped his black cowboy hat onto his head. "I'll go see what all the fuss is about."

"Who is that man?" asked Mia, referring to the stranger who had that morning ridden into the midst of their small wagon train.

"I don't rightly know," responded Jeffrey, "but I'll make it my business to find out soon enough."

Mia nodded. "Just don't be gone too long from me." She gave him a lazy smile. "I'll miss you."

Jeffrey's grin widened. "I'll miss you, too, honey. Now, stay here and keep a tight guard over those oxen."

"I will," she replied.

She regarded him lovingly as he touched his hand to his hat. Pivoting, he turned away. Mia's gaze at him was gentle and full of admiration as she watched him stride away. In truth, she couldn't get enough of simply looking at him, and she did so now, adoring his lean, handsome figure as he ambled off in the direction where the wagon master and the newcomer were speaking. Other men in their small, five-schooner wagon train were ambling toward the stranger, also, but none were as tall, or as handsome as Jeffrey.

The meeting lasted longer than Mia would have expected, but in due time, Jeffrey returned to her.

Was something wrong?

As he came in sight, she scrutinized his long, slow gait, noting that it lacked its usual cheery step. Moreover, he looked downtrodden.

Upon drawing level with her, he took possession of his whip, procuring it carefully from her grasp. But the action was done without uttering a word or even looking at her. Something, she thought, was definitely not as it should be.

She asked, "What's wrong?"

Jeffrey didn't answer.

"Who is that man?" she questioned after several minutes. "Why is he here?"

Jeffrey gazed away from her before he replied, "He's the trail guide for another wagon train pulling up our rear. It's larger than ours, and he reckons we might be wise to wait for his people to catch up to us so as to allow us both to join forces."

Mia paused. Her frown deepened. "Why?" she quizzed. "Is he suggesting there might be trouble ahead of us?"

"Might be," Jeffrey answered as he shrugged. "He says we're comin' into Injun country and a small train like ours don't stand a chance of survivin' an Injun attack. The more firearms and able-bodied men there are with the train, the better." Jeffrey took off his hat and smacked it hard against his thigh. "Wish we'd waited for a larger train of wagons when we were back there in Independence."

Mia didn't respond right away. Instead, after a moment's pause, she asked, "What's been decided then? Will we wait for the other wagon train?"

Still looking off, away from her, he answered, "That's what most folks want."

Dead silence. Jeffrey neither uttered another word nor moved a muscle.

"And you?" Mia prodded gently. "Is that what you want?"

Slowly, Jeffrey squinted up at her. "Neither of us," he began, his words a slow drawl, "rightly considered the danger of Injuns when we began this trip. Last I inquired about Injuns, I understood they'd been tamed by the cavalry and sent to reservations. But according to this trail guide, there's a large band of them still free and at large."

"Oh." Mia gulped. "That doesn't necessarily mean that they're hostile, does it?"

"Doesn't mean they're friendly either. That trail master said he'd seen a war party out this way."

Mia took a moment to digest this information, and Jeffrey didn't volunteer further details. After a pause, she queried, "What's on your mind, then? Something is. That's obvious."

He didn't deny it. Instead, he slowly turned his gaze away from her. "Fact is," he began, "I'm not sure I want to put you at risk, darlin'."

Mia swallowed hard. "I appreciate the thought, and I thank you for your concern. But what are you suggesting?"

He paused significantly, and it was at some length that he responded, saying, "Near as I can tell, we have two options. We can stay here, wait for the other wagon train and take our chances..

"Yes? Or...?"

"Or we could go back." Squinting his eyes, he looked up at her as he followed up that statement with, "We'd lose the five hundred bucks we paid to join this outfit, but it's not too late to return to Independence, if you want to go back."

"Go back? But we barely escaped the agents that my father sent after us."

"Yep, that's so, I guess," Jeffrey replied, still looking away from her. "But the truth is, I'm not certain it was your father that sent them after us...might've been Max Greiner."

Mia frowned. Max Greiner. No. Surely not Max. And yet... "Could be Max," she agreed, "but if that were so, why would you want to go back?"

Jeffrey didn't reply at once. As he placed his arms over his chest, he brought his gaze back to hers and scowled. "Like I said, I'm of two minds about it. Don't rightly want to be responsible for puttin' you into some kind of jeopardy. Now, Max Greiner might be all kinds of things that you don't like, but I don't reckon he'd try to hurt you. We could make our way back to Independence and wait a spell. Maybe the Injun trouble will die down in a few months and we can try makin' this trip next spring."

"But I thought the idea was to escape my father's influence."

"It was, but— Conditions have changed."

Mia bit her lip. "Is there any reassurance that the trouble will be gone by next spring?"

"Reckon so. The cavalry's on the job."

She hesitated. "Sounds fair, I suppose." She shrugged. "But if we go back the way we've come, and wind up again in Independence, there's every possibility that my father will force me to go back east. He might even try to annul our marriage."

"Not much chance of that. Marriage has been consummated."

Jeffrey's tone was so dry, so calculated and seemingly hard-spirited, that Mia's heart caught for a beat. The way he talked, one might have surmised that she was a prize to be won in a game of chance.

Quickly, she admonished herself. What a disloyal thought. She was Jeffrey's bride, and he loved her as much as she did him.

Didn't he? Fearing to voice that thought aloud, she inquired instead, "What about the life that we talked about? What about Oregon? Having our own land, our own place, starting a family?"

"I still want those things, same as you do." He made a grab for her hand, caught it, and took it firmly into his grip. "But I also want you safe. Don't know what your father would do to me if somethin' happened to you." His voice trailed away.

Mia frowned again, lapsing into silence as she tried to make sense of her thoughts. On the one hand, she was glad that Jeffrey was concerned about her welfare. On the other, she couldn't shake the idea that he seemed...what? Afraid?

The thought had her scoffing. It was a ludicrous idea. Jeffrey had seen action during the Civil War. He was a decorated war hero. He was also one of the bravest men she knew.

Perhaps it was the unusual circumstances that confronted them now that was the cause of his contrary behavior. Maybe...

Still, she couldn't shake the feeling that Jeffrey *was* acting out of character. Where was his flirtatious grin, as well as the spark of daring that usually gleamed from his eye, that look that said, "Just try to cross me."

Sighing, Mia wished—and not for the first time—that she hadn't been born a senator's daughter. She knew too much, was too practiced in the charm of reading men's thoughts. Because she had grown up in the country's capital, she'd had a varied education. True, she'd been properly instructed in the many fine arts of painting, music and poetry. But one of those arts taught to her had been the "aptitude" of recognizing the telltale signs of lying, and amongst those signs was a sense of panic and anxiety. Those clues were here now on Jeffrey's countenance.

Mia calmed herself. Something was wrong, yes, but maybe there was good reason for it. Perhaps this newcomer—this trail guide—had simply put the fear of God into Jeffrey. And why not? They were traveling into the unknown. It was entirely possible that this alone was causing him to show his agitation.

Not knowing what to do or say, Mia took refuge in the advice her father had often repeated, and she said, "If there's one caution that Daddy always made, it's that nothing's 'safe' in life. And although I thank you for your thoughtfulness, I think it's unneeded. Think, Jeffrey, if we decide to go back to Independence, it might likely be the cause of ending our marriage. My father does have his ways...."

Jeffrey nodded. But he didn't take back his words, nor did he attempt to comfort her.

"Jeffrey, please," she pleaded. "I don't want to put our marriage at risk."

"I don't either."

"Then," she suggested, "I think we should go forward, stay with the train. That way, whatever the danger is, we'll be together."

Again, Jeffrey nodded, but his features looked carefully blank, as though he were hiding something from her—something important. He might have enlightened her about it, too, but the chance to do so was suddenly lost to him. At that moment, their wagon master pulled his roan up level with their wagon.

"Mornin' ma'am," he greeted as he drew rein and raised his hat.

She smiled. "Good mornin'."

Focusing his attention on Jeffrey, he added, "Don't reckon you should cotton up to leaving, Mr. Carlson. That trail guide says there's a large war party of Injuns behind us, as well as in front of us. Wouldn't be safe to leave now. I know what you said earlier about leavin' us to go back to Independence, but I think you'd best stay with us."

Jeffrey listened without comment. At length, he nodded. Meanwhile, Mia gaped at the trail master. Had she heard that right?

"Ma'am..." The man tipped his hat in her direction, then issued the order, "Yah!" to his mount. As he rode off, it seemed to her as if the confusion of the dust and dirt that his horse kicked up echoed her own bewilderment.

Silence ensued between Mia and her husband until at last Mia gave voice to her misgivings, uttering, "Did you tell the others that we would be leaving to go back to Independence?"

"I might have."

"Without consulting me first?"

"Didn't seem necessary. Thought we'd agreed that I should do what I think is best for us both."

Mia didn't comment. Instead, she bit her lip. Premonition spurred a deep-seated fear within her. Was she wrong? Had she made a mistake in running away? Differences aside, she had left behind all she had ever known and loved: a father who doted on her in most ways, save one, and a nanny who was like a mother to her, who had been with her since her mother's death almost eighteen years ago.

Of course, there had been problems back East, and Mia had fled from them; her chief concern had been a man called Max Greiner, who, along with her father, was pressuring her to honor the marriage contract between her father and his—a contract drawn up at Mia's birth. It was an old-fashioned practice, and Mia, being of a new generation, had chosen to ignore it.

After all, this was not fifteenth-century Europe. This was America, she'd told her father; America, the land where one might exercise a little free choice. Besides, she'd fallen in love with Jeffrey Carlson. She would marry Jeffrey, or no one.

Her father had disagreed, had scolded her and lectured her on the responsibilities of her position within the family. He had backed up his cause by pleading legal repercussions if she didn't consent, even to the point of threatening her. But it was all for naught. In the end, all the words and the threats had proved useless. Mia was determined that she would marry a man she loved, and she had acted on that decision.

But now, for a moment, if a moment only, she wondered if she had only traded one problem for another. Her decision to elope with Jeffrey had followed fast on the heels of Max Greiner's attempt to enforce the marriage contract. He had set a date, announced it in the paper, had even made arrangements with a priest.

Looking back, Mia realized she really couldn't have responded in any other way than what she had; not and remain free and true to herself. It was either escape, or be forced to wed a man whom she could never envision loving.

However, her decision carried with it a stiff penalty. Overnight, Mia's social life had transformed from that of a coddled heiress to an overburdened and often ignored pioneer woman. While it wasn't that she objected to the downgrade of her character, it was more to the point to say that, now and again, she missed the gaiety and stability of her former life.

Catching Jeffrey's eye, she scrutinized him, watching for signs, any facial expression that might show his innermost thoughts: a quickness of eye, a fine sweat, an inability to focus. She had thrown in her lot with this man and had made him the center of her world. Had she made a mistake?

Her father had disliked Jeffrey, had branded him a liar and fraud, citing Senator Wilson's daughter as an example.

"The man told Wilson's daughter that he'd loved her, too," Mia's father had remarked on one occasion. "They had planned to marry. But when the senator lost his fortune, Jeffrey disappeared."

At the time, Mia had chosen to ignore such evidence, especially because her father was so obviously blind to Max Greiner's faults. Besides, she'd spoken to Jeffrey about it, and he had told her that May—Wilson's daughter—had fallen in love with another.

But such evidence didn't matter to her father. No, according to Senator Sheehan, the sun rose and set by Max Greiner. He was rich, stable, handsome in his own way, and a man who would be faithful to her.

But Max Greiner frightened her in a way she couldn't quite grasp. There was an untamed and raw quality about him, something that was almost inhuman....

At that moment, Jeffrey smiled up at her and winked. It was the sort of grin that comforted her, and Mia found herself melting a little as he said, "Sorry I didn't ask you about returning to Independence. I'll know better in the future."

They were words. Nothing more than words. But their utterance had a way of settling her fears, and she sighed. It was going to be all right after all.

Jeffrey let go of her hand and said, "Guess I'd better go determine what the rest of the train is fixin' to do now that we'll be staying with them."

Mia nodded, returning his smile.

As if to position himself in her good graces again, Jeffrey presented her with a look of heated passion, the one that she was growing to recognize and to love. Then he declared, "Don't forget, I love you."

"And I love you," she replied. But a little voice in the back of her mind still held onto its doubt, asking her, "Is it true? Does he love me?"

She pushed the rebellious thought aside. Certainly Jeffrey loved her.

But perhaps not enough to risk danger in order to keep me with him.

Well, no one was perfect, she argued with herself. Besides, it was possible that he'd had only her welfare in mind. He was all she had now; he was her entire world. They were married. The deed was done.

It only remained for her to give him all of her that there was to give....

Yes, she was sure that was right.

CHAPTER TWO

With the promise of game aplenty and the lure of a few days fishing, the small wagon train settled down to await the larger party of pioneers that was slowly heading their way. The newcomer had guided all of their wagons into the refuge of a beautiful canyon, one filled with shade and the wonderful scents of pine trees, cottonwood and willow trees. Even now, those willow trees were dipping their many branches into the lazy rush of a crystal-clear stream which wound its way through the valley. It was an idyllic setting in many ways.

The ground was level here, the grass was short and green, and the abundance of trees seemed to keep the hot sun at a minimum. Perhaps that was why the valley resembled a park rather than the wilderness. One could easily imagine taking a leisurely stroll here.

Added to the valley's beauty were the brown hills that surrounded the place, and the deep, beckoning purple mountains in the far distance. It was a perfect site for a rest...or an ambush.

Mia shivered. If it were true that danger from Indians confronted them, the new trail scout and their wagon master had picked a shelter that didn't allow for an easy escape.

But the scout had declared the spot to be a perfect one, and perhaps the other pioneers in the wagon train were only thinking of hiding and lying in wait, since it would be several days before the other wagon train would catch up to them. If concealment were the best option, then this place was perfect—better than the open prairie.

Not for the first time, however, Mia wondered at the wisdom of their small train setting out on the trail to Oregon without soliciting the aid of an experienced veteran of the Western trails. Back in Independence, hiring such a man would have added an expense of two hundred dollars per wagon. It was a price that none had been able to afford, not after surrendering the five hundred dollar fee to simply be a part of this wagon train, as well as another two hundred dollars for their rig.

At least it was a well-known fact that the way to Oregon was well-marked from constant use, and since their wagon master knew the path well, enlisting a professional guide amounted to an unnecessary luxury. Besides, one of the travelers, a Mr. Mario, was a merchant, and he had made the trip to Oregon and back from it more than once. Between these two men, their small train stood a good chance of arriving in Oregon with little to no trouble.

Until now, there had been no reason to doubt her and Jeffrey's initial judgment, and perhaps her doubts held no substance. One detail that Mia did wish for, however, was that there were more women attached to this train. Besides herself, there was only one other female pioneer, the rest of the prairie schooners being peopled with men engaged in the merchant business.

Peggy was her name, and, like Mia, she was newly married. At present, Mia watched as the other woman approached, and by way of issuing her a warm welcome, Mia stood up from her seat on the wagon and jumped to the ground.

"Good morning, Peggy."

"Good morning."

Mia held out her hands in greeting, taking Peggy's within her own. "I see that you've brought some of your knitting and darning with you. Come, I'll find us a blanket to spread over the ground, where we can sit and talk for a spell. I'll bring out my mending, too."

"That would be most kind, Mrs. Carlson," said Peggy. "Most kind, indeed."

"Please call me Mia."

"Yes, Mia." Peggy smiled.

Mia grinned back, and, turning aside, she stepped up onto the running board of her wagon, then crawled into the back of it to find a blanket. Where was it? She and Jeffrey had slept on that coverlet last night. Surely it was right here....

Reaching up, Mia picked up a lantern and some extra rope on the floor, looking under them. Ah, there it was. How had it gotten under that rope?

Boom! Crash! Blast!

Involuntarily, a scream escaped Mia's throat, and she dropped the rope as she fell to the floor of the wagon. What was happening? Those were blasts from guns and rifles, and they were close, as though they were right outside. Was the wagon train under attack, or was it nothing? Was someone merely hunting?

Please Dear Lord, let it be hunting....

Boom! Boom!

Mia wasn't screaming now, but others outside her wagon were; men were barking out orders, and other voices were wailing as though in pain. Carefully rising up to peek out through a crack in the canvas, Mia shrieked, then covered her mouth with her hands as the remains of her breakfast threatened to come up.

Out there, with her knitting scattered over the grass, lay Peggy, a bullet shot through her forehead. The image was almost impossible to accept as real. Moments ago, Peggy had been very alive.

What was happening? Anger, and a good dose of terror, took hold of her. Who was attacking them? And why?

Though Mia had barely known the other woman, tears formed at the back of her eyes. One of those tears spilled down over Mia's cheek, and it was only then that the thought materialized that she would be there, too, and perhaps in the same condition as Peggy, had the blanket been within easy reach.

Crack! Boom! Crash!

Mia felt the whiz of something shooting past her—bullets. In reaction, she fell again to the floor and covered her head.

"Mia!"

It was Jeffrey's voice. Mia rose up to peep out through a bullet hole in the canvas.

"Mia!"

"I'm here in the wagon," she shouted out. "I'm here." She rose up enough to crawl to the running board and look out from behind it.

That's when she saw them. Indians!

"Mia!" Jeffrey was running toward their wagon.

"Jeffrey, I'm here in the wagon!"

For a moment, he halted as his gaze met hers. In that instant, more heartfelt communication transpired between them than in all their past conversations. This was it. They were doomed. They both knew it.

"Stay there!" he yelled. "Stay down and put a blanket over you! You hear?"

"Yes, I will. Yes. Please be careful! Don't get yourself killed!"

"I won't! Stay down!"

That's when it happened. One of those detonating blasts struck him. It caught him in the arm, and, jerking back from it, he fell to the ground.

Mia screamed, and she kept on screaming as she flew out over the running board.

"Jeffrey!" She hit the ground in a run.

"Stay away, Mia!" he ordered as he came up to his knees. "And get yourself back in that wagon!"

Mia halted, hesitating.

"Get back in that wagon!" Jeffrey repeated, barking out the command as he took up a position on the ground, and despite the injury to his arm, he held a pistol in each of his hands. "Get back in there," he called to her again, "and don't come out no matter what!"

Mia backed up toward the wagon.

Another shot fired close to hand, and she watched as though outside herself as Jeffrey caught the blow in the back. With a cry, he went down. He didn't move.

No! Mia burst into action at once, rushing toward Jeffrey. The distance between them, though no more than a few feet, seemed great, and the mere minutes passing by felt like hours.

At last, she reached him. She fell to her knees, and picked him up in her arms. "Jeffrey! Jeffrey! Don't you dare leave me. Don't you dare."

"Mia," he croaked through lips that were red with blood. Mia had turned him over so that his face was staring up at her. He muttered, "Why aren't you in that wagon?"

Mia was crying in earnest now. "Jeffrey, I love you. Don't leave me."

"Can't help it, Mia. Can hardly breathe." Then his eyes met hers. "Know that I did what I did 'cause I love you."

"And I love you. I love you, Jeffrey."

He opened his mouth to utter something more, but the effort proved to be more than he could accomplish. A gargle sounded in his throat, and as he took his last breath, his eyes opened wide until at last he lay staring up sightlessly at the sky overhead.

"No! No!" But even as she screamed out the word, she knew it was no use. He was gone.

Grief shot through her, and tears gushed from her eyes as though a fountain were contained within her. Through her tears, Mia reached down to close Jeffrey's eyes, noticing that the blood from his wounds was drenching her dress. But she little cared. She was beyond that.

"I love you, Jeffrey," she muttered. "I'll always love you."

The tears wouldn't stop, nor did she try to control them. She bent down over him, covering him with her body, and although the peal of shots surrounded her—for Mia, time stood still.

Perhaps she should seek safety for herself, as Jeffrey had ordered, but the thought occurred to her that if the Indians were intent on killing them all, then she would meet her fate, too. It calmed her somewhat. Yes, she would confront her destiny here beside Jeffrey.

Crying, her sobs were drowned out by the sound of killing and the cries of the dying. Mia, however, was too lost in her own grief to spare too much attention to what was happening around her. It didn't matter anyway, because she didn't expect to live. Indeed, she assumed that soon a bullet would find her, too, allowing her to join her husband.

What was it? Something had startled her out of her own thoughts and grief. It was quiet. Too quiet; it was a silence that, like an omen, spread like horror.

She listened. Nothing. There was no sound to be heard. Was the fight over so quickly? Had the wagon train's resistance been so meager that they'd only been able to muster a few minutes' defiance?

But she was still alive. Surely she should be lying here dead beside Jeffrey. Without making any noise, she pinched herself to make certain of it.

Gradually, the quieter tones of men speaking spread around her, and she listened to the deep voices of those who had staged the attack. Peeping upward cautiously, she saw that they were Indians. But there was a thing odd about these Indians. Strange, because she could understand every word they said.

"Did cha see that one runnin'? Got him with a single shot." Whoever was speaking laughed.

A surge of anger filled Mia, the spirit of defiance rising up within her. How dare he find humor in the doom of others.

Carefully, slowly, Mia raised up her head, and with great care, she inched her hand toward one of the guns that was still clutched in Jeffrey's grip. Though it took more than a little effort to pluck it from his death hold, she was at last able to free it, and slowly, inch by slow inch, she brought the weapon in close to her bosom.

More snickering and guffawing filled the air, and it occurred to her that something besides murder was wrong. But what? How was it that these Indians spoke English amongst themselves? And with American accents?

Warily, she glanced up, catching sight of these "Indian assailants." She frowned. Did Indians grow beards? Hadn't she read somewhere that most Indians had little body hair, that even the men of these tribes grew no facial hair?

"Did ya see 'er? Did ya see the one we're after?" The voice was surly, low-pitched and sour.

"Kilt dead," replied another. "Over there."

A short pause, then, "Ya idiot! The devil take ya. We was told we could have our way with that one afore we kilt 'er."

"How was I ta know?"

"Ya numbskull. A bonus is what awaits us, if'n we could've gotten that one back alive. Alive, but ravished so much that she cain't see straight." He guffawed. "Only then, once she was thinkin' she was safe, was we ta kill 'er."

"Why didn't ya say somethin'?" asked another voice.

"Idiots! Show me 'er body. Maybe it's still warm."

Mia bent down again over Jeffrey, but warily, she kept one eye open, watching as the murderers approached. They didn't, however, come close to her. In truth, it appeared they didn't see her. Instead, they strode to the place where Peggy and a few of the other men lay.

"That's not the one," the big man with the hostile voice roared. He was kicking Peggy's dead body, causing another fury of outrage to rip through Mia. But her protest quickly evaporated as she heard another one of them say, "Hair's supposed ta be red, not blond."

Hair was supposed to be red?

Mia's stomach dropped. Her hair was red. They were looking for her?

But why? It didn't make sense. No, more likely they were searching for someone else—someone who had cheated them? Yes, that had to be it. If she remembered correctly, there was a man with the wagon train who was red-headed. But they weren't looking for a man, were they?

"Gotta be here somewhere. Search all the wagons."

Perhaps, Mia thought, it was just as well that she hadn't sought the cover that Jeffrey had so entreated her to take. Maybe out here in plain view was the best hiding place after all.

"There! Did ya see something move o'er that way?"

Mia's stomach turned over, sickening her as she felt blood pump through her veins. They were pointing in her direction.

All her senses jerked into alertness. Oddly, instead of fear, she found strength in the impending doom, and despite the fear that spread like a deadly disease within her, she discovered a power within her.

For, as though her father were here with her, she heard his words, *"The best defense is a strong offense."*

The memory of those words gave her strength, and, taking a deep breath, she sat up, carefully positioned the pistol into both her hands, and pointed it at her enemy.

"It's loaded," she croaked out through dry lips, her voice unusually high. "Don't come any farther."

Each one of the bullies halted as though in surprise. However, much to her distress, the shock didn't last long.

"Oh, looky," said one of them. "One of the little girly's still alive, 'n thinks she can kill us all."

"She's a looker, that one," commented another one of the murderers before he grinned. "And she's got the red hair we're lookin' fer. I'll be first one with 'er a'fore we do our duty. We was told we could."

"No one's going to be first or have their way with me," Mia managed to say, even though her voice shook with the effort. "Now, back up." She came up to her knees, and from that position she stood to her feet. She wobbled, then steadied herself. Her full height of five foot four wasn't going to intimidate them, but perhaps her knowledge of how to shoot might.

"Back up," she ordered again. Her cry, for all its trembling, rang out loudly. "And drop your weapons. I won't tell you again. I've been trained to shoot, and I guarantee you that I can pull this trigger faster than you can move to overtake me. So do as I say."

No one budged.

"Don't think I'm too afraid to do it. This here is my husband lying dead at my feet. I'm looking for an excuse, any excuse, to kill you all."

Amazingly, this last declaration had the desired effect, and she watched as the three filthy and bearded "Indians" stepped back.

She repeated, "I remember telling you to drop your weapons, too."

One of them reached out to unbuckle his belt, and the others followed suit, but she had only a moment's satisfaction before the whiff of unwashed flesh warned her of impending doom. Her stomach lurched painfully as she realized there was a man behind her, and faster than she could move, the man had pulled her off her feet. He grabbed for her gun.

In reaction, Mia fired a bullet before the weapon fell to the ground. It was reflex alone that had caused her to take that shot, but still, she enjoyed an instant of pleasure as she heard one of the bullies yell. Then the ruffian from behind her pushed her to the ground.

She went down with a hard thump, for her strength was no match for his. Drat! Her own inadequacy seemed to hurt more than the physical pain of having her body held in a vise.

"I'll be damned. She shot 'im. That little girly got 'im."

Good, thought Mia.

"Kill her!"

"No!" yelled the biggest bully, the one with the deep, crass voice. "Not 'til we've done as we was told ta do. 'Sides, I want my way with her."

"Me too."

"We'll take turns."

The bully from behind her snickered. He also held her down so tightly, she could barely breathe. Meanwhile, another one of them bent down to take hold of her legs. Although she resisted with all her might, he managed to part them.

But her legs and her hips were the strongest parts of her body, and Mia wasn't about to make it easy for them. She kicked out at them until, exhausted, her legs would barely move.

"Hold them legs of hers fer me!"

In the end, it took three of them to keep her down, and, as they raised her skirts high above her head, Mia screamed out her frustration. Was there nothing more that she could do?

She struggled, she bucked. But her efforts only caused them to laugh all the harder.

"Guess she'll be a good ride, after all." It was the same one speaking, the one who looked to weigh more than three hundred pounds.

Mia peeked up over the material of her dress to catch a glimpse of the murderer's ugly face, looking on in horror as he dropped his pants.

He caught her look. "You want a piece of this, Missy?"

Mia didn't answer. It wouldn't have done her any good anyway. He came down over her.

She screamed, expecting the worst at any moment.

He chuckled. "She's a wild one, this one is—" He started to say more, but it never came. Suddenly, he gasped for air. Then there was nothing.

What had happened?

All at once, she was free. The bullies had let her go. Without pause, without even thinking, she pushed her skirts back down around her ankles, and came up onto her elbows. What was happening?

The biggest one of them, the one who'd been about to do his worst by her, fell over her and it took all her might to push him to the side so that she was free to move again. He was dead.

She gulped, then looked away. There was an arrow stuck in his neck.

Seeing him, even hating him as she did, Mia almost vomited. It was a terrible sight.

"Curse it all," cried one of the other murderers. "It's Injuns. Real ones."

Of course. That explained the arrow. Mia almost fainted. Real Indians. Did that mean she was saved or...?

She'd read news stories about what Indians did to the women they captured. Remembering those accounts, she shuddered.

"Where are they?" shouted out one of the assassins. "Do ya see 'em?"

"You'll ne'er see 'em," answered another bully. With the tables turned, and becoming the hunted instead of the hunter, the man seemed to lose his mind, because he commenced emptying his lead into the trees that surrounded them. But his gun had no more than clicked empty, when an arrow caught in him the heart. "Damn!" It was his last word.

In the meanwhile, because the other two bullies were looking elsewhere, Mia rolled off to the side, stopping beside Jeffrey's still form. She took refuge beside him, lying next to him, and watching from the shelter of his corpse.

"I don't see a thing, do you, Jake?"

It was a pointless question. Another arrow, well shot, caught the one called Jake in the throat. She paid heed as the man looked down at himself, at the blood running down his chest to his pant legs, before he, too, fell over, dead.

The final bully who was left standing stared insanely at the woods. His eyes bugged out.

"Come out! Come out!" he called. "Do ya hear me?"

There was no answer. Like his dimwitted companion before him, he shot into the woods wildly, one blast following upon the other in quick succession, his target apparently nothing but phantoms. Also like his buddy, as soon as he'd emptied his weapon, an arrow caught him. It landed square in his ear.

Had there been no blood involved in the hit, Mia might have admired that shot, for the target was small. But admiration was not in her mind this day. She screamed.

The scream was followed by trembling, and she shook from head to foot. Still, she had the presence of mind to survey her surroundings. Nothing moved. Nothing happened. The woods remained silent. Did she dare hope that her rescuer or rescuers had moved on? Was he or were they unaware she was here, alive? No, they were out there, waiting. For what?

She could barely breathe. Gradually, the bushes that skirted the woods shook, then a hand parted the thicket and a buckskin-clad figure stepped forward. She caught her breath. There was no mistaking who this man was—Indian—from his braided, long hair to the fringed buckskin shirt and leggings he wore. White and black paint covered his eyes like a mask and a wide, red band encircled the top of his head. As though to seal his identity and heritage, she noted that his chin showed absolutely no hair. When he raised his hand that held his bow and an arrow, as though bringing it into position for a kill, she almost fainted.

But she didn't. Instead, she tried to swallow her fear and use reason. After all, somebody had rescued her. Was it this man?

Somehow that didn't seem right. According to her understanding of it, white men were not villains, and Indians were not heroes.

The man might have been a statue, for he initiated no motion toward her. Instead, he stood rigid, and had she not been so frightened, she might have praised the way he held himself, for his stance looked casual, even insouciant. Yet, contradictorily, he appeared ready to kill if the need arose.

He was tall. He also looked young, as though he weren't accustomed to a recent growth spurt. Yet, young or old, there was no mistaking his threat, for in his hands he held that bow with an arrow at the ready. Did he mean the arrow for her?

She whimpered, the sound of it high and loud in this aftermath of deadly quiet. But he did nothing except look at her.

What was she to do? Let him kill her before she could decide if he were friend or foe?

"The best defense..." she silently recited to herself as she did her best to gulp down the contents of her stomach. Slowly, so as not to alarm him, she reached for the gun that lay at her feet. As swiftly as she could, she came up onto her knees, took aim and cleared her voice, calling out, "Come any closer and I will kill you."

The young man showed no surprise by her words. And although he looked anything but alarmed by her or even intimidated, he held up the hand that was holding his weapon. He loosened his grip on the bow and arrow, and let them drop to the ground. Then he shook his hand as though to say that he was now unarmed.

It didn't quite appease her. What should she do now? Should she collect those weapons?

All at once, she caught movement out of the corner of her eye. She chanced a quick look over her shoulder. Dear Lord, it was another Indian. How many of them were there?

Swinging her gun around, she turned to confront an adversary who was clearly older than the younger man whom she had been studying. If she had been frightened by this first Indian, she was doubly so with the second one. His face was painted in a pattern of black and red, and when he raised his hand which held his weapon, Mia screamed.

That's when she saw another figure come out from the woods...then another.

She began to shake all over, and a tear escaped from her eye. She was clearly out-numbered. Was this what it was like to die? Scared to death?

She couldn't control the shuddering of her body, and she realized she could barely hold the gun. Another tear fell over her cheek. Still, she knew that if she were to die here, she would not end her life as a coward.

Swallowing hard, and sweeping all three of these newcomers with her pistol, she called out, "Don't come any closer. I promise I will kill you all if you make another movement toward me. Now, throw your weapons on the ground." Her voice trembled, but at least she'd gotten the words out.

No one moved. No one disarmed himself.

Physical tremors raced over her, and her voice sounded more like a croak when she commanded, "I mean it."

Still, no one budged. She sobbed. How was this going to end? In her death? Or with the loss of her feminine dignity?

Suddenly, strong, masculine arms came around her from behind and reached out to grasp the gun in her hands. The man removed it from her grip so easily, she felt as though she were a baby and the pistol was as lethal in her hands as a peppermint stick.

The young Indian. How could she have forgotten him? And how could he have come upon her without making any sound and without alerting her in any other way?

Spinning around, she found herself engulfed in his arms, and as fear took over any reasonable thinking, she screamed. He let her go, but it was too late. She collapsed, and was only slightly aware that those same arms caught her before she hit the ground. Then, blessedly, there was nothing....

CHAPTER THREE

Brave Wolf carried the woman to the side of the battleground, laying her on the soft grasses there, which would cushion her until he could find a blanket to place beneath her. Then, satisfying himself that she had simply passed out and that she would most likely recover, he turned away from her and trod back to the spot where the fight had taken place.

Cautiously, he stepped around each body that lay over the ground, bending toward each person to search for any heartbeat. Was anyone else alive? Had only the woman survived?

The awful stench of death would soon be upon this place, but for the moment, only a tinge of it hung in the air. Bodies lay in a scattered formation, twenty in total. Brave Wolf counted fourteen pioneers; the rest were their attackers—men who had dressed themselves as Indians. Why had they done this?

Even he, who was accustomed to the sight of death, found the scene before him oppressive, and he paced toward the side of the valley, away from the bodies. What a waste, he thought, a bad use of this beautiful place, and a ravage of all the life that had been here. With sympathy, he shot a glance from over his shoulder toward the woman, who still lay where he had positioned her, reminding him that he had come this way in search of a few blankets.

Letting go of a deep breath, he stepped toward a wagon and was pleased to find two spreads from within the wagon's inner sanctum. Then, striding back toward her, he bent over her. He pulled and twisted and pushed the blanket until it lay between her and the ground. Then he placed the second quilt over her, hoping to prevent as much shock as possible. Her hair was the color of an orange-red sunset, it being a hue he had never seen on a woman until this moment, and perhaps, he justified to himself, this was the reason that he ran his hands over the long, reddish locks of it.

She was youthful, he noticed; probably her age was close to his own, a little younger, perhaps. She had also been lying next to the corpse of a man whose youth appeared to be about the same as hers. Her husband?

Being this near to her, touching her, he thought he could feel the depth of her loss this day, and he imagined what he might experience personally if his own love, Walks-in-sunshine, were gone from this world.

Yes, war had come to this land, and he was wise enough to realize that this might only be the beginning. All he realized at present, however, was that he'd seen too much of it these past few years. Often his people, the Lakota, found themselves embroiled in skirmishes between his own people and the whites.

That his heritage was half white, he again dismissed from his thoughts. He had few happy recollections of that branch of his family, since those relatives had left this part of the country when he'd been a lad of only ten winters. He also remembered the anguish those people had caused his mother; he recalled her tears, as well as his father's attempts to soothe her hurt.

But the memories hadn't always been bad. Only after *she* had come had conditions on that side of the family worsened.

His mother's mother, his grandmother, had been living in the East, and had ventured west at the request of her soldier husband. He recalled now that the meeting had been far from what he had anticipated, for his maternal grandmother had fainted at the sight of him and his older sisters.

Her arrival seemed to change the Indian/white familial relationship forever. Before his grandmother's arrival, his family had often journeyed to the soldier fort to visit with his mother's father. He recalled the image of his grandfather well—a tall, strong man with blue eyes, a man who seemed to be as jolly as the songs that accompanied the white men's dances. Brave Wolf had loved him, had respected him.

And then she had come....

It had been a happy occasion as they'd traveled to the soldier fort that summer. His mother, especially, had been jubilant. The entire family had gone to meet his maternal grandmother: his parents, his two older sisters, and himself.

They had been smiling and laughing, trading jokes as they had awaited a grandmother that the children had never seen. As the wagon had pulled into the parade grounds of the white man's fort, he had recognized his grandfather, of course. But his attention had been given to the woman at his side.

She had appeared to be a frail woman. A frown had pulled her brows together, and the corners of her mouth were twisted downward, as though her thoughts were particularly sour. She had once been beautiful, Brave Wolf thought; her hair was the same color of dusty-blond as his mother's, except that the few locks of hair that escaped his grandmother's bonnet were splattered with gray.

He recalled that he had been anxious to meet her, and when his mother had called him to her, in order to introduce them to each other, he had stepped forward proudly, and had even managed to smile at this personage who was so closely related to him.

He had expected her to be joyous to meet him, for in camp, his grandmother on his father's side was his best defender, showering all three of her grandchildren with love and adoration. Truly, he'd had no cause to think this woman would be any different.

"Kristina, what is the meaning of this?" The question had been spoken in a high-pitched voice that was edged with accusation.

His mother had pulled him into her arms, and smiled. "Why, this is my youngest child, my son, Mama. His name is – "

"No!" The word had been screamed, and his mother had broken off, never to finish that introduction. "Is this some cruel joke?"

"No, Mama. Don't you remember that I married Tahiska, White Buffalo? This is our youngest, your grandson."

Brave Wolf noted that his father had come up beside his wife, and had stepped slightly in front of her.

"No!" His grandmother had yelled the word, swooned, and might have fallen to the ground, had not his grandfather taken hold of her before she fell. The woman looked up, into her husband's face, and had asked, "How can this be, Wendell? How could you have allowed this to happen?"

"Now, Margaret, don't you recall the day Kristina married the man

standing there beside her? Don't you remember me writing to you to tell you about each child of their union?"

"But they are Indian, Wendell. I had thought.... Indians! They are dirty and savage, and they cannot possibly be family of mine."

"Mama..." His mother had stepped around her husband and had paced forward. She had taken his grandmother's hand in her own, and had continued, "Why don't we put all this behind us and go inside, for we have prepared a feast in honor of your arrival. Mama – "

The sound of the slap had resounded within Brave Wolf's ears long after the fact of it.

"You are no daughter of mine!"

Brave Wolf still recalled his mother's cheek, red with the imprint of his grandmother's hand. He also recollected his mother's tears and the shock so clearly witnessed upon her countenance.

His father had turned toward him, had signaled him to escort his older sisters from there, to entertain them, and to look out for them. Then, Tahiska had taken command of the situation, and despite the Lakota taboo of a man and his wife touching one another in public, he had pulled his wife into his arms and had escorted her in the direction of their lodge.

In the days to come, Brave Wolf had watched his father comfort his mother, spending long moments within their lodge – teasing her, laughing with her, reminding her of their happiness.

With time, the incident had faded into insignificance, and his mother seemed to recover; her sunny disposition had returned, being as genuine as it had been before that fateful meeting. But Brave Wolf had never forgotten.

Within only a few months, his maternal grandfather and his grandmother had left the country. They had never returned. And Brave Wolf had forgotten them and more....

With the will of his mind, he had consciously divorced himself from all things the white man had to offer – including its language. Never again, he had determined, would he speak a word of the dreaded English. Truth was, he couldn't bring his tongue to say those words anymore. Always, they reminded him of a grandmother who had rejected him, and who had slapped his mother.

His mother, however, had never tired of trying to teach the white man's tongue to himself and his sisters. His siblings were better learners than he was, but only because he wouldn't allow a word of that language upon his tongue. Never, unless he had to, would he speak English again. Never...

As Brave Wolf stared off into the beauty of the hills surrounding this battle, he came back to the present. Occasionally, he wondered what had happened to his grandfather and grandmother, but he had never questioned his father about it, for to do so was the height of bad manners.

Sometimes, he puzzled over the mindset of these newcomers, the whites, to this land. Were these foreigners more like his grandfather, or were they more akin to his grandmother?

He hoped it might be the former, but whatever the case, he realized that the pale-faced men were here to stay. Further, the battle lines were quickly arising between them and his tribe. What would the future hold for his people, for himself and his family?

Dismissing the uncertainties of the future from his mind, he looked around him, taking in the clues that were left here. But what remained here was clouded in mystery. Why were these whites at war with one another?

Cautiously, he stepped from one dead man to the other. It was to be regretted that their small hunting party had come here too late. By the time he, his father and his uncles had arrived, all of the white pioneers had been killed. All, that was, except the woman. Truth was, had her assailants left her alone, it was doubtful their hunting party would have intervened.

Brave Wolf frowned. Why were these whites so willing to rape one of their own kind? Moreover, what demon had caused the evil ones to dress up as Indians?

He shuddered at the thought that his people might be blamed for what had happened here today. Had these white devils meant to bring even more fighting to the land of the Lakota?

Brave Wolf gazed on as Watapah and Strikes Hard scalped the bullies, as was their honor to do. It seemed that by mutual agreement, his uncles were leaving the innocent pioneers alone.

"Are you taking any scalps?" asked White Buffalo.

"*Hiyá*. No," answered Brave Wolf, shaking his head. "I am scout for this party. None here are mine to take."

"*Wašté*. Good." White Buffalo said, using both signs as well as words. "We are done here. It is time for us to return to our village with the meat we have procured for our families."

Brave Wolf nodded.

"Yet, we cannot leave this woman alone and without some one of us to watch over her. It is certain that she would soon perish if left on her own. But we cannot bring her with us. You know this, for she might cause danger to our people, since it is well known that the blue coats raid those tribes who are housing white women captives. Stay with her, my son. It will be best. Because of your mother, you can speak a little English, and so you might be of assistance to her. See that her needs are met, and when her grief eases, bring her to the trading post on the Kaw River where it meets the Big River. White men's boats run there. Perhaps she might ride on one of them, which would bring her back to her own people."

Brave Wolf nodded. "*Wašté,* good. I will do as you say."

Brave Wolf didn't mention his aversion to speaking the English language. To do so would have been discourteous, as well as rude, for one didn't question one's elders.

White Buffalo continued, "I will tell your mother and your sisters where you are."

"And Walks-in-sunshine," added Brave Wolf with sign and a few words. "Have my sisters tell her, also. Let her know I will bring home honors enough so that we can at last marry."

White Buffalo smiled, but only for a moment, before he said, "I will ask one of your sisters to tell her."

"*Wašté,* good," said Brave Wolf. "*Wašté.*"

"But beware," added White Buffalo thoughtfully, "the woman

here is an unusual beauty, and it appears that she lost a man in this fight. It is to be expected that she might summon your sympathy. Be aware that she might prove to be hard to resist on your journey to bring her to safety. It is also to be assumed that she will be missing her husband and the intimacy that a married couple shares. My son, recall well that a man who indulges in love-making too much can sacrifice his strength and ability to fight an enemy and win. Although Walks-in-sunshine might forgive you a short romance, you must ensure you guard your affections well, for this woman's safety, and for yours."

Brave Wolf nodded. "I thank you for your wise advice, my father," he acknowledged. "But my heart is filled with a love that is true for Walks-in sunshine. *Awicakeya,* indeed, I hold no fear of another woman catching my fancy. I have given Walks-in-sunshine my oath that we will marry upon my return. I will not break it."

"*Wašté.* Good. I am glad to hear it. Still," White Buffalo smiled briefly, "I would advise you to guard your heart well, for within our family runs a weakness for the beauty of the white woman." Gently, White Buffalo laid his hand on his son's shoulder. "Remember that not all white women will welcome the security of an Indian husband. Your mother is an exception." He grinned. "For that, my heart is glad. But these are troubling times; our country is at war, and a strange war it is, for we fight not only enemy tribes, but we, and our enemies also, fight the white man. Travel with care, my son."

"I will do as you say, my father."

Brave Wolf's father nodded his approval. "We go now," he declared simply, and with a signal to the others, he and the rest of their hunting party disappeared back into the woods, to that place where they had left their ponies hobbled. Brave Wolf knew that his father and his uncles would return to where they had cached the riches of their hunt, for their families awaited the meat. They would also bring the knowledge of this fight back to their chiefs.

Perhaps only then could the threat of what had happened here be analyzed. Meanwhile, he had best bring back to mind a few of the English phrases he knew. Were he a weaker man, he might curse the necessity of speaking the white man's tongue, but being in his right mind, he grasped that there was no other way....

***

Brave Wolf's father and his uncles had left long ago, and still the white woman lay unconscious upon the ground. After ensuring that she was simply sleeping and not unconscious, and that she was safe from the elements, Brave Wolf stepped farther into the camp, looking through wagon after wagon, for he was hoping to find clues as to why this fight had happened. But there was little here that provided him with what that reason might be.

He cut the straps that chained the oxen, then urged them to leave. He had no need of them, and there was little reason to let them die here because of confinement. The open prairie would feed them.

From the wagons, he had obtained food aplenty for the woman and himself, which meant he wouldn't be required to leave her to hunt for their sustenance. At least, not immediately. There was also a plentiful source of guns and ammunition, a rich find for a man who intended to travel upon the open plains.

It was strange, for nothing appeared to have been stolen. Nor was there any evidence that an attempt had been made to do so.

Why? Again, he wondered what could have caused this. A blood feud? An insult? An injury?

He ruled out all of these, since, had the assailants possessed revenge as their reason, they would have had no cause to imitate Indians. That action alone proved to him that the bullies who had committed murder wished no credit for their actions.

Briefly, he glanced again at the woman to ensure that she was still in the same position he had left her. Her vulnerability tugged at his heart, and he realized that his father had been wise to speak of caution, for the woman was a delicate beauty. But what his father didn't know was that Brave Wolf was committed to Walks-in-sunshine, whom he had loved since he was a lad. He would not betray her, for he had given her his oath. He would keep it.

Several hours later, after taking further inventory of what was left, Brave Wolf sat down in a position near enough to the woman to keep guard over her. In his hands, he held a small stick of wood and a knife. It was in his thoughts that the woman might have need of a comb, for women were known to desire such accessories. She might also like a walking stick, for they would be required to travel by foot to the nearest trading post. For safety, he had left his pony in his father's care, because when he and the woman left here, they would be open to predators, and horses could be too easily spotted on the plains, thus announcing his position to his enemies. It was a well-known maxim to the Indian: when scouting alone, one had best travel under his own exertion.

Hau, yes, a cane might help her. He would see that she had one.

***

Hunger caused Mia to return to the world of the living. She breathed in deeply, if only to ensure she was still alive. As the sweet taste of oxygen filled her lungs, she realized that it was not in her destiny to die here today. Was she happy with that fact?

She wasn't certain. Perhaps there was merit in dying alongside her husband, yet the welcome scent of oxygen taken into her body made her glad for a reason she could not quite define.

Was that wrong? Truth was, had death come to her this day, she knew she would have welcomed it. And yet...

She sat up as her stomach growled. Being alive meant she would require food to eat, and there should be provision enough in her wagon. But on the tail end of this thought came another: such nourishment would require a fire, and the good Lord help her, she didn't have the energy or the will to start one right now.

But there would be water in the wagon. That would have to be enough, she decided, at least for the time being.

Apparently she was alone, for there was little more than the stirring of the wind in the trees to hear. Rising up, she glanced down at her dress. The fact that the material was blood-soaked didn't bother her. It was Jeffrey's blood, and therefore, sacred to her. Indeed, she might never wash this dress. But she would change out of it. It smelled bad.

As she quickly surveyed the valley around her, the gradual stench of the dead was starting to permeate the air. She put her hands over her nose, as if the action might make the smell go away. But it didn't work.

Perhaps she possessed a scarf that she might tie around her face. It was either that or suffer it, since her only option was to stay here and await the other wagon train, which, if she remembered correctly, would be coming here soon.

She stepped toward her wagon.

"Hau."

Mia stopped deadly still. Someone had spoken. She wasn't imagining it. She knew she wasn't. Was it Jeffrey? Was he alive after all?

Slowly, she turned around. It was dusk, which made it difficult to see clearly.

"Hau. Yahíacipe manke." A man rose up from his position atop a rock.

Mia screamed.

"Wan ka wan! Yahíacipe manke." The man stepped toward her, his hands outstretched as if he were speaking with his hands alone. In broken English, he said, "I...no harm...mean you."

It was that Indian! The young one with white and black paint over his eyes and a red band tied around his head! She screamed again, and, spinning around, fled to her wagon.

She clambered into the back of it, toward the spot where she and Jeffrey had kept their weapons. There it was. A rifle. Was it loaded? Quickly she checked it.

It wasn't. With trembling fingers, she put a cartridge into it, and, clicking it closed, she pushed its muzzle through a bullet crack in the white canvas tarp. She breathed in deeply.

No! This wasn't right. The Indian might come through the back, or even use the front of the wagon to get at her. Worse, he was probably a better shot than she was.

Not knowing what to do, she sat back on her heels and cried. Had she lived through the worst of the day only to have to endure more? Was her future to be torture at the hands of Indians? Rape?

At last, not knowing what else to do, she called out, "I have a gun and I know how to use it. Don't come any closer."

"*Waunkinioinéktsni.*"

"Don't come any closer to me."

"I...have...with you…no...fight...."

"You stay there. I'll stay here."

"*Hau, hau.* Yes."

His voice sounded as if it came from a distance farther away. Had she frightened him?

Not likely. Well, she thought, there was nothing else for it. She would have to stay here on guard the night through. Drat! The water was in a keg outside the wagon.

Biting down hard on her lip, she sat back against her legs, shifting her body into a position that she might be able to defend, regardless of what direction he might choose to stage his attack. And an attack was brewing. She was certain of it.

But she would catch him before he could harm her. This she promised herself.

***

The smell of food awakened her. Mia jerked herself into alertness. Oh, dear Lord, she had slept! How could she? And why was she still alive?

The aroma from outside the wagon smelled wonderful, though. She recognized the scents of bacon and eggs and her stomach growled. Did Indians eat bacon and eggs? She had heard that they subsisted on nothing but buffalo.

Her stomach spoke to her again, this time with hunger pangs. Guardedly, she sat forward so that she could look out through the crack in the wagon's canvas. There he was! That Indian. His countenance around his eyes was still painted in a mask-like design, as though he were adorning himself for war, but at least he had laid his weapons far away from him. They weren't even within easy reach for him. Had he done this in order to tell her without words that it was safe for her to come out?

No, she couldn't go out there. He might kill her.

Ah, but the scent of those bacon and eggs... Her mouth watered.

The Indian suddenly glanced up toward the wagon, as though he could see her through the crack. Could he?

He didn't say a word, however. Instead, he smiled and gestured toward her where she kept watch in the wagon. Then using his hands, he indicated a spot next to him. He held out a cup of water toward her.

His actions spoke for themselves, and Mia gulped. Could she trust him?

No. Never!

However, she reasoned, he hadn't attacked her last night, when she had been at her most vulnerable. Slowly, with rifle clutched firmly in front of her, she stood to her feet and stepped out from under the canvas covering.

As she glanced toward him, the wind wafted toward her, bringing with it that fragrance of the bacon. Perhaps it was this which was her undoing, and she found herself speaking up, saying to him, "Do you have any extra food?"

Again, he smiled at her. *"Hau. U wo."* Then in English. "Come...sit...eat. I have...plenty."

Mia swallowed hard. She glanced toward his weapons that still remained far away from him, then at the fire and the food cooking. Her stomach rumbled.

That decided it.

Slowly, with the rifle held in a ready position, she climbed down from the wagon, keeping the Indian always within her view. Looking downward, she grimaced at the bloodstains on her dress, for she had been unable to change out of it.

But he did nothing more than grin at her, and, despite her

misgivings, she noted that he was handsome in a savage sort of way—at least she thought he might be beneath all that white and black paint, as well as that red headband he wore. And he was young, perhaps only a little older than she was.

The observation gave her a sense of ease...at least a little. She said, "I would like a bit of that, if you have some to spare."

He nodded, and again motioned toward her, picking up the cup of water and holding it out to her. One slow step followed upon another until she stood within a few feet of him. With her right hand, she held the rifle, not pointed at him, but in an ever-ready position. With her left, she reached toward the water.

She didn't wish to appear greedy, but as soon as the liquid came close to her lips, instinct took over, and she gulped down every last drop of it. Glancing up, she returned the cup to him, then wiped her mouth. Glancing up, she saw that he was studying her.

Once more he nodded, and he looked amusedly at her.

"It's good," she said, and not knowing what else to do, she returned his smile. There was a plate filled with bacon and eggs, and he gestured toward her, obviously asking her to sit. She wouldn't. She didn't dare.

But when he held the plate out to her, she found her hand stretching forward toward it. However, she couldn't hold the plate, eat and keep her weapon in a position where she could use it, if that were to become necessary.

He solved the problem by holding the plate for her. Tentatively at first, she reached for a piece of bacon. It took no more than bringing it close to her face for her to practically stuff the food in her mouth.

She didn't stop at one piece. She ate everything on the plate, including the eggs. Her body thanked her for her wisdom in not refusing the food. And, prayer-like, Mia silently thanked this young man.

Only when she had appeased her appetite did she see that he withdrew the plate. Then he offered her the water again.

Gladly, she accepted. "Thank you."

He nodded.

He started to rise. Alarmed, she stepped back and held up the rifle.

Holding up his hands, he brought himself into a position on his knees before he stood to his feet. He was a tall man, she noted once again, tall and slim with the firm muscles of an athlete. He wore no shirt this morning, she observed reluctantly, and her gaze lingered on the beaded necklace that hung down over his chest. A large claw hung there, and she could only surmise that it might be the claw from some huge beast. A bear?

She had once seen a bear at her home back in Virginia. The incident had so frightened her that she had never again ventured into the heavy woods that surrounded her home. Had this boy/man killed a bear?

The thought had her setting her rifle in a ready position, but he simply reached out away from her, to grab hold of another slab of bacon, whereupon he placed it on the skillet that sat atop a smoke-less fire. As soon as he had accomplished the task, he sat down again and looked up at her.

Pointing at himself, he said, "*Lakōl*". Then he motioned toward her.

"That is your name? Lakota?"

"*Hiyá,* no. *Lakōl*...my..." He frowned and muttered, "*Oyáte*...tribe."

"Oh. Then what is your name?"

"I...," he pointed to himself, "speak it...cannot. Manners...bad."

"I see. Well then, since I don't wish to cause you bad manners, I suppose I'll have to address you as Mr. Lakota."

When he didn't speak or protest in any other way, she bowed her head slightly in acknowledgement, and said, "But I should tell you my name so you'll know what to call me. Mia. My name is Mia."

He nodded. "*Hau,* Mi-a."

"*Hau*? Does that mean hello."

"*Hau,* hello. Also means...yes," he affirmed, then he gestured around their camp. "Your...husband...die?"

"Yes," she nodded. "Yes. He died." She swallowed back the gulp in her voice.

"I...stay to...help...you..."

"Why? Why would you help me?"

"Woman..." he gestured toward her, "...die..." He frowned as he obviously searched his memory for the right word. "...Die," he continued, "...if...if no help."

She came down onto her haunches and sat, her calves pulled into a position under her. She laid the rifle on her lap. "I think I understand what you're trying to say. That I might die if you don't help me."

He nodded.

"It is kind of you to be concerned about me," she said, "but there is another wagon train coming this way—it is behind us. I can wait here for them."

He frowned. Then training his gaze on her, he replied, "No...sea...of...white..." He shook his head. "None. Wagons...no."

"Perhaps you didn't see it. The guide said it was a few days behind us."

Again, the young man shook his head. "Wagon...train...none. Not...behind. Not...in front."

Mia furrowed her brow. Surely this wasn't right. Hadn't that trail guide told them that there was a wagon at their rear? It was the only reason they'd stopped here.

Then another thought crossed her mind. Had the man been lying? She blinked a few times. Then she looked up at Mr. Lakota. She asked, "Are you telling me the truth? That there is no wagon train near here? None at all?"

"*Hau*. Train...none." He nodded.

"I can't believe that. Why..." It came to her then. The scout—the man they had all trusted—might have been one of the murderers. He had left their small party to return to his own wagon train. But if there were no train, if he had done this only to—

She caught her breath. If he had been one of their attackers, then he would be here amongst the dead, dressed in Indian garb like the rest of his fellows. She hated to do it, to search over the dead, but she would have to do it. If that man were here, it meant that she and this small wagon train had been utterly betrayed.

She didn't say a word. Instead, she rose up to her feet, and turning her back on the Indian, she stepped out amongst the dead. She found the man after some little search. He was, indeed, dressed as an Indian, but he was also easily recognized.

She swayed. The truth was a hard matter to come face-to-face with.

That man had utterly deceived them. But why? Had someone in their midst cheated one of these murderers? Cheated all of them? Try as she might, Mia could think of no reasonable explanation for the slaughter, outside of— What was that they'd said about a woman with red hair? She couldn't quite recall what had been said now, but it seemed to her that it might have something to do with her.

Perhaps it was her lack of understanding of the motives involved in this slaughter, or maybe it was fear or anger that caused her to teeter on her feet. She felt oddly weak. She ran a hand over her eyes, realizing she was going to be sick to her stomach. Her knees buckled under her, and despite her best efforts, she fell to the ground at the same time that the contents of her stomach spilled up. But she didn't reach the ground.

Sturdy arms came around her to catch hold of her, and she was brought up firmly against the chest of her rescuer. Oddly, before she lost consciousness altogether, she was aware that his arms felt good around her.

What an unusual thought, she decided before the all-consuming blackness of unconsciousness engulfed her once again.

CHAPTER FOUR

When next she awoke, she was greeted by the tops of trees swaying gently in the ever-present prairie wind. Their leaves seemed somehow greener when contrasted with the steel blue of the sky above her. A subtle haze filled the air and lingered in the tree branches; moreover, the sound of the birds chattering and singing seemed to indicate that it might be early morning. If she turned her head, she could see that select rays of the sun were breaking through the pinkish and orange clouds that were scattered in the eastern sky, their magnificence seeming to lend not only color, but inspiration to the prairie. Perhaps these thousand different hues of pink, red, orange and blue had purpose, as though their beauty were there for no other duty than to lend courage to the inhabitants below.

It was an observation she had often commented upon to Jeffrey. One could feel the presence of something here on the prairie, of God perhaps. The brilliance of the sky and the unending roll of the landscape seemed to remind a person that God was alive, well and at peace with the earth.

She paused in her thoughts—sunrise? Hadn't it been afternoon when last she had recalled the day? Yes, yes. It had been late in the afternoon, and yet, the evidence that morning was stirring all around her could not be dismissed.

What had happened to the rest of the day? Had she slept so long?

Perhaps. But it seemed that it didn't matter. Her bed this morning was warm and snug, and she breathed in deeply, feeling as though she were wrapped in a warm cocoon. Strong, naked arms encircled her from behind, and the taut skin of her guardian acted like a cushion, fitting in perfectly to her body, shielding her. Sweet, gentle breath stirred the wisps of her hair at the crest of her ear, and the enticing, musky scent of a male body filled her senses. Jeffrey. He was alive. He was here beside her.

She sighed. *It had all been a bad dream – nothing more than a horrible nightmare.*

Smiling, she opened her eyes slightly and snuggled deeper into Jeffrey's embrace, treasuring the silky feel of his long hair as it spread over her shoulders and breast. Her eyes flew wide open.

Long hair?

Long hair meant... Without moving even an inch, she looked down. Those arms that surrounded her were tan in color, not white. They were also oddly devoid of hair.

With a power akin to that of a lightning bolt, the memory of the recent slaughter of Jeffrey, of her near rape, her escape from death, all rebounded upon her, as though her thoughts packed a physical punch. It was happening too fast, and her grief recoiled on her and smothered her. Like a bad play which keeps getting worse, she felt herself grow small in relation to the facts.

It had been no dream. This was not Jeffrey who was nestled up so closely to her. This was Mr. Lakota, the same boy/man who had stayed behind to help her, the same one who had cooked her breakfast. But why was he huddled up behind her? Unless... Had the worst happened that caused him to feel he had the right to?

Afraid of what she might discover if she moved so much as a muscle, she froze, her mind searching for a logical explanation as to why he might be lying in so close to her backside. The last detail that she recalled was what? Yes. Yes. If she thought hard about it, she would remember.

"No...move...," came the husky, low whisper, there at her ear. "We...being watched..."

Watched? No! Not again! By whom?

That's when she heard it, the slow steady stealth of an enemy, either man or animal, advancing toward them. What happened next was so swift, she barely had a moment to conceive of what had occurred, let alone see it. Suddenly, and without warning, Mr. Lakota leapt up and over her, letting go of a blood-curdling scream.

There was an abrupt, howling response, followed by the sound of fleeing feet or paws. And then there was nothing. Silence. Not even the wind appeared inclined to intervene.

"We...go...now."

What? Go? With Jeffrey not put in a proper grave? "No," she said. "I can't. I have to remain here and bury my husband and the rest of these people."

"No time. That...was wolf. He...be back. Bring others. We...go at once."

"I cannot. I must see that my husband has a decent burial."

"No. Wolf bring...pack...here. One wolf…alone not brave. Many wolves...very brave. We...go."

"But I—"

"Not...safe...here." He turned toward her and held out his hand. "Come."

She ignored that hand, and came up onto her feet unassisted. How dare he order her about as though she were mentally unstable. Did he think that because of what had happened here, she was not in complete possession of her senses?

She took a deep breath, crossed her arms over her mid-section, and declared, "I will not."

"You...must do as...I say."

"I don't think so. I'm not certain that I trust you to think for me and..." She frowned. "Why were you sleeping so closely to me just now?"

"You...cry in…sleep," he answered without hesitation, which she knew was an indication that he was probably telling the truth. "I...try to...pain...ease."

"I—I hope that was all it was."

He scowled at her, but the look was quickly gone. In its place was an expression of great calm, as though he were dealing with a willful child. He motioned toward her again, saying, "*Itó,* come."

But she stayed where she was.

"*Itó,* come," he gestured once more with a hand movement.

"I will not go with you," she stated flatly. "Leave if you must. But I will stay here. My beliefs in my God require that I put my husband and these people to rest properly."

Mr. Lakota turned more fully toward her and this time he glared at her. She stared right back at him, and because she held his gaze, she could discern that he was uncomfortable, that he was struggling with himself. Why? Was he wondering if he should pack her over his shoulder and leave? Or was he determining that his best course of action was to walk away at any cost, even going on without her?

At length, he sighed. "Husband... We...bury husband. Then go."

"No. I must see that they all receive a burial."

He shook his head. "Husband...only. Go...must leave."

Suddenly, it was all too much. She had to bury all those men from the wagon train, didn't she? Wasn't it her duty? But there were so many of them, she contradicted her own thoughts. Would it hurt the dead to let them lie? To bury Jeffrey only? Maybe not.

But there was another problem. Could she bring herself to leave Jeffrey so soon after his death? No, indeed not. And yet she had to. After all, she couldn't stay here indefinitely, and alone.

Or could she? Staying behind would mean her death most certainly, but was that such a horrible idea? Hadn't she wished only hours ago to join him in death? Yet she was still alive. Well, since she hadn't died with him, then wasn't it her duty to remain here with him until she sensed that Jeffrey had left to meet his Maker?

Confused and feeling more than a little unsettled in a world that had suddenly turned hostile, Mia felt the tears pool in her eyes. Soon, they were falling down her cheeks, and she brought her hands to her face, as though to hide them from Mr. Lakota. Despite what had happened here, she didn't wish to present him with an image of vulnerability.

Truth was, what did she really know about this young man? He was Indian—an enemy of the State. And yet, he was all that stood between her and death.

Head downcast, she muttered, "I'm not sure I can leave Jeffrey so soon after his death, Mr. Lakota. It doesn't seem right somehow."

Mr. Lakota, however, said nothing in response, and she wondered why, until she looked up. He was gone. All at once, she felt bereft. Had he taken the decision from her? Had he left her here alone? For the wolves? So easily?

But why shouldn't he? He didn't know her. He held no commitment toward her.

Perhaps it was for the best, she thought, as she fell to her knees and let the feeling of loss have its way with her. As the tears made a path down her face, she wondered again if it wouldn't have been best if she had perished along with Jeffrey.

Why, oh why had this happened? Again, the memory of the bullies' talk stirred in her mind. They had said they were looking for someone with red hair—a woman. Hadn't they? Had she really heard that? Could it have been her imagination? Could it have merely been an invention she'd thought she'd heard? Yes, that was it. She had no enemies.

She shook her head. She couldn't be certain of anything right now.

Suddenly, Mr. Lakota stood in front of her, and in his hand, he held two shovels.

"Me...you...show...how to bury?"

She looked up, staring first at him, then to the shovels. Slowly, she nodded.

He put both shovels on the ground, came down on his haunches in front of her, and without saying a word, he reached his hand out toward her. It was more than a simple gesture to help her to her feet. She knew it instinctively.

Peace. He offered her peace.

Gingerly, she placed her hand within his, liking the feel of his warmth and his strength in that single touch. Suddenly, she felt as though she knew him. What was more, she seemed to be less confused. It was as though a part of his being had joined with hers, and their meeting had provided her a little tranquility.

They both rose up at the same time, their fingers still entwined.

Suddenly embarrassed, she looked down at his hand, admiring the power and the beauty of it.

She said, "Of course I'll show you how to use the shovel. Thank you for bringing them here."

The lesson was quickly accomplished. But, to her shame, she seemed unable to stand on her feet without assistance, much less help him, and so sitting down, still crying, she watched as Mr. Lakota, alone, dug the grave.

Too soon, the moment arrived to lift Jeffrey into the open grave, his final resting place. She let Mr. Lakota do that also.

"Peggy..." she mumbled.

Mr. Lakota was kneeling by the hole that he'd dug into the earth. Casually, he glanced up toward her. There was a question in his gaze.

"Peggy should be buried with Jeffrey."

"Who...Peggy?" he queried.

Mia pointed toward the place where Peggy lay, then said, "She was the only other woman on the wagon train. Do you see her body there? Could you bring her body here and place it in the grave with Jeffrey? I can't leave her there."

Mr. Lakota nodded, and soon both bodies lay in the grave. Then, shovel by shovel, he filled in the dirt. Mia watched for a moment, but somehow, this didn't seem right, and although tears streaked down her face, she rose up, picked up the other shovel, and helped Mr. Lakota fill in the grave.

It was done too soon for Mia's peace of mind. This was her final good-bye to Jeffrey. She could barely stand the thought, but, swallowing hard, she pushed the digger into the earth, and, bending down, she traced a picture of Jeffrey's image in the dirt. It was a good picture of him, for she had long ago mastered the art of drawing. But it would be soon gone, for all it needed was a good rain to wash it away.

"When or if I ever return home, Jeffrey, I promise I will paint your portrait, so that I will never forget my dear husband. I promise." This said, she looked up at Mr. Lakota, and added, "I must say a few words before we go."

Mr. Lakota nodded.

Coming up to her knees next to the grave, she prayed, although her voice shook. Oddly, she began first with an apology. "I'm sorry about placing Peggy into your grave, Jeffrey," she murmured, "but I couldn't leave her here on the prairie at the mercy of the elements. I'm sure you understand. Besides, now you'll have company on your way to heaven."

Mia crossed herself after her short speech, and bent her head. "I love you, Jeffrey. I will always love you. I hope heaven knows what a treasure they are receiving at this moment. Dear God, I beg you to treat him well." She made the motions of crossing herself again, and coughed as she choked on a new bout of tears. At last, she threw herself full length over the dirt of the grave.

How long she remained there, she didn't know. It seemed no time at all had passed before she became aware that Mr. Lakota had squatted down beside her. At first, nothing happened, and then she felt Mr. Lakota place his hand on her shoulder, reminding her in a gentle way that they had to go.

He helped her to rise by lifting her up by her waist, and as soon as she came to her feet, she made a back-handed swipe at the tears that continued to stream down her face. When Mr. Lakota reached out to touch one of those tears, she drew back, but only a little.

"Dirt," he said, as he brought his hand up again to brush away the offending earth. "*Itó*, come," he coaxed, and he offered her his hand.

She bobbed her head a little in agreement, and, remembering that she had felt better after accepting his offer of peace a while ago, she placed her hand within his. He brought his other hand up to clasp hers. She stared at the ground.

Gently, almost tenderly, he raised her head until her eyes gazed into his. "One, maybe two moons...we...must travel.... Your...people...fight we...free Lakota...and Cheyenne. But me...I...promise you...with me...safe."

"I thank you. Yes, I had heard that there were still some Indians who were not on the reservation, and I guess these people must be your tribe. It is too bad they are fighting, for we mean you and yours no harm."

He squeezed her hand. "But...much harm...," he frowned as he obviously searched his mind for the proper word, "...happen. Many die...under...promise of...protection."

She shook her hand free of his grasp and glanced toward the ground. "I'm sorry." Tentatively, she raised her eyes to his. "I hope you'll understand that I am truly thankful for your help and that I am also grateful that you do not extend any antagonism to me."

He inclined his head. "Mother...white...also." This said, he jerked his head quickly to the left. "We go...now."

He let go of her hand and stepped away from her, turning only once to ensure she followed.

And she did fall in with his steps. What choice did she have really? Glancing ahead, she noted several facts about him: his height, which must be six foot or more; his youth—he was probably little more than twenty-two years of age; his steady gait, and also the evidence that he looked as though he were a walking arsenal.

Earlier, she had watched as he had stripped the dead of their weapons: a Colt .44, a rifle, several knives. She had seen that he had selected certain ammunition, had looked on as he threw the rounds into a belt that was crossed over his shoulders and chest. She had also witnessed him taking up another rifle, holding it in his hands as though to test its feel. These, combined with his bow and sheath of arrows, and the various and many bags thrown over his shoulders, gave him the look of a man about to go to war.

And perhaps he was. After all, there were several men left dead behind them. Obviously something war-like was afoot, as he had already mentioned. Besides, maybe he would need all these weapons. He would know better than she.

She, also, was armed. She had slid a pistol into the pocket of her dress, and Jeffrey's heavy rifle dangled in her arms. But its weight wasn't a consideration; she wasn't about to leave it behind. They would need food, it was true, but the notion of building a fire and then frying the food was, for the moment, more than she could easily contemplate. Besides he would know what they needed, and she was certain he would have made provision.

As she stepped forward to match her pace to his, she considered what he'd told her about himself. His mother was white. This explained why his hair was a deep, dark shade of brown, instead of the usual midnight-black of his people, and why his eyes were blue instead of the traditional dark brown. It also brought her understanding as to why he spoke a little English. But did she care to know so much about him?

No. Yes, she corrected herself. He was, after all, the only being who stood between her and a death that would be a terrible way to exit this world. She sighed. Of course she owed him consideration.

With this decided, she hurried to catch up to him, glad that he set a stride that was easy for her to sustain. But the tears, she found, were never far away, and she discovered that gradually, she fell behind, causing Mr. Lakota some trouble to backtrack to find her.

Although this happened several times, luckily for her, he never admonished her nor did he appear inclined to do so. Instead, he gave her a present: a cane.

"We be...long on trail. Walking...stick...might help."

"Yes," she responded, taking the staff in hand. "I am indebted to you." *In many ways*, she added silently.

Still, she lagged behind, causing him to return to her, over and over. Often, she fell to her knees, and at these times, he encouraged her to continue on by holding out his hand to her. Although she usually declined the invitation, the fact that he had offered was usually enough to see her on her feet again, following along behind him...

CHAPTER FIVE

Because their trek was situated within Lakota territory, and because the Lakota guarded their nation fiercely, the chance of encountering an enemy would be rare. Thus, Brave Wolf decided that they would begin their travels during the daylight hours. He would amend that in days yet to come, since the evening hours were a safer time of day to journey over the prairie. But because the woman was barely recovered from a near brush with death, and since she was clearly afraid of him, to make this journey in the darkness might cause her to cry out at the slightest noise. And this was a chance he couldn't take.

It was summer, a time for war parties. Although it was true that many warriors were now confined to a reservation, he couldn't take a chance that some young men hadn't escaped.

His pace was slow, with frequent resting, since he was uncertain if the white woman was used to walking the required long distances. Besides, her emotional frame of mind had to be taken into account. Although she made no complaint, she was never far from fits of weeping. Often, he would look back at her to find her eyes cast downward, and her face wet with tears.

Her gaze was almost constantly averted from his, as well. Even when they rested, he observed that she remained embroiled in her own thoughts, not speaking unless he addressed her first. But her responses were clipped, and usually she uttered only a short "yes" or "no" to his questions.

If he'd had access to any of the white man's fire water, he would have offered it to her. Although he couldn't be sure, he had heard that it could impart courage to a person when they needed it most, or could help to heal a broken heart. While she could surely use it, he had none of that white man's brew, nor did he ever want it on his person. Since he was a scout, with a scout's honor, he would never partake of a drink so full of false hope.

Crunch!

Brave Wolf stopped cold, accepting the feel of her body as she crashed into him. He reached behind him to take hold of her around the waist so that he might keep her still.

That sound had not been a part of the natural order of the prairie. It was as though someone or some animal had stepped on a dry twig. Not that unusual a noise in the wild, but it had been erratic, not within the order of things.

Turning slightly around toward her, he placed his finger over his lips, the universal sign for silence. Her golden eyes stared up at him, and as he gazed down into their honey-colored depths, he recognized her alarm. But he became too aware of another of her attributes. She was beautiful; utterly beautiful. Even though her eyes were red from crying, and her clothing stained with blood, he realized that her allure was not to be easily ignored.

He shut his mind to it, recalling only too well his father's warning to him. Briefly, he admired those words of wisdom. Yes, his heart belonged to Walks-in-sunshine, but the loveliness of this woman beside him might prove to be difficult on a man whose body knew only that a handsome woman walked beside him.

He wasn't happy with his thoughts or his body's reaction to her, and he steeled himself against her charm. He reminded himself that the woman was weak due to her loss, her grief. To look upon her in any other way was not honorable.

Besides, he thought to himself, Walks-in-sunshine was as lovely in body and spirit as this white woman. If only she were here with him now, instead of this woman. Alas, it was not to be.

The white woman opened her mouth to speak, but Brave Wolf placed a finger over her lips, frowning down at her at the same time. Then he returned his attention to his environment.

Something alive had made that sound, the slight noise being that of a stick or a dried vine beneath a footfall. He had heard it, he had felt it with his being: here was something or someone close by that was foreign to the prairie and to the life all around them. Bringing her with him, he bent down to a squatting position, letting the long grasses of the prairie hide them while he devised a plan.

Mouthing soundless words, he told her, "Something...not with...prairie moved...must go...see what...is. You...stay here."

"No!" The word was shouted, not spoken.

Again, he placed a finger over her lips. "Soft...speak."

She nodded, then whispered, "I will not stay here alone. Where you go, I go."

"*Hiyá,* no. If danger...better you...here...be..."

"And die here alone if you don't return? No, I go with you."

He breathed in deeply before he mouthed more words, saying, "Then white woman...must...swear to...no...not cry out...must make no...sound. No time...to teach...now...."

"Then don't go. Don't leave me."

He paused. It could be an enemy that had adversely affected the ever-present circles of the life on the prairie, the circles a good scout was trained to distinguish. And if it were an enemy that he had perceived, there was no doubt in his mind that this foe would find them and kill them. Yet, if she wouldn't stay here on her own, she might become startled and scream, which would give away her position and make her, and him, vulnerable to attack.

At last, he nodded his assent, and he said soundlessly, "You...hold to...me. Make no...*ahotaŋ,* sound. Promise."

She nodded.

Mouthing the words, he said, "Walk...this way." He placed a moccasined foot to the ground, toes first, and pointed inward. "We go...bent...like this." He demonstrated the position. "Make no...noise.

Slowly...we go."

Briefly, she inclined her head.

They crept forward, low to the ground, step by slow step. Perhaps, he reasoned, the woman would tire of this until she might volunteer to stay behind in the future. He could only hope it would be so.

***

Mia's knees felt as though they would buckle under her. Unaccustomed as she was to traipse about in such a bent position, she wondered if her calf and thigh muscles might give out completely. To add to the difficulty, the ground was not completely flat, and the new manner in which she was to walk, placing her toes on the ground first, kept her stumbling. Then there was the length of time it was taking to discover the danger, if there were any. Was it an hour or more that she and Mr. Lakota had been treading in such a fashion?

After her first fall, he took control of her body and held onto her tightly, her hand in his, her arm encompassed by his. How could he do this, she wondered? But he didn't falter despite the extra weight she cost him, and she could only marvel at his tenacity and his strength.

More times than not, she wanted to call out and beg him to bring an end to their progression. Couldn't they sit down to rest? If only for a moment? But she couldn't do it. She was committed. She, not he, had made it so.

At last, he stopped, but it was not the welcome break she longed for. Instead, they squatted on the soft ground, and her body screamed at her to forget her pledge, to collapse and let him go ahead of her.

But no. If they were truly in danger and if he were to be killed here, then she knew she would go in the same manner. She would never survive this prairie without him. If she had to die, then better it be fast and quick, rather than the slow, painful death of starvation, or worse, wolves....

He squeezed her hand, and she noticed that he was pointing at something on the ground. Slowly, she shook her head back and forth. She saw nothing—nothing but grass and mud. She smelled nothing but the fragrance of grasses and dirt, and though the scent was fresh, it was not pleasing.

Slowly, he brought his free hand to the ground, and, pushing the tender blades of grass aside, he traced a pattern over the soft mud. She let out a breath in frustration. What was he showing her? Whatever it was, she was blind to it.

He picked up a stick that had been laying close-by, and she noticed that it was broken. So what?

But he was persistent, and he placed the stick back on the ground, while his fingertips traced a pattern in the mud.

What was it? Was that a track beneath his fingertips?

"Bear," he said aloud. "Bear...going away...from us. Came here to...hunt. Found...small game...fox...."

"There..." He pointed at the animal's backtracks. "See small track...fox... Bear not...bother us."

"But how can you tell that? How can you be so sure the fox or the bear wasn't here yesterday or...."

"Print...fresh...made today."

"But why would the bear not bother us?"

"Look...close...at print...here...another there..."

"I am, but—"

"He favored...this leg." Again, he indicated the track. "Injured. He want food, then...go."

"But I don't see—"

"It all...there in...Mother Earth." He stood up, bringing her up with him.

"But—"

He placed a finger over her lips. "Too much," he spoke softly. "Too much...happen. We rest...now."

"Here?"

He nodded.

"But it's muddy here."

He sent her another quick nod. "Good spot. Come...we sit."

She sighed, realizing she had no choice but to be seated in the mud. The new blue dress that she wore, once so pretty, would never be the same. She glanced down and gasped. It was still blood-stained, and now terribly muddy, as well. How could she have forgotten to wash it, or to change into another garment before commencing on this journey?

She grimaced at the thought, but she sat as he had asked her to, and when he offered her water and the dried buffalo that he carried with him, she realized with a start that she was hungry. She sighed again, but she was only too glad to accept the food.

***

They made camp that evening under a sky littered with millions, perhaps billions of stars. There was only a tiny, silver slit of a moon to add to the grace of the night, but its light was faint, which caused the stars to appear as if a child had overturned a bucket of shiny sand on top of a blanket of black. The vision was striking, and the ever-present wind of the prairie added to the impression of comfort, for the breeze was gentle this night. Under normal circumstances, she would have been awestruck by such beauty. But it wasn't to be. Her thoughts were too inward, her loss too raw.

Inexplicably, she discovered that sitting in the mud wasn't as bad as she had thought it might be. He had produced a blanket from one of those many bags he wore over his shoulders, and he had placed the spread on the ground for her.

The gift gave her a mild degree of relief, but the constant wind of the prairie suddenly turned against her, for though it was warm, it carried the scent of grass and wildflowers, and, without willing it, memories of Jeffrey intruded upon the peace of this place. Once, she recalled, they had made love in a meadow, surrounded by the fresh aroma of blossoms and lawn.

A whole new bout of tears followed in the wake of that particular memory, and the exquisiteness of the warm, Kansas night became wasted on her. Her thoughts were too inward and too sad, and the Good Lord help her, she couldn't keep from crying.

As a sob escaped her throat, she placed her hands over her face, bending forward. She cried in earnest now. No more pretense. No trying to hide her hurt from him. She couldn't.

He had lit no fire this night, but it didn't matter to Mia, since the air was balmy and warm. As the tears fell, images of Jeffrey, tall, handsome and strong, wouldn't let her be. In truth, the reality of his loss was almost more than she could bear.

That was when she heard it, softly at first, but then with more and more strength. It was a song, a rather slow song and in a minor key, sung by a deep, baritone voice. Was this young man singing? For her?

Perhaps. Yes. Oddly, she knew that his words, though she didn't understand them, were meant to soothe, and possibly to bring peace to her wounded heart. It was an act of kindness she would never have expected from an American Indian; particularly so because their two cultures were at war.

Her weeping grew stronger at first, then the crying slowly ceased. Gradually, she chanced a glance up at him.

He nodded at her, and they stared at each other, their gazes locked. Strange. She felt as though she knew his mind as surely as she grasped her own. And it was good. It was as though they were speaking to each other without a word being said.

It was a peculiar feeling, yet quaint.

How many moments passed in this rather spiritual way, she might never know, but at length, he whispered, "I...*lowaŋ,* sing...you...sleep."

Yes, it was as she had thought. Another sob escaped her throat. However, this time it wasn't because of the tremendous loss she was sustaining. She was touched by his selfless act, and the delicacy of the moment caused more tears to appear in her eyes, only to roll down her face.

"You sleep.... Lie back, look up...at sky." He pointed. "Those...stars there...," he pointed to the Big Dipper constellation, "called seven...brothers. Legend say...they stars...because chased by bear. No...place to...go. They...escaped to...land of sky...people. Do you...like song I sing...about them?"

She nodded as another tear escaped her eye to fall over her cheeks. "It is a beautiful song."

"*Pilamaya,* thank you. You sleep...now. I sing...you...sleep. *Ćante śića yaun śni ye.*"

"What did you say?

"Do not have…sad heart," he answered.

"I fear that this is a rather difficult task to ask of me right now." She looked away from him. After a short while, she asked, "And how about you? Will you rest also?"

"*Hau,* yes..., but after you. I not...lay down...with you. Long day...tomorrow."

"I..." She glanced downward. "I thank you." She cried again. But she did lie down, as he had asked her to do, and amazingly, a feeling of calm came over her. Her tears quieted, too—at least for a little while.

CHAPTER SIX

"Ćante śića yaun śni ye.
"Anpetu kin le, mićante etan wowaglake.
"Nape ćlyuza pelo.

"Ćante śića yaun śni ye.
"Anpetu kin le, mićante etan wowaglake.
"Nape ćlyuza pelo."

"Do not have a sad heart.
"I speak to you from my heart.
"I offer you my hand."

"Do not have a sad heart.
"I speak to you from my heart.
"I offer you my hand."

As he sang to her, he watched her closely so he would know when she at last drifted off to sleep. Hopefully, she wouldn't cry out in her sleep as she had on the previous night. She hadn't understood nor liked awakening in his arms; obviously, this was a circumstance to avoid. Wisely, he had known that she wouldn't realize that he had attempted several different means to cure her shouts and her tears, and that only by taking her in his arms had she at last ceased crying. She had no knowledge, also, that she need fear nothing from him. Were he able to choose, he would pick Walks-in-sunshine to hold in his arms, not this white woman.

But he wouldn't think of these particulars now. Although his heart belonged to Walks-in-sunshine, he was honor-bound to safely escort this woman to the nearest trading post. Once there, he would leave her with her own people, whom he assumed would take responsibility for her, since they were of the same tribe. Only then would he be free to return home—and to Walks-in-sunshine.

Shifting his attention back to the white woman, he saw that she was asleep. Gradually, he ceased his song, watching her closely to determine if she would awaken again as she had on the previous evening, screaming. If so, she would need his attention. She might not know it, but he was well aware that her shouts could bring danger to them, even though they were still within Lakota territory.

But her breathing was smooth and even, and he sighed. Now, he could go about the business of making their camp safer. Rising, he began the task of landscaping their site with grasses and mud and sticks, using the materials at hand to construct a "roof" of sorts that would protect them from rain were it to become necessary. He labored with this work until the moon was high in the sky. Finally, satisfied that their abode was almost indistinguishable to the casual eye, he sat down to "stand watch."

At least she was sleeping soundly. It was good. He had been aware that she was exhausted, although she hadn't voiced a word about it. She was also not in her right frame of mind, and he understood that unfortunate loss was the cause of that. Still, although he could well understand why her mind was terrorized by bad memories, shouts and cries didn't bode well for their journey, since the noise proclaimed their position to any enemy that might be within hearing distance.

He wondered if the long trek to the nearest outpost might do much to set her mind back to recovery. He could only hope that it would be so.

Meanwhile, he would not sleep this night. There was good reason. He had not scouted the surrounding area properly to ensure its safety; thus, it would be his lot to sit up through the night, watching, on guard. Tomorrow, he would find a place where he could construct a better shelter that would protect them from both weather and foes. He would design it so that it would not catch the attention of an enemy eye. But, of course, he would first scour the environment to ensure there were no immediate enemies. Then he would sleep.

Yes, it was a good plan. He yawned, and set his gaze out toward the gentle wave of the long, green grasses. In the distance, a coyote yelped and a night hawk squawked, while the crickets serenaded their pleasure in the night. All was as it should be, he thought, and he let his muscles relax, if only by a little bit....

***

She awoke slowly, and to the scent of the fresh, wet dew that had settled over the entire landscape. There was a ceiling of sorts above her head—one made of long grass, yet the shelter didn't distract her from looking out upon the land to see a cloud-like moisture which hung over every blade of grass, vine and bush. It made for a gray morning, yet in a manner of speaking, it was comforting all the same. In the distance, the sound of many different bird songs filled the air with music, and she wished that she could distinguish one song from the other. But she couldn't, and she sighed at her inability.

Soon, a deep, masculine voice, raised in song, drifted to her on the breeze. Of course, the voice had to belong to Mr. Lakota. What time was it? Where was he? He sounded far away.

Already the low-to-the-ground moisture was giving way to the new day. Was that really a pinkish-orange sun showing through the scattering of the steel-gray mist and light-colored blue clouds? Obviously, it was morning, and soon they would be back upon the trail. Shame. She would have liked to linger here if only to "catch her breath."

She started to rise, but winced when her muscles refused to obey her. Fair enough, she thought, and she lay back down, only to find herself staring straight up. Through the cracks in the long grass that had been placed above her, she could see that dawn crept into the sky slowly this day, but even still, faint colors of orange and pink were settling into the gray-blackened sky. The feel of the wet mist touched her everywhere, bringing with it the scents of mud, grass and prairie flowers.

Below her, the ground was soft and giving, encompassing her weight with ease. The blanket that he had laid beneath her was warm, and, for a moment, she experienced a feeling of well-being.

But the awareness was quickly gone, replaced instead by the utter realization of her loss. The tears, which were never far away, blurred her vision. She sobbed, then she checked it. She didn't want him to know she was awake. Why she felt this way, she didn't understand. She only knew that these few moments felt important to her well-being.

Luckily, he appeared to not notice her at all, for his singing continued, his voice deep and baritone. In many ways, it was soothing to listen to him, but after a while, she began to wonder what he was doing, and why he was singing at such an early hour of the morning, and to whom was he paying tribute?

Turning silently and coming up onto her side, she peeped out through the shelter's opening. She saw him at last, and despite herself, she found the sight of him inspiring. He was facing east, his arms outstretched, as though he welcomed the misty warmth of sun into them. Perhaps he was.

She watched him for the spread of a few more moments, admiring the muscles in his broad shoulders. The red headband had disappeared, and two lengths of his braids fell down over his back, a back which narrowed in a V-shape into his breechcloth. An eagle's feather waved back and forth in the ever-present wind, and she was reminded that there was a beauty to this moment that even she didn't understand.

That's when she realized it.

He was praying.

She sat up smoothly, so as not to distract him. Was she wrong about that? No.

He was standing, his legs apart, his arms open. And he sang and he sang.

There was a beauty to the moment that reached out to her, but rather than such pleasure bringing her relief, her appreciation brought on more tears, which fell gently onto her bosom. That's when it struck her: she hadn't talked to the Lord since she had laid Jeffrey in the ground. Perhaps there was reason for that lack, for she couldn't understand why God had taken something so precious from her.

Watching Mr. Lakota carefully, she discovered a need in her to do the same. Perhaps a talk with the Lord might help her to understand her loss.

She rose up to a sitting position, and from there she came to her knees. After crawling out of the shelter, she stood to her feet. She took up her rifle, placing it in the crook of her arm as she stepped toward him, and, reaching him, she fell to her knees. With her head bowed, she brought her free hand to his, taking his in her own.

It gave her comfort to know he was there, to know that he, too, was praying. Perhaps between the two of them, God might smile more favorably on her—on them both, and perhaps He might forgive her the anger, the absolute horror, that even now stirred in her soul....

***

Her hand squeezed his, and he realized its gentle pressure brought him pleasure. It wasn't that he was surprised by her appearance by his side, for he had known when she had awakened, and he'd heard her footfalls, quiet though they had been. But her action in touching him was unexpected, and had created a flood of feeling within him that he was not prepared to understand. It was the first time she had reached out toward him, and he was surprised by the awareness that he liked it.

Leaving his hand held tightly within hers, he glanced down at her as she knelt by his side. Her hair, tousled from sleep, shone with a wild, reddish hue, here beneath the grandiose of the pink and golden sky. Her eyes were shut and her head was bent toward the ground.

He understood. She had come here to pray with him and to give thanks to the Creator for a new day. After a while, he gazed away from her, turning his attention back toward the early morning sun, as the misty world around them exploded with a myriad of colors—steel gray of the sky; orange, pink and blue rays of the morning light.

"Hepela hepela!
"Onsimala ye. Omakiyi ye.
"Cantéwaśteya óciciyin kte."

"Hepela hepela!
"Onsimala ye. Omakiyi ye.
"Cantéwaśteya óciciyin kte."

"Hepela hepela!
"Onsimala ye. Omakiyi ye.
"Cantéwaśteya óciciyin kte."

He finished the song, yet he didn't relinquish her hand. They faced the east thusly, each seemingly reluctant to bring the moment to a close. It was as though time itself had ceased to be, and although slow to acknowledge his feelings, he felt a part of him draw closer to her. From out the corner of his eye, he saw her make the sign of a cross over her head and chest, and he realized her prayer had come to an end.

At last, she looked up at him, and he turned his gaze on her entirely. Her eyes looked like large, doe-like colored jewels in her heart-shaped face; they appeared to question him, and he held that look, until at last, she gazed away. At length, she struggled to her feet and he took her weight upon him easily as he helped her up.

Neither of them spoke. There seemed to be no need. At last, she voiced, "Thank you."

He nodded briefly.

She let go of his hand then, and he surprised himself by the bereft feeling he experienced at its loss.

He explained, "Custom...it is to...welcome day...by giving thanks to...*Wakáŋ Taŋka,* Creator. You...may...be here with...me every...morning...if you...like." His voice, he noted, was husky, and he was stunned by that fact.

"I would like that," she murmured in a tone that sounded as throaty as his. She glanced toward the ground. "I would like that very much."

"Wašté, good," he replied with a quick motion of his hand away from his chest. "It...good. Now...we must...prepare. Long...trek we have...this day."

"Yes, yes, of course," she said quickly, glancing away from him before she turned to take the necessary steps back to the small shelter where she had slept. He watched her momentarily as she reached in to pick up the blanket that had buffered her from the ground during the night. He saw her fold it and place it in one of his bags.

That's when he realized that she would be wanting a bath. All creatures needed the cleanliness of the water, but women in particular seemed to enjoy these excesses with great pleasure, even when on the move. It would be his duty to locate a secluded place, free from the danger of enemy eyes, where she could freshen herself, perhaps even wash her dress.

Idly, he realized she would require freedom from his wandering glance as well. It was not a comforting thought to recognize that an image of her body, completely naked, entered into his imaginings. With force of will, he refused to think that thought again....

***

He astonished her. Before they set out upon their journey, he produced a pouch full of water, and, handing her a sprig of grass that smelled like mint, he showed her how to use the plant to clean her teeth. Next, he set out a small piece of buckskin on the ground, and made the signs for wetting it and washing the face.

"Yes, thank you," she acknowledged. "I understand. These are for me to wash and prepare myself for the day."

"*Hau, hau*," he said.

"But where did you find the water?"

"In *tataŋka*...buffalo...wallow."

"A buffalo wallow? What is that?"

"Place where...buffalo bulls fight..."

"A place where buffalo bulls fight? You mean those muddy holes I've seen across the prairie—where the bulls lock horns and go round and round? This water must be dirty."

"Water...clean...enough to...wash face."

"Yes, well, that might be a matter of opinion, but it doesn't matter. I am not in the comfort of my home, and I am certainly in no position to be picky. I thank you."

He surprised her again when he produced a brush. It was crudely cut, a wooden stick carved so as to mimic a comb, but in case she didn't realize its use, he used it to mimic combing his hair. When finished, he laid the "brush" out for her use.

"I...this is very kind of you, Mr. Lakota."

He nodded, and, leaving these items of comfort in her possession, he rose up to his full height and trod away from her. She stared at his departing figure, noticing idly that his masculine gait blew his breechcloth back and forth in the wind. At once, she was contrite for the observation, and she felt more than a little disrespectful to Jeffrey's memory.

Still, she hadn't thought to bring such accessories with her. When they had first set out upon the trail, her attention had been so introspective that to even consider what toiletries she might need had been beyond her ability. But he had thought to pack them. For her? Perhaps.

Whether for her, or for some other reason, she was thankful that he'd had the foresight to remember them. Slowly, with some apprehension, she picked up the "brush", and began the long process of chasing the knots from her hair.

Awhile later, Mr. Lakota returned to her, and, squatting in front of her, he produced a kit from another one of those numerous bags he carried. Opening it, he pulled out some "paint," and placed a red dot on the crease between her eyes.

When she looked at him questioningly, he explained, "Hot sun...protect against."

She nodded, and, gazing a little ways up at him, she again compared him to a walking arsenal. A rather handsome and human one, true, but he looked prepared for battle. He wore many of their bags around his shoulders as well as his bow and quiver full of arrows. Resting on his thighs were two rifles, and there were rounds of ammunition strapped around his waist.

He said, "We...go now."

"Yes," she murmured, her tone of voice guttural, which caused her to introspect. What was wrong with her?

He was still squatting in front of her when he replaced the red paint in a pouch, and produced similar pots of white and black paint. With a firm hand, he dabbed the colors on his own face, making a pattern that reminded her of how he had appeared the first time she had seen him.

She shivered. She would rather have not recalled that memory.

"Why do you use that paint on your face?" she asked quietly, perhaps with the hope that talking might distract her from her own thoughts.

"Stop sun...from burning...and...look...fierce...if meet...enemy."

She gasped. "Do you think we'll be coming into contact with an enemy?"

He shrugged. "Perhaps. Come," he encouraged as he came up onto his feet. "We leave...now. Long...walk." And with this short and to-the-point explanation, he turned away from her, his gait swift.

"Wait!" she called as she jumped to her feet and followed him. "May I carry one of those bags?"

He turned back toward her, a frown marring his countenance.

Quickly, his gaze scanned her from the top of her head to the tips of her toes.

"We...walk far. Bag could...be...heavy for...one not used to...travel...by foot. Also, one...who feel...grief."

"Yes, it could," she replied. "And if it does become like that for me, I will let you know so that you might help me."

He nodded, although he did give her a strange, searching stare. Nevertheless, he released one of the pouches from around his shoulders, took a step toward her and placed it gently over her head. However, he appeared to take much too much care to avoid touching her hair or her shoulders, or any part of her at all. For her comfort? For his? All in all, she supposed she appreciated his care.

For the pulse of a moment, he stood back looking at her with an appreciative glance. Was he admiring his handiwork, or was he approving of her?

"Look...good."

Briefly, she smiled, and was surprised to see that his gaze lingered over her lips. But the look was quickly gone, and, as he turned away, she asked herself again whether that glint of admiration was for her.

No. Probably, she thought, the sun had gotten into his eye.

CHAPTER SEVEN

She hobbled a little to try to catch up with him. He turned back toward her, squinting at her.

"You...find...leather of shoe?"

"I...I did not. I searched for it everywhere. But..."

He stepped back toward her, retracing his path. As he came up level with her, he commanded, "You...stay..."

"I am no dog, sir, to be told to sit, stay or roll over."

He grinned at her. "I not...confused about that."

She crossed her arms over her chest. "I looked and looked for the sole of my shoe, but I couldn't find it."

"I will...find it. You...here...stay."

"No. I'm afraid to be left alone."

His fleeting look at her was enough to cause Mia to realize that her defiance frustrated him. After four days of travel with this man, she had become used to witnessing the tiny nuances that told of this young man's emotional moods. Years from now, she reasoned, he would most likely master those miniscule flickers of concern.

For now, she was glad to have acquired some means to recognize his frame of mind. She said, "Please don't be upset with me. The pea vines and other prickly bushes are constantly stinging me and tearing at my dress. It's so much easier to find a piece of my clothing hanging from a bush, than it is to find the bottom of my shoe stuck in the mud somewhere. The tall grass alone makes it hard to find, for when I bend to look to try to find it, I get pricked."

He nodded. "You speak...true. This...why I go...find it. Easier for me. You...stay...here."

"I can't. I can't be without you."

For a moment, she caught a surprised light in his eye as he regarded her.

"Don't you see?" she went on to explain. "What if something happened to you? What if you didn't return? I would rather be with you and face what you face, even if that be death, than to stay here on my own, unknowing. Without you, I would die here in this world of grass and vines."

The curious look was gone, and in its place was a glimpse of what? Was that admiration?

He said, "Understood. Will try to...teach you way...of prairie. Then not be...afraid."

"Good," she acknowledged. "I would appreciate that, but that's in the future. For now, I must go with you."

He drew his brows together in a frown as he stepped toward her. Nevertheless, he uttered, "Then walk...low to ground. Like this..." He bent over double.

"All right, I will. But why must we spend so much time trying to find this? What difference does the bottom of a shoe make? Truly, who's to see it in this environment of dirt and grass?"

"Land full..." he waved his hands out and away from him, "...of Indian *toŋwéya,* scouts. If find shoe...they follow...our...trail. Us they kill...maybe."

"Oh," she frowned. "I see. Is that why you've had me go back over the trail so many times to find the pieces of my dress when I've torn it on the bushes?"

"It is so."

She sighed. "Then I had better help you, I suppose, and be more careful where I step, for it was in a muddy patch of ground where I lost my shoe's sole."

"*Wašté*, good. *Itó*, come."

Mimicking him, she grappled with the rifle to find a comfortable position, then she bent over at the waist, following him as they made a slow progress back over their tracks. Amazingly, she had no doubt that he would find that stray piece of leather, and he did not disappoint. Within a relatively short time, he held the wayward sole of her boot in his hand.

She limped toward him, and reached out for it, but he did not immediately give it to her. Instead, he made a sign to her, and, turning away, he indicated that she should follow him again, traveling once more in that bent-over position.

Shutting her eyes on deep sigh, she realized she had little choice but to do as he asked.

***

The deeply colored green grass waved above them in the prairie's ever-constant breeze, while a hawk circled above them, as if curious about the goings-on below. Crows flew here and there, their *caw-cawing* echoing loudly in the warm breath of the wind. Everywhere about them was the scent of mixed grasses, mud and sweet earth. The sun felt hot, since it was now in its zenith, but the surrounding shrubs and grass provided some shelter from its direct heat. Only moments ago, they had stopped on a piece of ground where a few large rocks littered the terrain. He sat on one of those slabs now; she resided on another, facing him. He held her boot in one hand and the sole of that shoe in another, and he examined the footwear and its missing bottom from every possible angle.

As she watched, she basked in the relief of simply sitting. Sadly, she'd left her bonnet behind in her wagon, and, in consequence, the sun glared down on her bare head, while the wind whisked locks of her hair into her eyes. With an impatient hand, she pushed those strands behind her ears.

She gazed away from him, not focusing on anything in particular. Simply, it seemed a better option than looking at him. Something about his hands, something about the delicate way he handled her shoes was devastating to her peace of mind. She sighed.

Frankly, she was fascinated by him. Too fascinated.

She rocked back, and let her aching calf muscles relax as a feeling of tranquility settled over her. It was the first time since Jeffrey's demise that she wasn't constantly reminded of that loss, and for a moment, if a moment only, the hurt subsided, but only a little.

It had been earlier in the day when she'd lost the sole of her shoe. At first, she had said nothing about it to Mr. Lakota. But, after discovering that blood had covered her hosiery and the sole of her foot, she'd at last confessed her problem to him.

She'd expected his anger, for it meant that the object would have to be found, which would only serve to slow down their progress. But he'd shown none of that. Instead, he'd calmly asked her to go and retrieve it. It had seemed a simple request, for she was accustomed to backtracking to retrieve bits of her dress after the material had caught and torn on a branch or vine. But this was different; she had delayed telling him about it, and the underside of her shoe might be as far back as a mile.

He might not fully realize it, but she would never go so far away from him. Not even during the day. It frightened her to be alone in this vast expanse of prairie.

Her thoughts caused her to stir uneasily, and she brought her gaze back onto him. At last, he looked up at her and muttered, "Cannot fix."

Her heart sank. What did that mean? That she was doomed to walk over this muddy, sticky and stone-littered ground in her blood-soaked, stocking feet?

All she said to him, however, was, "Oh."

"Better I make...moccasins...for you...walk in."

"Moccasins? You could make them? Here? That would be superb, indeed, if you could. But how is that possible?"

"Cannot fix...this. So...put together moccasins...for you."

"But to make them?"

"*Hau, hau.* You...cannot walk...prairie without moccasins to...protect feet."

"That's true. But I suppose what I don't understand is how is it possible that here on the prairie you could assemble moccasins? Do you have the proper materials?"

"*Hau.* Hold out foot."

When she didn't comply at once, he stated again, a little more softly, "Hold out foot."

Still, she hesitated. Was it unseemly to raise her skirt so that she could extend her foot toward him? Perhaps it was, but the rights and wrongs of such behavior seemed the lesser of two evils. With a shrug, as if she were releasing a weight from her bosom, she did as he asked. At once, she realized her mistake, for as he took hold of her by her ankle, placing it on his lap, her heart skipped a beat.

What was this sensation of delight? This craving for more of his touch? No, oh, no. This mustn't be happening to her. Yet, if she were to be honest with herself, she would have to confess to a frenzy of excitement that was even now cascading over her nerve endings.

No! Please no, she cried to herself. This was all wrong.

What was the matter with her? She should feel embarrassed because he was touching her, not elated. She gathered her skirt around her legs in an effort to minimize the exposure of the rest of her from his view. But it was a wasted effort; he showed no interest in looking at her there.

Taking one of the bags from around his shoulder, he brought out a moccasin and placed it up against the bottom of her foot. She gasped a little, for as soon as he touched her toes, tiny sparks of fire shot over her, from the tip of that foot to the top of her head.

Luckily, it appeared that he didn't notice her strange behavior, and he explained, "These moccasins...made for me...by Walks-in-sunshine. On journey...like this, need...many moccasins. I...cut this for you."

Mia, who was more than a little upset with the waywardness of her conduct, glanced away from him, speculating as best she could on what could possibly be the cause of her body's rapture. Truth was, she'd barely registered what he'd said.

Instead, her attention centered inward as she admonished herself.

Perhaps Mr. Lakota reminded her of Jeffrey. Could this be the reason for her misguided reaction to him?

Yes, yes. That was it; it had to be, for she was in love with Jeffrey, would always be in love with Jeffrey.

Still, cautioned an inner voice, this man didn't look at all like her deceased husband; he acted nothing like him, and she wasn't at all confused about who was who.

Or was she?

Wasn't it possible that some deep and uninspected part of her was a little muddled? After all, Mr. Lakota was a young man, and she had been a newly married woman. Plus, Mr. Lakota had rescued her from what would have been a gruesome death. It was only natural, wasn't it, that she might place her emotions for Jeffrey onto this other man?

Yes. It had to be.

Yet, she countered her own thoughts; she was more than aware that her reaction to Mr. Lakota was not simply emotional. It was sensuous, perhaps a little wanton in nature. Was it possible that her body, having been treated to the delights shared by a married couple, was flustered by the presence of this man? And that it was her body's reaction to him, not her own?

She sighed deeply. This was more than likely the truth. What she was experiencing was little more than a physical reaction.

Yet, again that inner voice cautioned, if it were no more than physical, if it were purely platonic, why was it that she was experiencing the joy of his touch?

Enough! Her thoughts on the matter were more troubling than the action of his touch.

Still, she wondered, what should she do? Should she withdraw into herself? Mentally lock herself away from this man's influence?

Nice thought, but hardly practical. Given their situation, and seeing that her life depended on this man's ability to get the two of them safely across the prairie, such introversion would hardly be possible.

All at once, he placed her foot back on the ground, ending their physical contact. Relieved, she breathed out slowly, expecting that the lack of his touch would improve her problem.

But it hardly mattered. Her body still tingled from the contact. Modestly, she shook her skirt free to place it over her ankles, hoping against hope that the action would settle her.

But it didn't.

Only the quickness of a moment passed, however, before he reached out toward her again, and said, "Need...other foot."

"Oh," she articulated. "Of course." She gulped.

She lifted her skirt up again, and guardedly placed her other foot in his hand. Abruptly, a similar thrill of excitement raced over her nerve endings.

She swallowed. Hard.

She needed a distraction, she decided. Perhaps conversation might prove to divert her attention. It was worth an attempt, she reasoned, and so she asked, "Did you say that someone called Walks-in-sunshine made these moccasins for you?"

"Hau, hau."

"Oh. Is she somebody special to you?"

"She...future wife."

Mia's stomach dropped, and she felt as if those words had delivered her a blow. So, this man was spoken for. Of course he would be, she reckoned as her thoughts raced ahead. He was young, he was kind and he was also handsome. What female worth her weight wouldn't do all she could to make this man hers?

She sat back as she asked, "Could you tell me about—what was her name? Walks-in-sunshine?"

He paused, and, as he glanced up to survey her, she thought his look might be wary. Nevertheless, after his initial hesitation, such watchfulness seemed to disappear from his countenance, and he said,

"She...beautiful. Wait for me. We...promise to...marry."

"To marry?" Mia almost choked on the words. She glanced away from him. She felt...jealous.

Was he aware of her reaction to this news? How embarrassing it would be if he were.

But he was continuing to speak, and he said, "She...I...love since we...children."

"I see," Mia responded. "Then what will she think if you cut up these moccasins for me? They are so beautifully made, and were especially sewn for you. Might that not upset her?"

"She...understand."

Would she? Mia couldn't help but speculate that Mr. Lakota might be wrong about that. If this man were her own, she would care.

He was continuing to speak, however, and he uttered, "She...not understand...if leave...someone...hurt when could...fix. Give me other...boot."

She complied.

"We...cache these." He held up her boots.

"Cache?"

"Bury them. Leave no...trace of us here."

He had set himself to work over the leather, and she felt odd as she sat before him, watching him cut the moccasins down with a knife and a sure hand. His fingers were strong, long and handsome, and she wondered how they might feel upon--

Abruptly, she pulled up her thoughts, and she asked, "Might I help?"

"Know how use...*takaŋ,* sinew and...bone?"

"Sinew? Bone? Have you no thread and needle?"

"One not...find needle...thread in nature."

"Oh," was all she said. Then, "You have none of the finer things in your tribe? Since your mother is white, I had thought perhaps she might keep something of the European culture around her."

"Mother...white, but...Indian through marriage. What mean...finer things?"

"They are items made by the white man's hand—like needle and thread—things that make life a little easier. I see you punching holes there in the moccasin and then threading the hole with the sinew. It looks to me to be slow and painstaking work. A sharp needle with thread would make your work easier and less time consuming."

"No...need for...finer things, when have…nature all around."

"Yes, I suppose I can understand that viewpoint. But think for a moment of a woman's joy over acquiring a new gown in a silken fabric that shimmers with each step she takes—gowns are clothing, by the way."

"What need of...gowns...when have soft animal skins?"

"Perhaps this is only a feminine reaction; a pleasure that only a woman would understand: To wear something that she knows makes her look pretty."

"Walks-in-sunshine already pretty."

"I'm certain she is. And it is kind of you to say so. But there are other goods that might be considered 'finer things'. For instance, a sewing machine could make this work fly by."

Without raising his eyes to hers, Mr. Lakota jerked his chin to the left, and said, "This slow...because I...little time…spent doing it. Walks-in-sunshine...quick."

"Yes," agreed Mia. "I'm sure that she is."

"Give me foot...again."

She hesitated, yet she did as he requested. However, instead of gazing at him directly, she looked up above his head. The tall grasses bent and waved in the warm, summer breeze, as though all of nature were performing a dance. She tried to concentrate on that.

Yet, as he touched her foot, the warmth of his fingers produced again that recognition of a passion she wished she didn't feel. Suddenly, he produced a piece of buckskin from one of his bags, and, wetting it, he proceeded to wash the bloody bottoms of her feet.

Oh, my. The sensation produced by this act of kindness was exquisite, and as bodily excitement swept over her nerve-endings, she became aware of a stirring of sensation, there in a place most private to her.

Surprise shot through her. And so upset was she, even though her body's reaction was involuntary, she could barely speak. Gulping hard, she knew she had to talk again, if only to try to dispel the guilt she felt. Changing the subject, she asked, "Why is the wind so constant here?"

"No thing to...stop it."

"There's grass."

"But no trees. No...hills...mountains. Nothing to...block it."

"At home, we of course experience the wind. But never so on-going as what the prairie offers. Here, it is always blowing."

She noticed that he had come down on his knees before her, as he fit a moccasin to first one foot and then to the other. It reminded her that Jeffrey had proposed to her from a similar position. But before she could explore that thought, he gazed up at her, and with one eyebrow cocked, he asked, "Have trees?"

"Of course."

"Have hills or...mountains?"

"Yes."

"That why. Stand now."

She was only too happy to do as he asked, and she rose up to her feet. As she did so, he pressed a finger over where her big toe hit the moccasin, then, as though he found fault with the shoe, he adjusted the back of it, his fingers tickling her there, creating havoc within her.

"How feel?"

She swallowed grimly, for she almost answered him with the honesty of her wayward emotions. "They are perfect," she replied in a voice barely over a whisper.

"*Wašté*, good," he acknowledged, echoing the word with a motion of his hand out and away from his chest.

"Does that gesture of your hand mean something?" she asked.

"Mean good. It good." He rose up to his feet, and came to tower over her. He said, "Take few...steps."

He had positioned himself dangerously close to her, and she could barely control the impulse to throw herself against him. She took a few steps away from him instead.

"Turn."

"Why?" she queried, although she did as he requested, and spun around in a circle.

"Moccasins must be…comfortable," he explained. "Still feel good?"

"Yes."

He nodded. "Then we...continue. Must find...shelter for night. *Hópiye unyánpi kta!*"

"What did you just say?" she asked as she glanced up at him.

"Said... 'all right, let's go'."

"Yes. Yes, that would be good. We should keep moving along."

He smiled at her then, and seeing it, as well as his so-obvious approval of her, she almost swooned. But she didn't. Instead, her thoughts turned inward once more, and she admonished herself. Briefly, she wondered why her sense of moral right and wrong was not standing her in good stead against this man.

At least he seemed oblivious to her stirrings. She bit her lip, wishing that she were blind to it, as well. Unhappily, it simply was not to be.

CHAPTER EIGHT

As he fit the last moccasin to her foot, Brave Wolf became all too aware that the action of touching her caused him pain; physical, sexual pain. He was not foolish enough to ignore such tangible evidence that he wanted this woman—and desired her in the most elemental way a man might.

But this was not the right time, the right woman or the right place for such yearning. In the end, he could only hope that she were unaware of his physical reaction to her. Thus, he remained in a squatting position before her, that he might hide the evidence of his arousal from her slightest glance at him.

He was not happy with the lustful feelings she caused in him, and he made a mental note to stay as far away from her as he might, given their situation. Sometimes, it was true, their path might require physical contact. During such moments, he vowed that he would be careful to force any association between them to be as quick and as occasional as possible.

He reminded himself that sexual stimulation knew no boundaries such as race or culture. But that didn't make it right. Unions were not only a matter of the heart, they must be a concern of the family, for the rearing of children demanded stability. Wasn't it well known that a melding of two different lifestyles would place hardship on that family and on those children? Though his mother was white, she had chosen to become Indian at heart. Thus, there had been no conflict.

But would this woman choose an Indian path as had his mother? What, after all, did he really know of this woman?

Sexual desire was easy, he reminded himself. Creating a family life that would nurture both partners and their offspring required dedication and a meeting of the minds, as well as love. Besides, this woman was married and was still committed to her husband, although that man no longer breathed in the flesh. He, Brave Wolf, was also pledged to Walks-in-sunshine.

Although his sense of right and wrong would not allow him to make an overture toward this white woman, he was concerned. Their trip would be long, and he could not deny that she moved him in ways that he dared not consider too deeply.

At least, he thought, he was old enough and wise enough to know that he must suppress the longings of the flesh, and that he must find outlets that would squelch the attendant physical misery. He only hoped she were unaware of his problem, for it might cause her embarrassment, and would create a barrier between them that need not be built.

He rose to his feet quickly and turned his back on her, so as to hide the physical stirrings of his body. Quickly, he stepped away to find a spot to dig a hole. There in the dry ground, he found a perfect place, and he attacked the job with gusto, using the butt of his rifle to dig.

As he worked, he considered the parting words of his father. At the time, Brave Wolf had thought the advice unnecessary. Now he realized his elder's wisdom. This woman could become a problem.

Therefore, he must envision ways to restrain the temptation that she presented. Not only because he was honor-bound to deliver her back to the white man's world in the same condition that he had found her, but as his father had pointed out, a man, having succumbed to the passion of the moment, could suffer a loss of energy. The consequence of that could be that he might become too weak to defend both himself and her in a life-or-death crisis.

Besides, there was Walks-in-sunshine and his devotion to her to be considered. He loved her. He had always loved her; he would always love her. And although she might forgive him a brief passion, she would not understand if he never returned to fulfill his promise to her.

Enough. Too much thinking, too little attention on the environment around them.

At last, the woman's boots were cached and covered with dirt, and he advanced onto the next chore, which was working over the ground, brushing the area with different patterns in order to erase the evidence of what the earth hid. He set plants upright and placed stones in careful positions.

It was done. Looking up toward her, he forced himself to turn a blind eye to the beauty of her, and he said, "*Hópiye unyánpi kta,* all right, let us go."

He spun away from her, willing the image of her pretty face from his mind. He was successful in the attempt, and his heart gladdened. Thus, as he again set their pace into a slow gait across the prairie, he felt pride in the awesome control he exuded over his physical self. The knowledge brought him some relief.

***

"Here...we spend night...." His words were low-pitched and soft against the breeze, and had she not been looking directly at him, she wouldn't have known he had spoken at all. She looked down, and only then did she realize that she had been so engrossed in her troubled thoughts, she had been unaware that she was holding tightly to the fringe of Mr. Lakota's shirt.

Once again, grief consumed her, and tears spilled down her cheeks. This time, however, her sadness held a double-edged sword. Not only was she left to cope with the sudden loss of her husband, she now felt isolated from good sense. Her husband hadn't been gone from this life long enough to merit her physical reaction to another man. She felt as though she were morally unstable. Was she?

Wearily, she realized she had no answers to the questions she posed, and she had little means to cope with the wayward emotions she bore. If only she had someone to talk to -- person like her father. What would he say to her if he knew of her dilemma? What would be his advice?

"Come home," he'd say. "Keep your distance from this young man and return home. All will be well then."

Yes. Go home. Indeed, she needed to get back to what was

familiar and so beloved.

Thank you, Daddy, for being here with me in thought, she whispered to herself. *I will return home as fast as I can. I'm sorry now that I ran away.*

It suddenly occurred to her that she had no idea where this young man was taking her. To his village? Maybe, but if that were true, why had he separated himself out from the others of his party?

It was strange that, until now, she hadn't even questioned him about his intentions: Where were they going?

But perhaps it wasn't quite so odd, she contradicted herself. She hadn't been in any frame of mind to think at all in the beginning of this trek, and she wasn't in a much better situation even now.

How many days had they been upon the trail? Was this only a week gone by? How much longer would she be in constant companionship with this young man? Could she keep a good distance away from him so that her emotions weren't stimulated?

Of course she could.

Without warning, he turned around toward her, and she gave him her attention as he spoke to her. He said, "Here we...camp."

Camp? Yes, that was right. He'd mentioned as much before she'd become lost in her own thoughts. He was looking for a place to set up a shelter.

"Here?" she asked.

"Good place."

"But—" She bit her tongue.

She was disappointed, yes, for she had hoped for a better bed this night than the harsh ground. But she tried to suppress the feeling of discouragement, remembering that whatever else he was, she was indebted to this man.

"We...build place for night...there. Do you see?" He pointed.

She frowned as she looked off in the direction that he was indicating. She saw nothing but grass and...

"*Itó,* come," he encouraged, motioning her to follow him. "I show you. Careful where step. White woman might fall...into crack. Hurt...might get hurt. *Itó!*"

He led off, but she stayed behind. What crack? Why might she fall?

He glanced over his shoulder at her, and seeing that she hesitated, he took the few necessary steps back to her. "*Itó,*" he repeated. He looked at her, seeming to hesitate before he finally held out his hand to her. "I...help."

Did she dare to touch him? Exhaling on a deep sob, she realized she had no choice. Reluctantly, she took hold of his hand.

Fire! A charge, not unlike the flash of a lightning bolt, rushed through her system, its force shaking her and confusing her all the more. What was happening to her? Was she losing all sense?

Although she tried to think logically, there seemed to be no way to stem the rush of heat within her. Already, her heartbeat had doubled, and she could feel its pounding in her chest.

Alarmed, she tried to pull back, but Mr. Lakota's grip was tight and she couldn't easily tug her hand back from him.

Oh, Daddy, please help me, she murmured silently.

She tried to remember to a few days past, when she had taken this man's hand in prayer. She reminded herself that there had been no storm then, no physical desire, no lustful imaginings.

She inhaled on a deep breath, trying to calm herself. *Home,* she thought. *Yes, home. I must go home. There I can come to terms with this.*

Luckily—for her own peace of mind—she recalled that she'd experienced a feeling of peace when she'd considered that she was placing her feelings for Jeffrey onto this young man. Hadn't she also decided that this would be quite natural, given their circumstances?

She fidgeted uneasily, and determined that if these unwanted stirrings kept happening to her, she would remember that it was her mind playing tricks on her.

But he had taken a few steps forward, and he was carrying her along with him, since he still held tightly to her hand. "See now?" he asked, seemingly unaware of her potent thoughts.

She looked downward to where he was pointing and gasped. Why, it was a coulee he was indicating, a gully that was carefully hidden by the tall grasses, the intertwining vines, and the shrubs of the prairie. The reason for his firm grip became clear now. Had he not grasped her hand so firmly, she might have fallen into that gulch, for the grade was steep, and the drop wasn't readily apparent until a person was right upon it.

She burst into tears. *Please Lord, help me,* she prayed. *Now I have another reason to like this young man and be indebted to him, for I would have plummeted down this incline were it not for him. Who knows what my fate would have been, if not for his strength.*

Mr. Lakota, seeing her tears, appeared to put the wrong interpretation to her grief, and he rushed on to say, as though to assure her, "Make shelter...safe. After I…erect it, I go erase our...trail."

His grip still held her firmly, and the flame that was even now racing along her nerve endings burned deeply into her heart. But his helping hand wasn't necessary at this particular moment, and she withdrew from him, placing her arm at her side. Quickly, she stepped back from him.

She couldn't speak. She couldn't even look at him. All she could do was stare at the ground and watch as her tears slipped down her face and onto her breast.

At last, realizing that he hadn't spoken to her as she had expected that he would, she looked up to find Mr. Lakota patiently awaiting her.

He smiled at her in a fatherly fashion, and as he turned to lead the way, she meekly followed him down into the coulee.

***

The ravine was probably twenty feet deep, and she cautiously made her way down into it, stepping a careful foot, as he had instructed her to do, so that rocks and dirt didn't create noise or a landslide. At last, reaching the bottom of the coulee, Mr. Lakota turned his back on her and without saying a word to her, he set to work.

She took stock of where she was. This place was not more than thirty feet across, and it was dry at this time of year. Espying a large rock, she paced over to it and sat. For a moment, she focused her attention onto Mr. Lakota, who was briskly at his work. He was moving stones, grass and vines from place to place, and appeared to be landscaping the ground around a shelter he was constructing. Was that an odd sort of lean-to he was building?

Perhaps. She noticed that he had found a deep cut in the coulee's wall which resembled a narrow-like cave, and that he was taking advantage of the spot, using whatever the landscape offered in order to create an entrance on one side of it.

She looked on with fascination as he positioned enough long grass over the top of the structure to form a roof. His actions were swift, yet exact, and it was with an inherent respect that she realized the numerous rows of grass and twigs he was creating, which were inches deep, would keep out the elements.

Without really realizing where her thoughts might lead her, she watched as he bent, then stood, then squatted while he concentrated on his work. His leggings were skin-tight, and he had discarded his shirt and now wore little more than a buckskin vest over his chest. His leggings came up high on his thighs, but were not far enough up to breach the naked gap where the outline of his buttocks and his thighs met....

All at once, she realized where her attention was centering, and she looked away. Self-incrimination was swift, and she worried again that something was very wrong with her.

Gazing anywhere but at him, she focused her attention on the dry stream which lay before her. Farther away, to the south, there appeared to be water in its bed. Perhaps she should investigate. It seemed a better option than monitoring the actions of this very virile man.

Rising up, she stepped toward the dry stream's bed, and followed it southward to where water still remained. Looking father away in the same direction, she could discern that the small river branched out into a full-fledged rivulet.

Perhaps some other waterway or underground source flowed into it there, for it looked to be about three or four feet deep. Maybe she would be able to bathe there, for it looked close enough that Mr. Lakota could stand guard over it, yet far enough away to provide her with some modesty.

Snarl, yelp, snap!

What was that?

Crack!

Fear washed through her. Was she in trouble?

"Mr. Lakota?"

No answer.

She swung around to glance back in the direction where she'd left him. But where was he?

Panic consumed her. Had he left her?

"Mr. Lakota!" She called again. Then, louder yet. "Mr. Lakota, where are you?"

Nothing... No answer...

"Mr. Lakota?"

"I am...here." The tone of his voice was deep, reassuring, but farther up the slope.

Relief swept through her. Still, it took several moments before she was able to respond, saying, "Where? I still don't know where 'here' is."

With that masculine grace which seemed to be as much a part of his stride as was his careful pace, he stepped out from the tall grasses that grew at the top of the coulee.

"Oh, there you are." She looked up. "But how did you get up there?"

"I climb. Did you not see...wolf?"

"No, I—"

"Wolf hungry...crazy. Watching you."

She caught her breath before she uttered, "A wolf, looking at me as though I were what? Food?"

"Could be. Had to...kill him. Not like to kill wolf."

"But how did *you* know there was a wolf there? Or that there was any danger at all?"

"My...duty to know."

"Yes, yes. However, I still don't understand how you could be aware that there was--" She cut herself off short, and paused. "You were so intent on building that lean-to. How do you do that? How do you know of happenings far away from you?"

He shrugged as he stepped down the slope and came down farther into the coulee. "I am...*toŋwéya,* scout."

He said these words as though they alone explained the world around them from his point of view. And when she encouraged him to expand upon that a little, and said, "Yes...?" he did little more than nod at her.

"Hear wolf growl?" he asked.

"Yes, but—"

"Wolf…pounce...on you before I kill? Spit and...howl? Bite you?"

"No."

His expression didn't change at all, as he said, "Wolf…rabid. Out of...mind. Had to kill."

The wolf was rabid?

All at once, the enormity of the danger she'd been in struck her. She swooned, but he'd come to stand close to her, and, clutching hold of his arm, she steadied herself.

"If it had bit me, then I would surely die a most horrible death." She swallowed hard and continued to speak as though the words were drawn from deep within her soul. "I am obliged to you once again, Mr.

Lakota. I—I hardly know how to repay you."

"No...claim on me," he said. "It my...duty." He touched her hand where she still gripped his arm, and he loosened her fingers. But as soon as she stood on her own, her knees buckled under her, and she fell.

He caught her before she reached the ground, and, as his arms came around her, she gazed up into his eyes. They were the color of a crystal-blue sky, and looked so foreign in contrast to the deeply tanned color of his skin. So strange a combination for an Indian.

Then it happened. His head came down toward hers, and his lips were only a fraction of an inch from hers. She was ready for the embrace, and she opened her lips in anticipation of his kiss. But it never materialized.

As though they had both turned to stone, neither one of them moved. Nor did either of them step away from the other. However, neither took action to close the miniscule distance between them.

Her whole body was on fire, and she could barely speak as she asked, "Are you going to do it? Are you going to kiss me?"

"I...dare not," he whispered, and so close was he, she could feel the movement of his lips on her own as he spoke.

She whispered, "For what you have done for me, I owe you much. If you wish to—"

He put a single finger over her lips. "Do not say it. You...owe me nothing. If I...kiss you, it...be because I want kiss you, not because you…owe me anything."

"And do you want to kiss me?"

"*Hau.*" He shut his eyes.

"That word means yes?"

He didn't answer.

"Do you not do it because of your pledge to Walks-in-sunshine?"

Again, no answer.

He let his arms fall from around her. With a deep breath, he stepped back from her, putting a little distance between them. When her knees wouldn't stand under her weight and she stumbled, he quickly moved to catch her, but he placed no more than a single arm around her waist.

He said, "No kiss...because one kiss not enough."

His words stirred her, caused her to realize that he was as moved by her as she was by him, and, in consequence, she might have gone to pieces and plunged to the ground altogether. She didn't. But only because he held onto her so tightly.

"These...words," he continued, "we must not say to...each other. Long...trek. Must not...touch again."

"Why?"

"Forbidden," was all he said. "Come. We set up...camp. You sleep."

"And will you sleep, also?"

"Not tonight," was all he answered, and when he let go of her to turn to walk back in the direction toward their camp, she found her feet were at last able to hold her, and she fell into step behind him, afraid now to be left alone.

So, she thought to herself, the problem between them wasn't all because of her lessening of morals. Apparently, he perceived the pull of their attraction, too. The only difference between them was that he intended doing nothing about it, while she...?

What was she thinking? She loved Jeffrey, not this man. Therefore, her intent was to do nothing about it, also.

Still, she felt almost helpless to stop admiring the beauty of that bare place where his leggings and breechcloth didn't quite meet. She did force herself to look away, and as she did so, she pledged that she would resurrect the lessons of her morals, which at present, seemed to be so lacking.

CHAPTER NINE

The shelter he'd built was ingenious, she thought, as she stepped closer to the temporary dwelling. Using the existing landscape, he had constructed a hideaway that included a makeshift entrance, and a combination grass/twig roof overhead. A soft, antelope-skinned blanket fell over the entrance that was a "door" of sorts. Moreover, if she'd not been shown that the refuge was here, she would have never discovered it, for the dugout fit so well into the environment around them that the eye glanced over it without seeing it.

Darkness had fallen, and a multitude of stars littered the sky. As she gazed up into the night sky, she was struck by the endless sight of those twinkling lights that littered the heavens. Extending from horizon to horizon, millions, perhaps billions of these tiny illuminations bathed the earth in a silvery image. The moon, she noted, was not yet in attendance, and the landscape was black, except for these tiny points of brilliance.

As he reached their tiny shelter, he squatted at the entrance, and pulled back the entrance flap. Looking up at her, he said, "You safe here. Noise...make none. I go to...erase...trail."

"No." She straightened up at once. "Please do not leave me here alone." She was aware that her lips trembled as she spoke, but she was far from being able to stop the shaking. "Please," she continued, "I have said this before, and I mean it now as much as I ever have, especially after that wolf—"

Mr. Lakota started to speak to her, but she rushed on, "Please, I must go where you go. Teach me your ways and I will do them as best I can. I am aware that I might be a hindrance to you, but I beg you to not leave me behind."

She glanced down at him where still he reposed on his haunches, and she attempted to determine what his reaction was to her words, but he did little more than stare at her. He stood to his feet, and suddenly his face swam before her. His was a handsome image, enhanced now by the ethereal glow of the night. Slowly, he nodded. "Understood," was all he said.

She let go of her breath, unaware until this moment that she'd been holding it.

"We go now," he began. "We go as...before. Step like this." He showed her the way it was done once more, with toes turned inward and then set down upon the ground before the heel followed. "I...show you how Indian...erases trail. *Itó*, come."

***

It was meticulous work, going back over their tracks, and erasing those in front and in back of them. Indeed, the moon had finally found its way into the sky when they at last came to the end of the day's tracks. Truth was, she had performed little of the work that was required, her main task being to step carefully back over her own tracks...at least those that he showed her. He erased them over the ground by means of constant brushing, and carefully placing grass and vines over them. She was thankful that he took the responsibility upon himself, for the truth was that she didn't know how to do it properly, even when he had demonstrated to her the manner in which it was done.

But as little as she did, it was still tiring work, and she felt as though she might yet sleep on her feet. More times than she could easily count, she wished the task were done. But he seemed to possess more energy and more patience than she, for he wouldn't stop until the task was completely finished. Indeed, so late was it, the Big Dipper Constellation was low in the sky before the chore was done. But now, with the work behind them, she relaxed a little as she crossed her arms over her breast.

"Now what?" she asked in a whisper. "If we left a trail during the day, won't we make the same kind of path going back?"

"*Hau*."

"But I don't understand. If that's true, why have we erased one trail, only to make another?"

He placed a finger over his lips, cautioning her to whisper. And indeed, she was reminded to heed his advice. But that finger brought attention to his lips, and as she gazed up at him, she recalled why it was that moonlight was supposed to be a girl's best friend.

It was also a man's, she reluctantly conceded. The moon had arisen at last, and haunting moonbeams painted him in a glow that caused him to look unworldly, as well as extraordinarily handsome.

She reminded herself that these thoughts would never do. She looked away from him, and took several steps backward in self-defense, falling onto her rump when she tripped over a pea vine.

He smiled at her as he offered her a hand up. But she ignored that hand, as well as the humor she witnessed in his eyes. Bristling, she found her own way up onto her feet.

He said in a voice so low that she had to concentrate in order to hear him, "Whole tribe...depend on...scout keeping them safe. Important I leave no…print to...follow."

"But if we make more tracks— I guess I just don't understand."

"We cover…tracks as we...go back."

"But—" She grimaced. "Isn't that double work? If we erase the trail we left during the day, then cover our tracks back to camp, why don't we simply erase our trail during the day?"

"When alone on prairie...daylight not safe. If…attention on tracks, then mind not on...world around...one."

"Then why don't we do our traveling at night?"

"You feel...safe with me at night?"

She didn't even hesitate when she said, "I think I would."

"Shadows not make you...frightened?"

"I—I can't say for sure."

"It as I...thought. So go...during day until…forced to travel at night."

"Oh? There might come a time when we will be required to journey during the night?"

"*Hau,*" was all he said.

"Why?"

"Be in enemy...territory. Only safe, then...at night."

"So there is some danger involved in escorting me across the prairie?"

"*Hau.*"

"That reminds me that I would like to ask you where you are planning to take me. I realize that I should have posed this question to you before now, but I guess it slipped my mind. Could you tell me please where we are going?"

"Later," he replied, "when we safe...in camp. We talk. Not now."

She nodded in agreement. If there were one lesson she'd learned, it was that this man knew more about this country than she might ever come to know. She would bow to his judgment and remain silent on the subject, at least for now.

It turned out that the work to erase their trail back to the coulee was as meticulously done as wiping out the previous day's tracks. But finally, after many hours, it was done.

The moon was now a low orb in the sky as they cautiously stepped down the ravine's incline, and a gray color had crept onto the eastern horizon, indicating the time of day was early morning. He held her hand now, for her exhaustion was such that she might have slid down the canyon's wall had he not lent her his support.

Unerringly, he led her to their shelter, and because she couldn't have distinguished one part of the structure from another, she was glad when he took up the entrance flap for her, and helped her inside, saying, "I go and…clean our tracks down...cliff."

"Do you promise you won't go farther away than that?"

"*Hau, hau,*" he muttered, but it was enough to settle her fears.

"But as soon as you return, we will have that talk about where it is that you are taking me?"

"Hau, hau."

With a quick nod, she bent over and crawled into their lean-to. He left forthwith, returning to her after several minutes. He scratched on the entrance flap to let her know he was there, but he didn't scramble into the little shelter, and, as she peeped around the deerskin flap, she saw that he sat a couple of feet away. His back was to her.

From the safety of their refuge, she asked, "Aren't you going to join me in here, where we can talk in private?"

"*Hiyá,*" he replied without turning around.

"What does that word mean?"

"Means 'no.'"

"But aren't you going to sleep?"

"*Hiyá*. Someone need...keep watch. That me."

"Yes, I suppose that might be— —"

He didn't answer.

"Might that not cause you to be drowsy on the morrow?"

"What mean...drowsy?"

"It means to be sleepy, not very alert."

"Alert enough. We travel far...tomorrow. You sleep."

"All right," she agreed, "but after our talk."

He gave a brief nod of his head, and she fixed the skin cover back with a stick, as she asked the question dearest to her, "Where are you taking me?"

He didn't speak at once, and his hesitation grated on her nerves, especially since his back was still turned toward her. Was it a secret?

With a deep sigh, she came up into a squatting position and crawled out from the protection of the abode; it took little time to join him, and soon she was sitting by his side. They were both silent. After a moment, she asked, "Where are we going? You seem reluctant to tell me.

Are you?"

"*Hiyá*, no. Needed...safe place to talk."

"Oh."

"We go white man's post," he said without looking over at her. "They your...own kind. They will care for you."

"I see." At first, his reply mollified her, but after a moment, she recalled the terrible incident from her most recent past, and a bully's voice saying, "Hair's supposed ta be red..."

She shivered. Her hair was red. Although it seemed a ridiculous fear, some small part of her wondered if those killers might have been seeking her. It was impossible, really, but try as she might, she couldn't pretend she hadn't heard the bullies speak those words. Plus...

I was the only woman on the wagon train with red hair.

Raw fear struck her. Should she tell him about it? Perhaps. Clearing her throat, she tried to voice the words, but in the end, she merely asked, "How far away is this white man's post?"

"One moon. Maybe less. Depends on...," he gestured to the sky, "...weather."

One moon, or rather one month, she paraphrased. Again, she debated whether or not she should voice her fear. Briefly, she considered the possibility that if she did tell him, might not the knowledge impel him to reconsider his commitment to her?

Probably not, she answered her own question. But if he believed there might be a danger he hadn't conceived of, would he possibly abandon her to her own fate?

No, he wouldn't do that. She was fairly certain of that. But, she countered her own chain of thought, why not?

Think logically, she cautioned herself. *There is no need to tell him anything*. People didn't attack an entire wagon train in order to destroy only one person. Such would be insanity. Additionally, she had no enemies. Certainly there was no one in her life that wished to see her dead.

"Hair's supposed ta be red..."

The words swam in her memory, and no amount of rational thought caused them to disappear. So it was that, although she feared the consequences of telling him about it, she couldn't quite help confessing a little of it, and she muttered, "Would those men who attacked our wagon train be attached to the post where you're taking me?"

He was looking away from her, out into the night when she asked this question. Immediately, he jerked his head to the side so that he could look at her directly. He frowned at her, and asked, "This...you fear?"

"I'm not certain." She shrugged, and, avoiding his eyes, she looked down into her lap. "They couldn't be... I mean those men who attacked us—do you think they were acting on their own?"

"Say what you...mean."

"Your English is getting better. Have you noticed?"

"Hump!" he grunted, then repeated, "You say what...mean."

"Well, I'm not certain because it all happened so fast, and I can't really be sure, but—"

She paused, and try as she might to tell him all of it, she discovered that she couldn't force the words past her lips. Perhaps once they were safely at the trading post? But he said nothing in the interim, and he did nothing as he seemed to await her to continue.

At last, she murmured, "Well, do you think that those men might have been doing the bidding of someone else? And if this be so, would a trading post be a safe place? For me?"

He didn't answer, but he did turn toward her so that he could stare at her, and his look was long and hard. At last, he inquired, "Is there other place that...better?"

"Yes," she whispered, and she couldn't keep her lips from trembling as a tear slid over her face. She whispered, "Home?"

"Where home?"

She hiccupped. "Never mind. It was an outrageous suggestion—a yearning that I have. It could not be, for my home is too far away."

He shrugged and turned his attention outward again. After a moment or two, he asked again, "If not home…another place better?"

She hesitated, then finally answered, "No, I guess not."

"When…reach trader post, I scout. See if safe."

"I would appreciate that."

"If safe, I leave you there."

"Yes, of course."

"Sleep now. We go far...on morrow. Soon, we travel during night. Will be in land…of Pawnee. Not safe during day then."

"Very well," she replied. "As long as you are with me, I won't be afraid."

"*Haiyé,* I am glad. Sleep now."

Perhaps it was because she was so tired that she didn't care that he had ordered her in such a matter-of-fact way, but whatever the reason, she found herself doing exactly as he commanded. Funnily enough she was able to rest peacefully so that soon she fell into a deep sleep….

CHAPTER TEN

"Cante śića yaun śni ye-ah
Wacécicicíya."
"Cante śića yaun śni ye-ah
Wacécicicíya."

"Do not have a sad heart
I pray for thee."
"Do not have a sad heart
I pray for thee."

Brave Wolf sprinkled sage over the place where he prayed. Although it was the custom to set fire to the dried herb and let the ensuing smoke drift up to the Above Ones, he didn't dare do it. He was too close to the land of the Pawnee, and though the Pawnee were supposed to be contained on a reservation, he could not chance an encounter with one of their keen scouts who would have no trouble in escaping the bounds of their reservation-type impediment.

Opening his arms toward the rising sun, he sang the prayer again:

"Cante śića yaun śni ye-ah
Wacécicicíya."
"Cante śića yaun śni ye-ah
Wacécicicíya."

"Do not have a sad heart
I pray for thee."

"Do not have a sad heart

I pray for thee."

Even though he didn't look around, he was aware when she ducked out from the shelter and stepped toward him. From his peripheral vision, he watched as she dropped to her knees beside him; she reached out for his hand at the same time. Then she bowed her head.

Tears fell over her cheeks, and as he witnessed them, his heart burst. Without pause, and without wishing it, he realized he truly cared for her. It was not a simple matter of duty that alone dictated his path now: he liked her.

Perhaps, he cautioned himself, he admired her a little too much in the physical realm.

But was that true? Might the feeling of affinity between them be due to moments like this, their ritual each morning? For at dawn, as he rose up to say his prayers, so, too, did she. Always, she took his hand before she spoke to her Creator, and her action endeared her to the very depths of his soul. It was as though she required his strength and his reassurance in order to communicate with her Maker.

Still, he realized that she would never take the place of Walks-in-sunshine within his heart. That simply wasn't possible, for his love for that woman went beyond the materialistic realm.

But he could not deny that he felt a pull toward this beauty who knelt so sweetly next to him. Enough. He blocked these thoughts from his mind, and he sang again:

"Cante śića yaun śni ye-ah

Wacécicicíya."

"Cante śića yaun śni ye-ah

Wacécicicíya."

"Do not have a sad heart
I pray for thee."
"Do not have a sad heart
I pray for thee."

Without another thought, he broke with tradition and came down to his knees beside her, squeezing her hand. He heard her whisper in prayer:

"Please, Lord, help me always to remember, and to understand. Help this man, too, whose kindness and skill have saved me so many times."

He listened to her swallow noisily, before she muttered, "Amen."

"Amen," he echoed.

She turned her head slightly to gaze at him, and as he caught her eye and witnessed her tears, he knew without a doubt that what had been before, and what should be in the future, had changed forever.

He loved her.

True, it was not the same sort of passion that a man might feel for a wife. He was not confused about that, for he still loved, would always love, Walks-in-sunshine; it was Walks-in-sunshine who would be his future wife. But he would be a fool if he were to deny the tenderness that stirred him so deeply—a devotion for this other being—this woman beside him.

After all, it was not unknown for a man to love many folk, many people. It didn't follow then, that a man need fear that he might shower another with sexual ardor simply because he loved. Did a man not love his family? His kindred? His tribe? All these were loved, but were different.

Thus, he need not fear this realization of love, and he could in clear conscience escort her to the trading post as promised, there to leave her so that she might return to her people. As he looked out toward the early morning sunrise, a red-breasted robin flew past his vision, its color reminding him of this woman beside him.

Slowly, softly he whispered to her, *"Zin-tká Áŋpo cíǩala."*

She smiled.

"It your new name," he murmured. *"Zin-tká Áŋpo cíǩala l.* You needed...Indian name. You have one...now."

"Thank you. What does it mean?" she whispered.

"Little Dawn Bird."

"Little Dawn Bird. I like it. How do you say it again?"

"Zin-tká Áŋpo cíǩala."

She repeated, *"Zin-tká Áŋpo cíǩala."*

He nodded. Then, after a moment, he added, "Brave Wolf," and pointed to himself. "Lakota be name of...tribe. This one's name Brave Wolf."

She squeezed his hand. "Brave Wolf. How do you say it in your language?"

"Caksi Cantét'iŋza."

"Caksi Cantét'iŋza," she echoed. "It is a beautiful name, for a man most beautiful."

He swallowed noisily before he jerked his vision away from her. Releasing her hand, he came up onto his feet, and without another word being spoken to her, he trod away from her, ensuring his back was to her.

Indeed, he might easily justify his love for her as nothing carnal, but the reality was less than he could explain away. Already, he was physically ready for her; it troubled him. All the more reason to keep a healthy distance from her, for honor demanded he not expand his fondness for her into another realm, the physical realm.

He would not do it. He promised himself that he would not.

***

As Mia watched his departing figure, she wondered what was

wrong with him. Why had he left her as though he couldn't get away from her fast enough?

Did she dare to follow him?

Not likely. For one, her fears were less here in the light of day, and she didn't feel the urgency to have him with her constantly. For another, his departure seemed to brook no argument. Without him having to say a word, she realized he required time alone.

Besides, a new reality had taken possession of her: no longer did she worry that he might suddenly leave her, to never return. Somehow, in some way, she had come to realize that she could trust him to his word. Although it was true that, by his actions alone, she could have concluded this, there was more to it. For a moment, if a moment only, when she'd looked up at him, she had espied an aura of devotion which had been directed toward her. Although the impression had quickly disappeared from his countenance, she'd seen it. She knew she had.

Likewise, if she were to be honest—and she must be—she would admit that she felt a similar kindliness for him, too. Indeed, what was happening with her in this regard went beyond a mere feeling of charity. However, this was not a matter she wished to explore; her emotions were too unstable.

What would be his opinion of her if he were to become aware that she held a regard for him that bordered on the sensuous? Would he form a bad opinion of her, since it came so soon after losing her husband? After all, it was doubtful that he would understand that what she was really feeling was the love for her husband, and that she was placing that affection misguidedly onto him.

Oh, this is all so confusing. It is also so very wrong.

Well, there was one aspect to it that could be her saving grace: she would never let him know. Never give him the chance to judge her. As she rose up to pace back to the shelter, she vowed that she would do her best to never let him know.

***

As she opened her eyes, she realized that the warmth of the day was upon the land, for there were some details that this shelter, regardless of how well it was built, could not disguise, and one of those was the heat of a Kansas summer. Peeping up through the cracks in the makeshift "ceiling," she could see that the sun was well past its zenith.

Why had he let her sleep so long? Usually, they were both up before the new dawn of another day made its appearance in the eastern sky. It was at this time that they would say their morning prayer and depart upon the trail. Sitting up, she pulled back the deerskin flap, speculating that Mr. Wolf might still be on guard, and sitting within a few feet from their shelter.

But he was not there.

Luckily, because of her conclusions last night, that old feeling of alarm did not materialize. Instead, she wondered if she might take advantage of being alone, for she would relish a bath. Of course, if she were to attempt it, she would have to make the trek to the water's edge in an alert manner; she would require her pistol, also, and the rifle, since there were too many occasions that demanded protection.

It would be a chancy exploit to attempt a bath out here in the wild, yes, but the idea of washing off the past few days' grime from her body was too appealing to be easily dismissed. Even fear of the wolf or some other creature took second place to the vision of cleanliness. And the water was so close by.

Besides, she thought as she glanced down at her attire, she might be able to wash off the brown bloodstains that still marred the light blue color of her dress. It was time, she decided, to try to erase the nightmare of the massacre, if not from her dreams, then at least from its physical evidence.

Briefly she wondered why Brave Wolf hadn't mentioned the condition of her dress. But then she realized that in her dealings with him so far, he had never criticized her. Perhaps this was because he felt it wasn't his place to do so, or maybe he was simply kind-hearted. Whatever the reason was, she was thankful for his lack of censure.

Scooting out of the temporary sanctuary, she paused while she fished back within the shelter for her pistol, pocketing it as soon as her hand came in contact with it. Then, grasping hold of Jeffrey's rifle, she positioned it under her arm, where it would be ever ready. Using her fingers to "comb" her hair, she threw the bulk of the curls behind her shoulders and rose up to her feet.

It was a short stroll to the water's edge, and she was glad to realize that she could see no trace of Mr. Wolf's presence. The water looked refreshing, even from this distance, and her spirits picked up. The grasses were long there at its shores, but stones dotted the gentle slope of the mud and muck as it fell down to a rather rocky strand of sand.

She decided it would be there, using those stones, that she might wash the blood from her frock. Wading through the waist-high grasses to reach the water's edge, she was well aware when the dirt and mud beneath her feet turned to rocky sand.

She heard a squawk, and, looking up, she espied a hawk circling above her. The sun was lazily forging a path into the Western sky, but it seemed in no hurry to arrive there. White, fluffy clouds dotted the sky above her, as well as the distant horizon, where their whiteness was only beginning to mirror a light, pinkish orange. Sunset was, indeed, still far away.

The wind whisked around her, but it was a gentle force, probably due to the lower ground level of the coulee. The air smelled sweet and moist, the scent of wildflowers and grass strong within it. She listened. It was quiet for the moment. With no sound of a wolf or a coyote, or any other creature nearby, she took a moment to admire the peace of this place.

A feeling of well-being accompanied the beauty of the environment around her, but the emotion was quickly replaced with an ardent sense of guilt. Had she forgotten that Jeffrey was gone? That he would never again see or experience the wonders of places like this?

She sighed; it was best for her tattered emotions that she concentrate on the tasks at hand. She needed a bath, and her clothes required cleaning. With a quick glance around to ensure that she was alone, she bent down toward the water and placed the rifle and her pistol close to her, but far enough away from the water so as to ensure that they would remain operational.

With care, she began the long process of undressing. Gingerly, still watching her surroundings, she unbuttoned her dress, then brought it up and over her head. The garment had once been of a light, aqua-blue hue, but now it looked a patchy brown all over because of the bloodstains which covered her skirts as well as the blouse of her dress.

As soon as she had discarded her garb, she glanced down at her underclothes and was dismayed to see that even her slip bore the brown stains of blood. Did she dare to strip down to her chemise so that she could wash her slip, as well as her gown?

Realizing that if she didn't clean the material now, she might never have another chance to do so, she set to work with speed. After all, the task required some time alone, and so far, she hadn't let Mr. Wolf out of her sight. It caused her to wonder if, once they were back on the trail, she might ever have another opportunity.

Because she couldn't be certain, it was this that finally decided her. She removed her slip, too, bringing it up and over her head.

She inhaled deeply, glad for the moment to be rid of the cumbersome clothing. Of course she was still dressed in her corset, chemise and hosiery, and she was saddened to note that even these garments bore the disfigurements of blood. Well, these articles of clothing would remain where they were; she did not feel secure enough to strip down into the altogether. But perhaps those spots might come clean while still remaining on her and hugging her body. At least she would try to wash them in this way.

She wet her dress and her slip, and, using a few stones, she began the cumbersome process of washing away the discolorations. The water was invitingly cold, but she ignored the call to bathe her body right this minute. It was best to not put her work aside yet. There would be time later.

Gradually, the bloodstains lessened as she diligently scrubbed at them. It was, however, a long process to be attempted without the aid of soap, and when at last it was done, she figured an hour might have elapsed.

Luckily, the summer days were long and the sun was still a large orb in the sky when she rose up to position the apparel over a few rocks. There her clothing would dry.

Turning back toward the water's shore, she waded into the water, her moccasins protecting her feet from the sharp rocks that littered the bottom of the stream. She was almost waist-deep in the stream when it happened.

In a short distance, perhaps no more than twenty feet away, a figure suddenly arose from the river, the level of the water hitting him thigh-deep. She stopped completely still.

It was Mr. Wolf. He was naked, he was incredibly male, and the sun above him highlighted the muscles and sharp planes of his chest and arms. His stomach was flat, tapering down to a masculine part that was longer and bigger than Jeffrey's and—

She pulled up her thoughts, and she knew she should look away. But alas, it was not to be. She stared straight at him.

He saw her almost at the same time that she'd become aware of him. He stopped mid-stride, seemed unable to move, unable to speak. Indeed, he looked surprised.

And then that male part of him grew bigger, thicker. Briefly, it astonished her. Hadn't she heard that man parts and cold water did not necessarily work well together?

Yet, there he was. He was aroused, and his masculinity grew ever larger, stronger.

Before she could look away, he took the necessary motions to execute a hundred and eighty degree turn, furiously immersing himself in the water so quickly that she barely registered the change before she noticed that he was swimming away from her. It took a moment for her breath to return to normal, longer still for her body to cease its wayward, yet highly sexual response.

Well, that didn't help me resolve to ignore the situation between us.

Thank goodness he'd had the wherewithal to turn his back on her. But it hadn't happened fast enough. She'd seen his arousal. And she knew: He wanted her.

What was she to do? Who could she turn to?

She realized the answer at once, and she whispered, "Oh, Daddy, forgive me. Help me to know what to do, how to act."

It was then, realizing there was one being above even her father who might hear her, she prayed, "Dear Lord, as you are a witness to my plight, I ask that you guide my path to return home at all possible speed."

And that's when she slammed full force into a realization: Yes, it had been wrong of her father to obligate her to a contract which was not of her own making. But perhaps she was mistaken to blame her father for an act he believed would be to her benefit. Wasn't she also amiss for running away from him? As she expected him to forgive her, shouldn't she also bear no malice toward him?

"Oh, Daddy, I'm sorry I did what I did to you," she whispered to the wind. "I miss you. I miss your advice. Certainly my life there in the East wasn't perfect, but at present, it seems more like a haven than the prison I had thought it to be. Oh, how I wish I were back there now," she murmured quietly, adding, "I am out of my element here, Daddy, and I don't understand what's happening to me."

She waited, as though she expected his wise advice to be brought to her on the draughts of air. But it wasn't to be.

She was on her own, and she was with a man who would be everything to her in this month to come. She knew that, without him, she would die.

But she was also aware that circumstances had changed between them: The truth was out. He wanted her, and the Lord forgive her, she wanted him, too.

Abruptly, she cried. After a while, her tears waning, she bathed herself, hoping against hope that the coolness of the water, and the blessed relief it might bring her, would quiet the yearning of her body.

But indeed, it was not to be...

CHAPTER ELEVEN

She knew. There'd been no means to hide his physical stimulation from her. At least, he thought as he turned the events back through his mind, he'd had the sense to turn his back on her, and had endeavored to swim away the carnal lust. That it had required a lengthier time than he had thought it might, was to be borne without rationale. But at last, although several hours had passed before he could trust himself, he felt confident that his bodily urges were under his control.

He stepped back into their camp. He knew what he had to do. He simply didn't want to do it. It might cause his sexual problem concerning her to magnify, yet there was no other way; it had to be done.

He had to talk to her, and do nothing more than talk. He had to tell her that he would honor his commitment to Walks-in-sunshine and that, although he might desire her, this one he called Little Dawn Bird, he would not take advantage of their time together.

Would she believe him? Or more importantly, would she trust him with the task of bringing her unharmed to the trader's post? As he trod back into their encampment, these thoughts troubled him.

Although he didn't immediately see her, he knew she was there; he could sense it. Most likely, she had positioned herself in the relative safety of the shelter he'd constructed for her.

Taking a deep breath for courage, he bent down at the entrance flap of the structure and scratched on its flimsy opening. It was the easiest way to let her know that he was there.

He asked, "Might I…come in...or you come out?"

She pulled back the deerskin overlap, and there he witnessed a strained smile on her countenance, before she replied, "Yes. Please, although which would you prefer? Shall I come out there, or you come in here?"

"It safer if I come in, do not fear. I mean only...to talk."

"Yes, yes, of course. I, too, think we must have words with each other."

"Pardon," he murmured, as he crawled into the narrow space and scooted into a position as far away from her as possible, given the smallness of the enclosure. Immediately, he wondered if this were a wise decision on his part. This place smelled of her, and he found the scent...invigorating.

Yet, determined he would control his earthy desires, he placed his arms over his chest, an action that indicated he might not be as calm as he might like to be.

He inhaled deeply before he began, saying, "We will...smoke, so that we will...ensure that words we speak are...truth. Do you agree?"

She nodded.

He produced a small pipe that he carried with him in one of his many bags. Appended to it was a tiny pouch which was filled with tobacco. Reaching into that miniscule sack, he took hold of little bits of the sacred plant, using these to fill the pot of his pipe.

Using a white-man's match, produced from another one of his bags, he lit the tobacco, then sucked on the pipe until the leaves began to smoke. Only then did he continue the required ceremony, and he said, "Because you not know…Lakota ceremony, I will...explain...ritual of speaking true. By letting smoke from pipe...drift up to...heavens, I...commit myself to the Creator, and...vow my words be only truth."

Because it was important to carry out the tradition exactly, he next held the pipe up toward the north, then to the south and finally to both the east and the west.

As he did so, he recited, "I…invite winds of…north, south, east, west...these, the four...directions to hear my words. By this and by smoking, I…vow what I say be...sure and true. No forked tongue."

He inhaled the smoke of the pipe, before he at last passed the vessel to her.

"By smoking," he told her, "you agree…only true words be spoken. If you agree…, inhale."

He watched as she sighed, and he wondered for a moment if she would do it. But at last, she took hold of the sacred instrument, and she whispered, "I agree."

She puffed on the sacred object and inhaled the smoke. A fit of coughing followed, and he could see that she tried to contain the involuntary reaction, but she coughed again and again until she sheepishly glanced up at him, and, still wheezing, said, "I have never—*cough, cough*—smoked before now."

He nodded. "Understood. And now that you...have done so," he added, "you give pipe back to me. Do not...pass it in front of...entrance."

She did as he requested, and he took it from her gently, ensuring he did not touch her fingers. Without delay and without emptying the contents of the pot, he placed the whole of it on a stone.

Briefly, he wondered how he should proceed, what words he should say to ease their plight. Then he remembered that complete honesty dictated that he come directly to the point, and so he began, "You saw...me. You now know...my secret. I am...sorry, for I meant you not to know."

"I—I—"

He held up his hand. "Your turn…speak come...soon."

She nodded.

"I mean not to...*kikśan*..." He paused as he sought the correct translation, "*kikśan*...violate you. Must keep distance from you. Love...I feel for Walks-in-sunshine. Touching...you, me...must not touch. Return you to your people...same as found you. Meant you not to know."

He sighed deeply, then, lifting up his glance to encompass hers, he continued, "Earthy...desires bad for man on trail. Cause him be weak. Must...avoid touching. This one," he pointed to himself, "...*huŋhuŋhé*..." He frowned, searching his memory for the right English word. "*Huŋhuŋhé*...regret that you know."

He paused as he gathered his thoughts together, hoping she had understood his meanings and his intent toward her. Finally, realizing he had said it all to the best of his ability, he gestured toward her and encouraged her, saying, "Your...right now to speak. What say you?"

At first, she did nothing more than glance down at her lap, and he wondered if she had understood him. As he watched her, he noticed without speculating on it, that she had washed both her dress and her body. All at once, without willing it, an image of her, naked and waiting for him, swam before his eyes, bringing with it an onslaught of longing. He looked away from her as he sought control of himself physically.

It embarrassed him, this lack of discipline he exerted over his own body's needs, and he determined that he would regain command. By the time he returned her to her people, he would have conquered it.

At last, she began, "Before I say what I must, I fear I must tell you that I believe that you will dislike me, or think bad thoughts about me if I tell you the truth."

He said nothing, as was custom and obligation. When it appeared that she might not say more than this, however, he voiced, "It not happen. I promise. *Yeyéé,* continue."

She breathed in deeply, let it out slowly, before she murmured, "I—I fear I have similar feelings to yours."

Passion, raw and sweet, washed through him, and he considered that perhaps he had been wrong. Maybe speaking of their problem would make it worse. But he schooled his features, endeavoring to keep hidden what was occurring with him.

"How can this be happening to me so soon after my husband's death?" she continued. "I don't understand it, and I am fearful that the only explanation I have for it is that I am not a good woman."

He shouldn't speak. Custom dictated that he wait until she was finished, yet he knew he had to set her fears at ease, and he said, "Only good woman…feel this way."

"Thank you for saying that, but I'm not sure this is true." A tear fell over her cheek. "I loved my husband. I love him still, but I am afraid that the root of your problem might be me, and that if I were not here—"

She sobbed, and, although he felt urged to say words of comfort to her, he knew he dared not. Not yet.

So he waited until she continued, "You see, I think I am placing upon you, in a manner of speaking, the love that I felt for my husband. That it is he that I want, that I love, but now is given to you, not because you have done anything to make me believe you might like it, but simply because you are here...and so am I."

Again, she cried. "The truth is that I am maddened by what I feel. Yet, I also realize that because we all influence each other, either for good or for bad, I fear that that I am the problem. Not you."

Her chest rose and fell with her sobs, and her tears fell gently on it. However, he was careful to note this without directly looking there.

"But please," she continued, "though I am afraid this be true, I beg you not to abandon me here." More tears, more sobs followed her plea, and her cheeks became wet with her grief.

However, so startled was he by her confession that for a moment words failed him. At last, custom came to his defense, and he said, "I will speak to you on this…only after you have said all you...wish to say. Have you?"

She hiccupped a reply that was inaudible. However, she nodded that she was, indeed, finished.

Although passion filled his physical being, he ignored it. Sympathy for her plight took precedence over all else, and he responded to her, saying, "It…natural this be so."

Her acknowledgment for his words was a steady stream of weeping, and his heart reached out to her.

"Do not fear this. Great…loss," he went on to say, "can cause one to...respond this way. My father told me…similar words before we parted. I...promise I not use this as...reason to... *kikśan*...violate you. I tell you this true. I not...abandon you here. I promise."

As he spoke, he saw that so great were the sobs that racked her body, she had placed her hands over her face, as though embarrassed that she should feel these anxieties so greatly. Compassion for her rocked him to the depths of his soul, and helped to cool his unwelcome physical response to her. Indeed, he became aware that his physical appetite for her seemed less, and that it was gradually fading as a reality. It was a good feeling.

He resumed his train of thought, uttering, "In one moon, maybe less, we be at…post. Until that time, we not...touch. Better for you. Better for me. You agree?"

She nodded, but she didn't look up at him. Although she no longer held her hands over her face, her gaze still centered away from him.

"Not always…possible we not touch. But we try."

Again, she nodded.

"Have you said all you need...say?"

"Yes," she whispered.

"Then it is done." Picking up his pipe, he emptied the ashes onto the rock in front of him. "Our talk is finished."

Only then did she glance up at him, and he met her amber-colored eyes with a nod and a smile, as if to allay her fright. "I go now. We leave…camp after sun sets. I go…prepare. You, too."

"Yes," she agreed. "Thank you for our talk."

A curt nod was his only reply to her, and, scooting to the entrance of their shelter, he pulled back the flap and crawled out through the small entrance.

He wouldn't think of their talk now. There was too much to do that would ensure their safe passage over this part of the country. He would concentrate on that work, and perhaps later, he might reflect on what they had said to one another. He felt comfort momentarily, for he believed it was their conversation that had set them onto the right path.

Sighing, he stepped forward into the remnants of a glorious sunset.

CHAPTER TWELVE

Days turned into a week; a week into another and then another yet. Since they had transgressed into the territory of the Pawnee, they traveled by the light of the moon and the stars. But that illumination was dim to eyes that were not used to such stark blackness; so she often stumbled, requiring him to backtrack to find her.

Sometimes, particularly if the night were cloudy, it was so very, very dark that she found she could not see farther than a few inches in front of her. At such times, she could only plod forward by holding onto his shirt. Tonight was such a one.

At least, she justified, when these times were necessary, she was careful not to touch him—only the buckskin of his shirt. Luckily, he never commented on it, although she realized this did cause him to slow his pace.

A night hawk hooted into the blackness of their path; it was a common sound in this environment of grass, vines and wildflowers. Yet this time it sounded close—too close.

"What was that?" she whispered as she caught up to Brave Wolf.

He placed a finger over his lips, the universal sign for silence. Then, catching hold of her hand, he put it over his lips, and he uttered silently, "That not...owl."

Her mouth gaped open in surprise.

Keeping her hand squarely over his lips, he said, still without sound, "We not alone."

She gasped, and she hoped the slight noise was hidden in the whining of the ever-constant wind.

He told her silently, "You stay here. I go find out who here."

No!

Quickly grabbing his hand, she placed it over her lips and commanded, "I must go with you."

The moon had peeked out from a cloud, emitting a shimmering ray of light, but it was enough that she could see his frown. Looking up at him, she was struck by the beauty of his features, as the heavenly illumination bathed him in its ethereal light. She closed her eyes against the sight, realizing that she was still as fascinated by him as she ever had been.

Because her fingers remained over his lips, she felt the words he said as he declared, "Could be…trouble. Not like to worry about you. If have to...fight."

"If you fight, then I fight, too. Where you go, I go.
If you die here, so do I."

He exhaled deeply. She could feel the warmth of his breath against her hand.

He was so close, she could see that he stared at her; she looked back at him, and her gaze was steady. She was determined to follow him; he should know this by now.

He said, still without emitting any sound, "We close to trader's post. If bad thing happens to me, you could find way there."

She didn't know why this suggestion was unacceptable to her. But it was, and she immediately answered, "No. I'm lost without you. I mean it. What happens to you I will ensure happens to me, too."

Again, she felt his warm breath on her hand as he breathed out.

He said, while her fingers still covered his lips, "I not…good protection if cannot keep you safe. *Éna uŋ,* stay here."

"I cannot. I will not."

She could swear that his eyes softened suddenly, and he spoke to her in that same inaudible way, "I care for...you. Want you to live. Stay here." Then he added, "Please."

She bit her lip. She swallowed hard. How dared he say that he cared for her at such a time. Not fair to use that plea against her resolve. Yet, she would have been made of stone to not be moved by his entreaty.

His soft, though almost indistinguishable features swam before her eyes as she gazed up at him beneath this fleeting, flattering starlight. He was so handsome, so very becoming, and his kindly manner toward her endeared him to her heart.

Should she let him have his way this once? Should she stay behind?

He seemed to wait for her answer with bated breath, and, at last, she grabbed hold of his fingers again, and brought them to her lips, as she replied, "All right. I will stay behind this once. But if you don't return within an hour, I promise that I will come to find you. I promise."

She felt his lips twitch up in a smile before he voicelessly murmured, "Then I work quickly."

"Yes," she responded. "Yes, please."

He squeezed her hand once before settling it back at her side, and then, in an instant, he turned away from her. She thought that he would leave her at once, but she was wrong. Working as silently as possible, he constructed a temporary hiding place for her, made with what was to hand: grass and vines. Then, before leaving her, he told her, "If I...do not return, you stay here 'til…morning. Go to post, that way." He pointed off toward the southeast. "Follow old buffalo trails. Neither Pawnee nor white man harm you…during day."

"Thank you, but you must know that I won't. Whatever befalls you, I will ensure happens to me, too. So do not get yourself killed."

He smiled at her then, and, squatting down in front of her, he took her by the chin, holding her face up to his as he brought his forehead down to lean against hers. He urged, "Go to post."

She bit her lip. "Maybe..." was all she promised.

And then, quick as the wind, he rose up and was gone. She watched the place where he had been for many minutes. Suddenly, she knew what to do: Coming up onto her knees, she bowed her head and began to pray.

***

He was back within moments. Indeed, so fast was his return, he found her still kneeling in prayer. He joined her there, and bowing his head, too, he echoed her, "Amen," as soon she whispered it.

"White man," he began silently, as he caught her hand and brought it to his lips so she might understand his words.

She shivered in response to the feel of his lips moving beneath her touch. But it had to be endured. At present, there was no other way to communicate.

She let out her breath, and asked, "Did you announce yourself?"

She felt that he grinned, and, as she glanced over toward him, although the night was so dark, she could see nothing but a vague image of his features. He replied, "Do I seem like fool? I not know…these men. They could be...murderers...thieves. Why would I take action so foolish?"

The word "murderers" caught her attention, and she asked, as she caught hold of his hand and brought it again to her lips, "Do you think they are murderers?"

"I not know," he mouthed. "But will not…reveal you or me 'til I know."

"I fear them," she gasped out against his fingers. "Please, when we get to the trading post, if they are there, do not announce me or leave me there."

"Calm...remain calm. I will not leave you if I believe there danger to you. I will scout. Not leave 'til white man's...*minwaŋca-peta*...boat of...steam comes for you."

"You won't?"

"I promise will stay...until then."

Her breath outward was quick and strained. A new concern surfaced, one she had not realized until this moment: She wasn't certain she felt safe to go all the way home without him. Worse, she realized with a start, she would miss him.

All at once, she entreated, "Come home with me."

Because her fingers still lingered over his mouth, she felt his deep intake of breath as he fidgeted.

To strengthen her position, she added, "I promise you would not regret accompanying me. My father would be pleased to meet you, and he would pay you well for what you have done to help me."

She was encouraged when he didn't immediately speak against the idea. Instead, he asked, "How long journey take to home?"

"A month," she replied. "Maybe two."

He didn't immediately give her an answer, and she added to her plea, saying, "Please..."

"I will think on it."

"Do you promise?"

"I do. Will speak of my..." he paused, then said, "*wowiyukcaŋ*...thoughts. Will tell you my thoughts after I consider it...before you go."

His promise to heed her request was more than she had hoped to achieve, and, content for the moment, she forgot her fears as she settled back against the backdrop of grass and bush. But her ease was short-lived as he insisted noiselessly, "*Itó*, come. We cannot camp here. Soon, we be at trader's post."

He had already come up onto his feet, and she followed suit, although she was slower to do so. After he had erased the traces of their temporary set-up, he stepped forward, and she was quick to catch up to him, reaching out to take hold of his shirt.

He didn't stop her from doing so, even though she realized again that her hold was a burden to him. Indeed, he made no comment on it whatsoever.

CHAPTER THIRTEEN

She felt the moisture of the Missouri River on her skin and inhaled its dirty fragrance long before the roaring, muddy water became known to her. Shorter grass grew here in this place which was southeast of the far-off site of the wagon train attack. Also, trees—a rare sight in the prairie's sea of green—had taken root here and were scattered over the landscape.

It was in the extreme darkness that foreshadows the dawn when they at last stopped their trek, and she didn't really need to be told that they had at last reached the outskirts of the trader's post. What would that place hold for her? Would it be the haven she hoped it might be?

A shiver convulsed her body. She feared that place; she knew why. Should she speak fully of her dread to Mr. Wolf?

Not yet, she decided. Not yet.

Suddenly, Brave Wolf came down on all fours and spread out his long form over the ground until he was lying flat on his belly. He motioned her to do the same, and she complied. The ground was moist and soft beneath her, perhaps because of the humidity from the river. He was scooting forward, and she followed his motions until at last they both came to the edge of the ground. Only then did she realize that they were high up on a cliff, overlooking the Missouri River. Looking down, she saw a big watercourse silhouetted beneath a million stars, which glittered like jewels in the sky overhead.

The water sparkled every now and again as the waves from its flow caught hold of a bit of the light from the heavens. At these times, it looked as though the water hid a thousand diamonds, and that every now and again, one of those surfaced, magnified beneath the pale glitter from above.

As the light transformed the sky into a silver-gray, she saw that there were trees down there that lined the water's shoreline, as well as a gentle slope of sand to its edge. Across the water loomed more trees and hills and a short grass that looked as though it were cared for by a hand other than that of the Maker.

But she knew that couldn't be so. That land would be as wild as the long grasses of the prairie, and only from this distance did it appear as if a gardener had attended to it.

Brave Wolf and she were still communicating in that strange voiceless way, and she reached for his hand to bring it to her lips. Impishly she wondered how he might respond if she were to give in to impulse and place a sweet kiss on those fingers.

She abandoned the urge at once. They had agreed to be on their best behavior toward one another, and they had come this far without betraying that trust. She would not do so now.

A gentle streak of smoke rose up from a cabin that sat close to the water. Though the structure was surrounded by a corral and a staked fence that housed what appeared to be two horses, it was not a large, going concern. It was hard to believe that such a tiny place was important enough to cause a steamboat to stop here. Perhaps she was wrong. Maybe this abode was reason enough, although—could it be that it was only the home of a trapper? So she asked, "Is that little hut down there the trading post?"

"*Hau, hau,*" he whispered.

She was silent for many moments. It was so small. Was it safe?

She was reminded that he hadn't yet given her to understand whether or not he would accompany her all the way back to Virginia. Dared she ask?

Not yet, she decided.

"When will we go there?" she inquired in a whisper.

"I make…visit there after I scout and...ensure all well for you. You not step foot down there…till…time to leave."

Listening to his deep voice, even though he was merely whispering, she was well aware that his command of English was improving. *Soon, he will be speaking the language as well as I.*

She asked, "Do you know if the steamboat has already made its last run?"

"I do not," he responded. "But it early in summer. I have seen it go up and down…Big River many times in this…season."

She turned over, onto her back, and stared up at the dark, dawn sky overhead. Turning slightly toward the east, she watched as the pinkish-blue clouds mirrored the beginning of the day. As well as the feel of moisture on her skin, the scent of mud and grass and even the fragrance of oxygen hung heavy upon the air. For a reason she couldn't quite define, these impressions imbued her with a sense of ease.

She asked in a quiet murmur, "Where will we stay while you scout?"

"I have…place in mind. We go there soon."

"Are we safer now that we are close to the post?"

"I not know. Only good scouting...prove if free from danger."

Once again, she longed to ask him if he might be coming back east with her, and she opened her mouth to put her thoughts to words. But she didn't. When he was ready, he would tell her; she was certain of it. Let him scout, let him have some time and space in which to mull over her request. If he didn't tell her of his decision soon, only then would she ask.

"*Itó*, come," he encouraged with a tap on her shoulder as he scooted back down the sloping hill. "We must find place so you can sleep."

"And you? Will you sleep, also?"

"*Hiyá*, not yet. Much needs doing now we…here."

She didn't say a word back to him, although she did wonder when the man rested, if ever. Always, he stood guard over her as she napped, and never did he occupy any of the shelters that he'd built.

But such was the way of it. He had his honor to uphold, and so did she—she hoped.

***

"Steamboat due soon. In few days."

Mia awakened to these words which had been clearly spoken, not whispered. She sat up with a start, and looked toward the entrance of the lean-to that Brave Wolf had put together in the wee hours of the morning. Oddly, constructing the shelter had taken less time than finding a safe piece of ground. It seemed as if they had traipsed over valley and hill for hours and hours. But at last Brave Wolf had discovered a place, and the shelter had gone up so quickly she'd hardly had a chance to catch her breath before it was done and awaiting her presence.

As she registered the nearly soundless scratching of his fingers upon the deerskin flap, she shook her head to rattle the wave of sleepiness from her mind. She leaned forward and peeked around the flap that separated them, realizing that she had slept through the day. Already, the sun was setting in the western sky.

"The boat will be here in a few days?" she asked. "That soon?"

"Hau, hau."

Bringing the hide blanket up and over her shoulders, she scampered forward and emerged from the temporary shelter. Briefly, she let the deerskin coverlet fall as she brought her hands up to run her fingers through the tangled locks of her hair.

Looking up at him, she was surprised to catch an image of intensity in his eyes as he gazed at her. He was watching her hands. But he looked away from her so quickly, she wondered if she had merely imagined the hint of passion that had briefly lighted up his countenance.

"Is it safe for me to go down to the trading post now?"

"Perhaps," he answered. "I find no...trace of white trappers we passed on journey here. All seems usual. Birds sing, game passes by here. There nothing to hint there trouble."

She nodded.

"But," he added, "this not mean there be no danger. There is...weighty...sense of wrong in this country which concerns you.... I try to find what that is."

"I see," she uttered; then she looked away from him. Her voice was barely over a whisper, when she mumbled, "I fear I have withheld telling you about a matter that might be important. I...," she paused, unable to put words to her concern. It was too personal, too frightening, and she feared that speaking aloud what those men had said at the wagon train fight might cause the nightmare to materialize. She struggled inwardly, knowing she should begin her story, but...

He remained silent; however, when she didn't speak out at once, he encouraged her, saying, "I am listening."

She exhaled deeply, then speaking slowly, she said, "Well, I—I heard those bullies at the wagon train fight say..." She gulped. "Although I try to tell myself that I am not the person that those men were referring to when they were speaking, I cannot quite convince myself of it."

He inclined his head, but he said nothing, as though by his silence he emboldened her.

She swallowed, hard. "After..." she began, her voice low and hoarse, "...after those bullies had engaged in murdering everyone there, except me, I heard them talking about someone they were looking for. Although I am not completely certain that I remember this correctly, I do believe they mentioned that they were seeking a woman. They had already killed Peggy, the only other female on that wagon train. But Peggy didn't have red hair, and when they looked at her body, I seem to remember that one of them said, 'Hair's supposed to be red.'"

She paused then, having been unaware of how those words had truly affected her until repeating them aloud. A quiver vibrated over her body, and she choked up, unable to go on.

But not by word or gesture did he interrupt her, and so after some moments, she swallowed down her hesitation, and gasped out, "My hair is red."

A tear fell down her cheek, and she was amazed to discover that her fear of the possible truth of this detail, buried within her for these many weeks, unsettled her to the point of grief. Silently, she sobbed.

He didn't at once respond to her confession, and it was some moments before he at last spoke, asking, "Any other person on…sea-of-white who have red hair?"

"Sea-of-white?" she inquired softly, then answering her own question, she replied, "Oh, yes, you mean the wagon train. There was a man, yes."

She saw Brave Wolf toss his head; it was his only reaction.

"But," she countered, "every time I recall what was said, this is what comes to mind, and I hear again, 'Hair's supposed to be red.' It haunts me because when it was uttered, they were looking at Peggy. At the very least, it implied that they were looking for a woman with red hair."

She hiccupped, and when she turned her gaze on him, he seemed unusually introspective, and his response to her confession was a difficult matter to guess, for he said no words at all for what seemed like hours, although it was in reality only minutes long.

"Of course," she went on quickly, as if to correct herself, "it all happened so fast that I could have been mistaken. Perhaps that gentleman with red hair, who was a part of our entourage, was the one they sought. Maybe he was wanted for some crime, and there were people who had decided to kill him. It's possible."

"But this not...explain or justify killing all people there."

"No, it wouldn't."

"And this not manner…you understood it?"

"No it is not. Moreover, I fear that if it be true, and that I am the one they sought, that I might be in some danger. Maybe you, too, because you are helping me."

He didn't respond to this last. Instead, he asked, "Enemies, do you have?"

"No. I can think of no one who hates me enough to send bullies after me. My father is a senator who is a sort of chief of our people. He is well-respected where we live, and although he might have political opponents, there has never been an attempt on his life or mine. That's why this all makes so little sense. Why would someone take the time to send men to find me and to kill me?"

He didn't answer her question; rather, he asked another one of his own. "Did you or father…insult another? Steal possessions?"

"No. Well, I did run away from home to marry Jeffrey. My father was against our marriage, but I hardly think my father's anger would be so great as to send someone here to kill me."

"There no one else?"

"No one, although I was engaged to another man—sort of."

"What this word, engaged mean?"

"Set to marry. But I had never agreed to marry him, and he knew it, and when I discussed it with him, he accepted it. When I was born, my father and a friend of his, Bernard Greiner, drew up a contract stating that when his son and I were older, we would marry."

Brave Wolf tilted his head in an agreeable motion, before asking, "Were one of those men who...attacked sea-of-white ...Bernard Greiner…or son?"

"No. Of course not. And Max Greiner is not the kind of person who would ever wish to kill a person."

"You certain?"

"Most definitely."

"When you go to home, what be your...fate?"

"My father will be glad to see me, I am certain, and I will resume my life there as usual."

"Does this 'usual'…include marriage?"

"Eventually, I suppose."

"To Max Greiner?"

"No. I could never marry him. Though he is kind and thoughtful and easy to talk to, I have never been attracted to him in that way. And I don't think I could marry someone without that spark of..." She didn't say the word. She couldn't, if only because that fire of which she spoke flared between the two of them. She let the sentence drop.

"How far away your home?"

"Far—very far. So distant is it that, if we were to leave now and walk there, we would not arrive at my home until the autumn leaves are golden upon the trees."

He nodded. "Your husband have enemies? Here?"

"Of course not," she said at once. But then, upon further reflection, she added, "Actually, Jeffrey was stationed in Kansas during the war, at Fort Leavenworth. Do you suppose he might have insulted someone, or refused to pay a debt or committed a deed that is equally wrong? Since it was a time of war, and because war is governed by no rules, maybe he carried out some crime, believing that there would be no retribution?"

She paused, then shook her head. "But no. Those men had been looking for a woman, not Jeffrey."

"Sometimes another feels he must…punish all who keep...company with person of his revenge," commented Mr. Wolf, "especially that man's family. Whole tribe sometimes pays for actions of one man."

"Yes," she agreed at once, but then she paused. What did she know, really, of Jeffrey's behavior, crimes or lack of them out here in the West? A moment passed as she tried to reason with her conflicting thoughts. At last, she uttered, "What you say could be true. Maybe Jeffrey insulted or even killed someone here during the war, and another, hearing that he was back in this country, felt it necessary to murder him, and those he loved, too. Could that be the reason for the attack?"

Brave Wolf shrugged. "It…might be. It known to happen. If true, you safer in...East than you are here."

"Yes, and I do so long to return home."

He nodded. "That is good." He cleared his throat; it was the only detail to indicate that he might be moved by their conversation. At length, he continued to speak, saying, "But come, there much work needs being done. You…require much dry meat for…journey. There still time to make it before boat arrive. I will hunt. Will show you how to make...meat to last for trip."

"Then," she began, swallowing back a note of panic, for he was speaking of her upcoming voyage in the singular, "have you decided not to accompany me back East? Is that why you talk of making meat— —for me only?"

He gazed away from her, and she watched him in profile as the lines between his eyes deepened into a frown. His Adam's apple bobbed up and down once, as though he were choking back his words. But when he at last spoke, his voice was clear, and he said, "It hard for me…be with you without touching. I belong to Walks-in-sunshine. But I...care for you. Long...journey to your home without touching, not possible. Cannot...betray Walks-in-sunshine."

His lips quivered as he spoke, and a tear fell over the hard contours of his face, a testament to the truth of his emotions. He'd said it to her once before, only days ago: He cared for her.

Suddenly, his face brightened, and he said, "You come home with me. You safe there. Be…second wife." He slanted her a look that seemed hopeful.

"Be your second wife?" She was stunned by the idea. "Are you permitted to have more than one?"

"*Hau, hau.* It is so."

Now it was her turn to catch her breath. "I don't understand," she responded. "If you may have more than one wife, why couldn't you still accompany me home? We could perhaps marry along the journey there. Then you could send for Walks-in-sunshine. No, that wouldn't work. My society wouldn't allow you to be married to two people at once."

He shook his head in the negative. "I gone then...long time from camp. She might...wonder what happen to me. Might try to find me. Bad for her. It betray her."

"You could send word to her through a trapper so as to ease her mind, and then you would be free to come with me. You wouldn't have to marry me, so it wouldn't have to be a betrayal to her. Maybe you and I could have an...affair, since we seem to..." Her words trailed off, for she was unable to complete the thought.

"What is affair?"

She bit her lip, then asked, "Do you truly not know?"

He shook his head.

"I—" She stumbled over the manner by which she should define the word. She cleared her throat, and catching his gaze, she began, "I admit that it is not an action to be spoken of lightly, for the word means to love and to make love to another without marriage."

His eyes turned stony as he peered at her, and he parried, "How can this be? To...make love to woman is to...marry her. Do you...*aikśiŋkiya,* insult me? Believing that I am such a one to ruin woman's...*oiglusica,* reputation?"

She gulped. "Well, no. You have not given me that impression. But in my society, a man might have a passionate relationship with another, without having to marry the woman, and only a few might comment on it. And so I thought..."

Suddenly, he sat forward. "Man who...do this to woman...hate her."

"I'm not certain that's true."

"It true. I cannot do that," he declared. "Would hurt Walks-in-sunshine. My mother, also, to think I would insult a woman I care about in bad way. You...come with me. Be...second wife?"

To her astonishment, she actually considered the idea. On many fronts, the thought of it was appealing. She would probably be as safe in his camp as she would be in her own home. Plus, she was not unaware of a naked truth: she desired this man in a purely physical realm. Ultimately, that desire might quickly turn to love. After all, he was a handsome man, possessing a masculine strength she had already witnessed. Yet, that vitality was tempered by a kindness that was as heartfelt as it was real. Life with him would be a happy one.

Or would it? Could she bear to live with him, knowing that she was second in this man's heart?

It was then that another, more forceful truth struck her: It wasn't simply that her society would frown upon a man having more than one wife; her faith, the foundation of her beliefs in this world, forbid it. Could she engage in an action out-lawed by God?

The answer was simple. No, she couldn't.

Well, that placed a final seal upon their fate, for what sort of a person was it who would flaunt the very essence of their being? No, her own feelings, and even his, didn't matter, be they pro or against. She could not, would not, go against the laws of God.

She bit her lip and exhaled deeply. She pulled her gaze away from his, looking down at her lap, as she answered him. "I am honored, Mr. Wolf, that you ask me to marry you," she whispered. "Truly honored. But I fear I cannot do it. For you see, my faith forbids it."

"Faith?" he asked. "Your Creator?"

"Yes, that's right."

"Because I am Indian?"

"Oh, no. Not that," she responded. "It is because neither a man nor a woman may have more than one wife or husband, as the case may be. It is forbidden by the laws of God, and I cannot in all conscience consider participating in a deed that the Creator has prohibited." She peeped up at him. "But come with me," she beseeched. "We could make overtures of peace to Walks-in-sunshine. We could send her pretty things to make her life easier. For you see, after all that has happened, I don't think I could bear to make my way home without you."

She watched him in silence for a few moments, then, she added, "Perhaps, instead of sending word to Walks-in-sunshine that you wish her to join you in the East, you might let her know where you have gone and why, and tell her that she is free to take another as her husband. We could then marry in good conscience. And we would be happy as a married couple, I think."

He sighed before he responded, "Yet, as time went by, you come to...distrust me if I would...withdraw my...duty to one I have loved so long. Love not love without trust. I cannot do it. I cannot abandon her. I cannot…betray her."

Mia shut her eyes as the enormity of what had been said, and the pain invoked by his words, consumed her. Then this was it? She would soon set foot on that steamboat, to never see this man again?

Tears welled up in her eyes, and a feeling of desperation devoured her. He had admitted that he cared for her; well, she cared for him, too. True, it could simply be that Jeffrey's loss, and the love she'd felt for him, was being bestowed upon this man mistakenly. But even the realization of this distinct possibility didn't abate the anguish of knowing she would never see Brave Wolf again.

"I—I..." She couldn't speak.

He rose to his feet, quietly, as gracefully done as ever. When she glanced up at him, she was certain that his countenance reflected her own, for his eyes were red, and she could clearly see the trail of a tear that had fallen over his so very handsome face.

His voice was shaky, when he uttered simply, "I must...hunt. Make meat for you."

So it was that, without further preamble, he left her there, walking away from her so quickly and so silently that, for a moment out of time, she wondered if she had imagined their entire conversation. Unfortunately, she knew it was real.

She gasped in air on a sob, and she longed to take back her answer to him, to say yes, she would come with him. She would marry him. Be his second wife.

But she couldn't. The very moral fiber of her life, her beliefs and all she knew to be true in this life, would not permit it. It appeared that there was no way out for them, she realized, but to endure the pain, for their separate viewpoints were as opposed as were their very cultures. No, in this there could never be a meeting of the minds between them.

A cry tore through her silently. Too much loss; must she endure so much loss? First Jeffrey, and now Brave Wolf. And it didn't help to remind herself again that it was Jeffrey's privation that was really the cause of her grief....

CHAPTER FOURTEEN

The trees were not many down there, being so close to the Missouri River, but what there were of them, were clustered together so thickly as to give the area an appearance of being a tiny forest. Here were oak and cottonwood, as well as the droopy branches of the weeping willow. Here, too, farther away from the shoreline, stood orange and brownish-colored clay bluffs. However, their depth was dotted here and there with the green of grasses and trees.

In the middle of the Big Muddy rose a large island, while smaller bodies of land sprouted up and surrounded it. It was hard to imagine what the terrain of those islands might entail, because they were so heavily wooded with trees. Idyllically, she wondered if the river were deep enough there to keep the steamboat from running aground.

Unwillingly, her inspection at last encompassed *Effie Deans,* the steamboat that was to take her from here. Anchored close to the trader's settlement, it offered her both hope and loss: Hope of regaining her home in the East; loss of the presence of this man, who had so endeared himself to her.

She deliberately turned her thoughts to less hurtful matters, and, as her examination of the terrain took in the trader's settlement, she realized that it would have to be situated well above the military post of Fort Leavenworth, because it seemed to be civilization's only refuge in this sea of wild. Why else would a steamboat, even one as small as *Effie Deans,* stop at such an out-of-the-way place?

The ship was due to leave port within the hour, and Mia's sense of loss was so great that she could barely look at Brave Wolf without bursting into tears. He didn't seem to be in any better frame of mind as he lingered next to her, standing first on one foot, and then on the other.

Neither of them spoke. It was pointless. They knew their two paths would part here, never to mesh again.

Over her left shoulder hung one of Brave Wolf's many bags, filled to overflowing with dry meat. There was a pistol in her pocket, but no longer did she possess Jeffrey's rifle. For, despite Brave Wolf's offering a hearty portion of buffalo meat and a new buffalo robe to the steamship's captain as trade, neither had purchased the price of a steamboat ticket, valued at two hundred dollars. Nor would the trader make up the difference by buying Brave Wolf's own rifle or ammunition, nor any of the knives or trinkets he possessed, so as to give Brave Wolf more bargaining power.

The ticket was a ridiculous price, she thought, for she and Jeffrey had only paid fifty dollars for a longer travel than what hers would be to reach Fort Leavenworth. Mia was certain the Captain of that steamboat was cheating Brave Wolf, but short of marching onto the decks of the boat and protesting, she was doomed to accept his dishonesty. As it were, neither she nor Brave Wolf wished to announce her presence here until the very moment of embarking on her journey.

She gave Brave Wolf a sideways glance and asked, "You have scouted all around the post down there, and it seems safe?"

"*Hau, hau.* I have seen no sign of enemy. No one but you… leave from here today."

"And the steamboat itself? There was no one on it that seemed suspicious?"

"White man always look...suspicious."

She thought that he teased her. Surely he didn't really hold that opinion. But another sideways glance at him showed his countenance to be perfectly serious.

"Surely," she observed, "you don't really believe that, do you?"

He shrugged. "My people at...war with yours."

"But—" Whatever her objection might have been, she let it drop. The argument was pointless.

After some moments, he enlightened her, saying, "Ten men on

boat. Five of them be boat men. Others are trappers from north."

A whistle blew, announcing the steamship's imminent departure, and a chill ran down her spine. Was he in much the same frame of mind as she? A quick look at him showed his countenance to be tightly controlled; there was no emotion there to be seen, making it impossible to read his thoughts.

He placed a hand on her shoulder, and, without saying a word to her, he moved forward, setting a pace down the bluff. She followed at a slower walk.

As they neared that wooded area in the valley, he led her beneath the branches of a weeping willow tree, effectively hiding them. Turning back toward her, he took her in his arms. He bent, and...

She gasped, and her heartbeat thrilled. Was he going to kiss her?

No. He only placed his cheek next to hers. But at least he held her tightly in his arms.

"You…be in my thoughts…*oíhaŋke wanil,* forever," he whispered in her ear. "And I would have my...image be in yours. Remember me by this." He drew slightly back from her, and tugged the single bear-claw necklace from around his neck before placing it in her hand. "When you wear...bear-claw, call to...mind who gave it to you. For you will never be far from...mind." He pointed to his forehead.

She wept, openly and unabashedly. She couldn't help herself, and as the hot tears escaped from her eyes, he brought up a finger, touching each path they made before their wetness fell onto her breast. Then he placed that same finger over his own eyes, mixing her tears with his.

"Do you see I bring your tears…to my eyes?"

She nodded.

"And now," he whispered, "our tears…bring us together. Always…" Leaning down, he settled his forehead next to hers. "I promise I always care for you."

She caved. She couldn't do this. "I can't leave you," she confessed. "I swear I can't."

He shook his head. "Yet, you must. One cannot...leave behind one's...faith. And I...I cannot...desert she who awaits me." His eyes swam with tears that he seemed unable to hide, and as they fell over his proud face, she knew that this was as hard for him as it was for her.

"You must go," he continued. "I cannot go with you...farther than this to...steamboat," he admitted, "without causing...alarm, but I promise I watch you until you safe on ...boat. I promise I will. Go now." He let his arms drop from around her.

"I...I–"

"Go now."

As it had come to be in the past, so it was now. She did as he suggested without further protest. But she had paced no farther away than a few steps when she swung around and raced back to him.

"I cannot leave you behind with nothing from me so that you, too, can remember me."

"I need...no object from you to cause that to happen."

"Still..." She hesitated. What did she have to give him that was hers alone? She'd left all her possessions at the wagon train fight. The only object that she possessed that was of any worth was her wedding ring.

Well, it would be his. Sliding the ring from her finger, she held it out to him. She murmured, "What I am giving you is of some value, for it is the ring Jeffrey gave me when we married. I give it now to you." She bit her lip, then gasped out, "So you see, we were both wrong. Because of this ring, we are married now—in part—whether you or I wish it to be so or not."

He brought her fingers to his lips, where he carefully kissed each one of them, before he took hold of the proffered jewelry.

"*Hau, hau,*" he whispered. "When I look at it, I will...think of wife in part...number one..."

He smiled, but she did not. His words tore through her, and she couldn't help the sob that escaped her lips.

She couldn't leave him. Yet she had to. What was she to do?

He took the decision from her as he murmured, "You must...hurry now," his voice caught on the words. "Boat leave soon."

She knew she had to do as he said. Difficult as it was, she couldn't remain here with him and be true to the values she considered sacred.

Tearing herself from his arms, she spun around and ran as though she were being chased by some form of a prankster—all the way to the ship's gangplank.

"Come back!" She thought she heard the words whispered on the ever-present, Kansas gusts. But she ignored this seeming act of nature. Though her heart was breaking, she knew she had to be strong, to be true to herself...and to him.

She had to go.

***

Brave Wolf felt as though his heart were being torn from his breast. If only he could call her to his side again. But he couldn't. He dared not. Their paths were as wide apart as the Big River itself, never to narrow.

He supposed he should be thankful for these few brief days with her, for, although the Creator had surely tested his strength of will, he would never forget the pleasure of her company. He congratulated himself on remaining courageous enough to let her go.

He watched Little Dawn Bird's figure as she stepped up to the deck of the steamboat. Briefly, she turned toward the place where he stood, and she looked there. She didn't wave, and he was glad that she did not. Instead, the distance between them contracted, and he was aware that they shared a moment set out in time; an instant where their hearts were as one.

Though it was unwanted, another tear fell from his eye, until, with a loud and sudden boom of its cannons, the ship pulled away from its mooring. Brave Wolf stood transfixed as he watched the large boat navigate out into the deeper part of the river, carrying her away from him.

He would never see her again. This was understood, and her loss was almost more than he had reckoned for.

But he cautioned himself to remain strong. Duty and honor would not allow their hearts to unite. He tried to tell himself that their parting was good, because she belonged in her world, and he... If only one or the other of them had been able to set aside their differences.

But no, such was not possible. Those disparities were the solid rocks upon which each one of them lived their lives.

She belonged in her own world. And he...he was a man of the West; he also held in balance the heart of a woman who awaited him, a woman he had admired for all his life; a woman who trusted him.

Reaching a hand out toward the steamboat, he prayed silently, "May your...Creator guide your path, and...though we be apart, may you be...happy in your life."

He turned away, intent on leaving this place with all possible speed. And then a thing happened. It was no more than a thought, but it was an idea that contained such an unfriendly intention, it rocked him back on his heels.

Someone else was here. As the impression became reality, he knew that another had watched Little Dawn Bird board that boat, and it had not been in a good way, for it was at odds with the environment. Who else was here?

Logically, he realized that this consideration did not originate from the mind of the trader who ran the post at this place. He knew that man's consciousness, as well as his heart, and it did not include harm to a woman who was so much weaker than himself.

Then who was it?

Where was this enemy? He reminded himself that he had scouted for miles around this place in the early hours of this morning, and he had not found or sensed another person, particularly one whose motives were dangerous.

Had he made a mistake? Perhaps he had, for there was a definite presence here—a thought, an impression that was antagonistic to her.

He acted immediately, and, slipping over the landscape like an invisible shadow, he scoured the environment for the evidence that was surely here. Nothing happened upon this earth that was not recorded by means of tracks and the ever-present concentric circles whispered in the winds. He would discover who this enemy was....

CHAPTER FIFTEEN

It turned out that the presence he sensed was that of another scout. But was the man an honored member of the Wolf Clan, in truth? No *toŋwéya* of any worth would leave as many tell-tale tracks as did this one. For, despite attempts to cover his trail, the man had yet left imprints; faint, it was true. Yet, a scout of any merit would leave none.

Brave Wolf bent as he traced the patterns of the highs and the lows that were left in the tracks, reading aspects about the other man as easily as a white man might read a book. Briefly, he admonished himself, and he could hear his teacher speaking, as he had so often done, saying, "Never focus on a task to the exclusion of your environment. Only by becoming a part of the consciousness all around you, can you come to know your opponent's thoughts."

Brave Wolf realized that the loss of Little Dawn Bird had caused him to lose touch with the spirit-that-moves-through-all-things. His awareness had centered on her, and he had become blind to his surroundings, letting another enter into the landscape without his knowledge.

Had he known of this other presence, he would have never let her board that boat. It was too late now. The steamboat had already pulled away from its dock.

Brave Wolf understood, also, that his task was now set. While he might long to return to the sanctuary of his home where he could mend his heart, he knew he couldn't do it. He cared for Little Dawn Bird too much to let a possible danger go unwatched.

So he set his mind to complete this last task that he owed her as her protector, her guide and a man who had come to treasure her. He would ensure her safety, and then, once done, he would return home in good conscience and, he hoped, to resume the happiness of his life with

Walks-in-sunshine.

Further inspection of these prints proved what he had already surmised: this man was a warrior who had placed himself for hire by the white man. The knowledge caused Brave Wolf's stomach to turn, for a true scout, trained and learned in the ways of the Wolf Clan, disdained such men.

Not only did these pretenders enlighten the whites of Indian ways, hadn't they also caused the massacre of whole peoples? No true scout would ever be the source of a matter so hideous.

Brave Wolf knew he had only two options: he could follow the steamboat and steal Little Dawn Bird from it, or he could follow this "scout" and learn why this man held hatred in his heart for Little Dawn Bird.

Although Brave Wolf longed to take the easier path and simply rescue Little Dawn Bird, he knew that wasn't enough. Could this scout-turned-traitor be connected in some way to the massacre of the wagon train?

Perhaps. Moreover, if that were so, was it not possible that if he, Brave Wolf, did not discover the identity of this foe, wouldn't Little Dawn Bird be in danger, regardless of where she went?

Suddenly, Brave Wolf grasped a truth: This man was already following along a course that would lead to his controllers. *And* because this might be the thread that would explain the murder of the sea-of-white wagon train, Brave Wolf's path could only go one way. At least for the present.

***

Brave Wolf raced over the ground, little caring that he failed to backtrack to cover his own prints. The other man was traveling south and west at a fast pace, and Brave Wolf could see that the scout-turned-traitor had ceased to worry over what Mother Earth recorded. Why? Why such urgency? What possible danger could Little Dawn Bird be to this man?

Day turned to night, and still the man did not ease his pace. Brave

Wolf had long ago caught up to the other "scout," and had him well within his sight. Always keeping himself well hidden—for a true scout would be shamed if he were ever detected or seen—Brave Wolf watched from the shadows as the man satisfied his hunger with bites of pemmican, washing it down with water from any nearby stream. At these times, Brave Wolf refused to nourish his own body's needs; always he snacked on the run, when the other man's alertness would be centered on other matters.

Never did this man appear to be aware that a true scout's eye was always upon him, and Brave Wolf felt pride that he had carefully hidden not only his physical presence, but even his thoughts. Within three days it happened.

Two buff-colored tents came into view, though they went almost undetected because they were situated in a valley surrounded by brownish clay cliffs, which mimicked their own hue. The camp looked to be little more than a temporary hunting lodge, for there was evidence of the hunt strewn about the place. Dead bodies of elk, deer and even a buffalo rotted in the sun, their meat ignored. Bones of past meals were thrown haphazardly about, and, even from Brave Wolf's distance, the place stank of putrid waste.

Brave Wolf watched the scout-turned-traitor and the goings-on in that camp. Hiding himself behind a tiny indentation in a near-by cliff, Brave Wolf had an ample view of the place. Plus, in order to ensure his presence would go undetected, he scratched out bits of clay from the wall of the cliff and added water to it from a pouch. Using this mixture, he painted his body with it, and, when he had finished, he effectively faded into the landscape.

The scout-turned-traitor signaled his arrival at the camp by emitting three owl hoots, one after the other. He was not left long for a reply, which came in the form of a series of three gunshot blasts. Glancing around him, as if to ensure he hadn't been followed, the scout-turned-traitor appeared to find nothing to alarm him, and, with a careful and slow pace, he approached the camp of this dirty, smelly enemy.

On his belly and using his forearms and elbows, Brave Wolf crept down the valley wall, one slow crawl following after another, until he was within hearing distance of the tents. As sunlight filtered into the tent, it highlighted the figures of three men who sat in upright chairs around a table. The scout-turned-traitor stood next to that table.

"What have you to report?" asked a deep voice, speaking in English. "You haven't been followed here, have you?"

"I...alone."

"Good. What news have you? Is she dead?"

"No. All...others die. Man killed...but not red-headed woman who...escape...death. She on...boat...on Big River...now...."

"She be alive?" The accent was American, but the voice was that of another of the men. "How c'n this be? How'd she get thar?"

"Indian...brought her. Lakota..."

So, thought Brave Wolf, the scout-turned-traitor knew that he had been present at the trading post. And why should he not? Brave Wolf had taken no measure to hide himself from either the trader or the captain of the steamboat; only she had he shielded from any prying eyes...until the last moment.

"A Injun brought her ta th' post, ya' say?" asked the third man. "If'n she is on th' boat now, that means ya' didna kilt' her. Why not?"

"You...say...find out what...happen. I find out. Lakota...find her...Lakota bring...her...to trader post."

"And where is that Lakota Injun now?" asked the man who had first spoken.

"He...leave."

"You are certain?"

No answer followed the question, and Brave Wolf could only conclude that the scout-turned-traitor's answer was a silent, "Yes."

"Well, go back now and kill her. If she is on a boat alone, it should be easy."

"Killing...white woman...not ever...easy. Need

more...whiskey...more food for...family. More...credit...at trader's post."

"Why, ya—onery, good-fer' nothin'..."

"Now Wingate, calm yourself. What our friend here asks is little enough. After all, the man we sought is dead, and Lone Fox has done us a great service. How much whiskey do you need this time, Lone Fox? And the food? Should I send it to the same tribe?"

Again there was no answer, and Brave Wolf concluded once more that the answer had been in the positive.

Suddenly and unexpectedly, a gunshot shook the white man's tent, and Brave Wolf watched in shock as the scout-turned-traitor slumped to the ground.

Surprise turned to bewilderment. There had been no reason to take the life of this man, especially after the one called Lone Fox had done these men a service. Disgust filled Brave Wolf's soul. It also served as a caution: these men were takers of life, and might stoop to any deed to accomplish their task.

The shot must have been straight to the head, thought Brave Wolf, for the scout-turned-traitor made no defense, not even to try to use his knife to take down one of the white men.

"What'dya do that for, Martn'? Now how are we gonna kill her?"

"Stupid Injun," responded the one who held the pistol in his hand. "Should've known better than to come here with the job only half-done. Better off dead, I say. Now, gentlemen," continued the murderer, the one known as Martn', "it should be a simple matter to kill the woman ourselves. We know where she is. We are three, while she is one. And this time, we will ensure the job gets done. Our benefactor insists that the man known as Jeffrey Carlson, his wife, and all those who have shown them aid must die. Do I make myself clear?"

"And how 'bout th' Injun? The Lakota, ain't tha' same as th' Sioux? Th' one thar' brought her to th' post?"

"You heard Lone Fox say he was gone. Probably couldn't wait to be finished with her, I say. Besides, why should we worry about one Injun, gentlemen? One against three? Besides, the Injun's race of people is, after all, as dumb as a buffalo stud in heat. Get your things together. We leave at dawn."

Repugnance overwhelmed Brave Wolf, and for a moment, if a moment only, he felt shamed by the white blood that flowed through his veins, remembering that many of his mother's people had been as hostile toward him and toward his father as were these men. All, that is, except his maternal grandfather. It was hard to remember at times like this that, amongst all men and all tribes of people, there are those who do good and those who do bad.

However, on one matter he was certain: regardless of culture or color of skin, he honored Little Dawn Bird. Moreover, he would not, he could not, leave her to a fate that might take her life. So it was that, lurking unnoticed in the misty obscurity cast by broad daylight, Brave Wolf watched and listened as the white men set their plans.

***

The white men were oblivious to the one who followed them. Making no sound, refusing to think too deeply, and thus by his thoughts be discovered, Brave Wolf kept to the shadows, although he lingered little more than a few feet away from the murderers.

They were traveling fast. Why the desperation? The boat was slow, easily overtaken.

Within the breadth of a single day, they arrived at the Big Muddy. Because the three white men had no way of knowing whether the steamer was traveling further north, or perhaps going south, and, because they didn't dare inquire at the trader's post, they agreed to break up into two parties, one man following the river north, the other party of two traveling south.

This presented Brave Wolf with a problem, for he could only follow one path at a time. Where was the boat? It should be headed south. Was it?

Pausing in the shadows, he expanded his knowingness into the land around him, becoming fused with the spiritual mind, and thus not limited by the boundaries of the physical world. Though he might be young in experience, his elders had trained him well, and he could connect with the spirit-that-moves-through-all-things. Thus, he found the boat at once, and "saw" that it was south and east of this place.

Ignoring the one murderer who had set out to blaze a path north, Brave Wolf pursued the two white men who were headed south. Afternoon gave way to dusk as the sun announced its departure in colors of pink, blue and orange. Though Brave Wolf might have liked to pause and give thanks to the Creator for the beautiful day, he dared not, for the two men hurried onward, not pausing until they had the steamboat well within their sights.

Then they camped, striking a fire for one and all to see. Such foolishness. Didn't they realize that every Indian within several miles' radius would see and smell that blaze? Did they hope to gather more unsuspecting Indians to their cause? Annoyed, Brave Wolf decided to take out his frustration on the whites by utilizing the best weapon a scout could employ: ghostly deception....

Although he might like to murder these men outright instead of merely deceiving them, his honor as a scout would not allow him this option. Only in self-defense—only if attacked outright, could a scout call upon his skill to fight. But make no mistake, those of the Clan of the Wolf were thoroughly disciplined both physically and mentally to out-master, to out-think and to win a fight, if challenged.

Besides, perhaps by simply feigning deception, he might scare these men into abandoning their deadly plans. It was worth the try.

So it was that as soon as the two men traipsed to the water to wash their dishware, Brave Wolf slipped into their camp and extinguished their fire. Erasing his tracks, he faded back into the shadows and awaited their return.

"What's th' matter with ya', Martn'?" asked the one who had been first to trod back into camp. "Didna ya' know'd how ta build a campfire? This-here inferno's little more'n embers. Ya and yer Eastern ways. Must I do everythin' fer ya?"

The one he addressed as Martn' shrugged as he, too, paced back into camp. "If you want a fire to last through the night, then build it yourself, Wingate. I am not your lackey, and you know it."

Tough talk had its effect, and the one called Wingate set about building up another flame. While that one's attention was centered on that task, Brave Wolf slithered up behind him, as silent as a snake. Reaching out slowly, he took hold of Wingate's knife, which had been thrust into a sheath on his thigh. Quietly, he placed the blade between his teeth, then crawled silently away, slithering back into the protection of the trees before he scooted toward the murderer of scout-turned-traitor, the man named Martn'.

"What'cha mean takin' my knife?" bellowed Wingate as he swung this way and that, looking for the absent weapon.

"I've done no such thing," answered the other.

Slowly, quietly, while Martn's attention was focused on Wingate, Brave Wolf laid the knife on a rock next to the killer's gun.

"What'cha doing, ya lying thief? It's sittin' right there beside ya!"

"Why you! Are you calling me a liar? I ought to kill you outright."

"Idjut," responded Wingate. "Do ya' take me fer dumb? It's right thar beside yer gun."

Martn' glanced downward, espying the knife at once. "What the—What's going on?"

"Hand it ov-ar, ya thief."

"What kind of game are you playing? I didn't take it."

"Yeah, yeah, it jest walk't there on its own, I s'ppose."

The killer's eyes widened, and he looked a little spooked. "I didn't take it, I tell you."

"Right, and I ain't seen it thar, n'ither."

While the two continued their argument, Brave Wolf lifted that knife again, and, slithering back into the bush, he snaked up behind

Wingate. Slowly, silently, he slid the knife once more into Wingate's sheath.

Suddenly Martn' frowned. "It's gone!"

"Wha'?"

"I tell you, it's gone. Look beside me. That knife isn't there anymore."

Wingate looked at the rock which had recently held his knife. His eyes bugged out, and a frightened look came over his face. Carefully, as though he feared what he might discover, Wingate placed his hand on his hip, and whatever he'd been about to say, died in his throat. "It...it's back in me holster."

"Quit it!"

"I tell ya, it's back in me holster. See!"

Martn' looked, even as a show of terror crossed over his countenance. Slowly, he uttered, "I've heard of places like this. Spirits of the dead in the form of owls that take hold of your spirit and—"

As though on cue, an owl hooted in the distance. A haunted look came over both men's faces. Almost in unison, they exclaimed, "Wha' the—"

Both men jumped to their feet, guns in hand.

"Who's thar?" snarled Wingate.

Brave Wolf again hooted like an owl, then quickly, silently scooted away as the blasts from the killers' guns made mincemeat of the place where he'd been. Splinters flew in every direction, one of the bigger targets lodging in Wingate's cheek.

"Damn trees." He shot another round into the woods, sustaining a similar wound. "Damn!"

Meanwhile, Brave Wolf slinked up close behind Martn'. He repeated the hoots, moving out of the way before either man could repeat those shots into that new section of wood.

One of the bullets must have nicked Wingate again, for he cried out, "What'cha do that fer? Ya got me in th' arm."

"Then move out of my way, you lug."

"Who's a lug?"

Meanwhile, Brave Wolf had climbed a tree that hung over them, and let go of another hoot.

"That is no owl," bellowed the killer. "That there's a ghost. This place is haunted."

Without even breaking camp, the two men jumped up and ran in circles senselessly, as though the devil himself were after them. Then, dispersing in two different directions, one headed north and the other west.

Brave Wolf smiled. He hoped he had scared them away from here for good, and without their deadly mission accomplished. But he doubted it. Still, it gave him temporary delight to have bested them—at least for the moment....

CHAPTER SIXTEEN

The Captain of *Effie Deans* had moored the steamboat in the deepest part of the Missouri for the night. Sitting about mid-center in the river, *Effie Deans'* position required the biggest and roughest of the two murderers, Martn', to row a smaller boat up to her. Wingate had stayed ashore, his ever-ready rifle trained on the boat.

Because the night is darkest before dawn, the two assassins had made their plans, and had awaited the deepest, blackest part of the early morning before making their move. Brave Wolf had listened to their talk during the evening hours, but, having no experience with steamboats and what fueled them, he had not fully comprehended the technology involved in blowing up the boat.

It was Brave Wolf's intention, however, to thwart the bullies' plans to kill not only Little Dawn Bird, but the entire crew of *Effie Deans*. If time would not permit him to foil Martn's plans, Brave Wolf would rescue only Little Dawn Bird, but his duty as a scout dictated that he should envision a move that might counter the mass execution of innocent men. To this end, he now swam underwater next to that small boat.

It was remarkably easy to climb up onto the first deck of the boat, since the lower part of the vessel sat only a few feet above the level of the water. Gaining his foothold on the boat's platform, and, keeping to the shadows, Brave Wolf tailed after the killer, Martn'.

Martn's destination was a short distance away, on this, the lower level of the boat. He opened and passed through a door, disappearing into an inner chamber. Brave Wolf slowly followed, ensuring that he cracked that same door open with little, if any sound. What met him was a shock.

The room was boiling hot and steamy. A large piston sat at the fore of the room. Currently it sat motionless, most likely because *Effie Deans* was moored. Off to the side of the piston was a large furnace, and before it bent Martn', a large shovel in his hands. Furiously he was in the act of shoving huge, black rocks into that furnace, sparking up a large fire.

As Brave Wolf stepped farther into the room, he espied a man who was draped upon the floor, looking as though he might be asleep. Gingerly, Brave Wolf bent down and placed his fingers over the pulse point on the man's neck, finding that the man was alive, and merely unconscious. But already there was a large, red welt rising on the back of his head, the source of that obvious.

What exactly Martn' was doing was unclear to Brave Wolf, but he did understand that whatever the black rocks were, they were causing fire and energy in that small chamber. Was this how the assassin was fixing to blow up the steamboat? And if that were the case, how much time did Brave Wolf have to rescue Little Dawn Bird and get her to safety?

Seeing that Martn's attention lay centered on the stack of black rocks and shoveling them into the furnace, Brave Wolf picked up the unconscious man and carried him out of the engine room. Using water from the river, Brave Wolf made an effort to awaken the man and was successful, leaving him as soon as the man started to regain consciousness.

He must find Little Dawn Bird, and fast. Her life depended on his ability to get both of them off this steamboat with all possible speed. Where was she? Pausing momentarily, he searched for her with his mind. Perhaps he was confused by what he didn't understand about this boat, and so he didn't find her presence as quickly as he would have liked. But finally, with his mind's eye, he "saw" her....

***

The scent of fishy, muddy water overwhelmed all other odors in this place, Mia thought as she climbed the necessary stairway that allowed her to gain access to the highest point on the steamboat. Every day, as had become her routine on the trail with Brave Wolf, she arose early so that she might welcome in the new day with prayer. Ascending to the upper deck of the boat, she took up a position that looked eastward, toward the light, silver sky. Briefly, she said her prayer, then shifted her position, strolling toward the starboard side of the boat, gazing out westward. It was here on most every day that she hoped to see Brave Wolf, always wondering if he might still be out there, following the boat. Today was no different.

The day was only beginning, yet already the warmth of the early morning sun beat down upon the top of her bare head, for she wore no hat. However, its heat did not bother her; the gentle wind that was created by the forward motion of the boat blew into her face, causing the loose tendrils of her hair to fall back behind her ears. It was a cooling breeze and it seemed kindly, animated, as if it endeavored to cleanse her spirit.

But such friendliness was wasted on her. Her life had forever changed. Too much had happened in this last month to allow the naivety of her former life to regain a foothold over her.

Was such a shift of personality for the good, or was it bad? She couldn't be certain.

Where was Brave Wolf, she wondered. Then she answered her own question. He would be setting a trail for his home; he would be hastening back to the arms of another woman....

Would Walks-in-sunshine welcome him home with love in her heart? She would do so if she were wise. Trustworthy, honorable men like Brave Wolf didn't happen along every day.

"Ma'am," hailed the captain, a Mr. Wentworth. He raised his hat to her as he stepped by her.

Jerked back to the present moment, Mia smiled, hoping that the gesture covered her surprise. She had been so lost in her own thoughts, she hadn't noticed the captain's approach.

"Ye look so sad, ma'am. But don't ye fret. We're only a couple of weeks out from Leavenworth. We'll make it thar all safe and sound, don't ye worry."

"Yes," she replied, as she forced herself to look happy. "I believe that we shall."

"How did ye get yerself all stranded in this part of the country, ma'am, if'n ye don't mind me askin'?"

"I...my husband and I were part of a wagon train heading for the

Oregon Territory when our party was attacked by—"

"Injuns?"

"No, sir, although I did think so at first. But the butchers turned out to be men dressed up as Indians. They killed my husband. Indeed, I fear that they murdered all the people on that train except me. I don't believe that they saw me at first."

"But they did discover yerself?"

"Undoubtedly, they did."

"Pardon, ma'am, but then how did ye escape? Did ye play dead until they left?"

"No, sir. Real Indians came to my rescue."

"Real Injuns? Ma'am?" He grabbed his hat from his head and whacked it against his knee. "We's at war with them Injuns in these here parts. Cain't imagine one of 'em rescuing ye."

"I know. Yet, what I tell you is true. The man who bought that ticket from you is the same one who not only rescued me, but who brought me here so that I might return home." She paused for a moment, then added, "I think, sir, that you might have cheated him regarding the cost of that ticket."

The accusation, though softly spoken, was met with silence, and she let the complaint stand without further explanation. Captain Wentworth seemed honestly surprised; however, at last he uttered, "I'm right sorry about that, ma'am. But I'm under orders t' charge high enough fees so that them Injuns don't beg an easy ride. I'll return the full two hundred dollars to ye, ma'am."

"I thank you for your kindness," replied Mia, "for I lost all of my possessions at the wagon train fight. But, although I appreciate your kindheartedness, please ease your mind. It is unnecessary. I have enough food to sustain me until we reach Fort Leavenworth, and my clothing washes well. Besides, once we arrive at Fort Leavenworth, I can send word to my father, who will ensure that I am taken care of and escorted home safely. Keep your money."

"No, ma'am. Couldna live with myself if'n I was to do that," he said. "Wait here, ma'am, while I get yer two hundred dollars."

Mia nodded and watched Captain Wentworth's departing figure as he disappeared down the stairs, taking two of them at a time. She breathed in deeply, and was about to lean out over the railing, when two incidents happened at once.

A wet, nearly nude, but achingly familiar body knocked her to the deck at the same time a bullet whizzed by her. The whir of that discharge, and its ugly blast splintered the wood at the exact place where she'd been standing, its impact showering her and her rescuer with the sharp fragments.

She screamed.

"Stay down!" ordered Brave Wolf. She could do little more than that, for he lay over her, using his body to protect her. Only a single instant passed before another deadly shot shrieked past them, this one aimed lower than the first.

Then came another round of gunfire, followed by a slight pause, then more of the same. On and on it roared, the howl of the noise and the racket going on for so many minutes that Mia felt as though the entire world were engulfed by the barrage. Suddenly, as quickly as it had started, it stopped. No shots. No backfire. Nothing.

"He...reloading. Quick, follow me!"

Brave Wolf plopped off of her, scooting onto the deck. Lying flat on his stomach, he used elbows and hips to inch forward; Mia followed, utilizing the same manner of crawling, and could see an open cabin door ahead of them. This must have been his destination. But what followed next precluded all attempts to attain safety.

A huge man, who might have been twice the size of Brave Wolf, fell upon her. She screamed, then again, and she kept on shrieking as he raised a knife. Even while she yelled out, "No," she felt certain that this moment spelled the end of her life. It might have been true, too, but for an arm that came up to block that blow.

"Go! Move! Run to cabin!" shouted Brave Wolf.

But she couldn't get away from the monster, for he held her down; he was probably three times her weight. She squirmed, she tried to get away, but she couldn't shake him off her.

What followed could only be an act of God, for it was humanly impossible. Yet, as she watched the events unfold, she saw Brave Wolf rise up as though with super-human strength; he picked up the man as though this two-hundred-and-fifty-pound bully weighed little more than a feather. Instantly, she was free, but it wasn't over. Brave Wolf hurled the monster across the deck. The fiend's weapon, his knife, fell to the deck, but not so the beast's gun.

As quick as an instant, the would-be assassin slid his pistol from his holster. He pointed it straight at her head, for she had not run away.

In a fraction of a second, Brave Wolf executed a quick, high leap, landing on the assassin and pushing him down, forcing him into a sitting position. Taking hold of the man's pistol-carrying arm, and forcing it high into the air, Brave Wolf ensured the bullet shot harmlessly into the sky. The two men wrestled with that gun, their muscles straining under the assault, and the struggle that waged between the two of them outlined every muscle in Brave Wolf's body.

Boom! Crash! Blast!

What was that? It sounded as if it were an explosion on the below decks of the boat. Was it? Was the boat, itself, under attack?

What could she do? How could she help? She couldn't leave Brave Wolf to fight this monstrosity all on his own. Or should she?

Was she in the way? Should she leave here as quickly as possible?

But no. She couldn't leave him, even though he had told her to. As she had often said to herself: whatever Brave Wolf's fate might be, so too would be her own.

This decided, she darted into action, and, sprinting toward the wrestling figures, she jumped up into a flying leap, and added her weight against the bully's arm. The momentum of her fall caused the beastie's grip to come apart and loosen. The pistol flew out of his grasp, but the firearm was cocked, and it fired as it hit the deck...

...Away from them.

In a show of power and brute force, the monster flung Brave Wolf off, and Brave Wolf rolled as he landed, coming up onto his feet, unsheathing his only weapon, his knife. Then, without even a fraction of a second passing, Brave Wolf hurled himself forward, attaching himself to the fiend's backside, his knife at the bully's throat. But the monster threw off Brave Wolf's grip, and the knife fell harmlessly to the deck.

It wasn't finished, and what followed, Mia could hardly believe. Weaponless, Brave Wolf used feet, hands, fingers, teeth and his jaw as weapons. He spit, clawed, bit, scratched and threw his arms around the assassin's neck while his nails bit into the brute's face. Though the beast tried to shake him off, he couldn't budge Brave Wolf.

Mia watched, shocked, as Brave Wolf bested the man who was as big as a bear. Like a weasel, he scratched the swine, bit him, choked him and kicked him as he wrestled him to the ground. The bully couldn't throw a punch; in fact, it looked as though he could hardly breathe. Already, his face was turning bright red, then it was blue.

All at once, it was over. The monster drew his last breath. He flopped to the deck and lay there unmoving. Brave Wolf, however, didn't wait to examine the result of this struggle for life or death. He grabbed up both his own, and the bully's knife, seized her by the hand and sprinted toward the ship's railing, dragging her with him as he fled port-side.

Mia ran as fast as she could, though she was stunned, having never witnessed such a bare-handed, tooth-and-claw fight against such uneven odds. Brave Wolf was easily the smaller of the two men by a hundred or so pounds, yet he had won and...what was probably most astounding, she was still alive.

Boom! Crash! Blast! Crack!

Another explosion from the below decks shook the boat, and she realized the craft was blowing out from within. Huge bits of wood flew everywhere, the shower of deadly and heavy splintered logs a real threat. Worse, a massive fire licked to life only a few feet away from them; it was swiftly consuming the deck on which they stood. The floor was going to give.

"Oh!" Mia gasped. Had Brave Wolf won the struggle, only to lose the war? If the floor beneath them gave, they would be swept below as it crumbled; they'd be impaled and crushed beneath fallen rubble and knife-like timber.

Frightened into immobility, Mia could only stare. But not so Brave Wolf. He swept her up into his arms and sprinted around a corner, ignoring the deck crashing about them. He endured the burning heat, and somehow he kept ahead of the ever-rushing fire, veering toward the port side of the boat, the side away from the paddle wheel. Still holding her in his arms, he scrambled up onto the railing, and without hesitation, he knifed feet first into the river, taking her with him.

Down, down they shot into the mildly cool and welcoming, but muddy water. Brave Wolf didn't wait to touch bottom. Kicking out, he swam down deep underwater, heading north, away from the boat. A deadly tow pulled at him, yet he evaded it, and dove down deeper only to have a whirlpool tug at them, threatening to drown them. Yet it didn't happen. Brave Wolf forded the underwater death trap with what appeared to be so much ease that one might have thought he were part merman. He held her by the waist now and pulled her along with him. Once he surfaced for air and she gasped in the needed oxygen; a bombardment of bullets met them from the shoreline, and he dove down, down deep, deeper, kicking out in a stroke that propelled them to the bottom of the river, swimming as fast as the water would allow him. She felt the path of a bullet as it nicked him, for it was to that arm where he held her. Although the shot didn't draw blood, it must have stung him. But if it did, he showed no signs of feeling it.

Faster they swam, she kicking out now to help him. North and east they fled, away from the deadly assassin bullets. But how long could she hold her breath? She felt as though she were turning blue, and she tapped Brave Wolf on the shoulder to indicate that she needed air. Once again, although this time more cautiously, he came up for breath, but he allowed her only a second to suck in that air before he dove back under the surface, knifing toward the very bottom of the river once again.

Surprisingly no one appeared to be following them beneath the waves, and she was reminded of the danger of the deadly whirlpools, currents and underwater tows beneath the surface of the Big Muddy River. It had claimed many a man's life. It had tried to take theirs. Was this why no one was giving chase?

Those deadly traps confronted Brave Wolf over and over. She felt their pull, was certain she and Brave Wolf would never survive this. Yet, they did. How he managed to use these dangers to his advantage, she might never know, for he swam through the tows as though he danced a jig with them. They pushed onward, Mia having to remind Brave Wolf on more than one occasion that she needed to breathe air, not water.

It felt as though hours had passed as they shot through these muddy depths, although it was probably not longer than minutes. Always it seemed to her that they headed north and, she hoped, out of range of those assassin's bullets. She was aware that Brave Wolf could hold his breath longer than she could, and he seemed to forget that she was not part fish; many more times than she could count, she had to tap him on the shoulder as a reminder. At last, when they surfaced for air, it appeared that they had put enough distance between themselves, the shoreline and the steamship, for nothing met them but the smoke of a boat that would never sail the Missouri waters again.

They both looked on at the wreckage, which was even now still afire.

"Why did the boat explode?" she asked softly, more to herself than to Brave Wolf.

But he answered her quickly, saying, "Man who try kill you use fire to blow up boat."

Shock caused Mia to remain silent, and, when she didn't answer at once, Brave Wolf calmly dove again beneath the waves. They raced, then, through the currents and deadly traps. Luckily, the water felt warmer now, though it became more and more littered with debris and swamp growth. This, however, didn't slacken their pace. So long had they been in the water that her fingers felt wrinkled, and her eyes blurred. But she never thought to complain.

She was lucky to still be alive, thanks to Brave Wolf. Why had he returned? When they were out of this mess, and had a moment to spare, she would ask him.

Their pace slowed at last, becoming more leisurely, and the water level became shallow. Within moments, Mia could feel the rocky sand and mud beneath her moccasined feet. Still, Brave Wolf allowed only the tops of their heads to come up above water level, as they lay full length in water, which was now only inches deep. Their bodies were hidden beneath a grove of weeping willow trees. She took note that he had never let her go, and she was still nestled at his side, within his arms.

Slowly, he loosened his tight grip on her and, with one small movement after another, he came up onto hands and knees in the water. She mimicked him. Then he rose up so very, very slowly, perpendicular to the water, bringing her up with him. One slow step after another followed, until they had attained the shallows of the water, only inches deep. Then, stooping over at the waist, Brave Wolf executed one creeping step after another, taking perhaps an hour or more to finally come up onto dry land. He held her closely by his side through all this, and she mimicked his deliberate motions.

Finally, he seemed satisfied that he had left no traceable trail on the shore, and his delayed pace sped slightly. Selecting a shady spot beneath one of the overgrown willow trees, he brought her up close to the trunk of the tree, its numerous sweeping branches hiding them. In one quick motion, he brought her around in front of him, and set her back against the bark of the tree, pressing her body in against it.

Then, without pause, without a word being spoken between them, his head descended toward hers; unerringly, his lips found hers, and he kissed her, long and hard. His tongue swept into her mouth once, again, over and over, his kiss performing an act of love. His breathing was sparse when he ended the caress, and so was hers.

He whispered, "Are you hurt?"

"No, I don't think so," she murmured softly. "But are you?"

He ignored her question. "I must...ensure it is so. Forgive me..." He pulled up her dress, saying, "Hold up skirt. I would see for myself that you are whole and unharmed."

What followed was more sensuous than it was a discovery. At least, that was how it was for her, for he felt her everywhere, from her feet, to her legs; up and over her thighs, to that place most feminine and private, but he did not linger there. Up and over her stomach, his hands searched her; to her breasts, around to her back, her neck and upward to her head.

Only when he had seemingly touched and explored every spot on her body, did he let out his breath, leaning his forehead down to set it against her own.

"I think," he muttered, "I died many deaths when that murderer tried kill you."

"As did I when I saw you fight him. You came back, Brave Wolf. I thought that you had left me."

"I did leave you, but only to discover who trying to kill you. I tracked them here."

"But...I don't understand. Them? Trying to kill me? How did you—"

"Later," he murmured as he kissed her again in a long, slow stroke. When at last he came up for breath, he uttered, "We will talk about this, but not now." His lips conquered hers again in one breath-stealing kiss after another.

Gently at first, but then, when she responded to him, her own passion matching his, his tongue became savage, sweeping over her lips, her teeth, her tongue, as though by this alone, they dueled in the ever-wonderful sensation of love. Briefly, his lips left hers, as he kissed her cheeks, her ears, her throat.

"I do not wish to live in world without you in it. Even if we live not…together, I would have you alive in it." And then he said the words that caused her to melt into his arms. "Make love to me. I need feel that for little while, you are mine."

"Yes," she agreed. Hadn't she ached for his touch these past weeks? "Oh yes. Please."

It was all the inducement he appeared to need. Without pause, without explanation, he brought her up high against the trunk of the tree until he was holding her there by her thighs and buttocks. With one hand, he folded her legs around him at his waist; he pushed her clothing out of the way, and then, without ceremony, he entered her.

She welcomed him into her body, and as he drove within her, she met him move for move. The bark of the tree was smooth against her, as though it welcomed their lovemaking. His lips, as he kissed her, echoed his seemingly savage taking of her, except that she responded in kind, and she whimpered, "Don't stop, Brave Wolf. More please. I can't get enough of you."

He obliged her, and they danced, and danced to the music of the act of love, there beneath the welcoming arms of the kindly weeping willow. Mia met her pleasure fast, and he followed her, thrusting up deeply within her and bestowing her with his seed. Over and over he bore against her, in and out, in and out, until at last, they both surrendered to the ultimate pleasure.

Neither one of them moved away from the other, and as they embraced there, still entwined, neither of them spoke. It was unnecessary; they were both attuned to each other.

It was a while later when he whispered hoarsely, "And now, you are wife, true, and I am glad, because, Little Dawn Bird, I love you...."

***

"And I love you," she echoed.

He exhaled deeply, bathing in the rush of pleasure those simple words gave him. Yes, it was wrong. It was terribly wrong. He knew it. Yet, it was right, too.

She felt right in his arms. Her kisses empowered him; they did not weaken him. In truth, loving her made him feel as though he might run the length of the world and back without becoming winded.

But, they were also worlds apart; their cultures were at war, their own ideas about life and how it should be lived, conflicted. Though it might be inevitable that they must part, their time together was not yet over. For this very brief space in time, they would have each other, if only because there were still two men who walked upon this earth, who meant to steal the breath from this beautiful woman's body.

Why? He must determine it, because unless he could discover what this was all about and bring it to an end, she would never be safe.

He whispered against her ear, "We are secure here for little time. Must leave here, travel fast before their tracks are lost to Mother Earth."

"Whose tracks?"

"Those who seek...do you harm. Are you ready to leave?"

"Yes, I believe so."

Only after she'd answered him did he force himself to leave the comfort of her body. As he did so, he kissed her fully on the lips, and it took almost more willpower than he possessed to tear himself away from her. Oh, what they might be to each other, if only—

It served no purpose, however, for him to dwell on the negative. She was here now, his to defend, and the best he could do would be to create a place with no immediate danger for them; a haven where he might accomplish little more than relish in this woman's company, regardless of how fleeting that moment might be.

He let her feet return to the ground, and he smoothed her skirts over her legs, but he didn't step away from her. "I had to shed, cache bags, food, most of my weapons and clothes…get to you before..." He found he could not finish putting words to the thought. "But not to…fret. We double back once we find, make powerless two who mean harm."

"You will kill them?"

"Only if have to," he responded. "I have plan to cut short their purpose without killing, but if have no choice, I not hesitate to fight them, kill them."

"Yes, yes, you are right. This must be done. But..." Her eyes filled with sadness as she glanced away from him.

"But...?" he encouraged.

"Well, do we have to rush about it without rest? Could we not catch our breath for a few days?"

"Not good plan," he sighed. "You be in peril so long as they seek you. If do not capture them, question them, you not learn who sent them and why. They here now. Let us find who is their master."

"Yes. I suppose you're right," she replied, nodding. "Though I fear what we might discover from them."

"It best to know."

"Is it? Sometimes I wish I could return to the innocence of my childhood. The real world can be too terrible a place for a person, don't you think so?"

"I not be scout if believed that. World beautiful. All life precious. Let us finish task, take traitors prisoner. Make you safe. Then I show you harmony of life around you, show you mind of scout."

"That sounds so very, very pleasant. Brave Wolf, are you implying that you've changed your mind? Will you escort me to my home in the East? If so, is it not possible that we might marry there?"

"Already," he responded, "we married. Walks-in-sunshine be good second wife. Come to my village, not yours. I promise use all my power make life good for you."

He watched her as she bit back a groan. She swallowed hard, and looking away from him, she murmured, "I wish I could. But you know I cannot do that. I owe you my life, yes, and it is true that I love you. But I cannot be your wife in fact if there is another woman waiting in the wings for you."

"What do words mean? Waiting-in-wings?"

"It is a way of saying that there is someone else who is awaiting your return. In this case, it is a woman who you will soon marry, as you both agreed."

"But you and I have...committed act of married people. And you gave me ring. Said we are married. Makes us married."

She smiled, and reaching up to him, she placed a kiss upon his lips. It was a sweet gesture, yet hot desire rushed through him, and his life's blood came to roost in that most masculine place on his body...again.

He, however, would ignore its carnal calling. He must. But still, he couldn't keep himself from pulling her into his arms. One kiss simply wasn't enough. He ached for her; his loins demanded closeness and the merging of their bodies again. He sighed as she spoke.

"No, giving you that ring does not necessarily make that so," she declared softly, the movement of her lips against his as she spoke creating emotional havoc within him, and he found her lure stirring his very soul. He was ready for her again.

But she was continuing to speak, and he listened intently as she said, "I thought I'd never see you again when I gave that ring to you, and I wanted you to have something of mine so that you might remember me from time to time. Yes, it is my wedding ring. But to marry in fact, we would need to go before God and ask for His blessing. You know I can't do that unless you agree that I, and only I, would be your one, true wife."

"But God," he countered, "already witness…our union."

"Has He? I'm not certain that's correct. Brave Wolf, please, help me with this. You must know that I love you. Indeed, I love you so much that I am almost bursting with it. But please understand, I am only recently widowed, and my behavior is...well, it's scandalous. And you..."

He discounted the negative of her words as a feeling of elation filled his heart, for this moment was precious, set out of time. She'd declared it again. She *loved* him. But even as his spirits soared, the joyous words were quickly overshadowed, as she choked on what she said next.

"I don't know exactly when I began to love you," she began.

"Perhaps it started that first time I saw you making a breakfast of bacon and eggs for me."

She smiled, and he returned the gesture with an easy grin of his own, calling back to mind the events of those days when they had first met.

"But," she continued, "even though it is true that you have stolen my heart, please understand that I cannot live with you. I cannot do it when you intend to marry another; not and remain true to who I am and to what I believe. I love you enough to not ask you to go against your honor. Please, my darling Mr. Wolf, don't ask me to go against mine."

He sighed as he shut his eyes against the passion of her plea. Now that he had her, he did not wish to lose her. But she was right. He knew it, yet a long moment passed before he was able to utter a word. "*Hau, hau,*" he muttered at last. "You are wise…remind me of this."

"I do not feel wise, and I do not want to argue with you about this matter, important though it is. Please let us agree to disagree. Could we not use what time is left us to make love? Because you see, Mr. Brave Wolf, if I could, I would like to feel that, for a little while, I am as much the center of your world as you are of mine."

He groaned. Such was his only response against the raw hunger for her that ransacked his body. He was not immune to her appeal, though the timing for what she asked was out of place. It took him many moments before he was able to respond to her, before he could at last say, "I, too. I, too, wish make love to you every day, every way love might show. But there danger here. Not yet safe to love again."

"Oh, but I—"

"Sh-h-h," he uttered, as he placed his forehead against hers. "Soon," he whispered, "I promise we will adore each other, same way again…."

CHAPTER SEVENTEEN

"Let me scout, find good place, build camp, make space, time...to love for short while. Then we leave, find two men, question them."

Mia swallowed hard, embarrassed that she had spoken out so openly to him. In truth, her plea for his love, though heartfelt, distressed her.

Yes, she wanted him. Yes, she needed to be held by him, to be loved by him. But to suggest that they engage in more lovemaking? Here, now, and in the future...

Her heart fell. Suddenly, she felt out of her element. What must he think of her that she should beg for his embrace so brazenly? She, who had been so recently happily married?

He might feel that they were married; they might act as though they were, but she knew it wasn't—and could not be—true. What did this indicate about her that she should yearn for him in the most elemental way? Could it be true that because there was no hope of making a future with him, that her begging him for his embrace was shameful?

And what about him? Could her actions here, now, cause him future problems? Would Walks-in-sunshine truly understand about them? Fact was, she and Brave Wolf were not engaged in a heartless affair.

They were in love; the essence of who and what they each were, their very souls, had touched. It was not a commitment that one could take back. They were involved in a most carnal sense. Would Walks-in-sunshine really not worry that this man had shared his secret self with another woman, had made love to her? It seemed impossible that she would not care, since Mia knew that she would.

Still, these were not easy concepts for her to grasp, for an Indian man's and an Indian woman's ideas of love and marriage seemed so different from her own. At least, it appeared that this were so.

"Brave Wolf," she began hesitatingly, "I...I worry."

"I am listening."

She sighed, then began, "Will Walks-in-sunshine forgive you for loving me, and for making love to me?"

He hesitated for the space of a moment. At length, he admitted, "It my hope she will."

Silence reigned as Mia groped to try to explain her fears to him.

"Brave Wolf," she began after a while, "please tell me, do Indian men make love to other women before marriage?"

He was silent and appeared to draw his attention inward, onto himself. At last, however, he murmured. "Most do, for man must be…experienced in matters of love. Widows sometimes welcome man this way."

"But I—"

He pressed a finger over his lips, asking her for her silence. Then backing up from her, he took hold of her hand and urged her to follow him. "*Itó*, come," he encouraged. "Let us seek cover for talk, for it understood is important."

The touch of his skin against her own was warm and moist as he held her hand. It was odd, too, for even though he did little more than lead her farther into the woods, that simple physical contact between them created shivers of ecstasy that ran up and down her arm, from her fingers to her neck. To her mortification, though she might envision qualms about the true nature of her feelings, she realized she desired to make love to this man all over again, and perhaps for the rest of her life.

Emotionally, she slumped. What was wrong with her? Although she might envision and speak about having an affair with him, and although she might understand it because this man had risked his life for her many times, her Faith did not sanction it. Should she tell him about the conflict that waged within her?

At last, he seemed to discover what he was looking for, and he stopped his trek to stand beneath a large and voluminous elm tree.

Pointing upward, he uttered, "We climb high enough so that it seem as though we have disappeared to any who…track us. In this way, too, wind will hide our words."

"But who would follow us here?" she asked, not understanding the need for such diligence. "We left no trail in the water."

"Those white men…hired one Indian to be wolf, scout, and find you. They might do again."

"But through the water?"

He nodded. "It can be done."

All at once, he let go of her hand, and he bounded upward to take hold of a low, but large and sturdy, branch of the tree. He secured his seat on that limb, then he leaned down toward her and offered her his hand.

She hesitated. Did he really mean to lift her in the same manner that one might pull up a bucket?

Yes, he did. But what if they both fell to the ground?

Her concern was short-lived. He lifted her as though she might weigh little more than a babe. As her feet left the ground, she struggled to help him, and, using her feet against the tree's trunk, she at last came into a position where she could give him aid in pulling her up. She was panting by the time she finally found her own seating on the same branch of the tree. But he looked as though the exertion had cost him little.

He pointed upward; next, he indicated that she should hold onto his ankle. Slowly, scaling the trunk of the tree, he maneuvered the both of them higher and higher until the combination of tree branches and multitudinous leaves hid them from any possible prying eyes on the ground.

There were two large limbs far up, one on the left side of the tree, the other on the right. Standing upright, he perched against the arm on the left, while she leaned back against the other on the right.

The two of them were close enough to hold hands, and she saw that he didn't hesitate to take advantage of the opportunity. He reached out, and, bringing her fingers to his lips, he kissed each one of them.

Though tremors of excitement fled over her nerve endings from the erotic contact, she reminded herself of the purpose of her talk, and tried to calm the urgent beating of her heart.

After a short span of time, he explained, "Tree is...precaution. One is at...disadvantage on ground, if our talk causes me lose...awareness of motions of Mother Earth, allowing another here without my knowledge. I would not have us caught by enemy."

She nodded.

When she didn't at once speak, he encouraged her by stating, "You worry?"

She let out a deep breath. "Yes, I do," she agreed. "I am concerned about many problems besides the obvious—that someone is seeking to kill me."

"I know," was all he said.

"One of these is... Well, it's my behavior. I know we have spoken of this before, but the feeling persists that there is a fault in my character that, so soon after my husband's death, I should fall in love with another man."

He inclined his head, but he said nothing.

"I fear also that I might ruin you for Walks-in-sunshine. It seems to me that I have interfered in your life, and because I really do love you, I don't wish to cause you problems." She cleared her throat. "Do you intend to tell her about me?"

"*Hau, hau.* I do."

She inhaled deeply. "And you think she will forgive you, and still marry you?"

"It is so."

"Why?"

"Because we have known each other, loved each other since we...children, and once, long ago, she loved another, a man not Lakota. He left her, hurt her. Besides my oath, it is why I must return...not betray her."

"Oh," was all she said.

"Once," he began as his hand tightened on hers, "you say you put love for husband onto me. That it is husband you love, not me."

"Yes, but I don't think—"

He placed a finger over her lips, making them tingle with desire, even as he continued, "I would...finish thought."

She bobbed her head.

"Your husband die young. Sometimes happens that man dies, wife must continue without him. She...rejoices in life they shared, not life without him. She goes on, marries another. So, too, with us. Let us have this time with each other, to...remember always. While we together, I will fill loss in your life. If you love him still, through me or not, it is not you...at fault, for all nature has thrown us together and time...matters not when there is love."

"But I was confused back then when I said that to you; I am not confused now."

She watched as his Adam's apple bobbed up and down, an indication that his emotions were deeply involved. He brought her hand to his lips, and kissed it once more, before, with a smile, he looked up and said, "White man has good...custom. Man kisses woman's hand. Smart man."

She laughed gently, and said, "You are an amazing man, Brave Wolf. Truly one of a kind, but I still can't help but feel there is a fault in my character."

He squeezed her hand. "It is said by my father that only a...pure heart will seek to...correct itself. Man whose heart is black cannot see, cannot...mend."

"Perhaps, but—"

"Too soon to know if love is for me or dead husband. There be trouble in your life and I...rescued you. Even wild beast feels love for man who saved life. What you...experience is right, natural, not weakness in you."

She gazed away from him, his words bringing a tear to her eye. She was more than aware that only a good man would seek to ease the pain of another, and whether her feelings for him were misplaced or not, it mattered little. She loved him now. She wanted his love now.

Even her body could not deny the truth of this concept. Besides, he would be in her life for only a little while. He was right. She was right, too. Why not enjoy each other while they might? Why not make good memories, instead of those filled with loss?

Would she regret it later? Maybe...but somehow she doubted it.

"*Itó*, come," Brave Wolf interrupted her thoughts. "Big River has many good hiding places. Let us find one that safer than this...more comfortable than tree."

She grinned. "Yes, I suppose there might be somewhere more convenient than the highest branches in a tree."

He smiled back at her. "Whatever...future holds for us, I love you."

"And I love you. I do not believe I am confused about that, Mr. Brave Wolf. But, as you say, I might be. I guess only time will tell?"

He swallowed hard. "It true, I think," he whispered. "I believe it so. But come, we must leave before tracks of two killers become lost."

His words, the change of subject, suddenly caused fear to wash over her. She supposed she should be grateful that a little more time would intervene before they would need to set out to discover where these remaining enemies were. But the idea of tracing the path of those bullies frightened her. Couldn't he let them go?

But no, she was quick to answer her own question. He was right. If he didn't catch those men and try to ascertain the reason for their violence against her and Jeffrey, she would always be looking over her shoulder, always be afraid of the assassin's bullet.

Uselessly, she wondered again why anyone would take such trouble to find and try to kill both her and Jeffrey. What had he...or she done to anyone?

He pushed himself away from the tree limb, and, squeezing her hand, he declared again, "I love you. Let us go now and find good shelter...quick."

She smiled as she looked up at him. "Yes," she agreed. It was all she seemed to be able to say at this moment.

But it appeared to be enough, for he grinned back at her, and she thought she had never witnessed a vision more beautiful than the friendly beam of a man so very, very dear....

***

She could hear the rush of the Missouri River as it hurled madly onto some southern rendezvous; she could smell the damp grasses, the oxygen-filled air and the musky odor of the earth; she could feel the humidity of this place, taste the dirt in the breeze. Huge weeping willow trees and cottonwoods, as well as those of elm, oak, and pine trees surrounded her in this wood of brown and green. She felt sticky, unkempt; even her hair hung about her face in lumps, matted with mud.

Temporarily, she wished for a bit of civilization and a mirror, if only to repair the damage to her appearance because of those hours spent swimming in muddy water. Of course, she had done her best, patting her hair into place, but the tangles, matted with muck and sand, had proved too unwieldy to manage.

Meanwhile, evening had fallen, the navy-blue sky quickly turning to a deep, dark gray. There was only one star on the horizon at present, but soon there would be more of those tiny specks of light, sparkling against a background of inky black.

Interestingly, night in the Missouri River Valley was not cooler than the day; rather, the dampness in the air seemed to cause the evening to feel hotter than the daylight hours. Though the heat troubled her, making her feel lazy and inactive, it seemed to not affect Brave Wolf at all.

She gave him her full attention now that he had found a place to set up camp. This spot was nestled within the dense woods which skirted the river at this junction. Yet the place was far enough away from the water to allow for an unhindered view of the stream. Close by was a hill of stones, with various trees having taken root in such an unlikely place, giving the area good shelter. It was against this backdrop that she watched Brave Wolf erect a dwelling to spend the night.

From fallen timber and rooted trees, he quickly placed logs and branches to form a base that backed up to the stone hill, then he set more heavy timber against the main structure. Willow and pine branches, leaves, as well as clumps of moss and grass, became the walls and the ceiling of the shelter. What followed next, she could never quite understand, for he placed other branches, moss and timber not on the refuge, but surrounding it. The effect, however, was miraculous, for their hide-out faded into the landscape of their environment.

Perhaps she should help; the thought did cross her mind, but as she yawned, she realized she could barely stand, let alone carry heavy tree branches back and forth. As she sat there watching him work, she felt more and more lethargic.

Sleepily, she watched him as he placed various willow tree switches onto the floor of the structure. This was then followed by long pine boughs set over the willow branches, and she came to understand that this would be where they would sleep this night. It occurred to her that he had constructed this hideaway with no tools, not even the two knives strapped securely to his waist.

Her drowsiness was almost more than she could control, and she glanced away for a moment. But when she looked back, so disguised was their temporary abode that even she, who knew where it was, could barely distinguish it from the rest of the woods.

Suddenly, Brave Wolf loomed in front of her, holding out his hand to her. "*Itó*, come, our *tepee* awaits your...presence."

She placed her hand in his and smiled up at him, but so exhausted was she still, her eyelids drooped. She yawned.

Immediately, he squatted in front of her and there was a twinkle in his eye as he said, "Turn."

"Turn?"

He nodded, and she, being too drained to argue with him, changed her position until she had presented him with her back. She jumped when his hands came up to massage her shoulders. But she quickly relaxed.

Oh, it felt so good, and soon, she leaned back against him. He scooted her forward a little, and continued his massage down her spine. Voluminous sensation fled over her nerve endings, waking her up, and she tingled everywhere.

She groaned, the sound low and breathy as it faded into the sweeping gusts of the wind. After their earlier crises of this day, his touch seemed a little like heaven.

"You have had much...adventure this day," he whispered against her ear. "For little while, let me take...your strain onto me."

"Hmmm...yes..."

His hands came up to run through her hair, and she closed her eyes, letting him knead her hair, muddy and tangled though it was. Oddly, the action brought to mind a concern, and though it seemed out of place, still she asked, "Brave Wolf, do your people take scalps?"

"My people often do," he answered softly.

"Do you?"

"I have."

She let this honest admission settle in momentarily. Then, she added, "White people? Like me?"

"*Hiyá*, no."

"Then who?"

"Enemy tribes."

"But aren't your people at war with mine?"

"*Hau, hau*, but you forget my mother is white, and my grandfather is soldier."

"Then you don't fight in those wars?"

"*Hiyá*."

"Is that why you and your party came to my defense? Because I'm white?"

"*Hiyá*, no. Those men...deceivers...bullies. Threaten you who are innocent."

She sighed. "Oh, how I wish..."

He remained silent, which seemed to encourage her to speak, and she went on to say, "Brave Wolf, I am feeling that perhaps I am wrong. Could it be that I owe it to you to leave my religion and my commitment to my God behind me? I am thinking that maybe I should become your wife in fact. Could it be that because I am so beholden to you, it wouldn't matter if I were your first or second wife?"

Tenderly, he turned her around to face him, and, with a single finger placed under her chin, he brought her face up until they could stare into one another's eyes. He whispered, "Your words touch my heart."

"Yes, I—"

"But," he silenced her again with that forefinger of his, placing it against her lips. "I would not have you feel you...'owe' me anything. What I do is because it right. Such, the Lakota way."

"Yet," she argued, "I cannot deny that I am only here on this earth because you have come to my defense more than once. Is my life not yours to take, then? In truth, I am starting to fear that I am wrong to deny you the second wife that you ask me to be. Could this be what God intends me to do?"

She watched him draw in a deep breath, and he seemed to choose his words carefully before he uttered, "Is it true that law of your Creator...forbids this?"

"Yes."

"Then...stirrings of heart must bow to...wisdom of your Creator."

"But I—"

Instead of his finger, he softly kissed her on her lips, silencing her.

"Always," he murmured, "you would regret this."

She looked away from him, and she couldn't help the tears that threatened to mar her composure. She felt weak, defenseless, and she didn't want to leave this man...ever....

Tenderly, he brought her face back around to his. He whispered, "Takes...courage to do right thing. Always, we will have this time together."

She shut her eyes, and the tears spilled down over her cheeks.

He rose up to his feet and held his hands out toward her. "*Itó*, come. Let us make...merry this time together."

He pulled her into his arms, and because she was brought up so close to him, his clean masculine, musky scent assailed her senses. Inhaling deeply of its fragrance, she made a mental note to remember this knowledge of him always...always.

However, instead of escorting her into their temporary shelter, as she had expected, he simply stood with her, as though he might likely dance with her. His arms came around her waist, and he said, "You...I dance?"

"Do you know how to do the white man's dance?"

"Do not forget, my mother is white. Sometimes, we used to...visit her relatives. They did jig, a waltz. I learned."

She smiled up at him, and he brought up his hand to place her arm around his neck. Then he put her other hand next to his, and he began to guide her around the small clearing that he had created here in the woods.

And they danced. They danced a slow waltz to the song of the wind in the trees.

The stars were alive with their tiny beams of light, so beautiful against the dark, backdrop of the sky. The moon became their lantern in this wilderness ballroom; the misty beams of its light bathed Brave Wolf in a fragile glow that made his blue eyes seem darker. He hummed the strains of a waltz, surprising her that he would recall a melody that must have sounded foreign to a young boy. After a moment, she joined her voice to his, for she recognized the tune; he smiled down at her.

His voice was husky, as he uttered, "Our bodies move well...together. It is as though we make love with song."

"Yes." Her eyes teared all over again. Indeed, it was true. It was as if they were made for each other, this union that never could be.

Around and around the clearing they floated, as if their feet were inches off the ground. Their dance seemed timed to the rhythm of the earth, and they frolicked until, at last, he stopped, took her hand in his, and led her to their evening abode.

He entered the lean-to first, and she was glad that he had done so, for, so well-disguised was it, she couldn't even see the dwelling's entrance. He pulled her inside, and she noted that there was only room enough to sit up at the entrance of their shelter, because the temporary housing graduated in a slope backward. He helped her to sit next to him, and never did he release her hand.

"I love you," he began, his voice soft and hushed. "If our lives were...different, I would not let you go. Let us then make this night as though there be no time moving forward...no future. There is only you and only me. For though our paths must part, you will always be here." He placed his hand over his heart. "Always be my first wife here."

She cried, condemning herself slightly for her constant fall into grief. And it took a considerable effort on her part to utter, "Yes." She couldn't say more.

His hands came up to hold her face, and he bent toward her, placing his lips gently against hers. It was a sweet kiss; a simple touching. But oh, how it stirred her.

"Dear Lord," she murmured beneath her breath. "How will I ever be able to leave you? For if I could, I would share all your joys, all your sorrows, even bear up under your temper...if you have one," she added, for she had never been witness to it.

But so soft was her voice, she hoped he couldn't hear her, for if he knew how much she admired him—

But all at once, he gained her undivided attention, for he pulled the top of her dress down to her waist, exposing her chemise and her corset to his admiring glance. He whispered, "You wear many clothes."

She grinned at him. "Indeed, I do, as a woman in my culture must."

"But," he said, "I would see you without these. How do they come off?"

"Not easily, I fear. Here..." She scooted around their tiny shelter until she had presented him with her back. "Do you see the hooks and eyes?"

"Ah..."

Bringing one of her arms around to her back, she indicated the row of hooks. "These are the methods by which this is kept in place, and these come apart, but it is difficult for me to do it. However, if you separate the hook from the eye, eventually, the garment will fall away of its own."

"Then let me...attend to this at once."

She giggled softly.

"Your laughter like music. Full of life."

She smiled, joyous. It was odd that she could feel his fingers shake as they attended to their duty with her corset. Was he nervous? If that were so, it endeared him to her all the more.

At last it was done, and her chemise, as well as her corset, fell to her waist. Quickly, he removed the clothing from her, and set it aside. And then, with his gaze, he adored her.

"You are...perfect, beautiful," he whispered huskily.

So is he. Outside of a necklace that was more choker than pendant, he was bare-chested, all masculine muscle and brawn, and she longed to feel the expanse of all that flesh against her own.

She sat up onto her knees, and, leaning forward, pressed herself in against him, glorying in the touch of the solidity of his breast against the softness of hers. She moved up and down against him, wishing with all her heart that she could attain a closeness that was humanly impossible.

He gasped in a breath as his arms came around her and he pulled her in. Looking up, she watched the handsomeness of his face as he closed his eyes.

In a quick motion, he pulled her skirts off her, throwing them haphazardly to the side. She didn't wear pantalets, hadn't for some time, having discarded them long ago as unnecessary. So what met his eyes was her nakedness complete...except for her moccasins, which he quickly drew off of her, as well.

He did nothing more than gaze at her. Moment after moment flew by as his look seemed to take in everything about her, from the top of her long, red hair to her neck, then lower to her breasts; lower still, to the junction of her legs.

He touched her there, his graze soft, as his fingers moved over her heated flesh. This was a place most sensitive, and she wiggled in an effort to try to feel the pleasure more intensely. With his other hand, he massaged one of her breasts.

In response, Mia thought she might go quietly crazy with the desire that flooded and cascaded over her nervous system. What was the meaning of her reaction? For his touch wasn't harsh; it wasn't hungry. Rather, it was filled with admiration, like that of one who might explore a beloved object. But she felt on fire.

His voice was gravelly when he whispered, "I may not wash my fingers ever again. Always then, they would remind me of you."

"But," she whispered huskily, "I don't think these places on one's body smell very good."

"Not so," he responded at once. "Your...fragrance there like white man's heaven."

How odd. Jeffrey had once told her the exact opposite, and she had assumed that he was right.

All thought along that line ceased as he held her up and brought her up over him. Quickly, he untied his only clothing, his breechcloth, and tossed it to the side. She saw that he was already firm, rock-like—and big.

His size might have scared her, but then she remembered that already they had made love, and that he had fit within her perfectly. He was separating her legs now, and that part of her most feminine felt wet beneath his touch. He then positioned her down into a squat over him. Barely able to contain herself, she complied at once, and took his manhood within her as though his body were a cherished part of her.

Both of them gasped. It felt that good.

They did nothing at first, but savor the sweeping impact of passion, the incredible inclusiveness of the act of being so close. It was almost enough, but not quite...

"Why do I feel," she murmured as she placed her lips against his ear, "as though I am still longing to get nearer to you?"

"Twist over me a little, and the feeling might...end."

"Or extend."

He groaned, and the deep sound of his utterance urged her into a frenzy, and she danced over him. Her breasts were at his face level, and he took advantage, suckling first one and then the other.

Slowly, it was building up within her. She strained against him. She wiggled.

Then it happened. At the same moment he burst his seed within her, she met her own pleasure. Over and over, they pushed against the tide of fulfillment, each moving against the other, each relishing in the beauty of love. The pleasure went on and on, until at last she fell in against him, exhausted.

That's when it happened. So close were they, his spirit touched hers, and the intimacy she had wished for became a reality. Never had she felt an experience more beautiful.

He brought her head toward his, then, and kissed her gently before he admitted, "I love you much, my first...pretend wife. You should know, though, if we make...baby, you will have to come home with me."

She whispered in return, "Only if I remain your one and only wife."

He sighed. But he said nothing in response. Perhaps, he realized that now was not the right moment to address the possibility of pregnancy. She knew, however, that the matter was not closed. He would bring up the point again. She knew he would.

And, she told herself, she had better be prepared with some argument, since she was already weakening in her defense of being his one and his only wife. It had better be a sound argument, too, since she realized that he could probably talk her into most anything.

CHAPTER EIGHTEEN

The two remaining men were trekking south and west at a fast pace. They out-distanced him every day, for Brave Wolf, of necessity, kept a slower, more diligent pace. Not only did Little Dawn Bird require time to rest, but a scout never knew if he, too, might be being trailed; thus, he erased all traces of their own passage over the land. Such took much time.

He made up the miles between their two parties at night, and eventually he surpassed the two of them. He had already surmised that they were en route to a nearby trader's post, and he knew the path to it well; thus, it became easy to go before them and examine the area around what their easiest trail would be. It was here that he would trap them.

Several days ago, he had returned to the place where he had cached his possessions, allowing him to dress in more clothing than his simple breechcloth. His chest remained bare beneath a summer sun, but he had donned his leggings, as well as his weapons. Guns and his bow were strapped around his shoulders, and a sheath full of arrows hung down his back. Bags fell over his shoulders, as well, although Little Dawn Bird had taken to carrying the majority of the lighter articles.

Routine had become that, late at night, as they camped and she slept, he cleaned his guns, checked his ammunition, tested his arrows and hatchet to ensure their ends were razor thin and sharp.

Already, he had erected a debris shelter for her, carefully ensuring that it disappeared into the landscape. Each night, he kissed her tenderly as he held her until she slept soundly. Most usually, however, rest came uneasily for her.

She worried, he knew, for he had told her that he would be gone throughout most of the night. She didn't like it, and had begged to come with him, but he knew she would be safe here, and there was danger in what he intended doing.

After several days on the trail, there came an evening when there was no moon, the sky being overcast. The lack of light stood him in good stead, however, for it would better hide his passage over the land.

He chose a spot along the trail where the multitude of trees and bushes would make the two men's passage difficult; it would cause them to create a path that wound in amongst a numerous patch of trees, since the way around the forestation encompassed many miles. It was here, along the most obvious clearing through the woods, that he would construct the man-pit trap.

The pit would not include any sharp objects at its bottom, for it was not his intention to kill these men. Scare them, yes. Intimidate them, yes. But he would only kill them if his or her survival demanded it. Being a *toŋwéya*, no other possible scheme would do, for a true scout killed no one unless he were pressed into action in a life or death situation.

He chose a spot where the ground was soft, which would make the digging easier. Using what tools he had to hand, he dug a large hole in the middle of the path that would be the most likely place the two bullies would be forced to take. The pit had to be deep; deep enough that a man couldn't easily climb out of it. In setting the trap, he had taken the precaution of tying a buckskin rope to a tree so that he could climb out of it, and then remove the rope. Lastly, he covered the pit over with branches, leaves and pine needles, tending to it until what lay beneath the ground became invisible to a mind that was untrained to expect the unexpected.

At last, he returned to his own encampment, carefully seeking out another path toward it, as was the manner of a scout. Day was barely breaking when he stepped into camp. She was still asleep, and he debated how best to awaken her without alarming her.

Food. He had secured a prairie chicken on his way back to their shelter. Let the scent of roasting meat bring her back from the land of slumber. Slowly, with painstaking deliberation, he built up a smoke-less fire.

***

"Hmmm... What is that I smell?"

Mia crawled out from the debris hut that they had both constructed last night.

She smiled at him. Then, continuing her line of thought, she softly said, "Good morning. I am glad to see you back here so early, for I was worried."

"I know," was his simple reply. "But work is done. Trap set. Soon, we will have two murderers trapped. Then I will...question them."

She gasped. "Is that wise? Isn't there danger in keeping them in a condition where they could overtake you? After all, you are only one, and they are two."

"*Hau, hau.* Could be danger, if I am not...careful. But I think not."

"Nevertheless, I don't see how you will be safe. If I understand this correctly, they will fall into a pit that you've constructed, still retaining their guns, their knives and any other weapons. They could fire at you. Throw a knife at you. They might do you harm."

"Is correct," he responded. "But I have thought of this, have...prepared for this, and if I do not do it in this way, I will...discover *not* who is their master and what this about. This, we must...learn, if you are to be safe."

She grimaced. She didn't know which was worse, the idea that these men aimed to kill her, or the very real threat they presented to Brave Wolf.

Perhaps it was both. But whatever the reason, she felt overwhelmed by the danger, so much so that she couldn't even put words to the fear that was even now consuming her. She swallowed down the lump in her throat, and at last managed to mutter, "Thank you for the prairie chicken. It will make a good breakfast."

They stared at one another for a long, few moments. In due time, he reached out his hand to touch hers, and slowly, he brought it to his lips. "You be with me," he said, "...not seen in...background. I hide you, keep you safe."

She inhaled a deep breath. "Yes, yes, but what about you? My concern is not only for myself. You could be... You could be..." She stopped. She couldn't bring herself to utter the concept that he might be placing himself in a position where he might be killed.

"This one," he pointed to himself, "will be...safe, too. Wait. You will see."

"I hope so, Mr. Brave Wolf. I do hope so. But be aware that if you lose your life there, so, too, will I. It is the same as I have told you in the past. If you die, I will ensure that I do, also."

Brave Wolf scrutinized her for several seconds, before he at last averted his gaze. It was a small victory. She only wished she felt better for it.

***

Long before they approached the trap he'd set, he knew it was sprung. He could feel this was so because of the disruption of the ever-present concentric circles in the air. The sudden and erratic waves that filled the silent bands in the atmosphere told of terror and fear, as well as the frustration which probably came from being unable to climb out of the deep pit. A sense of disgruntlement and fear carried over those drafts, as well. They told him that the trapped beings were human, not animals, for the thought waves were of intelligent origin.

Of course, he could be in error. Although he was almost completely certain that the bullies had both fallen into the trap, he was also clever enough to realize that only a full, physical investigation would determine the truth. Therefore, he would approach that deep pit with the slow caution of the scout.

Soon, his unknowing would become knowing. As a result, he would be able to track down the mastermind and put an end to this madness. She would then be free...to return to her home in the East.

At once, a sense of panic welled up in him. He pushed the emotion aside, however, deciding it would not do to think of that possibility now. Later, when he had accomplished his purpose, he would explore that thought.

He spoke up to her, remarking, "Men are trapped."

"They are? How do you know?"

"My duty to know," was all he replied. Then, "*Itó*, come, I make safe place so you can hear, not be seen."

"Could I not stay here, instead?"

"*Hiyá*, no. Must have you close. Attention will be on men.... You must be near to me, so if...danger happen to you, I can save you."

He saw that she bit her lip, an indication of her worry; but, to her credit, she said nothing. He turned away, and as quickly as he could, while maintaining his cloak of secrecy, he led her over the path toward the trap that he had set. Scout-like, however, the going, even when rushed, was exceedingly slow....

***

From the shadows of the simple debris hut he had constructed for her, she watched Brave Wolf as he sat cross-legged next to the man-pit. He tarried there, seemingly doing nothing more untoward than cleaning his gun.

It was a threat. She knew it, and so did they—those two who were trapped down deep in the abyss.

As soon as the two men had seen him, they had wasted no time in expending their ammunition, trying without luck to hit him, to kill him. But the slugs had missed their mark, for Brave Wolf sat carefully back, out of range. In truth, their shots had done damage to themselves, for their rounds had, more times than not, fallen back into the pit. Since what goes up must come down, each man now complained of wounds sustained due to their own stupidity.

"Why, he ain't nothin' but a damn savage," grumbled one of the would-be assassins. "What'cha plannin' fer us, ya ignorant savage?"

"*Wa cécicíciyapi.*" Because of the black, white and reddish paint which covered his face, his arms, his chest and even his back, he looked fiendish. She had watched him smear on that paint this morning; had even helped spread the mixture over his back, and yet, even she who knew and loved him, and who sat out of the way, in a safe place, quaked at the sight of him.

"What'd he say?"

"I don't know. Ask him."

"Ya know I don't speak Injun, Wingate. I thought you was taught all the Injun languages 'round here."

"I does, I tell ya. Still don't know what he said."

Brave Wolf set his gun so that the muzzle of it pointed downward, into the trench. Carefully, he inserted ammunition into that weapon. "I...pray for you," Brave Wolf said quietly. "That what I said. You...best pray, too."

"Ya speak English?"

Brave Wolf's smile was demonic. But he uttered no words to either confirm it, or deny it.

One of the men executed a short running leap up, reaching with all his might for that gun. But Brave Wolf had apparently dug the trap deeply enough to discount this sort of attempt, for Mia could see that Brave Wolf seemed completely unaffected by the effort.

He did inquire, "Who set you kill...wagon train?"

"We dinna kill no wagon train," said one of them.

"Sh-h-h-h, McWinna. Let's hear what th' pagan has ta say."

"He's gonna murder us," whined McWinna. "So what's it matter what he has ta say?"

"I no kill," offered Brave Wolf evenly, "if tell who sent you."

Dead silence filled the space surrounding the trap.

"If'n ya let me go, I'll give ya all the gold paid ta me."

"Gold?" replied Brave Wolf. "No use for gold."

"It ain't no good, Wingate. I's already told ya. He's gonna kill us."

Brave Wolf's smile was even more demonic as he asked, "Why hire...*toŋwéya*, scout?"

"Scout?"

Brave Wolf replied, "Lone Fox...Scout-turned-traitor."

"How'd ya know about him? Was he some relative of yers?"

"I know about you, him," was all Brave Wolf returned. "Who...hired you?"

"Don't know."

Brave Wolf became silent.

"I tell ya. We don't know."

"What man look like?" demanded Brave Wolf.

"I don't know," came the reply. "Neither of us knows."

Brave Wolf came up slowly to his feet, but before he walked away, he threw out a challenge, saying, "Tell me who.... Then, you may go. Not before."

"Cain't tell ya what I dinna know, ya ignorant and pagan savage."

Brave Wolf didn't answer, nor did he react to the insult. Instead, he walked away, only to return with his quiver full of arrows. Slowly, meticulously, he scraped away at those arrowheads, sharpening each point.

It seemed as if, for the moment, they had reached an impasse. But Brave Wolf would win in the end. She knew that he would.

***

"Hey, Injun, I'm thirsty!"

No answer. Plus, Brave Wolf wasn't anywhere to be seen. Where was he?

"Hey, Injun, ya out there?"

Silence.

"What's in this fer ya, anyway, Injun? What's a wagon train to ya? Ya got kin that was kilt dead there?"

Again, there came no answer from Brave Wolf. Where was he? Mia knew he hadn't left to investigate some other problem; he would have told her. But she couldn't see him, though she was certain that he could only be close by, knew that this was all part of a test of wills.

"I'm thirsty, ya stupid savage."

Mia watched as Brave Wolf at last trod into view. He stepped to the edge of the pit, and in his hand he held his water pouch. Carefully, deliberately, he opened the buckskin bag and let a few droplets of water fall into the hole.

A pained howl erupted out of the pit. "Ya tryin' ta drive us crazy, ya stupid savage?"

"Of course he is, McWinna. Jest shut up."

"Why not tell what this one..." he pointed to himself, "needs to know?" asked Brave Wolf. "Who sent you kill white woman?"

"How would I know? I's sayin' th' truth when I tell ya tha' we don't know. Now can we have all th' water ya hold thar?"

"*Hau, hau.*"

Mia watched as Brave Wolf dumped the entire parfleche full of water onto the two men. She heard the bullies scatter, as though they were trying to capture and swallow a droplet or two.

"I leave tomorrow. You stay here...meet fate. Or tell now and go...free."

"What's th' woman to ya?"

Brave Wolf turned his back on the men and walked away, out of sight—even she couldn't see him. He didn't come anywhere near her temporary shelter, either, which was probably as he had planned. In all probability, he was keeping her out of this as well as he could.

"I don't believe ya, savage. How does I knew yer'll keep yer promise, and let us'n go?"

In response, Brave Wolf turned back toward the pit and grinned. Then, in a voice that brooked no argument, he stated, "You know."

Well, that was that. Brave Wolf didn't go anywhere near the pit again, even hours later.

When darkness fell, and still Brave Wolf hadn't reappeared, Mia began to worry. Had he come to harm?

Briefly, she debated the wisdom of leaving the relative safety of her shelter to go and search for him. She couldn't simply sit here and do nothing, when she didn't know whether or not he might be in danger.

In the end, the worry overcame her, and she decided she would leave to go and find him. Having made that decision, she felt better for it, and she had crawled halfway out of the shelter, when Brave Wolf reappeared at the borderline of the trees. Strapped across his back was an animal that appeared to be an elk or a deer. It was hard to tell what kind of animal it was exactly, however, because the moon and the stars had yet to appear.

Slowly, one foot at a time, he paced toward the man-trap until he stood close to it, effectively presenting himself in full view of those below. He let the elk drop to the ground, then, sitting cross-legged beside it, he brought forward a knife, and proceeded to sharpen his knives until he was satisfied the instruments would cut easily.

Mia knew what he was about; he meant to skin that animal. Hadn't she watched him engage in this activity often enough? Over their travels, she had become used to watching him remove an animal's hide, making its meat available for nourishment and its tanned rawhide for blankets and parfleche bags.

But he was engaged in adding dramatics to what he was doing, and he commented, "Man's *uká*...skin come off like that of *heháka*...elk. Watch."

Here, he proceeded to cut the elk down its belly, whereupon the rest of the hide came off with ease. He narrated his task, saying, "If man still...alive—and he would be—great pain to be without skin."

The bullies in that pit were silent, and if it weren't for the constant and familiar chatter of the insects in the background, as well as the wind whistling through the trees, there would have been no sound. None at all.

Brave Wolf made quick work of his task, cutting up the meat, storing it into parfleche bags, and when this was done, he set about stoking up a small fire. She watched in awe as he quickly whittled a long stick and placed it upon two Y-shaped branches high enough over that fire so they wouldn't burn. Next, he put strips of the elk meat over the whittled stick, the fat from the meat as it dripped onto the flames causing smoke to curl upward toward the meat. Then he threw his buckskin blanket over the entire affair and enclosed it.

The scent of roasting meat was more than her empty stomach could experience. Its growling reminded her that she hadn't eaten any food since breakfast.

"I leave...first light. If you no talk about wagon train attack, good...luck. Scent of meat make wolves come...maybe hostile tribes. Maybe you live, maybe not."

Silence. Then, came a low voice, the words uttered in a whisper. "I'll tell ya what'cha wantin' ta know, Injun."

"Shut up McWinna...ya know what *he* said—"

"I dunna care. *He* be dead, I say. We saw th' boat blow up." After a brief pause, McWinna went on to say, "*He* gave us'ns gold. Said *he* was hired by man who was a government man; said this man was pretendin' ta be a trader. Man who hired us'ns was called Smith."

"Probably wasn't Smith," interjected Wingate.

"Probably wasn't. He had money—lots of it. Said the wagon train was nothin' but spies. Said this man, Jeffrey Carlson, an' his wife was all ta be kilt dead, an' anyone else helpin' 'em. We was promised ten thousand dollars in gold if'n and when we kilt 'em, an' anyone helpin' 'em."

"Who...is trader? Who...is government man?"

"Dunna know. Never named him."

"Where trading post...that government trader...work?"

"Dunno. Never thought ta ask. We gots ourselves gold. What did we care about who was th' man tha' hired Smith?"

Was this a dead end, then? By their own statement of it, reasoned Mia, these men weren't hired by the government man. Only Smith knew who that agent was, and Smith was now dead.

"Where," inquired Brave Wolf further, "man called Smith from?"

"Somewhere up north. That's where he met th' government man."

"Smith say why...government trader want you kill man and wife?"

"Said this man, Jeffrey Carlson, turned redcoat during the war 'tween the States. Caused this trader's wife ta be kilt. One turn deserves another, I reckoned. I understands 'bout revenge. We got Carlson, but not his wife. No more gold was ta be given us till she lay dead, too. "

This last statement was met with Brave Wolf's silence. Nothing was said. Nothing was done for several moments.

Mia's head spun as she realized two facts at the same time; the trouble was because of Jeffrey, but these two men still meant to kill her. Involuntarily, she shivered, while goosebumps raced over her skin.

At last, one of the turncoats ventured to ask, "Will ya turn us loose now, or are ya nothin' more than a Injun giver?"

"*Hau, hau,* you are free."

Silence ensued until one of the bullies observed, "Stupid Injun. We're still standin' in this hole in the ground."

"Always been able to go free," Brave Wolf answered with a grin, but Mia wondered, too, what he meant, for the two men were certainly still imprisoned down there.

"Stop talkin' jabber, Injun. We's told ya what we know. Keep yer end of th' bargain."

"You...always been able to leave."

"Stupid Injun. Do ya think we'd still be here, if'n we could get outta here?"

Mia could hear the smile in Brave Wolf's voice as he answered, "I tell you how to...leave pit. First, throw weapons, guns, knives, arrowheads to ground. Keep hands up."

This they did.

"*Wašté*. Now you," Brave Wolf pointed to McWinna, the smaller of the two. "Crawl up on man called Wingate's...shoulders."

"Wha' th'—" Though the two bullies might not understand the reason why this was necessary, they still obliged.

Brave Wolf went on to instruct, "Man called Wingate step up on...rock, there at side of pit."

Wingate complied.

"Now man called McWinna...reach up to tree branch and..."

"I see it. I see it." With muscles straining, McWinna grabbed hold of that arm of the tree and pulled himself up, crawling with difficulty onto firm ground. Once he had gained his balance, he leaned down and presented the branch down to Wingate. All the while, he was speaking, muttering, "Why, ya dirty, rotten savage. Ya tricked us. Made fools outta us. We could'a left that pit any time if'n we'd only known."

Brave Wolf smirked once more, but because his amusement was hidden behind the rifle he aimed at the two of them, the humor of the situation went missed by the delinquent two.

"*Heyáb iyá yo*! Go!" he said. "Run fast, faster than rifle can shoot."

McWinna and Wingate appeared to require no further warning, and they practically fell over one another as they scrambled away, falling and stumbling upon a path that was blocked with tree stumps, prickly vines and vegetation. Had that escape route, too, been sabotaged by Brave Wolf?

Apparently so, for Brave Wolf's laughter rang out clearly. It was infectious; Mia, too, smiled. Those two were to be congratulated; they jumped over dirt, fallen trees and rocks as though they had grown wings. And as they fled, their hilarious departure was accompanied by Brave Wolf's well-deserved mirth.

CHAPTER NINETEEN

"May I come out of here?" asked Mia in a voice raised barely over a whisper.

"*Hiyá,* not yet. Must be...certain men are gone. I will go now to...track them."

"I will come with you," she insisted, and whether he gave her permission or not, she crawled out of the small debris hut to step to his side. She sat down beside him. "So they could have left your trap at any time?"

"*Hau, hau,* it is so. *Aówehanhan wašté.* Good joke, I think."

"Yes, I agree."

He turned his head to look at her, and his look still mirrored amusement. "White man not take time to...observe. Sometimes red man, too."

She grinned back at him before she became more serious. A moment passed. "What do we do now?"

His grin vanished, and his countenance turned suddenly downcast. He gazed away from her, and it was some little while before he spoke. At length, however, he answered, "We make certain they have left this country. Then, must take you to white man's post, *i tókagata*...south, away from government trader in north."

"Yes, I suppose you are right."

"These men not know source of danger," he went on to say. "Who is man that is government trader? Only...bully now dead on boat knew. You not safe here. Man who...hired all still alive."

One instant followed upon another in silence, until at last, she asked, "Am I even safe now?"

"*Hau, hau,* with me. *Tuká* but must take you to white man's...fort in south. I stay with you...until you go home."

"Oh," was all she uttered at first. Then, she added, "And you? Will you go to your home, also?"

"Hau, hau, I will."

"What makes you believe," she asked, "that the fort south of here will be secure enough?"

He paused, then with seeming reluctance he replied, "I do not know. But fort there said to have *walówan*...singing wires."

"Ah..." At last she understood, and she went on to observe, "That's right. I had forgotten. It is said that this fort has a telegraph. I could send a wire to my father, and he could use his influence, I'm sure, to ensure that I return home without further incident." She swallowed the lump that seemed to have formed in her throat. "And that's where we will part?" The question was really more statement than inquiry.

"Hau, hau, it must be so."

She chanced a quick glance sideways at him, and was startled to witness a trail of wetness on his cheek. She reached out to touch the tear there, saying, "You could come home with me. You know you could. My father would welcome you, I think."

She watched him as he turned his head away from her touch, and her stomach dropped, leaving her feeling dizzy, as though butterflies had taken residence there. His lips quivered, and it was only then that she realized her own visage mirrored his.

"Many times," he began in a low, husky voice, his eyes averted from hers, "we have talked about this. Many times we have *yustán*...concluded that we must then part. Our *wicála*...beliefs war with each other. Would be *ecígsni*...wrong to force our ideas one on the other. Now, also, we have more reason you must return to home. We not know who...government trader is. You not safe, even with Indians, for traders...often come to village."

Of course he was right. Yet, although she understood the truth of what he said, it didn't make the reality of their parting any easier. She didn't have a response for this, and as she sat there beside him, so close to him, yet so far away, she quietly sobbed.

"But," he began, "we have *lehánl*...now, the present. Promised, I have, to show you ways of prairie. Let us enjoy each other and prairie while we trek to fort...in south."

She gulped and swallowed hard. Several times, she tried to speak, but with each attempt she found that her voice wouldn't work. And so she reached out to touch his hand, and, gripping it firmly, she took it within her own.

She whispered huskily, "You know that I will always admire you. Yes, yes, as you have pointed out, I might be misplacing the love I felt for my husband, giving all the fondness I felt for him to you, when it's really he that I praise. But, true or not, it doesn't seem to matter to me anymore. For, you see, Mr. Brave Wolf, I love you, and if I could, I would follow you anywhere, even to your home, and to Walks-in-sunshine."

"But you cannot."

"No, I cannot," was all she uttered.

"Then come," he declared as he stood up to his feet. Because her hand was still clutched within his own, he helped her to stand up. "We will make certain your enemies are gone, and then let us...pretend that there is only here, now. We will be *fyúsking*...happy, for we will always have this time to...remember, *oíhaŋke wanil*...forever...."

"Yes," she agreed at once. "We will always have this to recall—forever."

***

He kept his promise. As they ventured farther south, she observed that the grass became shorter, and they made their way through it a little easier. Yet, they never traveled on open prairie during the day. He insisted that it wasn't safe to do so.

"Am in territory of Lakota enemies," he had explained once.

And so it was that they traveled only at night. He set the rhythm of their passage over the land to a slow pace. Sometimes, she wondered if he were keeping their trek deliberately delayed. If so, she heartily approved.

Often he would bring their progress to a halt in order to point out a particular flower or a ridge in the earth; perhaps an unusual blade of grass or a strand of trees. Always, he encouraged her to touch the plant or tree, to take it in hand or to hug it, and to listen to it speak.

He taught her that this was the medicine way of discovering what power the plant held. A medicine person, he instructed, "always asks the plant what it does. Does it help the human body? If so, in what way?" Was it poison to the people? Was it to be avoided? Or did even the deadly ones hold a use, for there were those known to be poison to eat, while yet holding a capacity to heal the sick, if taken correctly and in small doses.

Once she thought she heard a plant answer, not with words, rather, the response was spiritual, as though it came from one mind to another. Startled, she began to look upon the life around her with new eyes.

He named several bird calls, and she learned to listen to and enjoy the songs of the night hawk, as well as that of the sparrow and the meadowlark, both of whom periodically filled the evening air with their nocturnal singing. Oddly, there was a feeling of harmony and security when one was roaming without light. And the feelings of fright, so common to her at first, gradually faded to become as nothing. Always, there was the music of the crickets and locusts to fill the balmy summer nights, as well.

Sometimes it rained, but that was occasional, and in the early hours of the morning, after an evening of travel, they made camp. Most commonly, before they lay down to sleep, they shared their admiration for one another in the ever-present physical demand of their bodies. Could a person become addicted to another human being? For in many ways, she wondered how she would ever live her life without this man, and she began to dread her return to civilization.

But at last it had to happen, and they came upon the sight of Fort Leavenworth—the white man's civilization. At present, they were looking down upon the settlement, stationed as they were atop a cliff overlooking the town in the valley below them. Several fires lighted up the numerous buildings down there, bringing with its smoke the aroma of roasting meat.

For so long, both he and she had satisfied their hunger with a daily supply of pemmican, and she was startled to realize that, up until now, she hadn't missed the white man's fare. But now her stomach rumbled.

In the distance, beyond the fort, lay the Missouri River, or that body of water which Brave Wolf called the Big River. It looked black now, except for the diamond-like sparkles of the moonlight that played occasionally over its waves.

Even though the darkness hid the two of them, they both lay flat against the ground, with only the tips of their heads showing above the ridge of the hill. The wind stirred her hair, since she had long been without a bonnet. But she had become so used to its lack now that this no longer bothered her.

The taste of moisture in the air was chased here and there by the ever-constant wind of the prairie. But somehow, this, too, she had come to appreciate, and she realized that her senses had opened up to the environment around her. Never again would she take such beauty for granted. With that thought, the scents of grass and dirt, as well as that enticing smell of roasting meat from the fort warred with one another.

Her stomach groaned loudly. She ignored it, and whispered to him, "Do you think it's safe to go down there?"

He replied to her in a voice barely audible, "I do not know...yet. But I do not think so. We will find safe place to camp for night while I scout. As I have told you before, I am in...territory of enemy. We must be...alert to danger. *Itó*, come." He tapped her on the shoulder, and, together, they scooted down from their perch on the hill.

Quickly, he found a camping spot and constructed a shelter for them. Oddly, she had become so accustomed to the numerous debris huts that he erected, that it had gotten so that regardless of where they were, she looked upon these small shelters as home.

It was no different tonight, except that they had arrived at their destination earlier than what she had expected. This meant that they had the night before them.

After settling her into a sitting position in the shelter, he handed her the parfleches of pemmican and water that he always carried with him. But neither of them indulged in the usually satisfying food.

Instead, he bent toward her, and, after placing a gentle kiss on her lips, he said, "Will see if fort, and what...lies around it safe."

She nodded. This had become their usual ritual each morning when they had at last brought their night's journey to a halt. Somewhere along the way, she had become braver, and she had grown to trust his innate sense of danger so well that she had ceased insisting that she accompany him. She would wait for him this night, too, but she couldn't help adding a caution, saying, "Remember, my darling Mr. Brave Wolf, that the soldier forts are well guarded. Please do not take any unnecessary chances."

"I will remember, and I...am grateful for your concern." He smiled at her. "May that never end." He kissed her again, then he stood up to his feet, and like a phantom, he faded into the shadows of the fragrant, summer night.

***

He reappeared within the expected time, scratching on the entrance to their refuge to announce his return. But he had no more than crawled into their hideaway, than she smelled it—roasted meat.

Instead of being pleased, however, she admonished, "You went into that fort, with all those soldiers, at a time when your people and mine are at war. Didn't you?"

"*Hau, hau*."

"Oh, Brave Wolf, how could you? Had I known, I...I—"

He took hold of her hand and brought it to his chest. "Do you see that I am still...alive?"

"Yes, but please, do not take any more chances. I beg you to not do that."

He grinned at her, and the smile was so crooked and so outrageously sexy, she almost forgot to be concerned. But the moment was fleeting, for she *was* worried for him. And even when he said, "Have you not yet...observed that white man does not see what is right before him?" she was hardly consoled.

He went on to say, "My wife hungry. Does she...expect me to do nothing?"

"But I didn't say to—" She broke off whatever she might have said. Briefly, she shut her eyes as she realized that, whether she admonished him or not, he was who he was, and he would do as he was trained to do. So many times had he told her that he was a *toŋwéya,* a scout. She sighed, and at last she voiced, "It does smell lovely."

He laughed, and so contagious was it, she joined in with the humor, and she chuckled with him.

What followed was a feast of roasted beef, gravy, and even a little mashed potatoes. She ate so much of it that she at length began to feel as full as a stuffed pig. He, on the other hand, consumed little of it.

Noticing this, she asked, "Are you not hungry?"

"Not for the white man's meat," he answered. "But," he winked at her, "I am hungry...for other pleasures."

She giggled as delightfully as any schoolgirl might. "Oh?" she questioned. "And what might those 'pleasures' be?"

He placed an arm around her, and asked, "Have you finished your...meal?"

"Indeed, I have."

"Then," he said, setting the food aside, "let me show you of what I speak."

"Yes, please."

He urged her back, onto the softened floor of their refuge, which smelled of pine boughs, leaves, grass and his "blanket" of silken deerskin.

He followed her down as his lips unerringly found her own.

Oh, to remember this always. Tomorrow he would escort her into that fort, where her society would surely part them.

But that had not yet come to pass. They still had this night to share.

As he came up over her, she inhaled deeply, consciously memorizing little aspects about him: his scent, and his touch as his fingers trailed over her cheeks, to her neck, to her breasts. Always would she treasure the look of love that filled his blue eyes, still so strange a sight against the tan of his skin. Always, she thought, she would savor the feel of his skin against her own, always she would remember his intoxicating scent, the madness of his embrace, as well as her struggle to merge their bodies into one.

"Brave Wolf, please," she whispered. "I need to feel all of you against me. Can we not shed these clothes?"

He laughed softly. "I would be most honored," he answered, then continued, "Do you see how easily now that I...remove your...blouse and skirt? The white woman's clothing no longer *wakȟáŋ*...mystery to me."

She laughed slightly, then she reached up to grab hold of the ties that held up his leggings and breechcloth. As she pulled at those strings, she observed, "And do you see, my darling, that your own clothing is no longer a mystery to me?"

He chuckled. "I do not believe," he began, "that my clothes are as difficult to take off as yours."

But the buckskin was heavier than she had estimated it might be, and in the end, it required him to reach up and whisk it away.

And then, ah...heaven. As his naked body touched her own, she gloried in the delirious sensation of his love. It was as though they met not only skin to skin, but soul to soul.

But it appeared that even this might not be enough, at least for him, for he pleaded, "Tonight when we love, do not close eyes. For this last time we have...together, I would know that it is I you see, that it is I in your *caŋté*...your heart."

"I won't," she whispered. "But oh, Mr. Wolf, do you really not know? If you do not, let me ensure that you grasp that I am not mixed up about this, if I ever really was."

"What does word mean...mixed up?"

"To be muddled, or confused about something, I suppose. But how is it that you seem not to know? Have I been so remiss in telling you how I feel about you? If I have, let me correct that impression. I love you. You, Mr. Brave Wolf. I promise you that when we make love, I know exactly who it is that I hold in my arms...and it is you. Nor," she paused as her voice caught. She swallowed, hard, before she continued, "Nor do I wish it to be anyone else."

She watched as he gulped, observed him as his Adam's apple bobbed up and down. He held her; he simply held her against his breast. At length, he whispered, "Oh, that our ways...not so different."

"Yes."

"Realize though we must part, you should be aware *oíhaŋke waníl*...forever," he murmured, "you will be within me, here." He held his hand over his heart.

She cried. This moment between them was precious, yes, but it was unfortunately intermixed with sadness. What was she going to do without him?

She sobbed, "Please, please just love me tonight, for I don't believe that I can bear to be separated from you. I fear that having known you as I have these past few months, I will never be the same again."

"I, too," he agreed. "I, too might never be same."

She brought her gaze up to stare into his clear, blue eyes, hoping against hope that she might take a piece of him with her. He met that look, and his own gaze softened as he stared back at her.

He went on to murmur, "But perhaps we will never be...apart. For, when one loves enough, one's heart lives on *o'hinni*...always, for the *wana'gi*...spirit never dies. *Óhinni*...always...I promise. I will love you."

A tear escaped from her eye, making a path down her cheek. Gingerly, he brought up a finger to trail its path.

"You go where you must. I, too." He shut his eyes. "I, too."

"Then tonight, will you also keep your eyes open?"

"*O'hiŋni*...always. It is how I know that you close yours. So great is my admiration of you, that I wish to see you in great...passion, for it is beautiful, as are you."

She wept even as she gloried in the feel of his stiff masculinity against her. *Oh, dear Lord,* she prayed. *Give me strength, for I do not believe I can leave him.*

He kissed her, his lips opening to trace his tongue over her mouth, her teeth, her inner sanctum, using this embrace alone to make love to her. Gradually, he let his caress fall lower over her body, showering her cheeks, her neck, her shoulders with the same endearment.

"You are so beautiful," he murmured.

"As are you."

"And I would know you...fully."

"Yes, please," she answered. But she realized, when his kisses ranged lower and lower over her, that she hadn't understood what his use of the word "fully" had truly meant.

As he scooted down, he at last came to her most personal femininity, and he implored, "Open legs to me."

"What?"

"I would have this...memory."

"Yes," she whispered, "but I don't understand."

He came up into a sitting position down there at the junction of her legs and the trunk of her body. He breathed, "I know. Do not fight me. I will show you."

She gulped. He parted her legs, and he looked at her there, as though he beheld a treasure. With his fingers, he worshiped her, and so intense was the feeling, she thought she might surely lose her mind. She felt herself give to him, and when she became ready there, she felt so embarrassed that she brought her legs together.

But he was insistent, and he parted them again, observing, "You are so *gopeca*...beautiful. Do not *aógluta*...close to me. Let me have this memory, also."

She nodded.

And then his lips found her there, and she swooned, glad that she lay on her back, for she was certain she would have fallen. Only one word came to mind to describe the sensation—intense. So ultimate was the pleasure, she met her release at once.

The feeling went on and on, and when at last it was over, he remained where he was, taking his weight upon his forearm, as his touch remained there upon her. He gave her a brief grin as he stated, "Never again will I...wash this hand."

She laughed softly. But if he wished to know "all" of her, she realized that she, too, shared a similar desire, and she whispered, "My dear Mr. Wolf, I believe I would have this memory of you, also."

Momentarily, he looked startled, but the impression was quickly gone, as a look of joy settled over his countenance.

"Brave Wolf, I do believe that we need to change positions."

"*Yazonta*...you flatter me."

"Is that all you think this is about? I assure you that I desire to imprint all of you upon my memory, too."

He inhaled deeply, yet slowly, they traded places, and as she repeated movement for movement all he had done for her, she heard the low growl that sounded in his throat. It gave her courage, and soon she had maneuvered her position until she became able to give him kiss by kiss a clear idea of the pleasure he had given her.

But the thrill was not all on his side; the act itself, and the musky scent of him would remain impressed upon her memory always. With her body, she did adore him.

Soon, it became apparent that the sensation was too much for him, and quickly, he pulled her up to him, reversing their situation. As he settled her beneath him, and as he joined his body to hers, he murmured into her ear, "Remember, do not close eyes."

"I will not do so, my love. I promise."

And so it was. As his thrusts within her became more and more rapid, neither one of them looked away from the other. Admiration, love and the beauty of who and what he was, impressed itself upon her heart. Forever, she knew, it would be so.

They stared so deeply into each other's eyes that it seemed as though they met and touched one another as independent spirits. Never had she known such exquisite intimacy as this. Never had she experienced such soul to soul adoration. If ever she had been in doubt of her love for this man, such qualms fled before the ongoing wonder of him.

Over and over, on and on, they adored one another. The physical exultation built into an excited fervor until, as though of one heart, they fell over the extreme precipice of love together. At that moment, so close were they in spirit, she knew his thoughts, and she suspected that he might be attuned to hers, also. It was beautiful. He was beautiful.

Yes, it might be true that they would have to part, and the imminent loss would be terrible, but always and forever, they would love. She felt this truth to the depth of her being. And nothing could ever take that away from her—from them.

Only time would tell, of course, but somehow, in some way, their coming together eased her pain, if only a little.

***

After a week of lingering in the shadows on the hills above the fort, and partaking in the many pleasures of the flesh, Mia began to wonder why they hesitated to approach the fort. Not that she was anxious to leave him; it was only that she didn't understand.

So it was that after a week's waiting and wondering, she raised the question, "Is there a reason why we do not go down there?"

He answered her at once, "*Hau, hau*, there is." But he didn't elaborate.

They were lying down within their crude refuge, and she reckoned that the time was somewhere around midnight. Earlier in the evening, they had made glorious love, and since then they had barely moved, were still basking in the warm afterglow of deep affection. For the moment, they were both stretched out naked on the ground, sheltered on all sides by their hideaway. His robe lay beneath them, but he had thrown no sheet or other covering atop them.

She had snuggled in closely to him, her leg, from the knee down, thrown over him. She murmured, "Will you share that rationale with me?"

"*Hau*, I will."

She waited for him to continue, but when that didn't occur at once, she asked, "And the cause of this is...?"

He sighed, as though he anticipated that his answer might be cause for friction between them. At length, however, he pointed to himself, and muttered, "This one must know if we make child. Must wait for *wiyáwapi*...month, or more. Woman will know. This one," again, he pointed to himself, "will know, too."

He was referring to her monthly menses, of course. Well, there it was, clearly stated; the problem of pregnancy. She'd suspected weeks ago that he would not let this matter go away easily, that in some future time, she would have to come to terms with his stand on this matter. Although she entertained mixed feelings about making a baby with him, hope that it might be true outweighed the negative. Of course, if true, this fact would bring on many more troubling obstacles that she would be required to face. But, after all, those problems would be more welcome than their eventual parting, wouldn't they?

He hadn't finished speaking out on the matter, however, and he continued, "Has Little Dawn Bird missed a month, yet?"

"Ah...no, I haven't. Last month, when that event happened, we'd had to stop on the trail until it was over."

"Because Lakota man cannot be with woman then. Forbidden."

"Yes, I remember you telling me about that. If my calculations are correct, I believe that my monthly menses is due in a few days."

He nodded. "Then we will wait for time it takes to...discover the *wówicaǩe*...truth of this."

"And if I am pregnant?"

"Then you will go home with me."

"And we will live there as a married couple?"

"*Hau*. This is so."

"And what will happen to Walks-in-sunshine?"

"She will be wife two."

"My darling Mr. Wolf, I cannot do it."

"I *wábleza*...understand. Child make difference. If there is child, we must not...part. All else not matter."

"But it matters to me."

"I know." He sighed. "Many...troubles this will cause. Yet, there is no other way."

"I—"

He brought a finger up to cover her lips. "May not be. We wait. If child made, then we continue this *kiciza*...fight."

She chuckled slightly. Leave it to this man to easily brush aside such a very important conversation. She couldn't help but observe aloud, "Yes, I guess we'll wait and see—and, if it is so, we will have that argument, I promise."

She could hear the laughter in his voice as he responded, "*Hau, hau*, I know. But it will be *kiciza wašté*...good fight.."

She laughed. She suspected he was right.

CHAPTER TWENTY

It wasn't to be. She wondered if the simple act of talking about it had brought on her monthly flow, because by morning of the next day, she was left in no doubt that she was not pregnant.

She didn't even need to tell him; he had informed her of the fact. She felt...disappointed. Yes, there would have been problems had they made a child, but the idea of staying with Brave Wolf and bringing a baby into the world with him so outweighed the idea of having to leave him. She'd even thought that she would welcome the inevitable disagreement.

But that was taken from her now.

Luckily for her, they waited a few more days until her monthly flow had ceased. But though those several days might have been filled with even more time spent with him, the reality was the opposite. As he had already shown her, Lakota warriors didn't associate with women who were experiencing their monthly time. He cared for her, yes; ensured she had food and water, but he left her alone.

However, it couldn't last, and the truth of their parting came about too soon. She had to go home.

It happened quickly. She had helped him to disassemble their temporary shelter, had even aided him in erasing the evidence of their stay. And with each footprint she wiped away, she shed a tear.

So this was it. On this day, they would part. Though she'd known this moment would have to come eventually, it didn't eradicate the loss—the extreme deprivation of his company, nor make it any easier to bear.

And now, here they lay, full length upon their stomachs, stretched out at the very top of a hill overlooking the fort. Tears filled her eyes. Gazing briefly at him, she witnessed that he fought a similar problem, for there was a wetness forming in his eyes, as well.

"Because we are at war," she asked, "what will happen to you when you take me down there?"

"I do not know."

"I won't let them do anything bad to you."

"You might have...little way to keep that from *akípa*...happening."

"But my father will be able to intervene," she answered. "He has strong and important ties to this fort. In that way, I believe I will be able to protect you."

He grimaced. "Do I look like I wear dresses?"

She giggled, the image of that so ridiculous. "Of course not," she replied. "But perhaps the time has come for me to ensure your safety, rather than the other way around."

"I do not need your...protection. *Itó*, come, let us arise from here, and see what this day yet holds for us."

"But, please, I thought there were stories told of warriors who have brought in white captives, and who surrendered those to the authorities, and that the brave men who had done this were then killed."

"*Hau, hau,* it is true."

"I will not let them do that to you."

He brought up his hand closest to her to run the backs of his fingers down her cheek. "What will be may be...difficult," he uttered philosophically. "But I must do as I have *wacín*...intended. I will fulfill my *yugalkiya*...oath to you, and lead you to fort. We must go now."

"No," she uttered. "I will take that path to the fort alone. No one will harm me. You stay here."

"Do you *aikśiŋkiya*...insult me? Do you think I would hide behind woman's skirt?"

"No, of course not. I—"

"Then, come. *Itó*." He stood. "We will discover if white man has any *wókinihaŋŋ*...honor."

Because she could think of no ready response to counter his statement on this matter, she came up to stand beside him. Reluctantly, although together—she following along behind him—they began the long trail that would take them to the fort known as Fort Leavenworth, the same one that the Lakota Indians called the "prison fort."

***

As the events of the day played out, the worst that she had envisioned evaded them. In truth, except for several curious stares as they made a path through the town of Leavenworth, their exposure went barely noticed.

To gain entry into the fort did require traversing first through the town of Leavenworth, and so it was almost an hour or more before they came to stand on the outskirts of the fort. Before her, she could see row after row of the two-story, white-painted, wooden barracks; the look of her own civilization. It was hardly a pleasing sight, since Mia was still of a fearful mind. What might happen to Brave Wolf here?

Before entry into the fort, a brown-haired, bearded soldier met them. But even this event went unmarked by any animosity. The soldier did insist that Brave Wolf disarm himself of his weapons: his rifle, his several guns and ammunition, his knives, his bow and arrows. Curiously, the guard did not insist that she, too, must follow this same protocol.

Brave Wolf frowned at their loss, clearly displeased, and Mia understood why, for she realized that he could not be certain what his fate might be here. Also, in all the time she'd known him, he'd made it well known that he considered it his duty to protect her. How could he accomplish this without arms? But, be that as it may, he surrendered his weapons without incident.

That seemed the worst of it, thank heaven. Armed or not, Brave Wolf stood at her side as she inquired where she might be able to send a telegram. Although the soldier pointed her in the general direction, he did not volunteer to accompany her there. This was left to Brave Wolf, who, leading the way, escorted her to the communications office.

The telegraph room was housed in the complex of the

commandant's offices, which stood alone from the barracks. Looking very much like the image of the other buildings in Fort Leavenworth in terms of architecture and color, the office they sought was clearly marked with a sign that read simply, "Telegraph."

Could Brave Wolf read? She wondered, because whether he was able to do so or not, he led her directly to the communications office without incident.

It was ridiculously easy to write the telegram and send it to her father, and it was accomplished within a few moments. Only after it was done, however, did she request an interview with the commandant of Fort Leavenworth, Nelson A. Miles.

Her inquiry was granted at once, for the commandant was "in," and no one seemed concerned that a young, American Indian accompanied her. Upon being shown to his office, Mia was surprised to find Commander Miles to be a young man, for she would have guessed that such a position of authority would have been occupied by a man of greater years. Brown-haired, with a mustache, he appeared to be little more than thirty. She could only hope that his youth would not affect the outcome of her interview adversely.

Her wish came true—almost.

Introductions were barely over, when Commander Miles observed, none too pleasantly, "I see that you have an Indian warrior there at your side, Mrs. Carlson. Is he your captive or are you his?"

Though shocked over the commandant's lack of manners, as well as his open antagonism toward Brave Wolf, Mia simply smiled pleasantly at him, stating, "This man came to my aid after our wagon train was attacked by white men, Commander Miles. I was the only survivor of that fight, and this man alone is responsible for bringing me here safely. Several times, in coming here, he has saved my life. I'm certain, then, that you will understand that I will insist that he accompany me, so long as I am at the fort."

Miles didn't acknowledge her request. Instead, he questioned her further, asking, "And how long do you anticipate remaining as our guest here?"

Although Commandant Miles's tone of voice was more than a little antagonistic, she answered him pleasantly, saying, "I cannot be certain of that. I have only sent a telegram to my father, Senator Sheehan, asking him to please wire me the wherewithal to buy a ticket home."

Commander Miles cleared his throat before inquiring, "Your father is Senator Sheehan?"

"Yes, he is."

"Well," Miles said, anger coloring his words, "why didn't you enlighten me of this at once?"

"I didn't think it mattered, sir."

"Of course it matters. It is important," he replied, the articulation of his words reminding her of that of a spoiled little boy. "I will see to it that you have escort and protection here at Fort Leavenworth as long as you shall stay."

"I need none of that," she answered. "Mr. Brave Wolf here will accompany me. I require nothing else."

"I will be the judge of that, Mrs. Carlson."

That said, Commandant Miles rose up from his seat behind his desk, and summoning his secretary, he requested a Lieutenant E. Johnson to be brought to his office forthwith.

It was quickly done, and Lieutenant Johnson turned out to be a somewhat older gentleman, who was perhaps in his early to mid-forties. Married, with no children, he took command of Mia's welfare at the fort, and accompanied her to his own married quarters. There he introduced her to his wife, Alice, who insisted that Mia be given a room of her own within their home. That this didn't include Brave Wolf troubled her.

But she worried without cause. Brave Wolf didn't leave her, nor did he allow the Lieutenant to direct his own actions. Instead, he set up watch at the entrance to Lieutenant Johnson's home.

A return telegram was not long in coming, and, within a single day, her father had made arrangements for her return home with all due haste. Lieutenant Johnson and his wife would accompany her.

It was all done quickly and without incident. No one bothered her, or Brave Wolf, and too soon, within less than a week, Mia found herself on the verge of boarding a train that would take her to Washington D.C. Gone was her overly soiled, blue dress. Being of a similar size as Mia, Alice Johnson had given her several dresses, some that fit her quite well. Though she still wore the moccasins that Brave Wolf had made for her, it gave her a feeling of pride that during their last few moments together, she stood next to him in a pink dress that wasn't tattered and dirty. Even her hair was styled in ringlets tied with ribbons, which was the current fashion.

The moment of parting had at last come, and there sat that big, black engine, which looked more like an enemy than the salvation it was supposed to be. The big locomotive was hooked up to four other cars, for she had learned that, for safety, she would travel home by special permit and military escort.

The train was due to pull out of the station within minutes. She was close to breaking down, and she knew she held herself together by a thin veil of control. Never far from grief, she wondered how she was to force herself to leave Brave Wolf. But leave him she must; they had long ago failed to reach a compromise. Though she'd long known this would come to be, still, she could barely believe that this was it. She would never see him again, and that fact felt as though it might completely destroy her.

Was she doing what was right for both of them? Perhaps she might be, for at last he would be free to return to his tribe and to the woman he had left there; he would arrive there conscience-free. Walks-in-sunshine would welcome him; at least, she would if she were smart.

And she? She would return to her home in the East, as she was meant to do. From this point forward, however, thousands of miles would separate them. Though it was surely the only right act for them both, it didn't stop her heart from breaking.

They stood together on a slight hill overlooking the train station. They did not touch, which was the Indian custom of proper behavior when a couple was seen together in public. He had been very clear on this detail.

But perhaps it was unimportant, for they were entwined spiritually, and maybe that was all that mattered.

"I," he murmured, his voice low and husky, "will say prayer for you that...journey be safe."

"Come with me," she pleaded one last time.

He inhaled deeply; a long moment of silence stretched out between them before he uttered, his voice still low and hoarse, "I cannot."

She swallowed hard.

He turned toward her, and, taking her by her shoulders, he brought her body around so that she faced him. He touched her forehead with a single finger. "Always," he whispered, "we be together here in memory, and," he brought his hand to his heart, "...here."

She cried. She didn't think she could do this.

"Doing deed that is right not...easy, very much." Even he was crying, and he added, his voice breaking, "Will always love you. Never will love die."

She sobbed, "I will always love you, too. I—"

Drat his adherence to the Indian custom of stoically showing no emotion in the open; it would have to be set aside, if only this once. In protest of the practice, she threw herself into his embrace, and, as his arms came around her to hold her, she cried, "I cannot bear to leave you."

"I, too," he uttered. "I, too."

And then he kissed her, long and hard, as if he, too, declared the Lakota practice outdated. He drew back from her slightly, bringing his forehead against her own. He murmured, "I will watch you...as you go. Will stay here till...mystery *travois*...train is gone. Have scouted. No trace of enemy. Journey, I think, be safe."

She didn't respond with words. Instead, she drew his head down toward her, and, standing on tiptoe, she reached up to kiss him. Her lips lingered over his, reminding her all over again of how much she loved this man. And then, before she lost herself to him completely, she spun out of his arms and raced down the hill, as though only in this manner could she bring herself to do the deed.

Tears streamed down her face, but she didn't bother to wipe them away. Perhaps these tears were her silent prayer of wishing him safety.

As soon as she placed a foot on the step of the train, the engine moved, and slowly—so very slowly—the long line of cars pulled away from the landing. She stood on the platform of the caboose, the last vehicle in the procession, her gaze trained on *him*. The train chugged and spat. Whistles blew, yet for all that, inch by slow inch, the Pullman carried her farther and farther away from him. Her heart aching, she prayed, "May life be kind to you, my love, my darling Mr. Wolf, my husband...."

For hours long after she could no longer see him, she remained where she was. She would never be the same. She knew she wouldn't be. With one last prayer, she said, "May God guide your path, and may your life with Walks-in-sunshine be good."

As was her belief, she made the motion of a cross, from head to belly, from shoulder to shoulder. With tears streaming down her face, she turned away.

***

Brave Wolf didn't immediately set his path to return home. Instead, he followed those railcars, her escort, for many miles, running beside it at a fast clip. Trees and shrubs hindered his progress, but he kept pace with the train, nonetheless. He saw that she never turned her back away from her vigilance, that she lingered on the platform of the caboose for long moments after he knew that she could no longer see the place where he had once stood. He stayed his path, next to and close to the railroad. He witnessed her prayer, then saw at last that she slowly spun away.

That his heart still beat, though it was breaking, seemed incredible to him. But so many times had they spoken of this moment, which they knew must come, and never had they reached an agreement on how to stay together. They could not. Their cultures were too different, their values too greatly opposed.

At least, he had been truthful. Never, not ever would he forget her.

Would she remember him in years to come? He could only hope that it would be so....

CHAPTER TWENTY-ONE
LAKOTA TERRITORY, THE PLATTE RIVER AREA
1874, Three Years Later—The Sioux Wars

Brave Wolf and his cousin, Speaks True, scaled the butte's wall that would take them to the top of the plateau which overlooked the Platte River. They had left their ponies, which were burdened with buffalo meat, at the foot of these hills. The morning was young, and both young men were anxious to honor the Creator with their prayers, for only in this way, with their hearts filled with good feelings, could they continue onward toward home.

"Truly, I was happy to learn of your favor," called out Speaks True in the Lakota language, as both men employed the use of their hands and feet to ascend the wall of the cliff. It was a dangerous climb they were engaged upon, yet they each set about the task with laughter and a feeling of camaraderie. "My cousin," continued Speaks True, "I feared your response to our marriage upon your return, as did my wife, Walks-in-sunshine. I know you loved her, and she, you. Only now, years later, have I courage to speak to you of it."

Brave Wolf shrugged, gaining a foothold and pulling himself up onto the high ledge. Squatting down, and lending a hand to his cousin, he helped him up onto the same foothold, then replied, "Ours was a love of our youth, and it was an affection that was destined to fade when countered by a more mature devotion. It is this strong love that she feels for you, my cousin, for I have seen how she looks at you and showers you with adoration when she thinks you are not looking. It is good. You are a lucky man."

"*Hau, hau,* that I am. Yet, I have worried that you would have bad feelings toward me."

"I understand," replied Brave Wolf, as both men stood up straight, looking out upon the vista. "But surely this does not still trouble you. Instead of hatred, we became *kola's* to each other, closer than even brothers."

"*Hau, hau,* it is so, yet I felt it important to speak to you about this, for I have a favor to ask you."

Brave Wolf nodded. "I will listen."

"This war," Speaks True began, "is bad. Almost daily, our people fight the bluecoats, and I have participated in many of these battles, never envisioning that I might not return. Yet for many suns now, I have come to fear for Walks-in-sunshine and our son. What would become of her and our child if I were to fall?"

"Her people would care for him, as well as your family, also."

"But if her own people, and mine, are gone, too? So many of our families have died in these wars."

As Brave Wolf gazed out upon the view from the top of this bluff, his stare took in the beauty of the rugged hills, the river that rushed through the valley below, the clear blue of the sky reflected there. Not knowing what to say, he remained silent. It was true. These last few years had taken a toll on his people.

"My cousin," Speaks True persisted, "I would share words with you as one man to another, for as you say, we are now *kola's*. Were my own brothers still alive, I might not have reason to seek your help."

Brave Wolf nodded, steeling himself for the words he did not wish to hear, yet suspected were coming.

Speaks True sighed, then carried on, "I would ask that you take Walks-in-sunshine for wife should I go into battle, never to return. Since I no longer have male relatives who would see to my wife's needs, I would ask that you consider shouldering the burden of my family should there be a need to do so."

Brave Wolf paused only a moment before saying, "I am honored that you ask this of me, for I would regard it my duty to care for your wife and your son, and I would shower Walks-in-sunshine with the love that you give her now, to the best of my ability. Realize, however," he cautioned, "that my heart belongs to another. Will always belong to another."

Speaks True looked momentarily taken aback. "But, my cousin," he responded, "how can this be? You are unmarried."

"I am not unmarried," Brave Wolf returned, "and I love my wife, still love my wife. But she is far away from here, in a place that I do not know. And because of this, I may never see her again."

Speaks True seemed suddenly tongue-tied, and he became silent, until, in due time, he asked, "Does anyone else know this?"

"My father does, but only because he suspected from the start, when I first met this woman, that I might lose my heart to her. I believe that my mother may be aware of this, also, for she once asked my father why I did not choose to take another woman as wife."

"Then it is well," rejoined Speaks True, "that I ask you to do this for me, since Walks-in-sunshine could bring joy to your life again."

"*Hau, hau*. My cousin, your words touch my heart. Yet, even in that time when she might bring light back into my life—were it to ever be needed that we join together—I fear that my spirit would still be burdened with grief. *Iho,* it was I who encouraged my wife, whom I still love, to leave me."

Once more, Speaks True met Brave Wolf's declaration with silence. How long they might have stood there in such a way was hard to determine, because slowly and silently, there upon the wind, drifted a scent of smoke, bringing with it another, more distinct and destructive odor: death.

Alarmed, Brave Wolf sought to discover its dangerous point of origin. He could not; it appeared that Wind was faster than Sight this day. He, who was trained to see events miles into the distance, could not physically determine the source. But the wind was blowing in from the south, which must surely account for the direction of the trouble.

Fear gripped him. A fight waged somewhere so close to their position here, that the wind felt bold enough to whisper the tale of death to them. Worse, Speak True's village was not far from here, and its direction was south.

Speaks True must have realized the threat at the same moment as he, for his *kola* said only, "*She* is in that camp."

Immediately, the two took to action. Speaks True practically jumped down from ledge to ledge, hurrying down the butte's wall. Brave Wolf clambered beside him, his descent as quick as his cousin's. Reaching the valley floor, and working together, they made a quick cache of the buffalo meat, then each one of them jumped onto his mount.

Either sensing their master's fear, or aware that something was very wrong, the ponies sped away with the least of encouragement.

As the two friends rushed toward the impending peril, Brave Wolf spoke a prayer beneath his breath. "Creator, let us be wrong about this. Let it be that the menace is not to our own village. Let it be little more than a prairie fire."

Even as he said the prayer, he feared the worst....

***

Their camp lay hours away, and, by the time Speaks True and Brave Wolf rode into camp, it was too late. The scent of burning flesh scented the air with sickness, and simmering fires still licked through the site as though greedy to destroy all living creatures, even to the skins of their lodges.

The once gay and happy village lay about them in ruins, and scattered ashes. Worse, bodies of Brave Wolf's Lakota kinsmen lay stretched out over the ground. Nothing sounded in this place except for the occasional crack of timber, as the fire sent lodge poles crumbling to the ground.

Nothing stirred. Not even a dog. Possessions were strewn about the camp in a haphazard and offensive fashion. Soon, too, these might succumb to the fiery blaze catching hold of all that had once been treasured possessions. Everywhere were the dead: women, children, babies, youthful boys and old men, who had died still clutching guns or arrows to their breast.

"Go find your family," ordered Brave Wolf to Speaks True, who in his shock, could barely move. "She and your son might yet be in hiding. Call for her. Let her know we are here. I will see to the others."

With tears streaming down Speaks True's face, his lips trembled as he whispered, "She must be alive."

Brave Wolf nodded, repeating, "She must be." He believed it, too, if only because it would be too difficult and too heartbreaking to believe she and her son might be found otherwise.

He would see to the rest of these people, his people; he would determine if anyone here were still alive. He choked back his own tears, for he had known and loved every member of this village.

He found no survivors. Had no one hid from the bluecoats? Women and children were taught from an early age to run and hide. As youths, their games included the sport of hide and seek. Surely someone would have.

Studying the tracks left behind, he could "see" the conflict as it had played out. The bluecoats had hit the camp in the inky darkness before dawn. It was all here to be read in the clues left behind.

They had assaulted the camp when the Indians were asleep, at their most vulnerable. There hadn't been time to hide. But surely someone would have managed it.

A masculine cry split through the air, and Brave Wolf shut his eyes against the pain, knowing what his friend had found.... Tears gathered in his eyes as he turned to pace toward his cousin, his *kola*, who would need Brave Wolf to stand strong. But even as he approached Speaks

True, tears streaked down his face.

This is wrong, so very wrong. None of these people ever harmed the society of the white man. They were a peaceful tribe of Sioux and Cheyenne; they never raised a hand to fight in this bloody war. By what reason, then, did the bluecoats justify this murder? That these people were merely Indian?

Hatred filled his soul, hatred at a society that arrogantly believed it was better than any other, and that all others needed to be destroyed; hatred for anyone in uniform, hatred for the white man. No, he could never hate the white man completely. His own mother was white, and he could never hate Little Dawn Bird.

But he could despise himself for still loving this woman who was his wife, and who belonged to the bluecoat society; he could hate this love, which even now he could not deny. As he slowly paced toward Speaks True, he braced himself for what was to come, for what he was about to see, for although she had married another, he would never think about Walks-in-sunshine with any other emotion than that of love.

His heart burst at the vision of the carnage here, and he said a prayer of thanks that this was not his own village, for he was only a visitor here. His people and camp, including his mother, his father and his two sisters, lay farther north of here.

Pacing slowly forward, he cried at the sight before him. Walks-in-sunshine lay lifeless upon the ground, her son at her side. He shook his head and jerked it to the left. Not only had the soldiers killed her and the child, the soldiers had raped her also. What manner of men were these, who would kill and disgrace the innocent?

Brave Wolf knelt beside Walks-in-sunshine's body; he pulled down her dress to hide the evidence of the white man's lust. In this way, he could bring her honor in death. Speaks True was bent forward, over her breast, crying as though his heart might never heal. Tenderly, Brave Wolf checked the pulse of the child, finding no life whatsoever, and that's when it happened: a vision of what could have been hit him as though it were a deadly blow. This could have been his own village; it could have been Little Dawn Bird lying here instead of Walks-in-sunshine, had he brought her home three years ago.

He shut his eyes against the pain of that realization, and momentarily, he was so stunned, he couldn't move. But eventually, he realized he could not give in to the weakness of the magnitude of this loss. Though he, too, wept, he knew he must begin the long process of honoring the dead. No one else was here to do it; Speaks True would require time with his love, to say good-bye to her in his own way.

Though other warriors would ultimately return to camp, and although they would lend their hands to the task of paying tribute to the dead, it would be his responsibility to ensure that each of these beloved people were dressed and well-prepared to walk the good road to the Sandhills, there to reunite with their ancestors.

Besides, he realized that there was much to be praised about hard, physical labor, when grief became too heavy. His elders had often advised this.

So it was that Brave Wolf set himself to the sad and debilitating task ahead of him, and he didn't stop to eat, nor to sleep, not even when other warriors came home. Some lent their strength in the duty of honoring the dead, but most bore too much loss to do little more than grieve.

This was a bad war, and he, being of mixed blood, felt it deeply. *She* had kept him from joining the Lakota in their fight against the bluecoats; until now, his love for her hadn't allowed him to raise a hand against her kind. But now, more than ever, he would enter into this battle, and he would fight to win. And if he died in the process of defending his homeland, then at least he might rejoice that, if that moment came upon him, her memory would perhaps never haunt him again....

CHAPTER TWENTY-TWO
TWO YEARS LATER
Washington D.C.
May, 1876

The little chit would do as told, or else....

He was tired of having to wait. But, although his patience was wearing thin, he would continue to bide his time, for their eventual union and the pleasure of the kill awaited only his expert touch.

The man's black, handlebar mustache drooped into a frown, as though it might imitate his ungodly mood. Standing back from the stately window of his office, his figure hidden to any discerning eye, Max Greiner pushed back the drab, silken curtain, watching as the red-headed senator disembarked from his buggy. The senator was of medium height, not quite as tall as Greiner's six-foot figure, and certainly not as slim or well-muscled as he.

Five years—for five years, he'd stood aside, pretending affection for the wench, waiting the necessary time for Mia Carlson's grief to heal. Yet, in all these years, he had yet to finagle himself into a state of matrimony with her.

Oh, yes, for all appearances, his heart was that of a man formerly betrothed, a would-be groom who would settle for friendship and the sharp edge of rejection. But that was about to change. The senator would bow to this new piece of blackmail, and his daughter would act as he dictated, or else.

Ah, the "or else" suited the black edge of his temper, and Greiner grinned, envisioning the exact pain, the exquisite torture that he might inflict upon her, once he had her. Ah, the pleasure of that moment when all his schemes would take fruition, suited his blackened heart.

And so it would come to pass, he promised himself. For this new piece of blackmail would ruin the senator and his precious daughter once and for all, unless...

His smile widened, but the gesture was hardly one of humor. Yes, the waiting was finished, done, no more.

Mark his words.

***

Senator Sheehan's countenance wore a frown. Worry lines had etched themselves into permanent wrinkles over his high forehead, and his steps, as he climbed down his buggy, were shaky at best.

He was too old for this, he told himself as he stared up at *Retrouvaille*, the sprawling Virginia farm that he and his wife had built with their own hands. *Retrouvaille*, a French word meaning "to rediscover an old love," was aptly named, for both he and his wife had found such joy in this land. It had become as though it were an old friend.

But this day, the senator's attention was far removed from the beauty of the landscape. Perhaps, his predicament might be less had he spent more time at home these last few years. Instead, he had stayed away from here, residing in the nation's capital, fighting for others' rights, instead of his own. If only his wife were here; if only she could add her voice and her wisdom to this new problem.

But it was not to be. She had gone on to another realm of existence long ago, and he was left as before, with only her image to guide him. In the past, he'd had a young daughter to raise without her mother. He'd done his best, for he loved his daughter as much as the woman, who after all these years, still haunted his dreams.

Mia's nanny, Miss Bailey, an Irish woman, was practically a member of their family, so close were his daughter and the woman. Once, there had been a time when he had considered marriage to the woman.

But he hadn't. He couldn't, for his heart knew only one woman.

Besides, Mia so resembled her mother, that he could never forget the one who had stolen away his heart long ago.

What was he to do?

He was only slightly aware that his usually proud figure presented a hunched image this day, as he walked up the steps and into the foyer of his home. So many scenarios crossed his mind that he was distracted from his usual joy at coming home. Over and over, he considered what he might say to her, what he might do to convince his daughter to do as Max Greiner demanded. Could he really demand that she marry the man?

Because of Greiner's father, the younger Greiner had always been a family friend. Certainly that man and his daughter shared an affectionate relationship, but the spark of desire, so necessary in a marriage, was clearly absent. Hadn't Mia made her feelings on the matter evident? Hadn't she fled into the West rather than bind herself to Greiner?

But there was no mistaking the threat. All of the senator's good work, all of his struggles to introduce legislation aimed at raising up the common man, would be for naught if Greiner went public with this latest scandal. Though Greiner hadn't stated as much to him in words, the menace that he might was very real.

The joke of it all was that it wasn't true. He hadn't accepted a bribe from the opposition. But without all of the facts coming to light, it could appear as if he had done exactly that. Indeed, the truth could be easily hidden. Hadn't Greiner stressed that point? Hadn't he offered to help hush up the entire affair?

But at a price.

Insistence upon the marriage in the past had caused his daughter to flee. What would she do now?

No, he couldn't do it. Not again. He loved his daughter, and even his work in the nation's capital paled into insignificance when set next to the affinity they shared. He would have to consult her. Perhaps she liked Greiner well enough to accept his proposal. Chances were slim, but he would ask; he would try to do it in such a way that she wouldn't sense his own problem.

He hadn't sent word to *Retrouvaille* of his intentions to return home. So it came as no surprise that no one was here to greet him. This was for the best; he needed privacy, not the problems of a household where he had been long absent.

As his footsteps echoed off the walls in the long hallway, he could only marvel that he had spent so much time away from a piece of the world that he loved so much. Paintings of his ancestors, several of his wife and young daughter, lined the great corridor. He stopped before his favorite canvas that carried the image of his wife. Looking at her now, he wondered if it were right that his work in Washington D.C. should take such precedence over his life here.

Was it really five years since Mia had returned home? She rarely spoke of the massacre that he'd known had taken the life of her deceased husband, and all others in that wagon train. Those who worked in his office had appraised him of it all those years ago, and he had assumed his own daughter had been killed there. Mentally, he had buried her.

Coming here now reminded him again of his joy when he had received her telegram, asking for his assistance in returning home. But Mia had arrived home a changed woman; no longer was she the frivolous youngster of his memory. Indeed, though she didn't seem to exude unhappiness, still, she rarely smiled.

He hadn't had the inclination or the time, all those years ago, to explore the details of what had happened to her. He hadn't wanted to, for he blamed Carlson for the change in her behavior; had felt that speaking to Mia about that man would have placed a shadow over her grief.

Let her heart heal, he'd thought. Besides, duty to the State of Virginia, to his people and to the Congress of the United States had held the upper hand in his conscience.

How had these past five years passed so quickly? He'd always meant to seek out his daughter and to help her come to terms with her grief. But he'd never done it, and his hopes that she would recover from her grief had never come to pass. Secretly, she cried. Miss Bailey had told him so.

Anger at that good-for-nothing Carlson briefly overtook rational thought. Personally, he'd never liked the man. Leave it to such a man to go and get himself killed, leaving behind a grieving widow.

Senator Sheehan sighed. Enough thinking. What he needed was more action. To that end, he decided he would retire to his office and seek an audience with Mia at all possible speed.

It was the only way.

***

Mia wasn't in.

"What's that you say? She is taking a walk through the woods?"

"Aye, that she is. 'Tis quite a common, yet queer activity that she be doing, make no mistake."

"When will she return, Miss Bailey?"

"To tell God's truth, rarely it is that she, herself, returns until after dark."

"After dark? My daughter? Trekking in the woods? And after dark? When did this start?"

"Has been this way, and no mistake, since she returned."

"Since she returned? But if memory serves me well, I recall that Mia has long held a fear of the deep woods that surrounded *Retrouvaille.* Were you here, Miss Bailey, when as a little girl, she came face to face with a bear in those very woods? Her only escape was to climb high up in a tree, and from that perch alone, scream and scream until I found her. The bear had gone by then, but not so her fear. From that time forward, I have never known her to set foot in those woods—ever."

"Aye," agreed Miss Bailey, "I remember that well."

Silently, he cursed his absence from here; he no longer recognized the changes in Mia. Had that massacre out West changed her so greatly?

Or was it still her grief due to the loss of her husband? Did she now not care that she might again face a bear in the forest?

"I believe," he told Miss Bailey, "that I have let my work in Washington D.C. interfere with Mia's recovery. Perhaps I might yet rectify that mistake. Maybe, while she is still out, I might let myself into her studio that I might find clues as to why, in all this time, she has not been able to lay claim again to her sunny disposition. Will you accompany me there, Miss Bailey?"

"Aye, Senator Sheehan, I will. For I have long been afeard that her heart is low."

"Yes, indeed." Placing his hand beneath Miss Bailey's elbow, he led the way to Mia's private room on the upper floor of *Retrouvaille,* her studio.

***

Retrouvaille boasted only the one room on the top floor, and his daughter had, since time out-of-mind, claimed the place as her own. Circular in shape, with three-hundred-and-sixty-degree floor-to-ceiling windows, the room had once been the favorite abode of his wife, for she, too, had been an artist.

But Mia had made the place hers a long, long time ago, and he had respected her privacy. The room had been constructed with the creativity of an artist in mind, for the chamber looked out upon *Retrouvaille's* own private mountaintop. Enchanted views and untouched forests demanded an artist's brush, and indeed, during her teen years, Mia had painted and had sold several of her oil creations.

Not knowing what he might discover in her studio, Sheehan, with the accompaniment of Miss Bailey, climbed the stairs to the upper floor, he with concealed anticipation, hoping he might uncover a clue as to why, five years after her escape from death in the West, she remained reclusive. He was not to be disappointed.

The door wasn't locked. Few of the rooms in *Retrouvaille* were bolted, for there was no need.

Throwing back the door, he escorted Miss Bailey into the studio first, then followed her into Mia's private domain. He had no more than stepped foot into the room when he stopped short. What was this?

Certainly he espied a painting of Jeffrey Carlson on display here, but there was only the one. Everywhere else—exhibited lovingly upon one easel after another—was picture after picture of the West. Yes, indeed, of the West. But more. In each of these paintings was the image of a young Indian man. Never painted in one pose, alone, his image in canvas was yet bigger than life; his face, his figure caught from every possible angle, always looking back upon the artist, as though she might catch his gaze forever.

Yes, over there were several depictions of the prairie, but in the distance was that same young man, bending, straightening, walking. Over and over again, it was always the same man. Indeed, even in young Carlson's painting, a faint image of the Indian stood at ease in the background.

"Who is this man?" Sheehan spoke his thoughts aloud.

Miss Bailey answered the question. "To tell God's truth, he is the man your daughter, herself, loves."

"Yes, yes," Sheehan answered. "I can see that well enough. I could not help but notice this."

Why have I never come here before now? How could he have been so out of touch with his own daughter these past five years, that this knowledge shocked him?

He put voice to his thoughts, saying, "I must speak to her at once."

"Nay," Miss Bailey replied. "And now I'll tell you, Counselor, and no lie, why I am afeard of your doing that. To tell God's truth, although this man saved her life, she, herself, cannot ever know the likes of him again, for she knows not where he is, nor from what division of his tribe he hails. I am afeard that speaking about him to her t'would do no more than cause her grief to become more troublesome to herself, right enough."

"Do you know his name?"

"Brave Wolf, Counselor Sheehan. He is a Lakota Indian, but from what band of that tribe, she does not know, and 'tis the trouble. Finding him again t'would be near impossible, if'n she might be wanting to."

"What do you mean?" asked the senator. "Is there a reason she might not wish to see him again?"

"He will be married by now, Mr. Sheehan. And though he would have taken our dear Mia for wife, she could not bear to share him with another, right enough. 'Twas the problem, for he had promised another his hand in marriage."

"I see," replied Sheehan. "Of course." He scratched his red-haired beard before declaring, "Come, Miss Bailey, let us leave this room to my daughter's private thoughts."

"Aye," replied the woman. "Right enough."

But a memory tugged at the senator's recollection. Hadn't he read something about the Lakota somewhere? As they descended the stairs to the main floor, the senator puzzled over it. Brave Wolf. Where had he seen that name before?

He sighed. He couldn't be certain, of course, but perhaps careful search might tweak his memory. He could only hope it would be so.

***

Once approached, Miss Bailey had been a wealth of even more information. It seemed that even though five years had passed, Mia had never raised herself up from her exploits out West. Alas, she seemed to be always on the verge of tears.

Sheehan listened as Miss Bailey explained that Mia, herself, had thought that she might put the remembrance of her time out West, and the recognition of her love for Brave Wolf, behind her. After all, she was Jeffrey's widow, and she had been of the mind that it might be her love for Jeffrey that she had mistakenly given to Brave Wolf.

But this was not Jeffrey's image he'd seen. This Indian, this Brave Wolf, clearly haunted his daughter's heart.

So she painted canvas upon canvas, commenting that she hoped to put his memory away. Yet it was Brave Wolf's image she committed to oil, and not merely one picture, but painting after painting; it was as though she might be fearful of forgetting what he looked like. Moreover, according to Miss Bailey, when Mia completed one of those paintings, she would cry, and often she would ease her pain by taking walks in the woods. Additionally, in all these years, the reality of her loss did not ease.

Several days later, thinking to gain more information, Sheehan sent a telegram to a Lieutenant E. Johnson, who, along with his wife, had accompanied Mia home. A return message had arrived only yesterday. It was the same story. The same man. Likewise, Sheehan uncovered the truth of Mia's emotional state upon her return journey to Virginia. She had grieved the entire time it had taken them to return to the East.

Brave Wolf. Lakota. Weren't the Lakota also called the Sioux? The Sioux... That same memory stirred his mind. Where had he seen that name before?

Suddenly, the memory was there. Congress—the president—a proposed treat—a delegation of Sioux. Was the name Brave Wolf on the delegation list? It must be, for it seemed familiar.

The senator reached for his bag, and, bringing it up onto his desk, he spread out stack after stack of papers. He flicked through one brief after the other. Hours dragged by until...

Ah, there it was. He brought the letter in close to him. Yes, here it was: A memo from the Indian agent of the Miniconju Lakota: A delegation of Sioux Indian chiefs from that tribe were requesting a visit to Washington D.C., their hope to gain an audience with the president of the United States with the idea in mind of securing a treaty.

The letter had gone unanswered and practically ignored by all members of Congress...until now. As Sheehan scanned down the list of candidates to head up the delegation, his finger shook. There it was: Brave Wolf, Honorable Scout of the Lakota.

Brave Wolf. Did he dare to answer this letter, to set up a meeting with the president? To bring the entire delegation here?

Perhaps a better question might be, did he dare not do it?

What if it were as his daughter feared and the man were married? Should he take the chance?

He had no way of knowing, of course. But there was one certainty to be realized: His daughter would never be the same again unless she could be reunited with this man. If he were married, and if she met his wife, might she then be more able to put the memories of this man to rest?

Perhaps. It would be hard to predict what might happen. Perhaps Mia's heartache might become greater.

Yet, he had to consider what he would have been inclined to do if he were in a similar situation as this man, Brave Wolf. Would he have married again, even if he could have? Or would he, like Mia, realize that his heart permitted only one person within it?

He stayed his hand, for if he did cause a meeting between his daughter and this young man, what would be his frame of mind if it ended in a bad way? He sighed; he supposed it was a chance he would have to take, because clearly, Mia might never regain her heart unless she could put the memory of this man behind her.

Yet, in the back of his mind was the knowledge of Greiner and the pending blackmail. Greiner would have to wait. He would simply have to wait.

This decided, the senator took up feather, ink and paper, and began to write.

CHAPTER TWENTY-THREE
Washington D.C.
August, 1876

Brave Wolf certainly didn't expect to encounter Little Dawn Bird in this white man's town. Yet, since alighting from the "medicine travois" that had carried their delegation of chiefs and the Indian agent to this place, he couldn't help noticing that one woman after another was of a similar figure to that of she, the woman who still haunted his dreams. At first, he had studied each of these women, but after a string of disappointments, he gave up the sport.

His relatives on his mother's side were expected to meet them here. Yet Brave Wolf was hardly impressed. In truth, he doubted that his mother's people would make the journey to welcome them. He, as well as his father and his mother, after disembarking from the train, had held back from the other chiefs. Without voicing his opinion, Brave Wolf watched his parents scan the faces of the people who had gathered to welcome the Western Sioux Chiefs to the city of the president.

But as Brave Wolf had feared, his relatives were not present. Carefully, he observed his mother from out the corner of his eye, fearing her disappointment might be great. His father stood stoically beside her, and, after a quick perusal of the personages here, he saw his father bend down to whisper in his mother's ear. She laughed.

Seeing that smile gladdened Brave Wolf's heart, and he hoped that her entrance back into the white man's world, even if only for a few days, would not cause her grief. Several councils were scheduled to meet soon, well within a few suns, and he had been made to understand that there would be celebrations in honor of the peace talks, even before they began.

But first, they were to rest and recoup themselves after their long journey to arrive in the white man's capital. Before them, in a line, were four strange-looking modes of transportation, what the Indian agent had called "buggies." Men dressed in black riding clothes held a pair of fine-looking white horses in check. Apparently, there was yet another journey ahead of them, this one shorter, being only several days in length. They were to travel to a "country" house, whatever that was.

The Indian agent had told them that it was there where the entire delegation of Indian chiefs and their wives could bathe, relax and prepare themselves for the coming councils. Brave Wolf's duty was not that of a chief, however, nor did he expect any relaxation. His was a special duty, for no one could be certain what truly awaited them in this white man's village. That each chief had brought his favorite wife with him showed their good intentions, since war between the white man and his own Lakota people still waged in the West.

But what of the white man? Here he was strong. Here he held command of armies. Here their own wise leaders might encounter an assassin's bullet. Brave Wolf's duty was clear: discover any such plots and disarm them before they could materialize.

And so, even while these important Sioux men and their wives stepped into and sat within the waiting buggies, Brave Wolf gave his father a signal before he lost himself within the crowd of white men and women, one lone Indian, who oddly enough seemed to be invisible to all but a very discerning eye.

***

The late spring air caught and held the scent of wildflowers, blooming trees and freshly cut grass. Although *Retrouvaille* had not been built on the top of a mountain, it was still positioned high enough up the knoll to look out over a vast array of hills and valleys, and the loveliness of its view had caught many an artist's eye, including Mia's.

Into this beauty was to come a delegation of Indians, and a party of two stood in front of a long line of various servants who were to attend to the needs of these people. Her father had hired extra people from the closest village to assist with the care of this delegation, and as many as fifty domestics waited in an extended column behind them.

Nervously, Mia glanced at her father. Of course, it was too much to hope that Brave Wolf might be part of the entourage that her father had invited to *Retrouvaille.* But the tribe was Lakota; it was *his* tribe, and at the very least, these people might provide a source of news about him. After all, wasn't it possible that Brave Wolf might be known amongst them?

At that thought, her heart beat so fast that she feared she might collapse. She reached out for her father's arm, and placed her hand upon it, partly for comfort and partly to steady her nerves. Her father petted her hand.

"It won't be long now," he said to her. "Do you see the buggies coming up the hill?"

"Yes, Father. I must admit I am excited that the Indians are to stay with us during their peace talks. You must know, of course, that it was a Lakota Indian brave who saved my life all those years ago."

"Indeed," Senator Sheehan uttered. "I have become aware of that fact. I only wish it hadn't taken me five years to discover it. Forgive me my negligence in putting my work first, before your own."

Mia smiled at her parent. "There is no need for you to ask for forgiveness, because you did what you thought best, Father. You are important to the people of our country, and there is no apology necessary." She paused. "Do you remember what band of the Lakota these people are?"

The senator shook his head. "Forgive me, my dear, but no. Perhaps the Miniconju? In truth, when I asked them here, I barely realized there were different divisions within the general tribe."

"Oh," was her only response. The Miniconju? Was that *his* tribe? Well, whether these people were from Brave Wolf's own hunting grounds or not, it would be an honor to be able to be amongst them, to talk to them, for they were *his* people. That alone would be reason enough to bring her pleasure. As she awaited the first carriage to pull into the lane that circled in front of her home, she made a vow to treasure each moment of their stay.

Mia had dressed for this occasion in her favorite gown of green and ivory. She had left her hair down, falling into tight curls at her shoulders, and she wore gloves of the same color of ivory as her dress. Perhaps it was wishful thinking, but she had donned her best costume, remembering that Brave Wolf had only once seen her in clothing other than that torn and stained, blue dress. In case he might be a part of this assemblage, she wished to correct that disheveled image.

Mia counted four buggies in all. They had each pulled into the one-way road that would bring them up the hill and into the circular drive that fronted *Retrouvaille*. The first buggy soon stopped in front of her father and her.

She held her breath as the door swung open from within, and even knowing that Brave Wolf couldn't possibly be amongst them, Mia's knees wobbled. Needing her father's assistance for support, she pressed her hand tightly against his arm.

The Indian agent performed most of the introductions, rarely including her in the presentation. Cordially, she smiled at each chief and his wife, refusing to take offense at the agent's slight. Soon, she realized that Brave Wolf was not a passenger in the first buggy, nor was he present in the second, or the third buggy.

What, after all, had she expected? The Lakota tribe was known to boast a large population of Indian peoples, and this included hundreds of "chiefs." What were the chances that Brave Wolf would have attained the status of "chief" at such a young age?

Indeed, how old would he be now? Twenty-seven or twenty-eight?

Mia ignored her disappointment, and pasted a warm smile of welcome upon her countenance as the fourth buggy pulled up in front of their home. But she caught her breath when out of this last buggy stepped a warrior, followed by his wife, who was a white woman.

Brave Wolf's mother was white. Was it too much to hope that this woman might be his mother? Or, if she weren't that personage, would she know Brave Wolf's mother? Why oh why hadn't she possessed the curiosity to inquire about his mother and her name when she'd had the chance?

But perhaps all was not lost. Couldn't she ask about this woman's children? About any other white women who were now living with the Lakota? Surely these questions could not be a social faux pas amongst the Indian nations.

As the two figures stepped toward her, she smiled at the woman first and at her husband last, greeting them both, saying, "Welcome to our home. I hope your stay here will be pleasant."

"I'm certain that it will be." It was the woman who answered, doing so in perfect English.

"My name is Mia," she supplied.

This woman, although no longer young in age, was still quite beautiful. She grinned back at her, answering Mia's unspoken question by saying, "And my English name is Kristina."

Mia smiled. "Welcome, Kristina. I'm sure we will have a great deal to talk about. And welcome to your husband, also."

Mia cast a quick glance at the handsome man beside Kristina, catching momentarily a strange look of recognition upon that chief's countenance, although the regard was quickly masked.

"*Haŋ,*" responded Kristina. "I am certain that we will talk. I will look forward to it." Turning to her husband, she introduced him, saying, "This is my husband, Mia. His name is White Buffalo."

Briefly Mia and White Buffalo exchanged nods.

Because she could think of nothing else to say or to do at present, Mia, still endeavoring to hide her dejection, backed up and started to turn away. She hesitated, however, when she heard her father speak in a quiet voice to the chief.

"Chief White Buffalo," he began, "might I ask if this is all of your party? There are only seven chiefs and their wives that I count here. I thought there were to be eight."

"Hau, hau," answered White Buffalo. "You are correct, and there is another. I am happy to say that he is here, although you might never have the pleasure of his company until it is time to counsel together, for he is secretive."

"Ah," replied Sheehan. "I understand. But tell me, is he to stay in our home, too?"

"That will be his decision to make," White Buffalo returned. "But I fear that the answer will most likely be no."

"Is that a fact?"

White Buffalo didn't answer.

"Please," her father continued, "I would be most honored if you might seek him out for me and tell him that I personally invite him to attend our dinner celebration tonight. It will give me great happiness, I believe, to welcome him."

White Buffalo inclined his head. "Although I cannot promise you that he will come, I will give him your message. I can only promise you that I will do as you ask. However," he added, his eyes twinkling with humor, "my wife might have more influence over him than I do. I will confer with her, also."

Senator Sheehan smiled, and, whether socially acceptable or not, he caught the eye of White Buffalo's wife, Kristina, and winked.

***

"My son," whispered Kristina, as though her words were directed to the air. "I would beg you to come and speak to me." Kristina had left her own and White Buffalo's quarters in *Retrouvaille,* in favor of strolling through the gardens that surrounded the stately home of Senator Sheehan and his daughter. She had known no other manner by which she might attain an audience with her son. Brave Wolf's duty as the selected scout for the chiefs would dictate that he remain in the shadows, unseen until the very last moment. He would not reside at this home during their stay, either; he would be as though invisible, 'til at last their people were to meet in conference.

She had no choice but to wait until he found her, and she knew that he would. Indeed, she had tarried only a few minutes, when he approached her, his steps as silent as that of a ghostly encounter. Because a stone bench had been strategically placed within the flowered terraces, Kristina had only recently seated herself when he appeared, taking a seat beside her. But Kristina was used to her son's ability to remain invisible until he wished to be seen, and so she didn't even start at the suddenness of his presence.

Softly, he asked, "Do you seek me out personally, my mother?"

Kristina glanced to her side and smiled at her son. "Yes, I do. Oh, how good it is to hear you speaking English without having to search your memory for the right words. Thank you for coming to me and asking for my help with the language five years ago. I believe the ability to speak it well will aid you in our talks here."

"It is so, my mother. I believe this also. I thank you for flattering me. What is it you would tell me, for I know you did not ask for audience with me to only speak about my use of the English language."

"*Haŋ*, yes, it is true. I have a message for you."

He nodded, giving her approval to continue.

"Our host has asked to meet you personally, and he requests that you favor him tonight by accepting his invitation to dinner."

"Does he? How can this be? He does not know me."

"He is aware that there were to be eight chiefs at our council, and he counted only seven."

"*Hau, hau*, this is an interesting turn of affairs, for I am unaccustomed to the white man being aware of the facts of the environment. I apologize. I did not suppose that I would be missed."

Kristina sighed. "But you were, my son, and I would request that you respond in a favorable manner to our host's invitation. Please come to dinner tonight."

"Of course I will do as you ask. Tell me, my mother, is it a formal affair? Should I wear my white buckskin tonight?"

"Yes, I do believe that your very best formal clothes would be in order this night. Come to your father's and my room before dinner, so that I might help you to dress."

"Humph! Do I look like a helpless babe, that I need a woman's help with putting on my clothing?"

Kristina laughed. "No, indeed, but I would like to give you my aid nonetheless."

He sighed. "Then it will be done."

"Thank you, my son." She didn't enlighten him as to which of the rooms in the house were assigned to herself and to White Buffalo. She had no doubt that he would find them well enough.

And so it was that Brave Wolf did as asked, and, to his mother's delight, she saw to it that her son experienced the pleasure of a warm bath for the first time in his life.

It was good.

***

Senator Sheehan's glance took in each personage in the ballroom. At the far end of the room sat a fine, professional orchestra, the musicians especially hired for this occasion. The harmonic strains from the string instruments had most recently filled the atmosphere with quiet, relaxing music while his guests had dined. But now, with the final serving of coffee and tea, the music had turned to a waltz, and it was expected that the dancing would soon begin.

He, of course, would be called upon to lead the others onto the dance floor, and so he would. But at present, the senator was nursing his despair.

Was he never to meet this man who had stolen his daughter's heart? He recognized each of the seven chiefs and their wives, but the young man who haunted each of his daughter's paintings was not here. Espying White Buffalo and his wife standing at the center of the festivities, the senator wove his way through the crowd, coming at length to stand by them.

He smiled at Kristina and then at White Buffalo. "Ah," he began, "the evening is yet before us."

"Indeed, it is," White Buffalo answered.

"Do your people know how to dance to the music of the Americans?"

"I fear they may not."

"But," Kristina spoke up, "my husband and I have long loved the dances, since my own relatives used to sponsor evenings of fun when we would visit them at Fort Leavenworth. How long ago that was, it seems. My children are also adept at this style of dancing, for I ensured they learned."

"Excellent," rejoined Sheehan. "Then might I suggest that your husband and I lead the way to the dance floor, that we might be the inspiration to open up the evening to fun and merriment? What say you, Chief White Buffalo?"

"I would be most honored, my host, but I would first ask that we wait a moment, since the one that you have inquired about should make his presence known soon."

As though White Buffalo's words had conjured up his son, Brave Wolf appeared soundlessly at his side. Senator Sheehan drew in his breath with a hiss, for he recognized the tall, young warrior at once. Here at last was the man whose countenance had been forever captured upon his daughter's canvases.

The senator was quick to realize that, in person, Brave Wolf exuded a raw strength of character that was only hinted at in Mia's paintings, perhaps because at the time Mia had known the man, they had both been little more than young adults. This man, now fully grown, was proud, confident and at ease. Yet it was clear that he endeavored to hide these traits behind a demeanor that showed no emotion. His was also a handsome visage; he was muscular with broad shoulders that tapered to a flat stomach. Skin-tight leggings defined strong thigh and calf muscles.

Brave Wolf was dressed all in white, and every inch of him screamed that he was proud of his Indian heritage.

It was easy to see why this man had captured his daughter's heart, for the young fellow's masculine good looks went far beyond what the "modern gentleman" might ever hope to achieve. His was a tall, straight stature and there was an air about him that was dangerous, though curbed at the moment. He would make a terrible opponent, and Senator Sheehan reckoned that during these wars between the military and the Lakota, he had been most likely that.

Yet for all his physical attributes, Sheehan secretly believed that it was more than this that had endeared his daughter to this impressive being. Though the young man might deny it if pressed, there was about him a sense of understanding and a look of kindness upon his countenance. Indeed, there was more to be seen here than mere surface impressions.

"Ah," began White Buffalo, "here he is now. Senator Sheehan, may I introduce you to my son, Brave Wolf? My son, this is our host whose home will shelter us while we await our audience with the president chief. This man, my son, is a very important chief amongst the white man."

"How do you do?" asked Senator Sheehan, staring even more closely at the imposing, slim, muscled and rugged young man. His skin color was that of a tan hue, his hair was a dark, dark brown, which at present defied the Lakota style of the ever-present two braids caught at the side of the face. His mane was loose, quite long, reaching well to his waist, and its length flowed freely down his back and over his shoulders. Although in the senator's own society such long hair might be considered feminine, the man before him disabused Sheehan of that notion entirely. His was a hard, firm, and utterly masculine appearance.

A single eagle's feather, attached by some means to his hair on the right side of his face, fell to his shoulders. Another eagle's feather stood upright at the crown of his head, creating even more of an image of height. He was dressed in buckskin white; his shirt, his leggings, and even his moccasins were elaborately beaded with blue, red and green beads, all in the same geometric pattern. His ears were pierced, and white, blue and green beaded earrings hung there, but the effect was clearly masculine.

Indeed, the man looked utterly American Indian, yet there was one exception: His eyes were crystal blue, a gift of course from his mother's side of the family.

Currently, Brave Wolf's gaze scanned the ballroom, and it took an effort on the senator's part to draw his attention onto himself, and even then Brave Wolf didn't look directly at the senator, as Sheehan was to discover later, was proper Lakota etiquette.

"Chief Brave Wolf," began the senator, "I am happy to meet you."

At length, the young man gave Senator Sheehan his full attention, and when he said in a deep, baritone voice, "I am honored to meet such an important man as you, our host. I thank you for your kindness toward my people, and for your welcome invitation to me."

"Ahem, yes, and—" Sheehan was on the verge of responding to Brave Wolf's elegant speech, and was about to ask him about his wife—if he had one—when he heard his daughter's delightful laughter from across the room. He had opened his mouth to say a word about Mia, but found that he had lost Brave Wolf's attention.

Brave Wolf stared at the place where his daughter stood. Her back was to them, and the senator was about to comment upon her, thinking to urge Brave Wolf to meet her, but he found the process unnecessary.

As though she could feel Brave Wolf's attention upon her, Mia turned slowly around, and for a moment, all was quiet, though conversations abounded around them. They looked at one another. That was all. From across the room, she and Brave Wolf simply stared at one another, their eyes locked.

A flush stole over her cheeks, and she blinked once, as though she doubted what her vision was telling her was true. Max Greiner stood next to her and was demanding her attention. Thus, she looked away from Brave Wolf but for a moment.

In that instant, however, Brave Wolf disappeared.

Where had the man gone? The senator gloomed, for Brave Wolf seemed as hard to hold onto as the wind. How was he to bring these two together, if he couldn't even engage the man in conversation?

And here Sheehan was, still wondering if the man were married or not. He reminded himself that there had been no woman by his side. Did he dare to hope that the man's affections might be free?

He sighed, and looking around him, decided to lead the way onto the dance floor, for in this way might he not give the young warrior a reason to approach his daughter? Gazing at White Buffalo, he questioned, "Would you and your wife be so kind as to help me begin the dance?"

"We would be honored," responded White Buffalo.

It was Miss Bailey that the senator asked to dance. Behind him came White Buffalo and his wife, as the four of them paired off, and paced out onto the dance floor. So it was that while the orchestra played a waltz, the two couples began to dance; step, step, sweep, their feet perfectly timed to the rhythm of the haunting, three-quarter beat of the music.

Gradually, others joined them in the middle of the floor, most of the dancers the personages from Senator Sheehan's society. Still, some of the Indian guests took note of what was expected of them, and, hugging their wives to them, they, too, joined in with the dance.

It seemed a joyous affair. The senator could only hope it would remain an evening of good cheer. Although it was probably a useless gesture, he crossed his fingers....

***

It was she. Brave Wolf was not mistaken about that. This wasn't someone whom he might confuse for the real person.

Little Dawn Bird was here...tonight. But what a terrible means to introduce her to him after these five years, for she was in the arms of another man. That man now touched her shoulders, her waist, her neck. That man's arms fastened around her, his manner clearly possessive.

Her husband? It must be. Did she have children with him, too?

Displeasure, as well as melancholy, filled his soul. That man's actions screamed that she was his.

Didn't she remember *him*, their love? No, that thought wasn't right. He had let her go. He'd had to. But right or wrong, it didn't matter; she should still be his. After all, was he not hers? Would always be hers?

Unreasonably, anger filled his soul, anger at her, and fury that she should marry another in his place. He did try to use reason, reminding himself that it had been he who had escorted her to that train all those years ago. Yet, no amount of argument with himself could convince him that it should be any other way than that she belonged to him.

He stood in the shadows of the room and watched her, admiring her, loving her, even though his ire was directed at her. If he had thought she was beautiful five years ago, she outshone that image a hundred fold tonight. Five years ago, he had seen her in only that one blue and stained dress. Tonight she wore a full, yet dangerously low-cut gown of gold that hugged the curves of her upper body, while falling in tiers, like a waterfall, to the ground. Her stunning red hair fell in ringlets to her shoulders, and caught the dim light of the torches and candles, and covering her hands were white gloves.

She smiled up at the gentleman beside her, and Brave Wolf experienced a wave of pure anger. He admonished himself, knowing his feelings were misplaced. She believed he, too, were married, and that she was under no obligation to him to remain single.

But such logic didn't help his mood, regardless of how intuitive that line of thought might be. He felt out of place here, and soon, he would leave here, never to return, never to see her again. But first—for a moment only, perhaps, he would face her, he would look at her, she back at him, and maybe she might remember....

CHAPTER TWENTY-FOUR

Had he been a figment of her imagination? She had only looked away from him for a second or two, but when she'd glanced back in that direction, he was gone.

Had she really seen Brave Wolf? It must be, for the man looked older that what she recalled, but so very much like the man she had fallen in love with all those years ago. *Dear Lord,* she prayed, *let it be he. And if it truly were Brave Wolf that she had seen, please send him back. Please.*

Max Greiner was speaking to her, and she turned around to give him her attention. That was when it happened:

"Hepela-hepela."

She froze. She would know that deep, baritone voice anywhere, and the words spoken came from close behind her. Was Brave Wolf really there? She had only to turn around. She was almost afraid to look over her shoulder, fearful that it might be no more than a mirror image she would find there.

But she did look, slowly pivoting around. She caught her breath. It was he. It was Brave Wolf. Even knowing that she had hoped he might be part of the Sioux delegation, the actual realization that he was here, now, standing before her, swamped her, and she almost swooned. But she didn't. Instead, she brought her hand to her throat, as though to still her pulse, for it was beating so fast, she thought her hand might shake from its pounding.

He was poised at an arm's distance away from her. Tall, handsome, dressed all in white; he loomed over her, and she could barely believe that the man she loved, that she had never forgotten, stood in front of her. She gulped. She couldn't speak. Somehow, her voice had deserted her.

Thank the good Lord that he didn't seem to be under the same inability, and holding his hand out to her, he asked, "Dance?"

Her voice still refusing to work, she simply nodded her assent, and as she touched his hand, tremors shook her body from head to foot. If he noticed her reaction, he didn't show it. Instead, still holding onto her hand, he led her to the dance floor, where several couples were swaying and waltzing to the enchanting music of the violins, basses, violas and cellos.

He began the dance of the waltz, and she recalled another time when they had come together in rhythm—back there as they'd camped close to the Missouri River. At that time, they had both hummed a three-quarter tune. She had been in a state of shock after he had saved her from a terrible death. But then he had twirled her around a makeshift ballroom, and such a simple action had calmed her.

Yes, she remembered it well.

His arms came around her now, and she could barely breathe, but luckily, her feet knew what they were supposed to do, and she matched her steps to his.

Neither said a word to the other as they became one with the pulsing beat of the music. At last, however, she found she had to know a matter most personal, and forcing her voice to work properly, she murmured, "Is your wife here tonight?"

"She is," he answered clearly.

She almost cried. Instead, she asked, "Oh?"

"It is so."

She inhaled deeply before she plunged in with her next heart-felt inquiry. "Where is she?" Mia scanned the crowd furiously. "Will she object that you dance with me?"

"She will not."

"But I don't see her. I—"

"I'm looking at her now."

Startled, Mia gazed up into his eyes, seeing that his focus was not on anyone in the crowd, but that he stared straight back at *her*.

"But I—" She missed a dance step, then corrected it. Perhaps her confusion was because she was so certain that Walks-in-sunshine was here somewhere, and it took a moment for her to understand. At the realization of exactly what he meant—and who he meant—her knees buckled under her. Unbidden, tears came to her eyes.

He held her up, his strong arms coming more fully around her, bringing her in closer to him.

"But I thought you married Walks-in-Sunshine."

"I did not. When I returned home, she had married another."

"Oh." She gasped. A tear fell down her cheek.

But he seemed unsympathetic to her plight as he asked, "Who is that man?" He nodded toward Max Greiner. "Is he your husband?"

"Ah...ah..."

"How many children have you now?"

"I don't understand. Why did you not marry another in her place?"

He sighed. "My people are at war with yours, and my life was and still is in constant danger. I would not make a widow of a good woman. Besides, how could I marry another, when my heart belongs to the woman who is my first wife?"

She gasped, she stumbled again, and she began to cry in earnest now. "Please don't be upset with me. I can tell by the manner of your speech that you are."

Again, he let out a deep breath. "I know. I am sorry. I will try to understand that you belong to another. After all, it was I who took you to the soldier fort, and I who watched you leave."

"No," she hiccupped. "You misunderstand." Tear after tear escaped from her eyes, falling down in streaks over her cheeks. Her lips shook as she gulped in air, and her body shook as she tried to explain, "Please, Brave Wolf, I am not married to that man. I have no children, for I am not married. Don't you see? I cry because it is I who is to blame for what happened to you and me. I should never have left you, for I've never forgotten you. Indeed, I fear that I've never stopped loving you, though I believed we'd never see one another again. It is because of me that we both have perhaps experienced unhappiness."

All at once, his gaze softened, and he seemed to hesitate before he answered her. In due time, however, he uttered, "*Hiyá*, you are not to blame. You did what you were honor-bound to do. It is oftentimes hard to do what is right, but you did it." He brought up a finger to trace the path of a tear, touching that same finger to his own eyes. Then in a gesture most sincere, he placed that same finger against her tears. Gently, he bent toward her, and murmured in her ear, "I am glad to discover that you are not married to that man. Do you see that, as I trace your tears, I bring that same finger to my eyes, mingling your tears with mine? As I do that, I bid that my strength will now be yours."

She broke down into grief in earnest now, unable to check the flow of tears coming upon her so quickly. She tried to continue the dance, but she felt out of control, and she literally sobbed.

"*Itó*, come, let us leave here, for you are quite wrong about your marital state. I fear you are very much married. Follow me and I will show you how married you truly are."

Manipulating his steps toward the French doors opening onto the balcony, he let his arm drop from around her, taking her hand in his instead. And then he led her out that doorway, away from the gathering, and into the night.

Mia followed him willingly, lovingly, for this was the man that she loved, would always love. *Thank you, Lord,* she prayed under her breath. *Thank you.*

***

Senator Sheehan watched the two reunited souls from afar. He felt helpless as he saw his daughter break into grief, watched as Brave Wolf calmed her, bit his lip with anxiety as he witnessed Brave Wolf take control of his daughter, and led her out through the veranda. He wasn't the only one to observe them, however. Both White Buffalo and Kristina had seen what was happening between their son and the white woman.

"Tell me," the senator said to White Buffalo. "Is your son married?"

"To your daughter, alone," he replied. "Long have they been separated, for he saved her from death many years ago. At the time when I bid him to lead her to a fort where she could return to her own people, I feared that they might forge a bond between them. They did. But they had to part, for I have come to know that each one of them was pledged to another."

"She is the one?" asked Kristina.

"*Hau, hau,*" enlightened White Buffalo. Then, after a moment, he asked Sheehan, "Is your daughter married?"

"Only to your son, my friend. Only to your son." Senator Sheehan let out his breath, unaware until now that he'd been holding it. And then it happened: He grinned a happy, happy smile.

"Come," said White Buffalo, "let us smoke a pipe of peace, that our children might settle their differences, and make a good life between them. If you have no objections, my wife will smoke the pipe, also."

"Good idea, my friend," observed Sheehan. "Of course I have no objection to that. Let me lead you and your wife to my smoking room."

***

The darkened atmosphere of midnight lent the familiar scent of pure oxygen to the evening. The night was balmy and near black. His touch, accompanied by the songs of hundreds of crickets, reminded Mia that she was experiencing reality, that this was not simply another dream.

Looking outward, Mia beheld a landmark most dear. She had always harbored a particular affection for the old Little Leaf Linden tree that stood majestically in the backyard of her home. Like a large sentinel, it guarded the entrance into the gardens at *Retrouvaille,* its heart-shaped leaves and unusual branches dipping down to the ground and forming a living curtain around its rather large trunk.

During the daylight hours, it was nearly impossible for a person to see through its numerous branches to the center of the tree. In the evening, such observation could not be done without a lantern.

Brave Wolf led the way to that tree now. He held her hand as he guided her to, underneath, and through the numerous tree branches, many of which had taken root in the ground, providing them a curtain of privacy. He backed her up to the tree's trunk before taking her face gently into his hands. And then he kissed her on the lips.

Oh, she would never forget this moment. Before she closed her eyes, his image loomed large before her. His mint-scented breath carried with it his own beloved fragrance, and she memorized that aroma and his taste, that she might hold it with her always. He smelled of deerskin and leather, and she wished she could bring him in even closer. Did he realize how ready she was for him, both physically and spiritually? As it was, she could barely breathe.

He murmured against her lips, "I have lived our moments together over and over in my mind."

"I, too," she whispered in return.

"I have made love to you in my dreams too many times to count. Moments ago, you asked me why I did not marry another when I returned to find Walks-in-sunshine married to another. I answered you that I could not love another when my heart is forever entwined with she who is my first wife...you...."

Mia gasped. "I, too." Tears fell down her cheeks, and her lips shook as she added, "If I had fully realized how deeply I loved you—you, not another—and that my love wasn't mistakenly given to you, I—I..." She choked on her words and though she tried to say more, she couldn't.

He took a deep breath. "It is true, what I said back there, but there is more I should tell you, for I would come to you with an open heart. I tried to love other women of my tribe, and I did endeavor to marry again. Because my people are at war with yours, and as I grew more and more to hate the white man, I began to hate myself, too, because I still loved you, and I could not put you from me. Many are the times when I wished to marry an Indian woman, and not the woman of my heart. But in the end, I could not do it. When I looked at another, I saw only you. When I envisioned holding another in my arms, it was always you in my mind's eye."

Her only response to his confession was to cry, and she bit back a sob.

"I have not been a happy man. I justified not taking another to my bed as wife because my life is always in danger. But I knew down deep in my soul that I could love no other woman but you, and I could not in conscience be half a man to another. I had begun to believe that I might die an old man who would never see his children growing in the belly of the one he loves."

She gasped, then whispered, "I didn't know. I, too, have been unhappy. In thought, I am with you always."

"As I am with you. But, you must know, and I must tell you, that I am not the innocent youth that I was when we were last together. I am at war with the whites, and as they have killed many of my people, so, too, have I killed them."

"But is that not the way of war?"

"Perhaps. However, I speak true when I tell you that I have hated you at times for the love I feel for you, and I have risked my life many times because I could not put your image away from me. There have even been moments when I wished for death so that I might end the vision of the white woman whom I will always love."

She gasped. She should have never left him. Had she only stayed, their lives would be so different now. More tears gathered within her eyes. Her voice quavered as she whispered a note of caution, saying, "But it is not only I who is white. So, too, is your mother."

"In race only," he answered. "In her heart, she is Indian. There is more. I want you. I want only my arms to encircle you. I desire you in my bed, and I would hope to see my children growing in your belly. You are my wife, even if I was slow to realize that we should have talked more, and perhaps envisioned that a path through our differences might be possible."

She gasped. "I, too, have dreamed of you in similar ways."

"Wait," he cautioned. "Do not tell me this yet, for you do not know all of what I must say to you, all that I must tell you that I have done."

Her response was a silent nod.

"I want to make love to you here, now."

"I, too. Please, please do this. Now that you are here, I can never let you go. This you should know."

"But you might have to part from me," he added, "for this is what else I must tell you. Unless this treaty is a success, we, the Lakota people, will continue our war with the white man. We must fight, for the survival of our people and that of our children lies in our ability to fight and to win. But if there is no treaty, I must not bring you back with me. I will return there, but you must stay here."

"No! I won't let you go again. I cannot."

He brought his forehead down and laid it against her own before he whispered, "Tell me, where would we live? If with my people, I might risk your life, for many share my hatred of the whites. If we were to choose to live with the white people, you and I could both be killed by those whose opinions are full of prejudice. And, for the white man, that malice is great."

"If that is so, then stay here with me," she pleaded. "We could start our life together here, for guests come here so seldomly."

He shook his head. "Surely you remember me well enough to realize I could never do that. Would you brand me a coward?"

"No, but must you always live with your people?"

"*Hau, hau,* of course." She felt his brows draw inward in a frown.

"Then I would have your mother teach me how to become Lakota, as she has."

He inhaled once, twice, before he commented, "My mother would be honored to do this for you. But there is more than this to the problem. In the not so distant past, our camps have been invaded in the early hours of the morning while the men of the village are out hunting, as they must do to support their families. At these times, all the women, children and old people in those villages have been as prey to the white man's guns, and they have been openly and viciously killed by the white soldiers. Walks-in-sunshine and her son met death in this way, while her husband, my cousin, was away from camp, hunting food for his family. This could too easily happen to you, I fear. I would not wish this upon you, nor will I allow it."

Tears, which had been accumulating at her eyes, spilled over her cheeks. "My dear Brave Wolf, I am sorry to hear about Walks-in-sunshine. I am so very, very sorry. I know you loved her."

"Yes," he admitted, "I did, but that was a young love. It does not compare to my devotion to you, nor to my admiration for you, a love which has never dimmed in these past five years, though I have often wished that it would."

She cried a new bout of tears. "I—I, too." She hiccupped. "But surely there is a manner by which we could remain together. I could come home with you. After all, your mother faces these same problems, and yet she remains there with your father."

"Because she has nowhere else to go. Her own father, a soldier, and her mother deserted her long ago. My father schools her in warfare and in shooting, it is true, but she is a woman, and she is weaker than a man. Always when he is out of camp and away from her, he worries about her."

"But Brave Wolf," she argued, "there is a part of my character that you might search your memory to recall. I will not let you leave me. If you stubbornly refuse to take me with you, I will follow you. I promise you I will. If you die, so then do I."

"And if you are with child, as I would hope to make you?"

She hesitated. "Please, we are here now together after a long, long time of being apart. Could we not celebrate our coming together again, and think of the future later?"

"*Hau, hau*, we could do this, but I must give you a moment to reflect on all I have said, for it would not be honorable to know of my mindset, and not tell you of it. Let me inform you of it clearly once again, so there is no mistake: If the council ends in a bad way, we will have to part, regardless of how difficult that may be."

"No. I will not let you go again. I would rather die than live without you."

He shook his head.

It was only then that she realized the difference in a matter about him, that up until now, she had failed to note completely; she had taken it for granted. She commented, "You speak English now as though it might be your first language."

He grinned slightly. "I became a shadow upon my mother's steps until she had no choice but to teach it to me. Until I met you, I never wished to learn that language or to speak it. But you, my wife, changed me in many ways."

"I am glad."

He backed away from her slightly, placing his hands against the tree at her shoulders. Though his face was only inches away from hers, she desired to have him so much closer. He whispered, "As we speak, we leave the matter most important, I fear, and I must return your attention to it, for I would have no misunderstandings between us, my wife. Only a man of no honor would bring a loved one into the problems that my people face, where death might await them at any moment. If this council ends in a bad way, you will have to wait here until the hostilities between our peoples cease. I will give you no quarter on this matter."

"You will have to make me."

"There are ways, and I would not hesitate to use them."

She sighed. "I will not agree."

"You do not have to, as long as you understand that my mind is set on this. Do you?"

She looked away from him and shrugged. She inhaled deeply before she admitted, "Yes, I understand you."

Curiously, he let out his breath, as though he had been holding it. "It is done, then." He brought up a hand to trace his fingers down her cheek. "I would ask you to do a thing for me."

"Yes, my darling. What do you require?"

"I would ask that you squeeze my hand so that I might be certain this is real and not another of my dreams."

She gasped before she shut her eyes against the overwhelming tide of emotion that swept through her. "Please, kiss me, my husband, for I can no longer stand to be so distant from you."

He moved ever so slightly so that his full figure was imprinted upon her, and as his lips came down to hers, his tongue swept into her mouth. She rejoiced.

She met him, move for move, kiss for kiss. Oh, how dear this man was to her. He might believe he must perform the most honorable action on her behalf, but he reckoned without full realization of how bleak these past five years had been without him. If it were in her power, she would never let him go. Not again.

He murmured, "I cannot wait." He pulled her up, off her feet, her back cushioned by the soft bark of the tree. "Tell me now if you do not wish me to make love to you...here."

Please," she murmured at once. "Yes, please now. I do believe, my husband, that only in this manner may I know that you are real, and that you are truly here with me."

"I, too," he uttered.

He heaved her upward, pulled up her skirt and settled her legs around his waist. "You are ready?"

"Yes," she mumbled. "Please let me come to be as close to you as two people can possibly be. I need this, my husband. I need this very much."

His fingers found her most secret place, lingered over her there, between the junction of her legs, and she could barely tolerate it. He loved her with his hand and his fingers until she tightened her muscles around him. "Please," she pleaded, "I would have all of you."

"I know," he muttered. "But I may be too quick, and I would ensure that you meet your pleasure also."

Suddenly it became too much, and with him pressed so tenderly against her, and her urgent need to be as close to him as possible, she met her pleasure at once, gasping at the intensity of joy from such a simple act. Oh, the love that she possessed for this man.

With her release, she heard him groan, and she knew that now was the time. He realized it, too, and he pressed himself upward and within her at once.

Oh, the feeling, the ultimate in love and pleasure, this sensation of being one with him. If only it could go on and on. But it was not meant to be, at least for this once.

He had spoken true. He was quick, and he met his need without further encouragement from her. He thrust upward once, then again and again, over and over, and, unbidden, she met him move for move, pleasure for pleasure as she welcomed his seed within her body. What beauty this was. He was beautiful. This was beautiful.

They didn't stir. As though neither wished to withdraw from the other, they remained where they were for so many moments, she lost count.

At last, with one more kiss upon her lips, he slowly withdrew himself from her, and as he did so, he whispered against her lips, "Know that we will always be this close, if not in body, then in spirit."

"Yes."

"But come, the night is young and our lovemaking has only made me hungry for more. If you are willing, I will take you to my private shelter."

"Yes, please."

As her legs disentwined from around him, she pressed her feet to the ground, and spoke, saying, "Yes, let us hurry. I fear that I wish to have no sleep this night, and perhaps all through the day tomorrow, as well."

She heard him chuckle. "I am yours this night and for days on end until the council," he whispered. "Please use me well."

"I intend to, my darling. I intend to."

CHAPTER TWENTY-FIVE

"Come in, Chief White Buffalo. Please come in, be seated."

White Buffalo opened the door wide, and stepped into Senator Sheehan's personal office, closing the door behind him. His long hair, caught in two braids at the side of his face, boasted of his heritage. A tall, handsome and imposing man, Sheehan estimated his age to be in his early sixties. But reaching his natural maturity seemed to have worked magic on the man, for his face bore few, if any wrinkles, and his countenance spoke of a wisdom that comes usually with age. No white man's clothes adorned this man, not even in accent. His garb consisted of buckskin shirt, leggings and breechcloth, not linen or even cotton. Each item of clothing was intricately beaded, as well as adorned with paint. In his right hand he held a red clay ceremonial pipe, and at his waist was a small parfleche bag which the senator thought might contain tobacco.

Had he sensed that Sheehan wished to counsel with him? Perhaps, for the senator had made a study of the red man in recent months, and had realized that the American Indian would not speak openly of matters of state without first lighting the pipe.

Wishing to come to the point at once, Sheehan stated, "I wish to speak with you, if you please."

White Buffalo nodded, though he still lingered by the door.

"Please, please do come in. Be seated please." Sheehan gestured to a chair directly in line with his desk.

Although White Buffalo nodded, he remained where he was, saying only, "I would beg your pardon, Senator, for I would feel more comfortable sitting upon the floor than in the white man's chair."

"By all means," responded Sheehan. "Shall I join you there?"

"If it is in your mind to counsel with me, then that would be most agreeable."

The senator pushed back his chair and came to his feet. Stepping around his desk, he paced toward the spot where White Buffalo stood. Gesturing toward the open French doors, he suggested, "Would my balcony be private enough for you? I guarantee that it is well protected from any hostile intentions, though there should be none of that here."

"I would be honored."

"Then, shall we? You first, since you are my guest."

White Buffalo strode toward the open doors, which were swung inward, allowing a slight breeze to ruffle the curtains that graced the glass window panes. He chose a spot in the center of the sheet-iron and stone floor.

With the two men seated, White Buffalo produced a pinch of tobacco from his parfleche bag, and, pressing it down in the pot of the pipe, he lit the mixture, using a white man's match. After inhaling briefly, he instructed, "The red man counsels only after we bless our talk by showing our gratitude to the Creator and to the Above Ones. Know that by smoking with me, we each take a pledge that only words of truth will come from our lips. Do you agree?"

"Certainly, I do," responded Sheehan.

Raising the pipe into the air, White Buffalo began, "I raise my pipe to the Creator, to honor He who made the world. Next I honor the four corners of the earth; north, south, east and west, and to the four winds, that all should know of what we speak here. By saying thus, I vow that only words of truth as I know it shall adorn my lips." He took another whiff on the pipe before passing it to the senator.

Taking hold of the pipe, Sheehan drew in a draft of the tobacco, and said, "I, too, vow that while in counsel, only the truth shall come from my lips." He then gave the pipe back to White Buffalo, who placed the sacred object next to them on the stone floor.

White Buffalo opened their talk by saying, "You wish to talk to me. Know that I will listen to all you have to say, and only after you have related to me all that you wish, only then will I answer. This is the way of my ancestors."

"Thank you, Chief White Buffalo. But tell me, before we begin, how do you say your name in your own tongue?"

"Tahiska," answered White Buffalo.

"Very well, then, Chief Tahiska. I have asked you here today to inquire of you if you might share any knowledge you have regarding our two children. I have not seen either of them since the night of the ball, and already five days and five nights have passed since that time. While I didn't know what to expect, I did hope that my daughter would have returned by now."

White Buffalo nodded, but said not a word.

The senator continued, "I would speak with your son, for I have concerns that I would say to him."

"I hear you," said White Buffalo. "But before I answer your inquiry, I will pause while you collect your thoughts, so that if there are any other ideas or questions that you have, you might ask them of me now."

Silence followed.

After a moment, Sheehan voiced, "I do have another concern that I would like to inquire about. If your son and my daughter are to be married in a fashion that I understand and condone, your son must seek me out to ask that a priest be found to seal their vows of devotion to one another."

White Buffalo inclined his head, but still he paused.

"I have waited," said the senator, "for Brave Wolf to contact me, but this has not happened, and I wonder if I am misunderstanding his intentions."

Again White Buffalo nodded.

"This is what I have to ask you. And now I would listen to what you have to say to my questions."

"It is good," began White Buffalo, "that you have sought me out to determine what might be happening between our children, for our cultures and our customs are as different, one to another, as a cardinal is to a blue jay."

"I had thought as much."

"*Hau, hau.* Please allow that, in the Lakota society, a boy and a girl who wish to marry leave the security of the tribe to find a safe place by which they may come to know each other better. Often they are gone for a month or more, as they enjoy, and begin to understand not only the new pleasures of marriage, but its demands on them, as well. When they return, they are married, and all within the tribe recognize this."

"I see," said Sheehan almost to himself. Then, in a louder tone, he asked, "It is not necessary for them to seek out a priest's blessing to seal their marriage?"

"It is not."

"Well, that explains much. Yet I must contact your son personally, I fear, for a ceremony is a necessity in my religion; my God insists upon it. Without their vows of devotion said before and blessed by a priest, I fear that our children's marriage isn't recognized by my God or my religion, and their offspring could be sent asunder, for they would not be thought of as children of God."

White Buffalo gave a single nod. He asked, "Has my son not yet left you any gifts?"

When Sheehan looked puzzled, White Buffalo added, "This is expected of him."

"No, I—" The senator paused, then inquired, "Is that what those are? Each day I have found Indian artifacts upon *Retrouvaille's* front steps. A bow was the first to present itself, then came a quiver full of carefully constructed arrows. There were two beaded eagle feathers the next day and an odd-looking object that is circular in shape, fashioned with leather and feathers, with ornamented concentric circles fixed in the middle of the thing. Today a beaded leather shirt was placed upon my steps."

Again, White Buffalo bobbed his head. "I am glad to hear that my son is diligent in his duty toward you."

"Yes, I hear you, but I wish to speak to him personally, and try as I might, I cannot envision how to do it, for he does not seek me out. I have considered going out into the woods, yet I despair of ever being able to find him there, for he seems to know the forest better than I."

Silence commenced until, after due respect, White Buffalo answered, saying, "I understand. Yet, going there is the only manner by which to reach him. If you enter into the woods with an open heart, and if you wait there for him, he will find you."

"He will what?"

"This is the custom by which it is done. Only if my son wishes to be found will another ever be able to locate him. It is his way."

"You are certain that this is all I have to do? I simply go into the woods?"

"*Hau, hau,* and of course one might be expected to seek out my son with good thoughts," added White Buffalo. "He will come to you. If he does not, seek me out again, and I will ask my wife to ensure that he finds you. He would deny her nothing."

Senator Sheehan bobbed his head up and down, saying only, "Thank you."

"*Wašté,* it is good. Have you any more concerns you wish to speak to me about? Let me again give you many moments in which to determine if you might have other thoughts that need to be clarified."

"That is all," acknowledged Sheehan. "I know what to do now. I thank you."

White Buffalo nodded, and, emptying the ashes from the pipe into another of his parfleche bags, he concluded, "Our talk this day is at an end."

***

Senator Sheehan stepped toward a clearing located deep within the woods. How long would he be required to wander about in the deepest part of this forest before Brave Wolf would show himself?

Though he had seen many a squirrel and several chipmunks, he had not been forced to confront a bear, thank the good Lord. He had beheld a red fox and a family of deer, even an eagle overhead. But no human being, and, in particular, no sign of Brave Wolf.

Perhaps if he made himself better seen within this clearing, he might increase his chance of encountering the young man. Stepping into the bright sunlight of the clearing, he moved forward to a small stream that cut and gurgled through the land. Squatting down, Sheehan cupped his hands and took a drink of the cool, refreshing water.

"Do you wish to speak to me?" asked a clear, baritone voice which was slightly raised in order to be heard.

Sheehan arose, turned around and looked closely at the deep woods which skirted this place. But he saw no sign of the young man, until...almost as though he had appeared in the flesh from nothing more than the air, Brave Wolf stepped forward into the clearing.

The senator was quick to note that Brave Wolf wore the same white buckskin clothes that Sheehan had first seen him wearing at the ball five nights ago. Perhaps this was his best ceremonial clothing. If so, it was impressive, for it was pure white and unstained, despite the man having to tramp through the forest. But he looked different this day.

Instead of his hair flowing freely about his waist and shoulders, he had pulled the length of it back, and had braided it there so that he presented a clean-cut visage—one that a person might espy in any Western town, the only difference being that his braid in back was quite long. As he walked forward, a single eagle's feather, attached to that braid, fluttered back against the wind.

He was a handsome man who seemed to be at ease with his imposing presence. Also, unlike many in the nation's capital, he seemed to be unaware of—or at least to be unaffected by—his good looks. His lips were full, his cheekbones high, his face almost a perfect circle. His blue eyes were so unusual in such a tanned face, and they held an uncanny wisdom within their depths that seemed at variance with his youth.

He, like his father, carried a red-stoned pipe in his arms, and attached to his waist were two to three parfleche bags. Clearly he meant to counsel.

"Yes," answered the senator at last, "I wish to speak to you, and I thank you for coming forward to hear me, for I have concerns that I would speak to you about."

Brave Wolf approached slowly, nodding. He said, "I regret that I did not realize this, otherwise I would have sought you out several suns ago, so that we might speak. I hope you have received my gifts and that they have done much to heal your heart."

"Heal my heart?"

"*Hau, hau.* It is true, I think, for I wish to take your daughter from you, if I can."

Sheehan smiled. Never had he heard marriage spoken about in such a manner. It was refreshing.

"What do you mean, son, 'if you can'. I fear you already have her."

Brave Wolf nodded. "Indeed I do, but perhaps not for long."

"I don't understand."

"I know," replied Brave Wolf, who had come to stand directly in front of him. Brave Wolf held up his right hand and turned it slightly right and left. "Do you see," he asked, "that I hold no weapon in my hand?"

"I do."

"Then let us smoke the pipe in council, that we might speak our thoughts to each other, and perhaps come to know each other better, for there is reason for you to come here. And if I am to be truthful, I, too, harbor a problem that concerns you."

"Yes," agreed the senator. "Let us begin."

They each sat cross-legged on the ground, and the necessary ceremony, attended to as custom demanded, was soon accomplished. Thus, they began.

"I believe," uttered Senator Sheehan, "that you and my daughter are married?"

"We are," Brave Wolf answered.

"It is as I had thought," said the senator. "But I am here to tell you, young man, that in the eyes of my church, you and my daughter are not yet joined in matrimony. Nor will the marriage be recognized here until your union can be blessed by a priest. That requires a ceremony."

"*Hau, hau,*" replied Brave Wolf, going on to ask, "How might this ceremony be attained?"

"Easily, son. Easily." Sheehan went on to describe how the church might bring this about, and how quickly that event could be possible. Not sensing any reluctance from his son-in-law, he was delighted that it appeared that his daughter might be properly married, after all. She and that good-for-nothing Carlson had sworn their devotion to one another by none other than a justice of the peace.

But Sheehan had reckoned without realization of Brave Wolf's mindset, and as the council wore on, it became apparent that although Brave Wolf listened diligently to him, and agreed with him on most of the details, he had yet to promise to take his vows before a priest.

"How would this Thursday be?" asked the senator when he had finished detailing why this was so necessary.

It took several hair-raising moments for Brave Wolf to answer the question, and when at last he did respond, he said simply, "I cannot do it."

"What?" Sheehan was taken aback.

"You speak well, my father, and you have made me aware of the particulars in how to bring our union together," said Brave Wolf. "But we have not yet discussed the problems that I and your daughter will face when we return west. The difficulties are many, and they could be dangerous for your daughter."

"I don't understand."

"I know it is so," answered Brave Wolf. "Hear me, my father, that I might tell you of what could await your daughter were we to return to the West without a treaty in place that will end the war that wages even now between your people and mine."

Sheehan nodded. "I will listen."

They talked then of the West, of the battles that had taken place, were still taking place; they spoke in detail of the deaths of almost half of his tribe. He graphically described the surprise attacks upon villages where only women, children and old men remained; he spoke with authority about each element of the many treaties which had been broken. But most of all, he depicted what might happen to his daughter if he brought her back into the West to live amongst his people.

Back and forth, round and round, they talked. So deeply engaged were they, it was well into late afternoon, and still their conversation raged on as each one of them spoke seriously about matters so dear to the heart. Their differing views of their marriage being proper were carefully dissected, their accounts of the problems facing the Lakota were brought out into the open. Brave Wolf even went on to detail his fears of bringing Mia back into the West.

The sun was a low, orange orb in the sky when at last, Sheehan gazed forward, toward this young man, whom he hoped to make his son-in-law. At length, he admitted, "Well, I can see that much depends on the success of making this treaty. Unfortunately, I cannot guarantee that all will be well in that regard, for these lands upon which your tribe sits, are coveted, I fear, by men who would own the land's water, grass and mineral rights. And this doesn't even take into account the average white man and his wife, who would welcome owning a piece of that property on which to settle and raise a family. I cannot say it will go well. I can only promise you that I will try with all my might to satisfy your chiefs' demands, and with all my influence in the halls of Congress, to bring about a treaty of peace that can be agreed upon by both sides."

Brave Wolf nodded silently. "It is all I can ask, and I thank you in advance for whatever efforts you might make."

"Indeed," returned Sheehan, "there is much at stake, for my daughter will not easily stay behind. You must realize that these last five years have been unhappy ones for her."

"*Hau, hau,* it is so. And yet," countered Brave Wolf, "what kind of man would I be if I were to bring her into the danger of these conflicts, where at any moment she might lose her life?"

"Yes, I understand, for you have stated your viewpoint clearly," Sheehan acknowledged. "And I will think well on it, that I might somehow envision a way that this could be resolved, if the treaty goes unsigned." He shook his head, and glanced straight into Brave Wolf's eyes. "She will never stay behind willingly. This you should know."

Brave Wolf nodded. "I do. Yet, I fear that only when the war has ceased by treaty, and both parties are satisfied, will we be able to have that wedding ceremony."

"And yet," countered Sheehan, "I think the official wedding vows must take place sooner. If you are willing, I will make the plans that will seal your marriage within the confines of my own heritage, and hers, even within the night. Do you agree?"

"In my heart, I am honored, and I would gladly take these vows. But all is not a matter of the heart in the West. I will not take her with me if the treaty fails, and I think it best that we do not marry in fact until we are certain."

"I disagree, young man. What you are doing now could cause a child to be born of this union. Better to ensure its place in this world, than to take a chance and have that child be the object of prejudice."

Sheehan watched as Brave Wolf frowned. Then slowly, Brave Wolf nodded, saying, "*Hau, hau,* of course. I should have considered this, but I did not, since a child—any child—is the object of love and affection to my people, and it matters not who the father is or the condition of the mother and father's union. I see now that this is not so in this society." He paused significantly, until in due course, he spoke, saying, "So it is that at last I agree with you. We must come together before this priest."

Sheehan drew in a deep breath. "Good," he acknowledged, letting his breath out in a sigh. "Should we say this Thursday?"

Brave Wolf grinned. "*Hau, hau,* it will be this Thursday.

And now," he continued, "I think it is time to end our talk, for we have now spoken for many hours."

"Yes."

So it was that, with this agreed upon, Brave Wolf performed the necessary rituals defining how to end a proper council. Lastly, he added, "It is growing dark. I will escort you to the edge of the woods so that I might ensure you return home safety."

"Do I look so old that you do not think I could find my way?"

"Indeed not," stated Brave Wolf. "But do you know these woods so well in the dark that you will not become lost?"

"I think so."

"And yet," countered Brave Wolf, "I would be most honored to escort you, for whether in person or not, I will follow you to ensure that you reach there without harm."

Sheehan laughed. "Put that way, son, I will be happy to accompany you to my home."

And so it was done.

CHAPTER TWENTY-SIX

A Thursday wedding never came. Instead, the President of the United States, Ulysses S. Grant, had decreed that Thursday marked the day that he would meet with the Lakota chiefs in council. This included Brave Wolf. For now, the priest, as well as a promise for a church wedding, would have to wait. Even Brave Wolf's father-in-law agreed it must be so.

A few days before this grand council was to commence, however, another meeting was urgently called by his wife's father, Senator Sheehan. White Buffalo, Kristina, Brave Wolf and even Little Dawn Bird were invited to this talk. What particulars were to be discussed was as yet unknown, but Brave Wolf assumed that this speaking together, since it was coming before the eminent council with the Great White Father, was important.

So it came to be that, on the day of this family meeting, Brave Wolf had awakened early, well before dawn. He had already dressed, had said his prayers, and had scouted through the woods, as well as around his father-in-law's home to ensure the safety of today's talk. Returning home, he had awakened Little Dawn Bird, and seeing that her first inclination was to prepare their morning meal, he had cautioned her against it.

"There is little reason to set about fixing food at this hour," he told her. "Time, I fear, will not allow this today, for I would arrive at your home before even my own father and mother arise. All must be well for our talk today. It is my duty to ensure it is."

"Yes, of course," she answered. She smiled, and then in a voice barely audible, she muttered, "I wonder what it is that my father is seeking. It must be some particular having to do with the great council with the president."

"*Hau, hau,*" agreed Brave Wolf. "I believe this, as well. Soon we will discover what it is. Now come, we must leave here now."

"But I am not dressed."

He leaned down and kissed her. "You are beautiful as you are, but if you wish to dress in the clothing of your society, you might do it at your leisure in your home."

She grinned up at him, and, sighing, she placed her arms around his neck and hugged him closely to her. "I suppose it was bound to happen that we would have to return to the world as we know it. I will miss our lovemaking today."

"I, too," he whispered, as his lips moved softly over hers. "I, too. But I think," he added, "that it will soon be evening, and then..."

She laughed.

"Come, let us leave here and arrive at your home early enough so that I might ensure that our meeting with your father will be filled with much love, and that it will not be disturbed by any enemy."

"Yes," she agreed. "Yes."

He nodded, and he gave her a brief smile; then, opening the entrance's soft, leather flap, he helped her out of their private haven, their little debris hut that he had erected so lovingly and so deeply in the woods. Crawling out of this little "home," into the fresh air of morning, he breathed in the cool, moist atmosphere that greeted him.

His mind was anxious, alert, but as was his way, he set his countenance to reveal none of this. Indeed, grinning at his wife, he winked at her before setting out into the woods.

***

Senator Sheehan had done his homework. In the year of 1871, the United States government had relegated the making of Indian treaties to a thing of the past. Different acts of Congress—even a few Supreme Court rulings—had effectively done away with the making of treaties with the sovereign Indian Nations. Instead, agreements between the President and the Tribal Chiefs—all properly signed and sealed—ruled the procedures.

Senator Sheehan, having a stake in the outcome of the coming talks, had used the time given to him to study various and different

Treaties made with several bands of the Sioux. By candlelight and oil lamps, he read Treaty upon Treaty, which extended from early in the eighteenth century to the present day, paying close attention to any recent Agreements between the Executive Branch of government and the Tribal Chiefs.

While he understood what his own society should have to gain from bargaining with the Indian Tribes, he couldn't grasp what the chiefs and the people of these Nations had to obtain from these talks. In each Treaty or Agreement, more land—which was Indian wealth—was ceded to the American Government. This in itself, wasn't alarming, however.

What was most disturbing was that the American Indian received "more" than the "peace" he believed due him. Indeed, each treaty contained language that allowed for the tools of destruction to fester and grow in the American Indian's way of life. These "tools" were in the form of European-type authoritarian schools, where only English was allowed to be spoken; Euro-American agricultural tools, which were foreign to their tribal culture, were "generously" endowed; Shakespearian-type merchants, who were documented to cheat the Indian out of his wealth, gained footholds; doctors and hospitals that degraded the American Indian's Medicine Men openly flaunted disdain for traditional cures; white flour and carbohydrate foods that were foreign to the American Indian's appetite and digestive system were largely and freely given. In each treaty, large tracts of the tribe's land were ceded to railroads, to merchants, to the army, to bankers and lastly, to the American settler.

What he couldn't understand was why did the Sioux people even desire to enter into these talks? Clearly, in his opinion, they did not stand to gain any treasure outside of a "peace" that was at best another type of war...a silent war.

True, it was the Lakota Indian Agent who had asked for the Tribal Delegation to make the journey to Washington D.C. Was the man truly concerned about the welfare of those under his care? Or did this agent hope to gain personally from these talks? The more Sheehan read, the more uneasy he felt about it, and certainly he came to understand that no good would come from any such treaty.

What the Senator needed was information from the Lakota Chiefs themselves. What did they hope to achieve? Were they aware of the danger inherent in these Treaties? Perhaps if he asked his new relations to parley with him, he might stand a better chance of helping them.

It was early morning. He had been studying and piecing together facts about these Treaties and legislation well into the wee morning hours. He had awakened only moments ago, having fallen asleep in his chair, his head down on his desk.

When he awoke, dawn was only beginning to paint the sky in its silver-colored glow. Rising up to his knees, he stretched, yawned and then came up fully to his feet.

It was time to get dressed. Today he and his newly formed family would counsel. He was ready for it, and in truth, he was looking forward to gaining their perspective on what their people hoped to gain from this parley, for only in this way could he foresee a future that could be bright for his daughter and for his own future generation.

***

Brave Wolf opened the door to the uppermost room of his father-in-law's home. The door swept forward easily, and Brave Wolf quietly stepped inside.

Until this morning, Brave Wolf had never considered expanding his scouting investigations into his father-in-law's home, since such forced inspection violated his own sense of privacy and duty toward his wife's father. But today was different. His father-in-law had asked that he and his relatives counsel with him. This, in turn, brought about Brave Wolf's duty to ensure that no danger from an unforeseen source might mar their talk.

This was the last room that required his examination, all else he had scouted thoroughly. As he turned to face into the room, he came to a sudden stop as shock-wave after shock-wave took hold of him. What was this? He could hardly credit what he looked at. Here was display after display of paintings, so real in image, that he could almost smell, touch and experience his own beloved prairie. It was as though he could even hear the constant wind of that place, taste the humidity in the air, feel the hot sun above him.

Slowly he stepped forward into the room, coming to pause in front of the nearest painting. He reached out to run his fingers over the dried strokes of the paintbrush on the picture. Here was a likeness that captured the image of him at full figure. In the background was the gold, pink and red colors of the prairie at sunset; another over there was of him that showed his back turned. One picture, lovingly painted, exhibited his face as the only subject, with nothing else in the background. Over to his right was an artist's rendition of their dance, back there in the wilds of the Missouri River Territory. He remembered it well.

To his left was an image that forever caught a look of passion and love upon his countenance, as though he were in the act of making love. There were hundreds of these honorable drawings. Indeed, the room could have been likened to a shrine in his honor, for he was to be found in each portrait.

Of course there was only one person who could be the artist of all this, and he could only marvel at her skill and her ability to make the past come alive in illustration form. Another realization came with each vision of these works of art, and had he ever been in any doubt as to the intensity of her love for him or her devotion to him, such misgivings fled as before the light of day.

Of course he had understood that she loved him. And he loved her. But this? This was the power of love magnified.

It was then that a flash of unanticipated awareness struck him, and he knew. He could not leave her behind. Regardless of the war in his own country, regardless of the outcome of this treaty-making, he could not let her leave his side, and the reality of this sudden knowledge was like a slap in the face.

She had once told him that she would follow him, that he would be unable to stop her. Only now did he realize the utter truth of her words. Worse, he grasped that it would be a crime to force another separation between them now, even though the good of her safety might suggest otherwise.

He now knew. She would not fare well if they were to part, and if he were to be honest, neither would he.

That's when another hard dose of reality hit him. His father-in-law had been here. It was as though his father-in-law had left a portion of himself here. He had seen this. He, too, knew.

And now Brave Wolf came into a new understanding: this trip to the white man's nation was of his father-in-law's making. The knowledge brought Brave Wolf to his knees, and he squatted on the floor as wave upon wave of recognition washed over him. Worse, he was torn in two. He could not take her with him if these talks turned bad. But he could no longer believe that he could leave her behind.

Although he had not painted picture after picture of her these past five years as she had of him, her image had never left him. When time might have caused his love and her image to fade from his mind, it never had. Always she had been there; always in his thoughts and in his heart.

He inhaled deeply as his gaze took in the extent of these paintings...so many of them. He could only fathom one resolution to this problem: the talk with the Great White President must go well. He must give this cause all of his energy, his devotion.

It had to be. And so, although he had always hoped these talks would go well, he now realized that his task was to ensure this. Silently he vowed that he would bestow all of his strength and his power to their success.

Humbled, he made this promise to himself, to his father-in-law, to his wife, whom he loved beyond all else.

***

"What is it your people hope to achieve by this coming counsel?" asked Senator Sheehan, his question directed to both White Buffalo and Brave Wolf. "If I am to ensure a successful outcome of this meeting, I should know what it is that would make this get-together agreeable to you and the other chiefs. Perhaps I should have asked the other chiefs to this meeting, also, but first I wanted to speak to you as my newly acquired family. Then we must inform the other chiefs of what we speak of here, so that we may act as one in unison."

The family conference, having been properly opened by Indian custom, was well under way when Sheehan had asked the question only moments ago. "I ask this," continued Sheehan, "because in studying Treaty after Treaty that our two peoples have made together, always land, water rights, mineral rights are the particulars that you trade away for—" He paused. "Truth is, I cannot grasp what your people gain from these agreements, and so I little understand your desire to 'make peace.'"

Both White Buffalo and Brave Wolf nodded as if of one mind. It was White Buffalo who stood to his feet, and who spoke. "Once," he began, using both words and the gestures of sign language, "in the days of my father, the land of the Lakota was rich with game, with buffalo and with the great mysteries of the Creator. Once, my people were prosperous and independent, for all their needs were fulfilled by He who made this world. In those days, it is true that there were threats of Indian wars between hostile nations, but never in the memory of my people, has there been such devastation as these wars with the bluecoats. No camp is safe from these soldiers, and the Lakota man, having to travel long distances to fulfill the needs of his family, is long gone from camp, making all within his tribe vulnerable to the terrible guns of the white man.

"We do not like to see our loved ones killed, and yet we must not allow our families to starve, either. The bluecoats are different from us; they come here with few women and almost no children in their forts that require their attention, thus they are free to center their industry on conquest alone. These soldiers do not parley once they have killed. Instead, they go on to attack another village, sometimes with more vigor than the one before. Even in peace, and certainly in war, they disgrace our women. They take no one prisoner; they kill all with equal vengeance.

"Peace for us requires a man being able to hunt without fear that his family will be murdered while he is gone. It helps also that food, even if it be the white man's fare, is distributed within the tribe. Are we willing to trade some of our treasured land for this peace of mind?

"Some say it must be. Some demand to continue to fight. But the wise men in the seven bands of our tribe know that we cannot long sustain this war, for our young men must be well nourished if we are to fight. Also, for every soldier that we strike down, another takes his place; it is as though the white man uses his people as carnage without thought to his individual life. This confuses my people, for to us, all life is precious, and when one of our young falls, it cuts into us deeply, as though each one of us were struck down, also.

"To answer your question, I tell you now that we parley so that we may yet live; so that our young people may look to the future with 'good eyes,' and so that our beliefs and our customs, different as they are from yours, will survive. This, I believe, is why we seek to council." He paused before he ended, saying, "I have spoken."

The Senator shook his head up and down briefly, his attention inward for the moment. At length, however, he spoke again, saying, "My son-in-law, Brave Wolf, have you concerns regarding this treaty-making that you would like to add?"

"I do," answered Brave Wolf, and he rose up to stand much as his father had done. He began, "We have now seen reservation life and the evils that attend it. We have beheld that when our people give up the fight, the white man brings his liquor to us, causing our people to go crazy. When we give up the fight, we see that he takes our children away from us, and sends them far from us. When we give up the fight, we have seen that some of these children die, yet we are helpless in these matters, for who knows where they have gone? When we give up the fight, we see that those children who do survive the white man's cities and schools, return to us changed, without knowledge of how to survive by the conditions of our environment, and some of these have perished because of this. Some of our children even return to us ashamed of being Indian. These are bad conditions, and yet, if we do not give up the wealth that we hold of value to us, we will surely die from the bluecoat's guns. Giving a little of land, yes, this is necessary. But we ask that there should be no taking our children away from us, no white man's schools, no white man's tools to dig up our Mother, the Earth, and particularly no white man's government, for we would rule ourselves."

Senator Sheehan breathed in deeply before he let his breath out in a sigh. Remaining seated, he paused briefly before stating, "What you are asking is not a part of any Treaty thus far made between our two peoples. Always, there are schools, traders, sheriffs, police, priests, land offices and bankers. These are all part of the agreements. Are the chiefs who have come here so anxious for peace that they will sign away not only their land, but their progeny? For I have not yet read or studied a Treaty that does not include it."

When both White Buffalo and Brave Wolf remained silent, Sheehan went on to say, "My dear family, it appears to me that those in Washington D.C. are of the mind to make over the Indian into a sun-tanned version of his own image. For why else would these Treaties contain elements of the seeds of his own destruction? If we are to meet your demands, and accomplish a document that is well for our family, and one that your chiefs might sign, we will need help from someone who is part of our troops, who is yet sympathetic and knowledgeable of the Indian mind-set. For I believe our President will not listen to you or to your chiefs' entreaties—only to such a man who might bring your cause to his ears. Do you know any such person?"

Silence ensued, and so quiet was it in the room that when a feminine voice softly spoke up, saying, "My father might be such a person, if he can be convinced to come here," it was as though she had shouted.

"Might he?" asked Sheehan, uncaring that Brave Wolf's mother might be flaunting tradition by speaking up. But then, this was a family meeting, and all were welcome to announce their thoughts aloud.

"I believe he might," continued Kristina. "He is still connected with the military, and he was once stationed at Fort Leavenworth, so he is familiar with the Indians. Further, there was a time when he was sympathetic to them. Perhaps he might be persuaded to attend the council on our behalf? For he lives close-by to our Nation's seat of government. I believe that he and my mother make their home in Maryland."

"Ah...," returned Senator Sheehan, and for the first time, since beginning their private council, the Senator's countenance broke out into a smile. "Mayhap we might send him a message."

***

"But how do we ensure he receives a message from us in only a few days' time?" asked Sheehan.

Brave Wolf stood to his feet. Here, he realized, was his chance to put his resolve into motion. He began, "I will take your message to my mother's father. Give me a map showing me where he is, and I will find him and do all I can to persuade him to our cause."

"I will go, too." It was Mia speaking, who rose up to stand beside him. She took his hand in her own.

Brave Wolf's initial impulse was to forbid her to accompany him. Firstly, he would travel faster on his own; secondly, he didn't possess a knowledge of the safety of their situation here. Were there others in this town who stood to gain from the Indian's loss? Could there be men who might use any means available to stop him and his chiefs?

Yet he held his peace. He would deny her nothing. If she insisted that she accompany him, he would do all he could to ensure their success.

"Ah, my son-in-law, I accept your pledge to find your grandfather, and seek his help. But I would caution the wisdom of taking my daughter with you. We do not know the lay of the land, so to speak. There could be dangers having to do with this treaty-making we have not foreseen."

White Buffalo rose up to voice his agreement with the Senator, and he said, "I, too, believe this could be a mission filled with unforeseen danger. It is possible that those antagonistic to our proposals might recognize that my wife's father could pose a threat to them."

"*Hau*, I am aware that I will need to be alert to the possibility of danger, and yet..." Brave Wolf brought his wife's hand to his lips and kissed her fingers, one at a time before he continued, his voice barely over a whisper, "Although I believe that she who is my wife should stay here, I will not leave her behind." He smiled lazily at Little Dawn Bird then, before he ended, saying, "Never again."

Both he and Little Dawn Bird ignored the possible shock that such an open expression of love might bring to the others; especially since Indian culture forbid such a display. Would their parents feel embarrassment?

However, it didn't matter, for they both were aware momentarily of only one another. And as his wife glanced up at him to gift him with a happy grin, he felt his spirits lift. Softly, almost as a prayer, she repeated, "Never again."

It was then that he knew she shared a promise similar to his own. From this moment forward, they would live the adventures of life together.

Ah, what a woman...

CHAPTER TWENTY-SEVEN

The day was sunny, but blustery and the wind seemed to echo a warning as to what the day might hold. Indeed, it was not exactly the best conditions under which to begin treaty negotiations with the Great White Father. Yet, it could not be helped. This day in July, 1876, was the agreed-upon date.

It was still early morning, and the delegation of eight Indians and one Indian agent reposed around a long table set up in the center of a room that was so large, that not even Senator Sheehan's ballroom could compete with it. All the chief's wives were in attendance, for none of the chiefs would counsel without their wives being in attendance; to do so would be as to strip the heart from the meeting.

At present, the women and were seated along a wall to the right of the table; this included both Kristina and his own loving wife, Little Dawn Bird. To his surprise his maternal grandmother was in attendance there, also.

His father-in-law, as well as his grandfather loomed large in presence. They were both seated, and between them were the papers that they both had labored under; here they exchanged notes, here they conferred with one another in soft whispers.

To the left of the table were long, rectangular windows, which appeared to magnify the winds from the out-of-doors. Exquisite lights lit up the room, the scent of kerosene strong in the air. Large and looming paintings of past presidents adorned the walls, as though they were here on display for moral support against an enemy. The floor in this place was made of hardwood, the walls were painted white, and here and there a mirror displayed the room, causing it to look even larger than it already was.

No one spoke, for tensions were heavy in this place. They awaited the Great White Father.

At last Ulysses S. Grant entered the room. Several men strode at his side, and one of them Brave Wolf recognized as the man he had once mistaken for Little Dawn Bird's husband. Although this man's presence here surprised him, not by word, gesture or countenance did Brave Wolf give an indication as to his astonishment.

Did that man's presence bode ill-will for this meeting? Despite the fact that Brave Wolf had come to realize that the man was a family friend, he sensed evil in the man. However, there was no opportunity to warn the others of his suspicions, for this was a meeting between the chiefs. In truth, although Brave Wolf was, indeed, a chief, it was not his place to speak here.

His duty was to their safety, although he admitted this might be a difficult task, since each Indian had been disarmed of any tool or object that might resemble a weapon; all divested before entry into this room. Not so the Great White Father, for he wore a long sword at his side, and Brave Wolf was more than aware that his father-in-law's family "friend," the one who accompanied the President, bore the unmistakable look of concealed weaponry, for it bulged beneath tight-fitting jackets.

So, too, were the other men who accompanied the Great White Father, armed. Brave Wolf was at once alarmed and alert. It was apparent that all was not as the government might like it to appear to be. Was this a trap? Was the meeting to end with the loss of life?

He would have to hold his own counsel on the matter, for the time to speak to his father or his father-in-law about his suspicions would have to wait. Perhaps the Great White Chief was merely afraid, although what damage these elderly chiefs might present him was in question. After all, the chiefs had given their word that there would be no violence. Too, it was well known that an Indian's word of honor, once pledged, was inviolate.

It began. Minutes turned to hours, and still the talk went on and on, neither side able to concede to an agreement. Though Brave Wolf followed the logic of both sides of the negotiations, he was yet aware that there was an unspoken agenda behind the Great White Father's talk. Luckily, Brave Wolf's father-in-law hammered out most of the needs to the Indians, and inserted them into the treaty, despite protests from the man known as Greiner. Why was that man here? What gains from these talks did the man hope to achieve?

Indeed, there was a bad energy about that man that set Brave Wolf's heart to pounding in his ears. He sensed that there was yet a price to pay from that quarter, but what that might be, he could only speculate.

Hours passed uneventfully, as no compromises were yet in place. A break for the mid-day meal came and went, with still no inroads into negotiations, for although each side had hammered out their demands, neither side was willing to concede in even a small way.

During the mid-day break, however, a thing had happened. While the Indians had been adamant about their demands for no interventions into their lives, the Great White Father had inserted demands into the Treaty when the chiefs were least looking.

In exchange for peace, the Great White Father demanded schools for their children in far-away places; police and doctors for their people; jails and churches and merchants to trade, and lastly of all, banks and a Land Office to govern their reservation. It was unacceptable. Indeed, White Buffalo and the rest of the chiefs held a brief council, and Brave Wolf listened to them; heard and agreed with their plan to walk away. To them, the fight at home at least retained their dignity and their sovereignty.

So it was with a shock that they heard a voice—which had been silent until now—speak out. It was former Major Wendall Bogard, who had once commanded Fort Leavenworth, which had once been the farthest west outpost of the military.

As he was given the floor, he cleared his throat before he began to speak. After a moment, he said, "Mr. President, I must protest this action of inserting these demands into the Treaty at a time of brief leisure with the noon-day meal, when it was least expected, and the Indian's guard was down. These men here, these chiefs, are honorable men to a fault, and they will not sit still for such a betrayal. Have they not already told you that they desire to have no white man's schools, nor do they wish merchants to come among them and peddle the liquor and other of the evils of our race? Have they not already spoken of retaining their sovereignty? In exchange for peace, and the giving of certain of their lands, they wish only to retain their own culture, and I believe it is little enough to ask. I promise you that if these demands are left in this Treaty, they will not sign; the war will continue and you will lose forever that land which you seek to control."

"But I am told that there has never been a treaty without these demands," came Grant's response.

"Then let this be the first. I ask you, do the lives of those soldiers under your command, mean so little to you that you gamble with their right to live unto old age? Is wealth to be bought at such the price of murder, for that is what this would be.

"I know the hearts of the men of these tribes, and I know they will fight to the death to protect what is theirs. I also know your own Christian heart, and I implore you to remember Christ's words of instruction, which is to love others as one loves himself. Strike these phrases from this Treaty, and let it be written down in history that you were the first President to end these wars with honor. I remind you that one day you will have to face your Maker. Let this deed of honor be one to set before Him, to speak well for you."

These words, though wisely spoken, were met with silence, as the Great White Father stared at Major Bogard, Brave Wolf's grandfather. Many moments passed in utter silence. Then, with a gesture of urgent calling, the Great White Father took up the quill and ink. With grand fury, President Grant struck the phrases from the Treaty.

Only then, with the last stroke put to paper, did he glance up at Major Bogard and smile before he uttered at last, "Does this please you now?"

"It does," responded Major Bogard. "Indeed, it pleases God also."

And so it was done. Along with Major Bogard and Senator Sheehan, each chief signed the Treaty. It only remained that President Grant must sign it also, and the room was as silent as the prairie at rest, when it was at last accomplished, and President Grant scribbled his signature to the Treaty.

It was a first, and indeed, it appeared that at last there was to be peace.

***

"No! I will not sign this evil document!"

This declaration came from Max Greiner, who was supposed to be merely a witness to the Treaty-making, not a participant.

At once, Brave Wolf came silently to his feet, and as unobtrusively as possible, he strode toward a corner of the room, placing himself at Greiner's back. It was as he had thought: Greiner thought of himself as more than a by-stander. Exactly what his role was, Brave Wolf was not certain. But he was convinced he would soon discover it.

It was President Grant who spoke to the man, admonishing, "You are here merely as a witness, and only at your request. Your ideas and decisions about the Treaty were never to be a part of this, for you are merely the holder of the Note, which will purchase the supplies and other goods to be paid to this tribe. You are not a representative of the government of the United States."

But his speech fell upon deaf ears, for Greiner raved on further, threatening, "I will kill you for this." He drew a gun and pointed it—not at the President—but at Mia. He further ranted, "I will not take this loss to my dignity without a fight. I was to own that land and every water and mineral right upon it. Do you now mean to strip me of everything that should rightfully be mine? *She* should be dead. Didn't I ensure it? And yet, here she stands today, not in disgrace for breaking her contract with me, but in good standing, despite the hardship and heartache she has caused me to suffer." The sound of arms, clicking into place, was loud against the quiet of the room, causing Greiner to wave his weapon toward the gentlemen assembled before him. "Do not think to save this woman," raved Greiner, "for my gun is cocked and I can kill you before you can fire at me."

Brave Wolf crept up slowly behind Greiner, one careful step after another.

"I will take her life now, as is my right," babbled Greiner, and he pulled the trigger, but he hadn't seen nor reckoned with Brave Wolf. Using his full body's weight, Brave Wolf jumped into the air, kicking Greiner's arm with the full force of the attack, causing the bullet to go wild of its target.

A feminine scream wafted through the air, while the gun fell from Greiner's grasp, but before Greiner could grab hold of the pistol to take another shot, three other fire-arms discharged, their target Greiner, for Senator Sheehan and Major Bogard had not been disarmed; White Buffalo, as well, had stolen a pistol from one of the President's bodyguards, and had added his bullet to their target.

Greiner fell to the floor, but life was still in him as he called out, "She should be dead. She should be..." But that was all he managed to utter before the throes of death overcame him.

Brave Wolf, as soon as he had heard the womanly scream, had fled toward Mia, and finding her safe, had looked up to watch as Greiner fell to the floor. It was then that he beheld the evil spirit of the man flee from his now useless body. He understood it now. This man was the cause of Mia's misfortune, for he'd had the means to hire those assassins five years ago. Brave Wolf shuddered to realize that he had unknowingly sent Little Dawn Bird back into the realm and influence of this evil one.

And evil, he was, indeed. But the dark one's power was broken, for, as the truly wise men know, no justification for a wicked deed will prevent the retribution of divine karma; for the violent acts against others always come back to roost upon he who would dwell in debauchery. Only a devil would pretend otherwise.

Perhaps Greiner's spirit might never again eclipse the world with his hatred. Brave Wolf could only hope it would be so.

CHAPTER TWENTY-EIGHT

Margaret Bogard had been removed from the White House, and had been taken to the Hospital. It was she who had received the assassin's bullet. Gathered around her now were her family, Kristina on one side of her, Major Bogard, her husband, on the other. Both Mia and Brave Wolf, as well as White Buffalo and Senator Sheehan resided off to the side, allowing those closest to her to give comfort. Mia reached for Brave Wolf's hand, taking it into her own for strength, as she listened to Margaret Bogard.

"Come here, Kristina," Margaret pleaded to her daughter. "I don't know how much time I have to live within this world, and I would tell you this while I am still a part of it."

"Yes, mother, I am here."

"Please forgive me. I am sorry for how I have treated you over these years. I fear now that I have been wrong to ignore you and your husband and children for so long. I had thought to lure you away from your husband. Please, I beg you. Tell them this, that I am sorry. And please find it in your heart, if you can, to forgive me."

"Of course, Mother. But there is no need to forgive. We have all loved you despite the parting of our ways."

As though these words had given her comfort, Margaret Bogard shut her eyes, her head falling to the side.

Was she still alive?

"She sleeps now," Kristina informed the rest of the family, as though she were aware of their question. "But I will stay here with her until she awakens again, and until she is well."

"As will I," vowed Major Bogard.

"And I," joined in White Buffalo. And when Kristina glanced up at him to grace him with a thankful smile, one might have thought that their love, alone, might bring calm into this very troubled world.

Perhaps for that very moment, it did.

EPILOGUE
South Dakota Territory
July, 1877

The sun shone down brightly on a part of the Western Prairie that had been purposefully cleared for this special day and for this important event. Two people were to say their vows today, and all of the chiefs, all of Brave Wolf's people, were here to celebrate this wonderful occasion.

Brave Wolf glanced up at Senator Sheehan, who lingered toward the back of the crowd, awaiting only his daughter to walk with him down the aisle. Beside Brave Wolf stood an altar, adorned with roses of white. Behind that altar posed a priest. Also in the crowd was the woman known formerly as Miss Kate Bailey, Mia's long-ago nanny. But she had a new name now, Mrs. Kate Sheehan, the Senator's new wife.

On Brave Wolf's side of the altar stood his father, White Buffalo, and his mother, Kristina. What was more, Major Bogard and his wife, Margaret, reposed in the background. Margaret's arm was still wrapped in a bandage, but she seemed to have recovered well enough from that now famous stray bullet.

This land which hosted the ceremony today lay adjacent to the Lakota land, which had been set aside for his tribe. This part of the world was his and Mia's. Even the Major and his wife had bought a piece of property near-to-hand, and it was rumored that the Senator had plans afoot to buy yet another property.

At last the moment had arrived, and Brave Wolf watched as Mia appeared toward the back of the crowd. She was dressed not in white, but in a shade of pale coral, signifying that she and he were already married. Her red hair was caught up in long ringlets, which fell to her shoulders. She smiled at him, and with it, she made his world a little brighter.

Then to the tune of the birds overheard, and to the music of the ever-constant wind of the prairie, his wife stepped slowly toward him, her arm entwined in that of her father's. Yes, at last a promise would be fulfilled: a priest would marry them this day.

As Mia stepped up to him, and as he took her hand in his, they both dropped to their knees and he was reminded of when they had been alone on the plains; they had prayed each morning, much like they were now. Little had he known then, that a trust had formed between them, one that neither one of them would ever break.

As they rose up, as they turned to each other to kiss, he murmured, "Always, from this day until forever, will I love you. Never doubt it."

She grinned at him, and gazing up into his eyes, she vowed, "And I will love you from this day until I cease to exist. And my love, that may be a very long time."

He laughed. "Oh, how I love you."

"And I, you."

And so it was that the family was at last united. It is said that Brave Wolf and Little Dawn Bird lived to an old age with many children and grandchildren, who are alive even to this day.

Yes, because of their love, the world was a happier place.

THE END

NOTE TO THE READER

Perhaps you might have noticed that as our hero is learning English, the reader is also learning a little Lakota. Often my books provide a dictionary of terms at the end of my stories, for the ease of the reader. However, in this story the English word usually comes directly after the Lakota word, and so I didn't feel it necessary to repeat those definitions here.

In using Lakota words, I referenced three different sources for the definitions and pronunciation of these words.

DICTIONARY - OIE WOWAPI WAN

Of

Teton Sioux

Complied by Eugene Buechel, S. J.

Edited by

Rev. Paul Manhart, S. J.

1983

Copyright 1970, 1983

Red Cloud Indian School, Inc.

Pine Ridge, South Dakota 57770

A GRAMMAR OF LAKOTA

The Language

Of the

Teton Sioux Indians

By

Eugene Buechel, S. J.

Saint Francis Mission

Saint Francis P.O., South Dakota

EVERYDAY LAKOTA

An English-Sioux

Dictionary

For Beginners

General Editor, Joseph S. Karol, M.A.

Assistant Editor, Stephen L. Rozman, Ph.D

Second revision, March 1997

First revision, April 1974

Previous Publications of Joseph S. Karol:

Red Horse Owner's Winter Count

One note of worth: Some words in the Lakota Language have both masculine and feminine ways in which they are spoken. One of these words is a common one, *Hau*, which might have several different definitions: yes, hello, fine, good. The way I have written it here is the masculine version of the word. You might have noticed that when Kristina appears toward the end of the book, she says that word a little differently, *Haŋ*. This is the feminine way of speaking the same word.

Another worthy note concerns the way in which the name, Walks-in-sunshine is written. I am aware that this might not be the most agreed upon way to write this name in English Grammar, which would prefer that it be written Walks-in-Sunshine. However, in my experience – particularly among the Crow Tribe – I noticed that these hyphenated words were more commonly written as such: Walks-in-sunshine. And so, in telling this story, I determined to write this name as I had more commonly seen names written in Indian Country.

Hope this helps to clarify any questions which might arise from the usage of the names and Lakota words.

Karen Kay

2018

About the Author

Multi-published author, Karen Kay, has been praised by reviewers and fans alike for bringing the Wild West alive for her readers.

Karen Kay, whose great grandmother was a Choctaw Indian, is honored to be able to write about a way of life so dear to her heart, the American Indian culture.

"With the power of romance, I hope to bring about an awareness of the American Indian's concept of honor, and what it meant to live as free men and free women. There are some things that should never be forgotten."

Find Karen Kay online at www.novels-by-karenkay.com

Lakota Surrender

By

Karen Kay

As she heads west to join her cavalry officer father at his Kansas outpost, Kristina Bogard eagerly anticipates new adventures—and her first glimpse of wild Indians. She has long dreamed of flashing black eyes, skin-covered lodges and buckskin and leather.

What she finds in Fort Leavenworth, though, is a far cry from her Indian nanny's thrilling stories. What few natives are left are crushed, brokenhearted shadows of their proud past. Except for one, a handsome warrior who stirs up a whole new set of dreams.

Tahiska can't take his eyes off the green-eyed beauty whose graceful hands are fluent in his native sign language. Except he can't afford to let anything distract him from avenging his father, who was killed by two white soldiers.

Though anger fills his mind, Kristina steals into his heart, igniting a wildfire passion that must remain their desperate secret. For soon comes the day of reckoning, when justice will be served...or a travesty will shatter their love.

This book has been previously published.

Warning: Sensuous romance for the romantic at heart.

ISBN 978-1-98335-0-320

Made in the USA
Monee, IL
25 July 2022